The Dragon Forest

R. A. Douthitt

What people are saying about *The Dragon Forest*:

"The author does an excellent job at making you feel that you're part of the war. You can visualize the battle field and the enemy. You can feel the men fighting for king and kingdom. As you read, you can almost watch Peter grow into a man. Great read."

"*The Dragon Forest* is one of the most exciting stories I have read in some time. Douthitt really knows how to blend action with narrative. Her universe has a *Lord of the Rings* kind of feeling, but stands on its own. I would definitely recommend this tale to all fantasy readers and those who enjoy an exciting tale with loads of inspiration and hints at what is to come. I can't wait for book 2!"

"Read the book before the moves comes out. *The Dragon Forest* reads like a movie with the details of the entry into the mysterious forest to the battle scenes that take place between Good and Evil. The tension between these two forces will keep you turning each page to find out what happens next. You will find this book difficult to put down until you come to the last page and then you'll find yourself wanting more..."

DEDICATION

To my son, Nathaniel, my inspiration
for all things adventurous.

To my husband, Scott. Thank
you for your constant encouragement
through the years.

To my Lord Jesus Christ- thank
You for giving me
this story. May it
bring You glory.

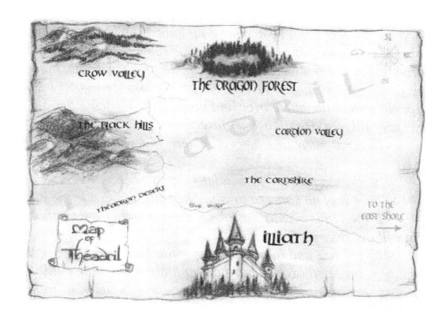

The cold and dark cave was lit only by the fire pits stoked by the elves. The master elf, a smith by trade, waited for special instructions from the two strangers before him.

"You must do this work now," the stranger said, handing him a carved box. "And you must do it quickly."

The master elf nodded and took the elaborate box and opened it. Inside the box was a sword. He took it into his hands. The blade glistened. The handle, made of ivory, felt good in his grip. He turned the blade over and noticed the intricate design, a most rare filigree. He studied it closely.

"I've not seen this before. Where did you get this?" he asked.

The stranger shook his head nervously.

"That is of no concern to you," he said.

"I knew this was a mistake," the second stranger spoke. "He will discover us."

The elf, tall and thin with long white hair braided over his shoulders, adjusted his robe to protect himself from the cold. He watched the anxious strangers and motioned for them to follow him into the cave.

"I will do this work," he said. "Follow me."

The strangers gathered the remaining carved boxes and turned to see if anyone had followed them. When they saw that no one was near, they quickly followed the elf into the dark cave.

PROLOGUE

In the beginning stood the mountains rising out of the western lands blocking out the sun as it set, casting long black shadows over the desert plains. Upon seeing the sight, the first settlers named the mountains "The Black Hills" when they compared the silhouette of the mountains against the violet sky of sunset. They surveyed the lands, the rolling grassy hills, the flatlands for farming, nourished by a river of blue waters, and hemmed in by a mysteriously dark green forest standing to the north.

Here the kingdom Théadril rose out of the dry desert plains east of the Black Hills, encompassing the vast grasslands heading out toward the sea. And it was here that the settlers, men and women and children, began their work. They had come after fleeing the darkened lands behind the mountains to claim their own region. They had bravely evaded the menacingly dark presence by passing through the elfin kingdom of Vulgaard and by traipsing through the great mountain gorges, until finally finding their paradise. Time and again this kingdom of man stood firm against invasion from the west by enemies who sought to destroy all that had been built.

In those early years, ten leaders arose and divided ten regions. Certain boundaries were set, as they always are where land is concerned. One region faced the sea while another took the hills to the northwest. Another region claimed the desert plains and more took the eastern lands.

But one particular leader claimed the grassy hills facing a patch of green forest for reasons unknown. Deagan of Illiath and his family obtained the land south of the forest for themselves. Each region, with its own customs and traditions, came together as one when called upon. These lands and the people therein shaped the kingdom of Théadril much as it is found to this day if it is found at all. It was at this time when leaders chose to chronicle their lives in the kingdom as they had learned from the Elves who had mastered the art of letters. This is how the history of Théadril had come to be long before it passed into legend, long before legend passed into myth.

§

One thousand years had passed in the land as peace reigned. In the later years, large castles of grey stone were built by the rulers of the ten regions where they faced the endless sieges of the dark knights named Baroks, their wolf-like Zadoks they used to attack, and, of course, the dragons.

These monstrous flying beasts, with black talons and leathery wings spanning several feet, would swoop down and breathe their fire onto the farmlands destroying everything in their paths: all the harvest as well as the villagers. Occasionally, the ogres from the desert plains pilfered sheep, and the trolls from the mountains alarmed the regions with their brooding packs, but nothing caused more grief than the threat of the dragon.

But one Dragon stood out from among the many. Year after year it rested within its cathedral of trees in the patch of forest green north of the kingdom of Illiath, son of Deagan. Appearing only to protect Théadril from certain doom, this Dragon destroyed all the Baroks with their steely black armor and kept the ogres and trolls to their own country in the desert hills. Because it protected the people, it earned the respect of the villagers and certain Kings, but it instilled fear in the hearts of the other dragons, keeping them at bay. The harvest grew. The Kings ruled. Peace had come to Théadril.

The ten rulers of each region gathered together annually to seek counsel from the great Dragon of the forest for they knew only the Dragon could help them keep the peace.

But, as with all kingdoms of man, the peace did not last. The vanity of man entered into the hearts of the rulers who sought power to rule over their lands without the help of the Dragon. All turned to their own ways except one: King Illiath. He ruled with humility and taught his son, Aléon, the ways of the Dragon Forest.

And as a result, only he and his heirs could enter into the forest realm.

At this time, the rulers of Théadril sought more powerful

weapons from the hands of the mystical Lord Bedlam for they feared the rulers across the seas. Lord Bedlam, a mysterious ruler from the far west lands near Vulgaard, had survived the darkened times that caused the settlers to flee for their lives. Some say he survived with title and lands in tact because he entered into accord with the darkness. With his sorcerer's ways, Lord Bedlam forged great weapons of war as the rulers fought against neighboring kingdoms for wealth and more power.

With time, each ruler died one by one, passing onto their heirs the desire for power. But when Illiath died, he had passed to his heir, Aléon, respect of earth and of the Dragon. Aléon did not trust Lord Bedlam for good reason: Lord Bedlam sought the scales of the Dragon for himself. For the scales of the Dragon were more powerful than any weapon forged by man.

In order to show his respect for Théadril, Lord Bedlam bestowed great and wonderful gifts to the sons of the ten rulers.

Ten swords were given. Ten Kings stood together and vowed to respect the lands and live in peace.

Glaussier the Brave
Aléon, Son of Illiath
Baldrieg, Son of Glenthryst
Théadron, Son of Ulrrig
Mildrir the Warrior
Byron, Son of Gundrehd
Beátann the Wise
Hildron the Mighty
Niahm, Son of Egan,
Naál, Son of Leámahn

After the swords were graciously bestowed upon the rulers, Lord Bedlam retreated to his land where he lived in quiet solitude. All was well within the kingdom once again as the sun rose and set on many prosperous days. But wise Aléon was not deceived by the impressive swords of Bedlam with their intricate designs carved into the steel blades. Hiding his sword away deep inside his castle, he waited patiently for the appointed time to use it in war.

§

Over time, a change came to the land. Subtle at first, many storm clouds hovered in the air above the land as a strange darkness approached. The moon remained new and the winds blew cold. There were no more harvests and the stench of death was thick in the air as the people began to starve. Then the people remembered the legend of their fathers about the darkness that caused them to flee. But Aléon, son of Illiath, studied the strange phenomenon and suspected Bedlam. So he ordered a meeting of the ten rulers.

But the vanity of man is a powerful thing. The ten rulers refused to listen to the reason of Aléon, for they loved the weapons of Bedlam and the power they wielded. With no where else to turn, Aléon sought the counsel of the Dragon. And in its counsel, Aléon was warned of the coming of war.

Lord Bedlam deceived the Kings and, in his betrayal, met them in battle, vowing to destroy the Dragon Forest. But when he reached the threshold of the forest, it was the Dragon who put the siege to an end. Bedlam was spared. He fled and the darkness lifted.

Three rulers fell, but seven held fast. After the wars when they buried their dead, the seven rulers came together and swore an Oath. Never again would they put their lust for power ahead of the land and the people. Together they vowed to protect the Dragon Forest at all costs and leave it in peace. They vowed never to enter into its realm.

As they stood beneath the stars on the highest hill in the kingdom of Théadril, raising their swords into the sky, they sealed the covenant of Théadril with their words, with their swords, and with their blood.

Seven swords remained. Seven rulers returned to their lands:
Glaussier the Brave
Aléon, Son of Illiath

Baldrieg, Son of Glenthryst
Théadron, Son of Ulrrig
Mildrir the Warrior
Byron, Son of Gundrehd
Beátann the Wise

Three swords were lost.

This is the legend of Théadril, the legend of the Dragon. As the years came and went, the legend became myth, and the myth passed into history. The legend was written down in a book for posterity. But as generations of Théadril passed on leaving behind no remembrance of the swords or the covenant or the Dragon, the legend was soon forgotten.

When the skies grow dark, some say it is the coming of winter, but others say it is Bedlam returning for the harvest, to claim the scales of the Dragon. The time of the Dragon has come to an end. The time of man is only beginning.

And the Dragon Forest remains.

1 THE MYSTERIOUS WOODS

The trees that stood on guard in the forest were nothing extraordinary in appearance with their deep green hue that drew cautious approaches by the villagers. Outwardly, the forest was nothing to behold, but inwardly…the mystery deepened.

§

The young boy felt the chill of the wind strike his face. His muscular steed trampled the earth beneath his body. The tan horse with white mane galloped with the confidence of a champion over the grasses. Together they rode in desperation to try and make it home in time for dinner.

"We must hurry. My father will be angry if we are late!"

He had forgotten the time while he hunted in the green hills of the valley with his trusted quiver and arrows. His empty quiver dangled on his back and an empty sack flapped as they rode. The hunt was unsuccessful. So, he decided to return quickly while a sliver of sun remained on the horizon.

Its neck wet with foamy sweat, the horse tried to keep riding while the boy tugged on the reins to stop. Finally, the beast reluctantly obeyed. The boy stood by the entrance of the forest as the colorful leaves swirled in the breeze. The enigmatic woods, the great mystery of his youth, remained quiet. A small wooden sign splintered with age, windstorms, and rainfall through the years, with letters scrawled in black paint stood near the path. The boy stooped to try and read the faded words. BEWARE THE DRAGON FOREST. He ran his fingers along the grain of the wood, but he did not heed its warning to trespassers. The boy knew it from legend. He hesitated.

He could feel the change and smell the dampness in the autumn air. The wind blew colder. *Snow is coming,* the boy thought. He gazed up at the towering trees staring back down at him in a menacing way, or was it his over active imagination? The sun continued to set. He knew he had to make a decision quickly because the day would soon give way to nightfall. He decided to risk entering the forest in order for his horse to drink of the lake. The boy knew of the legend, but he did not fear what was inside the mighty wooden columns whether it be a temple for a Dragon or not. The forest somehow seemed to call to him.

No, he did not fear...at least, not yet.

The trees towered over him and hid the departing sun and, suddenly, it became very dark. The indigo mist rose in the darkness from behind the trees. Black crows hovered over the tree tops in their undisguised disapproval. Black as midnight they flew. He tried to remember the mythology of the crows. *One crow is a bad omen,* the boy thought. *Or was it two?*

He saw the mist all around the lake and slowly led his horse to drink. With each footstep, the mist gave way to reveal the dark earth beneath them. They heard the soft breeze echo across the width of the blue water and the echoes of the horse's hooves clomping in the moist dirt below. His horse stirred. The clouds had parted to reveal the waxing moon. Its partial face glowed a white light glaring down as a sort of spotlight guiding the way to the lake. Rising high above the trees, the moon caused the trees to cast the blackest of shadows all around them in a web-like pattern on the ground. The boy felt like trapped prey, waiting for a spider. So he made his way out of the shadows and into the clearing. From time to time the crows entered into the silvery light of the partial moon. Fear began to penetrate the boy's brave façade until, finally, he surrendered.

A chill moved across his flesh. His horse hesitated and neighed nervously. The boy questioned his decision to enter in, and he quickly changed his mind. In his repentance, he turned to mount his steed to quickly leave this place, but as he turned, he lost his way and could not remember from where he entered the forest. The trees, with their black bark, seemed to have engulfed him and hid the point of his entrance. *Could it be that they were watching our every move?*

He became even more dismayed with this thought as the wind became colder on his skin. He sat down by a tree and realized his escape would not happen. His body stiffened as the thought of what was out in the night paralyzed him. The mist grew denser all around the lake like a thick veil. *Is this the great creature's breath?* He now feared that he had proof of the Dragon his father had warned him about, but now his father was far away and was most definitely very angry with him.

He closed his eyes in deep thought. His room with its soft feather bed and warm pillow ran through his mind. He closed his eyes even tighter and pictured the window of his room yellow and glowing warmly from the lantern placed beside his bed. He missed his toy soldiers carved from wood and his little wooden sword. Oh how he wished he had it with him at this moment. All he had was his bow, an empty quiver, and nothing to show for his hunt. His stomach growled when he thought of the smells of the kitchen and the warmth of its fire. He rubbed his belly. It ached from emptiness as he thought of all the wonderful food. Oh, how he missed the food!

Just then his father's face appeared and he opened his eyes. He missed his father most of all.

With eyes wide open, he heard a slow elongated hiss from behind him. It startled him, and the wind blew through the trees causing a black crow to flutter away. He jumped at the sound of the wings fluttering and the "caw" of the obnoxious black bird. The tree, with its scary web-like shadows on the ground, enveloped the boy and his horse as the branches rose up across the black sky lit only by white moonlight.

What is going to happen to me now? He shivered as the breeze touched his bare forearms so he wrapped his small arms tightly around his bent legs until his knees were under his quivering chin. His horse stood nearby with nostrils flared and ears bent back with caution. Its eyes darted back and forth through the trees. *Oh, come quickly bright sun!* The boy closed his eyes. Realizing he would have to stay in the forest all night until the sun came up, he sighed from frustration. Daybreak seemed forever away.

From behind, he heard the hissing sound again. It was nearer to him now. Deep within his soul, he knew someone or *something* was watching him. He turned and quickly asked, "Who is there?!"

No one answered. The blue mist enveloped him now.

"Who is there, I say?" He asked again, but only the wind whispered through the trees. "My father is the King!" He hoped this would scare away any robber barons hoping to harm him.

Suddenly, and as quickly as the blinking of an eye, there before him was a small fire burning. He jumped to his feet and watched the orange fire glow cut through the darkness. He supposed it came from the trees nearby, but how? He looked all around but saw no one…only the flickering of the flames. Smoke rose high into the night sky as the small fire illuminated the trees surrounding it. The details of the tree trunks in the orange glow of the firelight could be seen. They weren't monsters waiting to wrap him in their looming arms. They were just trees, after all.

He looked down at his feet. Something on the ground sparkled in the firelight. A small scale glistened in the fire glow. Sparkling like a jewel on the ground, the boy wondered if it could be a dragon's scale. He picked it up and admired it closely. It was iridescent in appearance. *Maybe it came from its neck? Or the tail?* He fingered the smooth scale a second longer and then put it in his pocket for safekeeping.

He sat beside the fire, feeling the fire's warmth and comfort from the darkness and cold wind. The orange sparks cast off from the twigs of the fire twirl high into the air, traveling ever higher and higher like the fireflies of summer. When he glanced up at the many stars in the sky, the trees hanging overhead no longer frightened him. Instead, they made him feel safer. He blinked harder and harder as his eyelids grew heavier. The flames danced into the night sky above him. He slowly lay down next to the fire and soon fell asleep. His loyal horse kept guard over the small boy's sleeping frame as the fire remained safely lit all that night.

2 THE KING OF ILLIATH

Many years had passed since that night in the mysterious woods, and the boy grew in stature and wisdom. This boy, Alexander, never forgot his night in the Dragon Forest. Soon after, King Aléon of Illiath in the land of Théadril, died. Alexander inherited the kingdom and ruled with all fairness and humility as his father had before him. Years later, Alexander loved Lady Laurien of Glenthryst and the two wed. A few years later, King Alexander fathered a son. After nine years of bountiful joy together, one winter his beautiful queen became ill. The King and the Prince mourned her death.

Now, with a young son to rear and a kingdom to rule, he found himself at a crossroads. Once more evil had entered the kingdom as the inevitable rumors of war spread through the valleys and between kingdoms as the scales of the Dragon were still coveted by man.

King Alexander sought to protect the forest green and leave it in peace.

§

"Where is Master Peter?" The steward hustled through the kitchen. "He is to eat his lunch now."

In the large steamy kitchen of the great castle, the busy servants looked at the steward and then at each other. They shrugged because they did not know where the lad had squandered off to this time. Always hiding from the servants who wanted him to eat or do his school work or clean his room, Peter was a master at hiding in the large castle.

The Great Palace of King Alexander sat high on a hill overlooking the different lands it governed. Many other kings thought Illiath, King Alexander's grandfather, foolish to build his castle so low to the river's edge instead of carving it out of a mountain peak to ward off enemy attacks and sieges, but Illiath knew that in order to build his castle out of a mountain, he would have to build it away from the Dragon Forest. And this was not a possibility. He insisted the forest remain in his sights at all times. Rolling hills covered in grasses painted the landscape in green hues like an artist's canvas.

The Castle, made of grey limestone, brick, timber, and earth, took decades to complete, but it was worth the toil and labor. Illiath, for whom the kingdom was named, hired masons and stone workers from faraway lands to construct a manor worthy of a King. Enormous walls surrounded the outer court as a ring of defense. Here the archers and foot soldiers stood with a clear field of fire in case of attack. Past the first ring of walls and towers stood the second ring of grayish stone walls and wooden gates which led to the main castle entrance. The two rings made the castle imposing, so that one would approach with apprehension were it not for the gates facing North, South, East, and West. These gates allowed the citizens from the nearby towns and farms to enter with leisure in order to conduct trade and commerce.

Surrounding the castle was a mote dug deep and filled with river water to prevent enemy attacks over the walls. A drawbridge was constructed to be lowered when the main gate was opened in order to allow villagers entry at will. The courtyard was an open thriving place of business for the people of Illiath. Here was where the stable grooms looked after the horses of the King and his knights. The blacksmiths made horseshoes and other metal objects of use. The Armorer mended the armor and weapons of the knights so they would always be ready for jousting games or battle. The Chaplain had his chapel next to the Solar and this is where the King had his own private quarters. The Chaplain, who led services for the King's garrison, knights, and squires, lived on the other side of the courtyard, as did the servants in their quarters.

Huntsman and falconers trained daily to perfect the hunt as they knew at any time the King himself would join them on their next adventure for pheasant, wild boar, or duck. All the game they brought back each day would be stored in the Keep next to the kitchen. The cook and his scullions prepared the food for each meal. Not only did they serve the King and his men delicious meals, but they prepared food for all the soldiers and servants. The smell of fresh bread always lingered in the courtyard as the bakers and their assistants were busy baking all day and into the night.

The wine was supplied by the vintner, and the King's butler took charge of the wine cellar hidden far beneath the Castle's foundation. The wine and spirits flowed every time the knights and their squires celebrated a victory in the great hall. Amongst all the fuss and noise and business in the castle court were the women workers who spun sheep's wool into thread to help sew up the torn uniforms of the knights and soldiers. They made clothes for everyone who lived in the castle as well as washed the clothes and repaired them. It was a lowly job, and so the King always made sure these women and their families dined with him and his family every Harvest Moon. He appreciated all the hard work of his servants in the Palace.

Woodworkers, tax collectors, soldiers, and servants worked hastily every day as the farmers bought and sold their hogs, sheep, and goats all within the castle courtyard. It was a small city within the walls. It was a peaceful and prosperous time in the land. As each soldier stood along the outer curtain walls of the palace, they could behold the Dragon Forest to the north with all its mystery and beauty.

Peter hid in his usual place in the castle this afternoon. Still small for ten years of age with his mop top of thick brown hair, he peaked out from under the massive mahogany table in the center of the large meeting hall. The noon sun shone through the large colored cut glass of the windows and its light cast down on the checkered floors. The floors were so shiny that Peter could see his reflection in them—and the reflections of others too.

Prince Peter knew all the perfect hiding places of the castle. For all these ten years, he had many excellent opportunities to search them out. His father was very busy fending off threats of war and attack. Peter chose this place on this day because he knew his father, the King, would be meeting here later that day.

"Caught you!" The steward quickly lifted the red tablecloth up to reveal the Prince.

"Time…for…lunch!" He sternly took Peter's arm and pulled him from underneath the table when the trumpets sounded. "Too late," he mumbled. "Your father is here."

Relieved, Peter scurried away when the steward released his arm and stood at attention to greet the arriving King. The huge wooden doors swung open and revealed King Alexander followed by his many knights and their servants in waiting. Their armored bodies clanged loudly as they walked by, and their armored shoes made such a clamorous commotion along the floors of the entryway that all the nearby servants peaked out from behind the walls to see what was happening. The faces of the knights were serious and rigid, leaving the impression that this meeting was most urgent.

"Your majesty." The steward bowed his head toward the King who hurried by him. He noticed a distressed expression.

When the steward turned to see if Peter was still nearby, alas, it was no use. The Prince was off to find another hiding place.

§

"Attention!" the head knight exclaimed as soon as they entered into the great hall to hear what the King had to say.

The hall was grand indeed. The ceilings, almost fifty feet high, loomed over a large painting of The Dragon Forest on one wall and the beautiful portrait of the Queen fair on the other wall behind the King's throne. Great arches framed the doorways and halls. Long velvet drapes hung alongside the entryway held open with cords of fine silk thread. The walls near the entrance were decorated with royal crests of each of the ten rulers made from hammered bronze and framed in mahogany wood. A few sets of full armor suits stood by the crests as memorials to past armor designs of Alexander's father and grandfather. Standing in the middle of the Great Hall stood a large table big enough to fit all the King's knights around it. A thick and heavy red table runner with the King's lion crest stitched in gold lay on the table. Fine tapestries—gifts from visiting overseas dignitaries—hung near the windows. Burning torches resting in iron sconces lit up the great room.

On this particular day, all of the knights eagerly gathered around without patience even to sit. Their armor reflected the light of the torches and candles, sending streams of light bouncing throughout the room. It was an awesome sight to see these warriors together in one room. Peter found it hard to conceal his delight.

The King's forehead wrinkled and his mouth formed a solid frown. The news he announced was not good. He had been to a meeting with his spies earlier that day. The most distressing news was about the illusive Lord Caragon and his plans.

"My Lord, we must have those scales!" Sir Peregrine pounded his fist on the large table. The crash of fist meeting table sent a loud echo throughout the hall. All their eyes were on the King.

Sir Peregrine, the head knight, had been the King's most noble and, indeed, his bravest knight for many years. He had fought alongside Alexander when he was still a young Prince in the Battle of Cornshire. It was this battle that impressed the

young Prince to name Peregrine his head knight once he became
King. Knighting Peregrine was one of the first acts of
Alexander's rule. Now the two of them faced possible war again.
The King was glad his brave friend was beside him once more.
With Sir Peregrine on his side, he felt they could win any battle.

"It is our only chance," another knight replied. The men
looked worried and agitated. "Here, here!" the others shouted in
one voice.

Many of the King's Royal Knights lived outside the kingdom
in their own nearby estates. They had earned the respect of the
local villagers for they were men of great wealth and prestige.
Now they were gathering once again with their King to have their
voices heard.

Peter, watching from up on the balcony near his room,
overheard the knights' words and gasped. Hoping they did not
hear him, he continued to listen as his father explained his plans to
his knights. Peter's hands were tightly wrapped around the stair
rails as he pondered the idea of an impending war with all its
consequences and destruction to the lands.

Sir Peregrine laid out his detailed plans. He desired to enter
into the Dragon Forest with some archers and foot soldiers to
capture the Dragon for the kingdom in order to have the scales for
themselves.

"The enemy must not have them, sire." He walked around the
large table. "If they obtain those scales before we do, all is lost."
His silver armor glistened in the light of the many candles above
them. Of all the King's Royal Knights, he was by far the bravest,
having won every joust and battle for the King and kingdom.

"You would dare enter into the forest where no man has
entered before and lived to tell his tale?" the King asked. "Well,
no one except one boy…" he smiled.

Peregrine stood silent.

"All is not lost," the King said. "We must not take what is not
ours."

He paced the great hall as his men discussed the news. Their voices grew louder and louder as their frustration grew. The King understood their desire for the scales and for battle. Lo these many years, they have gone without war and the idleness of peace has caused some of them to dangerously lust for war while others, blindly led by their complacency, craved peace. *But a wise King must always hesitate to reflect before going into any battle. He must carefully weigh the costs involved.* Alexander thought. *There is a high price for this kind of wisdom that every King must face...alone.*

The King found himself standing before the portrait of his late wife. Gazing into her lovely face, he missed her wise counsel. As he stood still, he could almost hear her voice. In the fine portrait, her long black hair lay across her bare shoulders of white skin and he could almost smell her scent of wild cornflowers, jasmine, and lavender.

His thoughts then turned to their son and all the families in the village. As King, it was up to him to protect those families. As he turned to make his way back to the table, he saw the large painting of the Dragon Forest across the room. Its beauty was mystifying as well. Its haunting presence had been with him all his life. What lay inside the wall of trees was unknown to all except the young boy who grew to be King. He stared at the massive, detailed painting in its enormous frame covered with gold. He could almost smell the mist. The memory of the black crow and its "caw" stirred him from his trance. He realized his men were staring at him now in silence. With head down and hands folded behind his back, he cautiously walked over to the table.

"We have truth and honor on our side." He studied the large grand painting of the Dragon Forest once again. "With these attributes, as well as justice for our shield, we will not fail. We will not be defeated."

"Here, here!" the loyal knights shouted in agreement.

"I, as King, have the awesome responsibility to protect all the people of the village. I have sworn my life to the cause.

Therefore, I must weigh all the costs involved in war. It is a heavy task indeed. One I do not take lightly," the King finished.

Tapping his gloved fingers on the table, Sir Peregrine sat somberly and patiently listed. Avarice deep inside his heart for the scales of the Great Dragon had changed him. It was incomprehensible to him that his King wanted to protect the beast he had never seen at all costs only because of a legend and myth told to him long ago. He wanted to say this to Alexander, but he knew it was of no use. No one could change the King's mind once it was made up.

He searched for the eyes of those who were in agreement with him and gave them a signal. They nodded in approval.

Peregrine stopped tapping his finger. "But I am afraid you do not see the urgency of this moment!" Peregrine stood. "We know Lord Caragon is already devising a plan to enter into the forest, strike the Dragon, and use the scales against us. We are defenseless without those scales. There is only so much we can do to protect the land."

Many knights nodded in agreement.

The King would not relent. "We will go to war to defend our land, but we will not take what is not rightfully ours in order to do it. We can stand on our own…and we will!" The King shouted.

His beloved friend looked on with anger. Something had happened in that instant between the two men. The King thought it just a disagreement, but Peregrine saw it as the beginning of the end. How he could continue to serve a King he no longer believed in?

§

Peter's heart began to race in his chest and he could hardly stand still. He wished he could be part of this meeting. He felt he was ready to stand with his father. His grip around the stair posts tightened until his knuckles were white and his fingers ached. He watched a little while longer as they argued on into the afternoon.

He ran to his room and opened the window that overlooked The Dragon Forest. There it was. His window framed the forest now as some sort of gilt frame around a painting in the hall. The sun was lower in the sky and the trees were a dark green. It looked so mysterious and yet so ordinary at the same time. He had stared at the forest since he could peek out this window. He could still hear his mother's voice telling him all the secrets of the Dragon and its lair. Picking up his small wooden sword in his hands, he gazed out at the great forest green and dreamed...

All his life he had heard the tales of the forest and the Dragon who lived there. Tales he had heard from his father, his mother, the servants, and the knights swarmed in his head. He had wished he could fight alongside his father in battle, but he was still too young. He lined up his stuffed toys and wooden soldiers along his bed and told them of his plans for battle. They listened to their master in silence. He grabbed his sword and raised it high above his head. He then pretended to fight the Dragon as his toys looked on. His sword sliced through the air as he imagined slaying the mighty beast and taking its scales. He climbed up on his bed as if climbing a mountain. He leaped down as if charging the great Dragon. He raised his sword and stabbed the great beast with one fatal blow. It was done. The kingdom was saved. Then he climbed on his soft feather bed, lay down, and dreamed of what real battle must be like.

"I wish I could slay dragons, don't you?" he asked his toys, but they remained silent.

Their silence was deafening. He stared at them wishing he had someone to talk to. His toys never laughed with him or made up games to play with him. He rolled over and stared out the window as he dreamed of what was out there. Hours had passed and the sun was low in the vast sky casting long shadows throughout the room. Light bounced off the bed and the shelves in Peter's room as he daydreamed.

He remembered when he and his father would play together in his room. They would laugh and play until they were so tired they could not laugh anymore. But, lately, his father had been so busy with things about the kingdom that they had very little time together. He missed his father. He wished he had an adventure. He wished he had a friend.

Then the Dragonslayer fell asleep.

3 PETER'S RIDE

"All this, and for what? Loyalty to a creature he has never seen? Loyalty to the Oath he was never a part of? This is madness. We must have those scales before Caragon gets them," Peregrine told his men as they secretly met in a small room on his fine sprawling estate outside the castle walls. A man of good fortune, Peregrine prided himself on his wealth and position as a Knight to the King's court.

"When the King takes his men to the valley to begin battle, we will volunteer to hide by the forest entrance with our archers at the ready. This will give comfort to the King as he will assume we will be with his archers. But we will secretly enter into the forest and capture the Dragon scales for ourselves…and for Théadril, of course." His face revealed his true feelings towards his King, and could not veil his ambitions any longer.

"Enter the Dragon Forest?" asked one of the knights. "But Sir Peregrine, no one Knight has entered and lived to tell! How can we secretly enter into this mysterious realm?"

Peregrine slowly turned to face the inquisitor. With eyes of a piercing blue made more intense by his dark hair and eyelashes, he stared at the knight and walked over to answer the question. "Well, my dubious friend, it appears you will just have to trust me now, won't you?" Peregrine said as he approached the doubtful Knight.

"I trust you, my Lord," the knight stuttered as Peregrine's intense eyes stare right through him. "It is just that I have heard about the forest all my life. I have heard the tales of men entering into the woods and a bright blue flash of light followed…and then the men were never heard from again." Most of the knights had heard many tales of unfortunate souls deceived by their cupidity and lust for power entering into the Dragon Forest never to be seen again. Not one of King Alexander's men had ever dared to enter into the woods.

"Yes, it seems that what I am suggesting is rather dangerous, isn't it?" Peregrine placed his arm on Sir Leonard's shoulder as he looked around the room at all of the knights present. Some nodded in agreement while others chuckled under their breath. "Far be it from me to ask my knights to partake in such a *dangerous* mission."

Many of the Royal Knights laughed.

"But, Sir Leonard, if you are too afraid or if you do not feel this mission is for you," Peregrine stated. "Then perhaps you shouldn't be a part of it!" And with that, Sir Peregrine grabbed the tunic of Sir Leonard and quickly lifted him up off the stool he had been sitting on. "You coward!"

Peregrine then rudely shoved the knight out the door of the small room, startling all the other knights gathered there. Leonard fell to the ground as the door slammed shut behind him.

"Now—" Sir Peregrine wiped his hands together as though he had tarnished them. "Will anyone else be joining Sir Leonard tonight?"

No one said a word.

As the butler laid out pheasant and bread on the table before the men, they ripped into the bird and bread. But Peregrine did not join them. He was expected later at the King's table as he entertained Lords and Ladies from the Valleys nearby.

The servants lit a fire in the fireplace and their shadows danced along the stone walls. The torches on the walls were lit and cups were filled. After eating, the men stood near the fire's warmth and listened intently.

"What shall we do with the scales once we have them?" asked one of the knights as he warmed his hands by the fire.

"In due time, my friend. I will explain everything in due time." Sir Peregrine smiled at him. Then he patted his companion's back as they all returned to the discussion as well as the development of the final plan.

A knock on the door stirred them. The servant looked at Peregrine who nodded for the door to be opened. "Ah, Sir Leonard," Peregrine said as he drank his wine. "Will you be joining us after all?"

Sir Leonard looked around the room and lowered his eyes. "Yes, my Lord," he answered. Peregrine smiled.

§

Peter heard voices outside of his door. It was darker now in his quiet room as the sun began to set. He realized that he had fallen asleep and the steward had let him nap right through to lunchtime.

Agitated, he arose and saw that his window was still open. Looking out at the valley below his window, Peter could see the Dragon Forest. In its serenity, it seemed to call to him.

He glanced down and saw his wooden sword and quiver of arrows leaning on his bed. He quietly stepped over and picked them up. As he admired the craftsmanship, he remembered when his father had given them to him for his birthday. The King called them his Dragonslayer weapons and told him only to use them when slaying Dragons. Now the wooden sword looked so real in his hand. His fingers wrapped around the smooth wooden handle tightly. He felt a burning inside and his heart pounded in his chest. He looked at all his stuffed toys still staring at him from his bed. It was as if they understood: It was time to test his sword. It was time to help his father, the good King.

Now was the time to be the Prince he was meant to be. He grabbed a pillow sack from under his bed and filled it with a blanket for the cold nights, a favorite toy for companionship, and the compass his mother had given him just in case he became lost. His father's astronomers had taught him to search the stars for the direction at night and to heed the moon above. He took one last glance around his room as if to say goodbye, for he did not know when he would return to its comfort. He looked at his toys as his friends. He glanced over at his books on the shelf. All of them he cherished.

No more dreaming of fighting dragons, now it would be a real adventure. He was amazed at how he had no fear at all.

Then he slowly opened the door, and with one last glance he snuck out of his room. He stopped to listen for voices in the hallway, but heard none. He crept over to the stairway leading to the great hall. No one was there any longer. Candles in the sconces and burning torches glowed and their reflections in the shiny floor cast enough light for him to make his way down. He made his way past the great hall, into the corridor and on his toward the kitchen. There was a loud commotion coming from the kitchen as the servants, cooks, and pantlers frantically prepared for the dinner the King was hosting that night. Several valley leaders were invited for dinner to discuss the plans for battle.

Peter slid into the kitchen unnoticed by the busy cooks and maids. He found a large table used for carving, and waiting for the right moment, crawled underneath the table. The delicious smells were plenty! Pheasants, pigs, and turkeys were roasting. Venison, peacocks, grouse were also being prepared. There were meat pies and stuffing made with bread. Breads baking in the brick ovens were removed and laid out on a large wooden table. Peter's empty stomach could barely take it all in. His mouth watered as he hid under the large wooden table where the butlers were preparing to serve the first course. The Royal Taster was busy doing his unenviable job. He was paid very well for this risky job and for good reason. As the servants quickly made their way with large trays of food, Peter reached up and grabbed a few rolls, leg of lamb, and an apple. This would be enough food to get him through the day of battle. He hurriedly put them into his sack.

The meat carvers were hastily cutting pig, lamb, and venison into chunks and throwing the parts into a large black cauldron hanging over the fire. The cooks were making a spicy meat stew for the soldiers outside guarding the castle. The pages rushed in to help serve wooden bowls of the spicy stew to the men. Bowls disappeared as each young page grabbed them off the table. There were several hundred men to feed any one night.

Peter sat underneath the meat carvers table. All he could hear above him was the loud *thwump* of the hatchet as it met with the table. Then he saw the cooked pig's head and feet fall to the floor. The ghastly sight made Peter gasp out loud, but everyone in the steamy kitchen was too busy to notice him. The meat carver just picked the parts up and tossed them to the dogs waiting by the doorway.

Peter waited as the servants scurried in and out of the kitchen hall. The pots and pans clanging and all the chatter of the cooks covered the noise Peter made as he crawled out of the kitchen. He was careful not to startle the women who were preparing large cakes and fancy pies for dessert. They gossiped and snickered and didn't even notice the small boy creeping along the floor. The striped cat did notice him though, but it was too busy cleaning its paws to bother him.

When he made it out of the kitchen and into the small damp mud room where all the servants kept their muddied boots, brooms, and cloaks, he noticed it was cluttered with mats, large spools of thread, hats and gardeners gloves. The mat weavers sat here on cold days making their straw mats for the kitchen. The Spinners used this area to spin thread onto spools. It was here that Peter grabbed a water pouch hanging on a peg. He filled it with water from the well outside.

Now he was set for his journey. He gazed up into the heavens and saw the full moon following his every move. He often thought that the moon was his mother watching over him. There was a slight breeze which gave him a chill on his bare arms, and he quickly put on his suede coat. He passed many squires and foot soldiers as they walked around the courtyard of the castle. Many of the soldiers were climbing the narrow stairs leading to the Curtain walls which surrounded the entire castle. It was here these loyal men stood watch all night. One by one they were changing shifts so they could eat the hot stew being served. They were too hungry to notice the Prince as he made his way past them.

Peter saw his loyal horse, Titan, tied up for the night in the stalls and he crept over to him. A large horse, Titan was grey with dark spots on his hind quarters. He was a strong animal bred for farming, but the Queen gave him to Peter as a companion and the two were inseparable. The crest of his neck was arched confidently with his glossy grey mane swept to one side. He had strong shoulders that held his head high with pride as though he knew he was a horse to a royal prince. His straight front legs were lean and muscular with ample knees and fetlocks that were only slightly bulging with hard sturdy newly shoed hooves. He had a slightly swayed back that led to hind quarters that were large and rounded from running and jumping with Peter in the fields. Titan was a strong sturdy horse for a young boy.

The horse whinnied when he saw the prince. Peter gently stroked his old friend's long grey mane. He scratched the white spot on its nose. Because he was a large horse he was a steep climb for any ten-year-old boy. After he harnessed Titan, Peter tied his sack onto the leather saddle lying on the stable ground. Peter placed his horse blanket onto Titan's back, causing the horse to whinny again because he knew a night ride was coming. Then, lifting with all his strength, Peter managed to carry the saddle over to his horse. He grabbed a stepstool and quietly lifted the saddle onto his horse's back.

Some of the stable boys turned to see what the noise was, but Peter hid behind Titan's large body. After he buckled the saddle under Titan's belly, he led him over to the fence so he could mount him without any trouble. The other horses whinnied as though they, too, wanted to go out for a moonlight stroll.

Some of the stable boys and groomsmen heard the horses, but went back to playing cards near the barn doors. They had built a small fire in the stone pit so they could stay warm. They were too busy losing money to notice Peter.

Once he was on Titan's back, the two carefully walked away from the castle stables as the other horses looked on.

"Shhh," Peter said to them as he grinned. They whinnied back and jerked their heads up and down. He winked at them then led his horse to the main gateway. The moon was already high in the sky as the sun made its last appearance over the hill. Four black crows hovered in the night air and cawed out to him. He just stared at their silhouettes flying through the moon's face.

Peter looked up at his window and saw the familiar yellow glow from the candlesticks on his bookshelf and the torches on the wall. His heart was really beating fast now. He scanned for the King's guards, knowing that if they saw him, they would stop him. They stood by the front gate which was still open after all the valley leaders had ridden through. Several townspeople were walking back and forth through the gate with their horses. Some pages were walking by as well. These young men were Peter's age, lived in the castle courtyard, and were studying to become knights one day. The guards were too busy talking of battle to notice Peter.

Once passed the gate and over the lowered drawbridge, they came to the rushing waters of the Blue River. Peter grabbed a handful of grey mane tightly in his fists and swallowed all the courage he could swallow as they galloped over the bridge and across the river. His heart pumped blood through his veins and sweat covered his forehead. He glanced back at the castle gate and around the land outside of the palace once again. No one had followed them.

Once the coast was clear, the two galloped away as fast as they could in the moonlight north towards the Dragon Forest.

4 ENTERING THE FOREST

The King rose to toast his guests as they sat around his large dining table in the center of the grand dining hall. It was decorated with the banners of each region represented there that night. The fine tapestries his fair Queen had collected on her travels hung on one wall while golden sconces held burning torches which glowed and lit the dim room. Portraits of the Kings of the past hung on adjacent walls. King Alexander's father, Aléon, posed impressively for his portrait with his beloved stallion, Audun. This enormous painting filled one wall behind the present King's eloquent chair.

As their great King stood, dressed in his finest silver armor with scarlet cape draping to the floor, all the guests stood out of respect for their host. All the golden goblets were filled with red sweet wine and the guests lifted their cups high as the King spoke. Sir Peregrine lifted his goblet the highest.

"This is a great night indeed. As we all gather here tonight to discuss our plans for protecting Illiath, and finally Théadril, from the enemy, unity is key to the survival of our great land, and we all have a duty to serve our people."

"Here, here!" the leaders said as they began to sit down. One leader, Lady Silith, remained standing.

"Your Highness, as the grateful representative of the great Cardion Valley, I cannot properly express the utter joy and relief of my people upon hearing the great news of your willingness to protect us against Lord Caragon, who at this precise moment is planning his evil takeover of every Valley we know." Lady Silith's burgundy velvet gown trimmed with gold thread glistened in the candlelight, revealing to all the great wealth of the people in the Cardion Valley. They were famous for their fine silks, velvets, and other materials brought over on the merchant ships. Many men of the Cardion Valley would take wagons over to the Eastshire port and bring back these treasures they traded.

When she finished speaking, she sat down to the right of the King—an honorable place setting indeed. Her father had served alongside the King's father, Aléon, during the wars against the many barons who attacked from the east. These Gothic brutes tended to rob the merchants who were bringing the Cardion people shipments from overseas. They had fought with great brutality. Many of the King's men were lost in these wars. Lake Silith is named after her father. The Cardion Valley was a peaceful valley filled with small stone houses with thatched rooftops. The people there grew much of the kingdom's wheat, corn, and other grains for its breads and flours. Windmills used for grinding these grains littered the valley landscape. Many of the women were fine seamstresses and its men were known for smithing its metals and iron.

Next, Lord Byrén rose to speak. He bowed with respect. "It is an honor to be in the presence of the King at this time in history."

"Our great lands are uniting to defeat the enemy once again, my Lord. As leader of the Crow Valley, I am here to inform you all that we will be as one with the Kingdom of Illiath in battle. As you all know, our small valley is most vulnerable to Lord Caragon. He has, at times, cut off our water supply from the Black River and threatened us with famine. My people are frightened that he will invade our valley and use our lands as an outpost of sorts for his army. This we cannot allow to happen!" Lord Byrén slammed his fist upon the large table.

The humble Crow Valley lay near the mountains by the Black River. The valley's townspeople bred fine horses for the King's stables. They also grew large trees to supply the King with wood for building projects, and grew hay and oats for the horses. They relied heavily on the river for water supply. Lord Caragon's castle, Hildron, stood ominously to the west of the Crow Valley.

"Here, here!" Many shouted in agreement.

The King nodded.

Sir Peregrine listened intently, but without comment. This silence did not go unnoticed. The King's eyes were upon the Knight.

"I, too, am here to express the concerns of my people." Lady Godden rose out of her chair. She was the eldest of the Godden family who lived in the Cornshire just east of the Kingdom. The tranquil Cornshire lay nearest the castle. With acres of green hills leading into the mountains near Lake Silith, the land was beautiful. To the south were the crystal clear waters of the Blue River that encircled Peek Island. The river fed row after row of corn and hay that grew full and tall in the bright sun for many a harvest. These cornfields, once the site of the bloodiest battle of the Cornshire war many harvests ago, were once again the place of peace and plenty. The people lived in tall houses made of mud bricks. Each owner had tree lined farms fenced in with wooden beams. Horses and livestock grazed openly on the fields. Lady Godden's long white hair was pulled tightly into a bun at the base of her long neck. She was dressed in the finest of silk dyed to a deep dark blue. Silver threading and embroidery decorated her long royal gown. Her hands were bejeweled with the oldest and rarest jewels in the land. They glistened as she gestured. Her appearance displayed the regality she had earned.

"Your majesty, I have come not to speak of war, but of peace," continued Lady Godden. "My people are weary of battle. We no longer see the need to see bloodshed on the battlefield as our only option for peace. We must find a way to appease Lord Caragon of his demands. We must do anything to avoid battle and the death that comes with it. All our valleys have seen too much death and bloodshed...too much loss. We have all seen war and its results. Who here has not been affected by war's ravages? Our land has thrived lo these many harvests. War would only cause famine upon the lands. My people have worked too hard to allow that to happen. War never causes benevolence, only death. Nothing good can come of it. Here and now we can stop the imminent threat of war. It must come to an end. I say, let us meet with Lord Caragon and discuss this as peacekeepers."

Mumbles of disagreement from all the other guests filled the dining hall. Heads shook from side to side in contempt of Lady Godden's speech. The King stood, and when he did so, Lady Godden bowed in respect then sat down in her chair to the left of the King.

"Friends, friends, please." King raised his right hand to silence the mumbles of disapproval. "Please, we must remember, this is a venue for all to speak as they feel. All are free to speak on behalf of their people. Lady Godden has done just that."

Sir Peregrine rested his gloved hand on his chin as he sat emotionless while the people spoke.

King Alexander left the great table and walked around his guests who remained seated. "Lady Godden, if I may be so bold, has come here on behalf of the great regal people of the Cornshire to ask me to avoid war at all costs. Am I correct my Lady?"

"Yes, Sire." She nodded in agreement. Her eyes remain lowered out of respect of her King.

"And may I assume that you have also come here to relay to me that your people, the fine people of the Cornshire, have a deep desire to allow Lord Caragon to enter into the Dragon Forest if this, too, means avoiding war?" the King asked.

Lady Godden's eyes widened with amazement. "Why yes, my Lord."

"And, am I also safe to assume that your people have implored you to come here to beseech me to let Lord Caragon slay the Dragon of the Forest if that is what he so desires, to avoid going to battle? Is this true?" He walked over to the large window overlooking the night sky. The full moon was high in the sky as its glow hovered over the Dragon Forest.

"Why yes, your majesty. The Dragon, after all, is a threat to all peoples everywhere," Lady Godden stated.

The King slowly turned towards the representatives of his great Kingdom. He looked each one in the eye, and as he met his eyes with theirs, they quickly lowered their gaze. "There is no appeasing evil, my Lady. What Lord Caragon has done is evil in the sight of my people and his very own. He has gone against the Treaty of Cornshire which your father and my grandfather both wrote in order to keep the peace. He was ordered not to build an army, and yet my spies have relayed to me that Caragon has spent the last eighteen moons doing just that. He has acquired a vast army. For what purpose is this army? I pay no heed to its purpose, only its illegality.

"He has over-taxed his people and horded all the money to supply this army while his own people starve and are forced to become like robber barons hiding in the Black Hills waiting to pounce on any travelers in utter desperation." The representative of the Black Hills nodded in agreement as the King continued.

"He has enslaved people and the Ogres and turned them out of their lands in the Théadron desert. He has gone against all that is good and kind to all of us who cherish these things. His desire is to enter into the Dragon Forest, not to slay the unseen Dragon whom you fear, but to control all of Théadril. His desire is to control all that we have. I refuse to enter into the Dragon Forest. I refuse to bring war into the peaceful forest in order to obtain that which is not mine to obtain. I have already spoken of this with my knights. This unseen Dragon has caused you no harm, my Lady. Nor will it cause us any harm so long as I govern." With this final statement, the King finished. He looked at Lady Godden who stared at her plate of uneaten pheasant and bread stuffing which the servants had placed on each plate.

"So, you see my Lady. There is no appeasing evil. One must strike at evil quickly. That is the only way. "

"Here, here!" All the guests stood at their feet and clapped in approval of their King's statement. Even Sir Peregrine rose with respect.

Lady Godden remained seated at first, but slowly rose as she watched her King walk back to his chair. She, too, stood clapping. But her gaze averted the King and his guests in disagreement.

"Now, please, all sit and let us eat this fine feast my staff has been preparing since this morning." The King sat down.

Sir Peregrine took a leg of pheasant and ate it heartily. The meat, flavored and roasted with butter and herbs from the Cornshire, melted in his mouth.

As all the guests began to eat and drink, they continued to discuss the matter at hand, when suddenly, a high pitched squeal resonated from the corridor and echoed through the Great Hall and interrupted the King's speech. Everyone looked around and gasped at the interruption.

Recognizing the voice as that of his son's nanny, the King asked the butler to find out what was the matter. But before the man could leave the room, the nanny entered huffing and puffing as she was out of breath.

"Begging your pardon, your majesty." The nanny bowed. "I regret to inform you that I cannot find Peter anywhere. His room is empty and I do not know where he is! All I found was a note on his pillow."

"Where is this note?" The King held out his hand.

She handed it to the King, curtsied, and waited as he read it. When he finished, he gazed out the large window and into the darkness. The King eyed Sir Peregrine and yelled for his guards.

"Ready a search party!" he ordered and quickly left the hall. Peregrine nodded in submission and followed his King.

As the note fluttered its way to the floor, the butler picked it up and read it:

Dear father,

I believe it is time to put my sword to good use and be the Prince I was meant to be. I will be back soon with the Dragon scales for your army.

Love, Peter

"Oh dear." The butler rolled his eyes upward. "He's just like his father."

"He must have heard the meeting the King had with his knights," the nanny said. "That poor boy is out there all alone in the night. Whatever shall we do?" she asked.

"Don't worry, my dear. The King will find him," answered the butler.

The butler stared at all the distinguished guests. He bowed respectively towards them, feeling all eyes on him. He rubbed the nape of his neck. "In all my years of service to the King, this is the first time I did not instinctively know what to do."

"Perhaps we should all pray for his safe return." Lady Godden rose from her seat.

"No worries," answered Lord Byrén. "Prince Peter will be back before we know it. I say we continue eating this fine meal."

§

"A search party?" the Knights asked as their squires and pages helped them quickly put on their armor. "Whatever for?"

"Well, the Prince, as young as he is, has decided to enter into the Dragon Forest this very night." Sir Peregrine watched his men get ready. Smiling, he removed his sword from its sheath and ran his fingers over the long blade ever so carefully. "It seems he has decided to retrieve the scales for the King himself."

"What?" They chuckled as their boots were fastened. "You cannot be serious?"

"That foolish boy! What does this do to our plans?" one knight asked as he angrily buckled his belt and adjusted his sword. "Everything will be ruined!"

Peregrine returned his sword to its sheath and considered the dancing fire glowing in the fire pit. He slowly walked over to it.

With the poker he moved the logs around to rekindle the fire's warmth. A sudden burst of flames lit up the small quarters. The heat felt good on his hands.

"Be patient, my friend. Nothing is ruined." He grinned as he played with the fire.

"The impudent lad has simply caused our plans to be put into effect sooner rather than later. Actually, the boy appears to have more sense than his father."

The men laughed.

"We will enter into the forest to retrieve the boy, or so the King will suppose." Peregrine held the red hot poker by the handle. "But in the end, we will have those scales."

He held up the burning poker close to the ruggedly handsome features of his bearded face until the orange glow reflected off his countenance. "So help me, we will have those scales no matter what the cost."

Relieved, the knights nodded in agreement. Their plans had been constructed carefully after much advisement. They weren't about to let a young boy ruin them this night even if that boy was Prince of the kingdom. Too much was at stake to let go of all they had already conceived. Many of Peregrine's men had fallen into debt and would have lost their estates had it not been for their leader's generous offer. Those scales meant money in their hands.

When they were fully armored and had their shields and torches, they headed out the estate doorway and to the stables where their squires were leading their saddled horses out to meet them. The night air was cool as the moon lit their way. Peregrine joined his men at his stables. He mounted his horse and joined his men in riding out to meet the king.

§

The King's men rushed out to the stables, interrupting the stable boys' poker game. They accidentally overturned their table sending their cards flying into the air. Quickly, they helped the knights saddle the horses and lead them out into the courtyard. Each knight mounted his anxious horse in the cold night air and rode over to the castle gate. There they saw the King mounted on his majestic white steed, the envy of all the land. It breathed heavily in the cold air and its breath could be seen as mist leaving its nostrils. The King held the reins tightly. His horse tugged at the reins and dug its hooves into the dirt. King Alexander knew it was ready to ride. Dressed with breastplate for protection and royal cape with the lion crest of Illiath embroidered onto it, King Alexander represented his land well.

"We will split up into two groups. One group will approach from the Cardion Valley, while the other approaches from the Northshore. Call out when you have reached the threshold of the forest. No one is to enter the forest. Understood?" he ordered.

The men all nodded in submission to their noble King. Then they all rode off in one accord, not knowing what lay ahead of them. None of them had ever approached the Dragon Forest before.

§

Peter rode as fast as he could that night as he watched the Dragon Forest appear larger and larger before his eyes. His horse breathed heavily in the cold night air. Although they were moving quickly, the night air seemed peaceful and still. He stopped before entering the Cardion Valley and turned back to look at the castle. He could see the mill tower where flour was made and near it he could see light coming from the Marshall's tower. As he spotted the light from his bedroom window, he could faintly see men with torches aligned on the castle walls guarding his father and the people.

He rode through the Cardion Valley first. This was the first time Peter had ever ventured this far away from the castle. He had been to the Cornshire once with his father for a memorial to the knights who died in battle. But he had never been this far away from home. As he rode through the quaint Cardion Valley, he pictured his father, the King, toasting his guests back at the castle dining hall. Peter slowed Titan to a trot as they entered into the valley. He wasn't sure if anyone there would recognize him, but then he realized that most people had never seen his face before. He was only allowed to stroll in the Castle courtyard, but never outside the gates. Here he saw small houses with thatched roofs as it was supper time for the people and most were inside now. Wisps of smoke came from all the brick chimneys. Peter could hear Titan's hooves slosh in the muddy road beneath them. Once in a while he heard an owl far off, but it was so peaceful here in the Valley.

He passed a house and peaked into the window from a top his horse. Together they stood outside of the home, curious as to what was happening inside. They heard laughter, a child's laughter. Titan's ears perked up. Peter leaned forward to see inside the small house. He saw a mother stirring a black pot by the large kitchen fireplace. She was talking to her husband who was playing with his small son. They sat at the dinner table, which was smaller than Peter's feather bed. The mother served the hearty stew into the bowls and the steam rose from each bowl. Then, the child and father bowed their heads to pray, giving thanks for their portion.

Peter stared at them for a moment. In silence, he sat there watching them, almost envying them from afar.

"Peter, say thank you before you eat your meal," his mother, the Queen had said to him once. She sternly looked at her young son, then smiled at him. Peter dutifully bowed his head and whispered a prayer of thanksgiving for his meal. As he prayed, the King entered into the dining hall. A servant held out his chair and he sat next to his beautiful wife, Queen Laurien. Peter sat by watching his mother and father spoke to one another of the day's

events. The three of them sat at the south end of the long mahogany table lined with plates of food and pitchers of wine.

Titan whinnied softly and woke Peter from his memory of family before Lord Caragon brought so many problems to the land. *I can almost smell the food at the table,* he thought. Back then, the King had time for his son. Peter missed their time together as a family. He could barely remember his mother's voice.

Titan stirred more vigorously. Peter realized a bit of tear had welled up in his eye and he quickly wiped it away.

"Come on now, let's go," he told Titan, gently prodding his horse. Peter tugged the reins towards the left to turn the horse around. They went down another street.

Together they walked slowly through the town in silence. Most of the homes had families sitting to supper, just like the one before. Peter rubbed his belly. It ached from nervousness. He wasn't sure what he was feeling inside. The moon above lit up the hills to the east of them. As Peter and Titan rode through the town, a man outside of his small home gathering firewood for the night called out to Peter. "Hey," he said to them. "Are you lost, son?"

"No, I am not lost," answered Peter. He tried not to make eye contact with the man. He did not want to be recognized. "I am just passing through town." Then he jerked Titan's reins, grabbed a handful of his dark thick mane, and turned the horse around. As they departed the small valley, they rode off together toward their goal.

While riding over the small green hills north of Cardion Valley. Peter could see his own breath in the night. The air grew colder as they approached the Dragon Forest.

At last hey reached the entrance to the forest. There they stood, Peter and his horse, the two of them about to begin their first adventure.

The trees stood as ominously as ever as they guarded their secret with fierce loyalty. They were such a dark green, Peter thought they were black. The moon was high now and giving off its familiar yellow glow in the cloudless sky. The perfect round orb illuminated the way for Peter as Titan slowly approached the edge of the trees. Peter climbed off Titan, grabbed the reins, and led him through the trees with his wooden sword in hand. The hooves in the dirt and leaves made a squishing noise—the only noise to be heard besides the caw of a black crow above him perched on a tree. The occasional breeze moving through the trees and scattering the dead leaves around them startled Titan. The midnight black crow stood there on its branch watching their every move. It appeared to be laughing at them. Peter frowned.

Thick and hard to navigate, the trees with their branches caught Peter's cape once or twice, tugging at his neck. It startled him as it almost felt like the trees were grabbing him and trying to keep him from going any further. He knew he must keep going. He untied his cape and left it dangling from a branch. *To get those scales for father is my only mission. To present him with those scales would make the King so proud of me. To do this one thing would stop the threat of war with Caragon and his men. I just know it.* In Peter's mind, it was the only way.

As they continued in, they could see the trees thinned and revealed a clearing of the forest. The blue mist grew thicker now and surrounding them. The cooler air went through Peter's tunic like light through a shade, leaving his skin chilled. Finally, the lake was before them. Its surface was like a smooth sapphire stone. A cloud approached and quickly blocked out the moon's glow, making it difficult for Peter to see where he was going. Coming in from the east, another breeze put a chill in the already cool night air.

They continued walking, searching for the Dragon's hiding place. *Would it be in a cave? Or would it be hiding in the trees?* Peter thought hard about what it would look like. Was it really one hundred feet tall as his history tutor once told him? Was it green with red eyes? Did it breathe fire and exhale smoke from its nostrils? Or was that just another tale? No one knew for sure.

Peter stopped by the lake as the cloud moved with the wind and the moon made its appearance once again shining brightly on the lake. As the water moved ever so gently in the breeze, thousands of sparkles of moonlight danced on the surface of the waters like glitter tossed into the air. The blue mist rose just above the water almost like a downy blanket. Peter had never seen such beauty and if he were never to see anything else in his whole life, he would not be sad because he was finally living his dream. He was inside the Dragon Forest.

"Have you ever seen anything so beautiful?" he whispered to his horse. Together they looked around the sapphire lake in quiet solitude. The trees encircled the lake like guards. They towered over the pair in an almost regal state.

Their silent repose was broken by a whispering voice from behind them.

"Did you hear something?" Peter quietly asked his horse. Titan looked at him and remained quiet.

"Is someone there?" Peter asked the darkness.

Silence.

"Is someone there, I say?" Peter hesitated.

"Is someone there, I say?" The darkness echoed.

5 THE RESCUE

The King and his men galloped across the lands passing the quiet Cardion Valley. Clops of mud flew into the air as the horses trampled the wet ground. Heading over the hills and toward the entrance of the Dragon Forest, they could see the rows of quaint little houses with smoke wafting from their chimneys

As they approached the entrance, they stopped to hear their King's instructions. They all gathered there to listen. The breath from their horses filled the air as their large chests heaved in and out. They had worked the beasts hard on that night.

Before heading on, Sir Peregrine directed his men toward the King to listen. The King saw his head knight approach.

"Your majesty," Sir Peregrine said approaching on horseback.

"Peregrine, take your men near the Northern entrance and we will enter here. Meet us in the center of the Forest near the lake. Mind you, it is deep. The way can become like an illusion. The Forest, it comes alive."

"Enter in?" Peregrine asked. "My Lord, is it wise for the King to enter into the forest?" The men were silent. "Perhaps you should allow me and my men to enter first."

As King Alexander pondered this idea, a rider approached from behind. It was the King's messenger.

"Your Highness," the boy huffed as his horse slid to a stop in the muddy earth. Then he spoke with great urgency. "A message

...from your scouts... in the Black Hills." He dismounted and handed the King the note.

Amazed that this young man had ridden the great distance from the Black Hills, the King read on. The message must be urgent indeed.

The King dismounted his horse and rushed toward the exhausted messanger. Taking the note, he eyed his knights. They looked confused.

He paced as he read the words scribbled on the note:

My Lord, as your loyal scout, I have asked this devoted messenger to bring you this most urgent warning. Lord Caragon's men have been hiding in the Black Hills. Only I and a handful of my men have survived. Caragon's men have left Hildron castle and are headed toward the Cardion Valley and, as I write this, they ride with the intent to destroy all in the Valley as they head toward the Cornshire and, finally, the Castle of Illiath.

There is not much time to act. I pray you meet Caragon's men before they enter the Valley.

Your loyal servant...

King Alexander stood silent with his back toward his men. He had never felt more alone. The dilemma was staring him straight in the face.

How could this have happened? His mind raced. He raised his eyes toward the Forest with its black trees staring down at him. The moon was now covered by dark looming clouds. Several black crows encircled them above, cawing and breaking his concentration. He alone knew what the forest possessed. He knew what his son faced. He also knew the capabilities of Caragon's men, and how the men of the Cardion Valley were mostly farmers, not soldiers. They would be no match for the evil knights of Caragon's army of Hildron riding toward them now. He pictured the people asleep in the small thatched homes unaware of the events about to take place...all the faces of the women and the children of the village.

Something had to be done.

"Sire." Sir Peregrine dismounted and walked toward the King.

"Caragon's men," Alexander whispered. "They tricked us. They saw us leave the castle and are now headed toward Cardion."

Alexander searched Peregrine's face, but found no surprise. Puzzled, the King turned toward his knights. "We've not much time."

"Yes, sire. What about the Prince?" Peregrine asked.

Faced with this dilemma, the King had to weigh the importance of his young son's foolish night ride and the evil that headed toward his people.

"You there!" The King motioned for the messenger. He put his hands on the young rider's shoulders and gazed deep into his anxious eyes. "Ride back to the castle. Ride as fast as you can. There isn't much time to waste. When you arrive at the gate, give the constable the note. Tell him to prepare the Castle for siege and to send a garrison of my knights to meet us in the Cardion Valley hills. Tell them of the urgency. Now ride!"

With that, the messenger hopped back on his horse and shouted at the frightened animal to move. The men watched him ride off toward the kingdom. Then they turned their eyes on the King.

"We've only minutes to spare. All of you will ride with me toward the Valley. Sir Peregrine?" The King turned toward his head knight.

"Yes, my Lord!" He shouted in reply and placed his hand over his heart. "I will lead my men into the forest and retrieve your son."

"Do nothing out of foolishness, Peregrine," Alexander said. "The Dragon is real."

"We will approach with caution, your majesty." Peregrine bowed his head.

The King wanted to hear just that. Relieved, he mounted his horse. He looked regal on his mount as his silver armor glistened and his scarlet cape flowed in the slight breeze. The Sword of Alexander was safely inside its sheath attached to the King's belt. His heart told him to trust his old friend, Peregrine, once more. At sixteen years of age, they had fought together in battle. Peregrine fought as a squire, Alexander as the Prince. For his courage, Alexander had knighted Peregrine there on the battlefield after he became King. From that moment on, Peregrine had sworn allegiance to Alexander and his bloodline.

Alexander would have to trust him once again—this time with his son's life.

"I trust you will bring back my son?" He asked his head Knight and all the men with him.

"Yes, sire." Sir Peregrine knelt down in submission to his King. "We will find him or die, my Lord."

He placed his hand over his heart.

"So be it." the King said. He jerked the reins of his stallion and rode off with his band of men.

6 LORD CARAGON'S WAR

Lord Caragon's dark castle, Hildron, was carved out of a colossal rocky mountain just west of the Black Hills. Once one of King Illiath's most loyal advisors, he had remained in exile since before Alexander's birth, where his heart became dark in thought and deed.

What makes a heart of flesh become a heart of stone? Lord Caragon's heart turned against the kingdom for vain reasons. During the Battle of the Cornshire, he took the leader of the Edonites aside and joined their cause. Desiring the land east of the Cornshire, they had cut off all access to the Blue River. Caragon secretly supplied them with the battle plans of the kingdom. He requested nothing but a piece of land for himself in return.

Then, he stood by and watched as new King Aléon's men died at the hands of the Edonites. The soul of Caragon blackened on that day.

When King Aléon discovered Caragon's deeds upon the defeat of the Edonites, he decreed Lord Caragon to be executed for his crimes against the people. But his father, Illiath, relented. He showed pity for Caragon. Instead, Illiath exiled him to the Black Hills, decreeing that he never again return. Off Caragon went into the desert lands west of the Black Hills, taking with him a few men tempted by lies of promised wealth and power.

Low these many moons, Caragon remained in silent exile. The leaders of the Crow Valley and the Black Hills lived in peace. But many suspected that his heart was growing darker and more evil with each passing harvest. Black clouds were always present over the hills and near Hildron castle. Many whispered of dark and evil deeds being performed inside. No one dared to enter the evil realm.

Secretly, Caragon's kingdom began to grow. He put together an army of creatures with hearts as black and twisted as his own and created many new weapons. With mystical powers as the source, he created weaponry unseen by any warrior. Rumored to be working alongside Lord Bedlam, these weapons were the most lethal in battle. The tainted black metal could not be shattered by the steel swords of man. Yet Caragon still coveted the scales of the Dragon. These, the foretold weapons of the greatest army, still remained unseen.

To achieve his evil plans of conquest, he enslaved and overburdened his people, causing many of them to escape into the mountains in desperation. He cut off access to the Black River for the people of the Crow Valley in order to ruin their crops and force them to starve. He then horded all the water for his army and attempted to overtake all the lands.

The dark clouds remained over the Black Hills and Hildron castle as the people feared for their lives. War was looming once again in the kingdom of Théadril.

§

When the King's messenger arrived at the castle, he hastily gave the message to Constable Darion who then told all the King's men to prepare for the battle. Darion, a young man with no family of his own, served the King in the tradition of his fathers. He quietly lived within the palace walls with his books and collections of rocks and shells from his travels. He loved the King as a brother and remembered with great fondness the Queen. Ordinary in appearance and physical strength, Darion was more intellectual than soldier and was pleased that way. He made his way up the ranks of servanthood by using his mind to great effect by inventing the spyglass and perfecting the telescope used by the Royal Astronomers. His inventions were greatly admired and used throughout the kingdom. King Alexander trusted Darion without reservation for he had proved his loyalty and fidelity time and again. Now, as Darion held the King's message within his hands, he knew his time of true testing had come.

§

The King had taken a hundred men with him on the search for Peter, but now he needed the garrison of archers and foot soldiers to prepare for war on Caragon's army.

The Lords and Ladies present in the castle were all escorted to the steward's tower where they could stay for the night. Lady Silith grieved for her people. She wanted to return, but the King's steward warned her of the dangers. She agreed to remain at the Castle.

The Castle became a frantic mess in no time. The archers all readied their bows and the pages and squires gathered thousands of arrows for the battle. They all readied the mangonels, the wooden structures posted along the battle lines for the King's archers to hide behind while they shot their arrows. Crossbows were prepared as well as spears, lances, shields. The blacksmiths were summoned to the Keep where the Constable ordered them to ready their fires in case any armor needed to be repaired. The blacksmiths were in charge of making helmets, armor, shields, and other metal objects alongside the Armorer. They ran to stoke their firepits. The Groomsmen readied the horses, feeding and hitching them all. The loud clanging of hammers against anvils echoed throughout the courtyard as Blacksmiths sharpened swords, axes, and daggers.

In the old Keep, the constable went over food supplies with the Butler and his Pantler. They overlooked fuel, food, and weapons stored in case of battle. Hidden down a spiral staircase beneath the castle floor was the dark and musty old Keep. There they inspected rows and rows of old barrels filled with blasting powder and fuel like oil. Trunks filled with preserved food lay next to rows of sacks filled with grain and potatoes. If the siege to the castle lasted for many weeks, the constable knew the people could starve if not enough food stored properly in the old Keep. His was grateful when he saw that his men made proper precautions.

Now the time to warn the other villages of the siege had come. On top of one of the tallest towers of the castle stood a large lantern made with tar and wood, only to be lit as a warning of any approaching trouble. The constable quickly gave the order to light the torch as a warning to the people. The young soldier understood the order and he quickly ran up the stairs leading to the torch. He held a smaller torch in his hand to be used to ignite the flame. As he huffed his way up the lofty perch, he finally approached the enormous pile of wood soaked in black tar. He lowered his small torch onto the surface and immediately the fire spread across the warning signal and sprang up into the starlit sky. The warning signal burned thirty feet into the night. The soldier hoped the other villages would see its light. He could feel the intense heat on his face. Then he quickly turned and headed down the stairs.

The constable stood on the North facing wall of the Castle alongside the garrison of soldiers waiting with bated breath. The sky over the villages below remained darkened except for some glowing orange lights coming from Lord Caragon's approaching army. His heart sank at the sight. *Perhaps it is too late*, he thought.

Just then, from the Cardion Valley, the soldiers could see the torch—the acknowledgement that the people of the Cardion Valley had seen the signal and the people knew of the coming siege. In a matter of time, the people would head toward the Castle and safety.

One by one, the torches lit up the night sky. The Crow Valley torch, the farthest and most difficult to see, burned as well. The people would remain there and fight to save their land. A journey to the castle would be far too dangerous for them. They would ultimately come face to face with Caragon's army if they tried to go through the desert plains. They decided to stay and wait. And pray.

§

The torch of the Cornshire cut through the night sky as the people entered into the Castle courtyard to safety. The constant stream of villagers with their carts pulled by oxen, donkeys, and people on foot lined the road toward the Castle. The people carried everything precious to them as well as woolen blankets, pots of water, and tools. Most important of all were the animals. Sheep and goats followed by chickens and geese all streamed into the courtyard. As the people entered into the once peaceful market, they saw soldiers running to find position, carpenters building reinforcements near the tops of towers and gates, and food and water being rushed into the storage rooms of the Keep. They smelled the fires from the Armorer's pit as the men swiftly hoarded together more and more freshly made swords and arrows for the soldiers.

Many had never been inside the castle walls. Amazed at how high the stone walls stood into the sky, the people began to feel hope. Constable Darion shouted orders to the garrison of soldiers to carry extra supplies of arrows and lances with them up to their positions on the castle walls. Other soldiers gathered in the Chapel where the Chaplain was offering a prayer of safety for the men.

Realizing there was little left to do as Caragon's army approached, the constable waited and watched.

With the final order given, the last villagers made their way through the gates and the main gate closed. The soldiers and villagers watched in awe as the towering wooden bridge rose into the night sky and ultimately sealed the palace walls. North, south, east and western gates were all closed immediately upon Darion's orders. Having never seen the gates in the closed position, the people were suddenly filled with fear. They worried about their homes, farms, and the village itself they had left behind. Would they ever see their lands again? Mothers held their children closer and their men held them tight. Each hoped for the safety of their King, who faced Lord Caragon's army even as they stood there.

Sadness crept over the kingdom as a black cloud gathers before a fierce storm. Everyone knew what Caragon's men were capable of; they knew the hatred and greed that bred in the black hearts of his men. For years, they had seen the evil in the form of a gathering gloom hovering over his dark castle.

Four hundred soldiers remained atop the castle walls. More waited within the courtyard. The outer curtain walls were several yards thick and made of stone. They could withstand a battle. Nevertheless, soldiers and archers stood at the ready. The wind stopped. The eerie stillness settled over the walls and over the land. They knew the walls held their fate. The soldiers would risk all to ensure that the enemy would not find their way over those walls.

"Look!" yelled one foot soldier as he pointed out towards the desert plains. The full moon moved outside the clouds and lit up the horizon. From along the castle walls, the soldiers could see an immense and growing orange glow from the fires of Caragon's army as it burned the Cardion Valley.

The siege had begun.

7 FACE TO FACE

Peter stood in frozen silence from the whispering voice he heard. *Was it just an echo of my own voice? Or was it someone else...?*

Titan looked around the forest near the surface of the lake for any sign of an approaching creature. His skin quivered from fear as well. A black crow continued to circle above them with his ever present *caw* descending down through the trees. The black bird made Titan nervous and he whinnied and shook his long dark mane. He pulled on his reins to signal to Peter for them to get moving.

"Yes, alright," Peter agreed as he walked Titan around the lake. The mist followed them. Every once in a while the surface of the water danced in the breeze and moved in every direction. Peter, anxious that something would arise out of the water, was troubled that his imagination was getting the best of him. So, together, the two adventurers continued to walk the area of the lake. The black from the forest peered at them from all sides and their old friend, the crow, continued his song above.

"Blasted crow," Peter whispered to Titan. "It makes me nervous." He eyed the circling bird above while he walked cautiously around the lake. The tops of the trees framed the crow as if it were a painting. The sort of painting no one wants. The moon was their guide, illuminating the whole area for the time being. Clouds hovered near the moon waiting to blanket the glowing orb and make it near impossible for Peter and Titan to continue their search. But for now, the moon stayed out in the open.

The crunch of the leaves underfoot was the only sound heard above the gentle breeze swaying the trees. Peter and his faithful horse stopped to figure out their direction. Then a sense of calm came to the forest...

Suddenly, the branches shaking violently in front of them, ending the calm. Several small birds quickly departed the darkness and flew up into the air, flittering by Peter and Titan. Peter waved his arms in front of his face while the birds flew past. The trees continued to tremble. Peter and Titan froze as they waited for something to happen. And it did.

There, from between the branches of the trees, moved a set of glowing yellow eyes, each one about the size of Peter's head. They stared right at Peter and his horse, unblinking in the moonlight. Peter's mouth was open; he turned to see if Titan was experiencing the sight as well. Titan's eyes were large and his nostrils flared as his ears were pointed back. Together they stood, staring at the yellow eyes glaring back at them. The dark pupils were vertical slits that reached from the bottom to the top of each glowing eye.

Then they heard it.

A low ominous, growl penetrated from behind the trees. The eyes rose from a few feet above the wet earth to just near the tops of the trees. They blinked as they rose. The growl grew louder. Then a hot mist from between the trees shot out towards the Prince, who was near tears in his fright. His body shook. The short blast of mist warmed Peter's skin and made him and Titan take a few steps back.

"Do not move," a low voice hissed. It seemed to come from the glowing eyes, which were nothing but slits now peering from the tops of the trees. "It is important that you are here."

Peter's knees shook; he eyed his faithful horse. Titan neighed nervously; his whole body quivered. With ears pointed back, he nervously shook his grey mane and whinnied. His hooves clawed at the mud beneath him as he huffed air out from his nostrils in defiance.

"Steady, boy," Peter said as he tightly held the reins.

Titan's bravery gave Peter his courage back as well. From his belt, he quickly pulled his wooden sword from its sheath and lunged toward the ever present eyes.

"Who goes there?" he yelled.

The yellow eyes moved rapidly up the trees and high into the night sky with the moon highlighting the tough, scaly skin of the giant creature's head and body. The hot, misty breath, spewed forth from its nostrils, exhaled in frustration, toward the boy and his steed. Larger than any other dragon known to terrorize the kingdom, the Dragon of the forest had four long limbs and a set of wings attached to its back. Gazing down at them from its lofty perch above the trees of grand forest green, it could see the fire glow from the torches of Lord Caragon's army approaching from the west. The Dragon of the forest knew the time had come.

Peter and Titan, in awesome wonder and amazement, stared at the giant creature as it stood many feet above the tops of the trees. Their eyes moved downward in order to see its giant feet now protruding from the trunks of those same black trees. The shiny claws glistened in the moonlight as they dug into the mud. Its colossal head had rough scales all over the surface, some bent grotesquely over the eyes and down the slope of its long snout leading to the protruding nostrils. Blue mist eased out of those same nostrils. The larger hardened scales made their way down its long giraffe-like neck and onto its humpback where the wings folded over its sides. Small horns made their way out of its skull behind the eyes, but they were short and dull, perhaps from battle.

The loud rustling noise throughout the forest came from its long tail as it moved back and forth. The end of the tail provided the final resting place for the larger more prominent scales to form sharp spikes. Even with the larger hind legs bent underneath its enormous body, it stood high into the night sky. Peter did not want to imagine the creature's full height. He froze in his dread. Titan whinnied and shook the reins from Peter's hands as he backed up in astonishment and fear. Peter grabbed Titan's reins once again. Just then, together, they remained frozen as the realization before them came to complete fruition: The Dragon of the Forest lives.

"We've not much time," it spoke. More steam came from the nostrils.

Peter looked at Titan. *Astonishing. Could it be that it spoke to us? Are we dreaming?*

The Dragon lifted one foot and with sudden force slammed it into the ground. The earth shook beneath them. A shot of fire eased out of its nostrils and lit up its roughened face made of scales and snake-like skin. The glow from its fire breath reflected in its shiny scales. They appeared to be made up of many different colors. For a slight moment, Peter surmised the scales were more beautiful that he had ever imagined.

The Dragon lowered its mammoth head toward the two before him, and his tongue slithered between its enormous teeth housed inside the giant mouth. The hot misty breath shocked Peter into complete attention to anything it might say if it meant it would not eat them both in one swallow.

"Listen now," it stated rather calmly. "I know why you are here."

"Yes." Peter nodded through his fear.

The Dragon studied him.

Peter swallowed hard as the yellow eyes narrowed.

"I need your assistance," it said, raising its head slightly upward. At that same moment, Peter could see its entire face in the moonlight. Its eyes were gentler than he had first thought. Although its hot breath and large teeth seemed frightening, somehow he was reassured they were not meant for him.

"*My* help?" Peter asked.

"Yes." The Dragon hissed. Just then, it spread its wings open wide, revealing the translucent skin between tough tendons and claws. They were immense in size and caused a breeze that ran across Peter and Titan's faces as the wings moved over the Dragon's body. This giant beast could have squashed them both with one gesture of its claws, yet it was somewhat tolerant of how they had trespassed into its forest.

Gazing up over the tops of the trees, the Dragon saw something in the valleys to the South. Peter waited for further instruction.

"War has come to the Kingdom. Caragon's army is coming," it said, swallowing hard. Peter watched the lump in its the throat slide down toward the large belly. From head to belly must have been the size of the castle courtyard, Peter assessed.

"War?" Peter faintly asked. Suddenly, he was ashamed to be missing from the castle. He sorrowfully looked down at his feet. He felt foolish.

"It is good that you are here," the Dragon said, as if sensing Peter's sadness. "You have come at the right time."

Its giant foot dragged the claws into the mud. Large piles of mud surrounded each long claw like the termites' hills Peter had seen in the desert one summer. He remembered each hill as being taller than his father and these mud hills were no smaller. The sliding of the claws in the mud echoed deep into the forest. Peter stared at the yellow eyes and wondered what the Dragon could have meant.

"What can I possibly do to help? I'm afraid I have ruined things for my father by running away. He is looking for me instead of attacking Caragon's army." Peter sighed.

"Why did you come here?" the Dragon asked. Blue mist eased from its nostrils.

"To—" Peter hesitated. "—Find you, to be exact." He looked at the sword in his hands. His fingers were firmly entwined around the handle. He reexamined his intentions. He suddenly felt sick. *A wooden sword against a giant beast?* He looked down at his feet and shivered from the cold. He felt....ten years old again.

"And so you have succeeded," the Dragon said as his tongue slithered out between its teeth once again.

"Yes, but I wanted to find you in order to…take your scales." He winced and waited for the fire to consume him.

But the Dragon moved its giant body and lifted its feet toward the two little creatures in front of him. Titan took three steps back as the beast made its way through the trees and into the clearing. A puff of fire came from its mouth and the firelight blew across the surface of the water as it illuminated the entire lake. The sound echoed off the surface of the lake. Titan reared up onto his hind legs in fear and confusion.

"No, Titan!" Peter yelled. "He won't hurt us!" He ran and grabbed the reins to his horse's harness. He pulled the gentle horse to him. With their heads together, Peter gently stroked the muzzle of his friend. "Trust me. All is well now."

A calm had gone through Peter's body settling his spirits. He no longer was afraid of the Dragon. A peace went through his soul and he now knew things would be okay with the Dragon here in the forest. The legend was true after all. Perhaps his father had been taken care of by the giant Dragon when he was a boy just like he had told him. Perhaps that is why his father never wanted Caragon or Peregrine to enter into this realm.

The Dragon hissed as it moved to the other side of the clearing. Peter and Titan stirred swiftly in order to get out of the way of its body and tail. The Dragon's sinewy muscles underneath the tough outer skin twitched and pulled the massive body along. The Dragon's claws dug deep into the mud as it moved. The earth trembled with each step. The beautiful scales twinkled in the moonlight. Shiny black clawed feet and long wings made a breeze on Peter's face as they went by him. The eyes of the beast were lined with tiny rows of scales; the rims of its eyes were reddened as though they were tired or old.

"How old are you?" Peter asked.

The beast continued to move its way over to the lake. "Very old," it hissed.

Peter considered his grandfather and great-grandfather and how they knew of the Dragon. "You knew my grandfather and great-grandfather?" he asked.

"Yes," the Dragon answered. "I am two thousand of your man years."

The notion of the Dragon being so ancient shocked Peter.

He placed his wooden sword in its sheath and quickly mounted Titan and galloped alongside the Dragon to keep up. Not wanting to miss anything now, he rode with the beast.

The three made their way around the lake and toward the entrance of the forest. The Dragon looked down at the horse and rider it had befriended. It stopped and motioned to Peter. Needing Peter to see exactly what was happening, it lowered its head and motioned Peter to hop on top. Peter dismounted Titan, carefully and cautiously walked over to the Dragon's large head, and climbed on top. Titan whinnied and moved back a few paces. Peter grabbed the small horns behind the Dragon's eyes and lifted himself to the neck of the beast. He discovered the scales were smooth and cool in the night air.

The Dragon slowly raised its head to prevent Peter from falling. Higher and higher it went into the air. Peter held on tight to the Dragon's scales as he watched Titan grow smaller and smaller. Suddenly, he saw the entire forest in the moonlight. The crystal clear lake and the trees seemed to go on forever. Then he turned his head south toward the Castle. His heart sank deep into his chest at the sight.

The Cardion valley engulfed in flames. He could see Caragon's army moving toward the palace and his father's soldiers fighting with them. The sight of flaming arrows and homes burning amidst the shouts of men in battle made Peter gasp. Peter could not believe his eyes. He remembered of the families he had seen. He envisioned their plight. Now he knew why the Dragon wanted him to see the view from up high.

"As your father returns to the Castle, the siege begins," the Dragon said.

"No." Peter shook his head. He covered his mouth with his hands. They were cold from the night air. "What can I do?" He asked as he lowered his hands.

"Lord Peregrine's men will enter the forest from the north in order to destroy me and take my scales." The Dragon slowly turned its head toward the north.

Peter could see the torches and riders swiftly approaching. He wondered if they could see the massive Dragon high above the trees.

"Quickly! You must bend down or they will see you," Peter shouted.

The Dragon stood motionless. "They will be upon us soon."

Us? Peter thought. *What will we do to stop them?*

The Dragon began to lower its head. It took a few steps into the clearing.

"They must not see me, but they must find you safe," it said as it lowered Peter to the ground.

"I want to stay here with you and help," Peter said.

"Patience, I need you… in the forest to help me… with this battle." The Dragon slowly answered.

Peter hopped off the large head of the Dragon and staggered a few feet back. He was a little dizzy now. His sword still dangled in its sheath, Titan whinnied, as if glad to see him back.

"Remove your sword," the Dragon ordered.

Peter hesitated a moment, then obeyed. Not sure what the Dragon saw in the little wooden sword, Peter wondered if it mattered. He slowly pulled the sword out and, with embarrassment, held it in his hand. His fist clenched around the handle.

"Hold it up high," the Dragon said as it lowered his head toward Peter. Its mouth stood a few feet away from Peter. "Hold it tightly."

Titan, with nostrils flared, trotted next to Peter and quietly observed the Dragon. Peter held onto the sword with both hands now eagerly anticipating what the Dragon would do.

Suddenly, the Dragon inhaled the night air deep into his massive lungs. As the chest cavity expanded more and more, the sound resembled that of a wind storm and Peter's hair blew in toward the giant mouth. The Dragon leaned its head back as it inhaled the air. A hissing could be heard. Peter closed his eyes, not knowing what to expect. Titan turned his head away.

Then, the Dragon's mouth opened and spewed out a thin blue flame of fire from between its teeth as it exhaled onto the sword.

SSSSSwhoooooosh!

The flash of fire hit only the blade of Peter's sword and nothing else. The weight of the force from the blue flame almost knocked Peter off his feet, but he held fast and strong leaning into the flame. The blue fire enveloped the small blade only, Peter opened one eye to see what happened.

He felt on his face that the flame was not hot. Indeed, it was ice cold! The blue flame was penetrating the wooden sword and changing it somehow. It grew heavier and heavier as the Dragon breathed upon it. Peter could feel the handle becoming colder and colder in his hands as he watched his sword transform before his eyes. *What is it doing?*

SSSSSSSSSwoooosssssshhhhh.

As quickly as it started, it ended. The Dragon hissed and inhaled air once again, only this time it raised its head away from Peter. Titan turned slowly to inspect the damage to his master only to find him in one piece still clutching the sword in both hands.

Peter opened his eyes wider now in amazement while he studied the sword. He could not believe what he saw. The blade was no longer made of wood. Now made of the shiniest metal he had ever seen, the blade was double-edged as well. He held it up into the night sky and turned it in his hands back and forth as the metal blade glistened in the moonlight. It was so shiny, Peter could see his reflection in the blade. He had a *real* sword now!

He raised his hand to touch the blade.

"Careful," said the Dragon. "The blade is very sharp," it warned Peter. Clearly pleased with itself, it bent down to inspect the work.

"But how?" Peter asked in utter amazement.

The Dragon was silent.

Just then the three heard some movement through the trees. The Dragon jerked its head and turned to look into the black forest. The glow from Peregrine's torches could be seen.

"I must go now. Do not fear, for I am with you." The Dragon gently removed something from its shoulder with its mouth and slowly moved its head toward Peter. In its front teeth was a shiny scale from the Dragon's shoulder. It motioned for Peter to take it, but Peter was scared. He slowly walked toward the creature's mouth, which was full of large teeth stained with age, and saw the scale up close. It was thick as a shield and hard as metal. He used both hands to remove it from between the Dragon's teeth for it looked heavy. Then took a few paces back. The Dragon's mist coming from its mouth was still cold as before.

Peter inspected the scale and saw that it indeed looked like a shield or buckler. It appeared large enough to cover most of his body, and yet it wasn't heavy. He turned it over and saw that his arm could fit inside the back slope and hold onto the short tendon as a handle. He held the shield in front of himself as protection. Then he realized that this must be what the Dragon wanted. He completely understood why Peregrine wanted the scales for his army. They seemed to be unlike any armor Peter had ever seen. The scale was beautiful, solid, and strong.

Then Peter saw where the scale had been; in its place was a dark hole in the Dragon's shoulder. Peter gasped when he understood what this meant. *The Dragon could be pierced in that very spot. He was unprotected!*

"No! Wait! You mustn't. The hole will leave you vulnerable to Peregrine's lance! You must take the scale back." He ran to the Dragon holding the scale up. But it was too late.

The Dragon quietly turned, hissed, and made its way into the trees with phantom-like movements then disappeared from sight. Peter could not believe that the massive creature he saw before them could simply walk into the night and blend into the darkness perfectly. Only the yellow glowing eyes of the Dragon could be seen between the trees, unblinking in the moonlight just as before.

"Be brave," the Dragon whispered. Clouds of the familiar blue mist returned to the forest and began to cover the ground around Peter's feet in waves.

Peter mounted his horse and together they stood firmly waiting for Peregrine to find them. What would happen next remained a mystery, but with one hand tightly clenched around his new sword and the other behind the scale shield, Peter felt ready for this adventure to begin.

8 THE SIEGE BEGINS

The King rode quickly toward Cardion and Lord Caragon's menacing army. He jabbed his heels into his horse's ribs and it lurched forward. Alexander's intent remained on his son's whereabouts. He hoped Peter would be safe in the forest because of the Dragon, but something inside him doubted Peregrine.

"Sire!" a knight yelled at the King to get his attention. "Look!"

The knight was pointing toward the Dragon Forest. Blue light from deep within the trees rose high into the sky. The knight tried to ride forward while looking back. He seemed frightened.

"Do not fear!" answered the King. "All is well. Look forward where you are going."

The King knew the blue light belonged to the Dragon. And he knew what the blue light meant. Deep inside his heart, he knew his son safely waited with the Dragon.

§

The Black Banner of Caragon's army waved in the night breeze as his men moved forward to battle. The golden crest of Caragon, made up of two small dragons intertwined and facing each other, gleamed in the moonlight. Beneath the intertwined dragons was a human skull symbolizing death. Many of his men were on foot and behind them rode the Black Knights called Baroks trained in the art of battle. Their black armor would have been invisible in the darkness were it not for the light from torches they held in their hands. Armor covered their faces and bodies, weighing them down so that their feet left deep impressions in the earth. They held shields before them and had lances in every hand. These metal suits of armor could not be penetrated by any lance or arrow, so the legend said. Yet they had never been truly tested in battle. The time had come for his men to finally meet their fate in the hills of the Cardion Valley. Huge catapults several stories high were pulled by large oxen. The thunderous cadence of the marching enemy echoed throughout the land and could be heard from the Crow Valley.

At the threshold of the valley, they stopped and soaked their arrowheads in black tar. One thousand Black Knight Archers lined up outside of the valley and lit their arrows in one swoop of brush fire. Then they raised their arrows high into the sky as they waited for the order to come from their master. Horses nervously neighed and reared from impatience. The riders had to fight hard to keep their horses steady.

Caragon sat mounted high on his black stallion. Together they stood on a low hill to the north of his archers. His men were anxious to begin the battle. But Caragon waited until the opportune moment to commence his plans of revenge on King Alexander and the kingdom of Illiath. His black horse tugged at the reins as Caragon tried to steady him. The cold breath blew from the stallion's nostrils as it weaved back and forth on the low hill. Lord Caragon slowly removed his black helmet. The wind blew his long dark hair over his face. His eyes, surrounded by dark hardened features, focused in on the Cardion Valley. With teeth clenched and jaw tightened, he turned his gaze southward to the Castle. He could see another thousand of his soldiers hastening their way to begin the siege. The tall limestone towers of the Castle glistened in the moonlight. Amusement filled his darkened heart while he imagined the fear and dread of the people within the walls.

Just then, a single black crow circled above Caragon. An omen. Or one of Lord Bedlam's spies? Its shrill interrupted the dark Lord's thoughts. He watched the bird fly overhead. He smiled. Then the dreadful Lord Caragon looked to the North toward the Dragon forest. Near the tops of the trees he saw what he had been waiting for all these years in exile. A blue light shone from deep within the trees and rose up as a crown over the forest. It cut through the night like a blue flame of fire. Caragon knew the time had come. He placed his helmet back over his head. Then he raised his arm high into the night sky as his generals waited for the signal. The archers steadied their arrows as the flames flickered. Their heads faced toward their targets as their eyes turned in their sockets to see the signal. The hand of their leader lingered there only for a slight moment. Then he quickly lowered it in a cutting motion the ground.

The archers bent their bows back as hard as they could and then released their flaming arrows into the cold night air. They caught the breeze coming from the west behind them and rose farther into the sky, where they reached their pinnacle before bending down again to the will of gravity's pull. Many arrows met the thatched roofs and began to burn the helpless straw into nothing but ashes. More reached the ground and set it aflame. The savage fires rapidly spread across the farms and roads leaving nothing behind. Caragon had hoped to see the people running for their lives, but the people had long ago entered into the Castle for safety. The archers reloaded, but behind them came the others rushing into the village carrying their black banners. They made their way in before the second wave of arrows flew. The trumpets of Caragon's army signaled the commencement of battle.

§

The King and his men had *ridden* around the Cardion Valley to the East. There they watched the fire devour the land as Caragon split up his men. The Black Knights entered into the small village, ransacking all the deserted homes, searching for the townspeople.

"Baroks," the King murmured as he angrily watched these evil Black Knights, mutations of man and beast, make their way through the dirt roads and destroying farms and homes along the way. It became too much for him to take. He knew the time had come to end this war with Caragon once and for all. He removed the sword of Alexander from its sheath and held it firmly in his hand. He could feel the power of his fathers before him emanating from the grip.

"He has unleashed the Baroks!" Alexander shouted. He motioned to Sir Thomas to move his men north and for Sir Andrew to head south away from him where he had set up another group to enter the battle from the front. On his orders they were to ride in, flank the enemy, and surprise the Baroks.

With swords drawn and shields up, the King and his men stood ready. The King raised his sword high into the night, then lowered it in a slicing motion. The knights saw the signal and began their attack on the brutal enemy before them. Sir Thomas led the King's men northward into the village. Many knights and squires followed him. Their horses screamed and the men yelled with passion as they entered the battle.

The Baroks saw the approaching men and ran toward them with lances held high. Their eyes glowed with hatred and magic from within their black helmets. Arms and shields were held high as man fought furiously against Barok. The King watched Sir Andrew enter from the south as riders clashed with enemy footmen in what appeared to be a slaughter.

Sir Andrew swept his sword into the approaching enemy and struck down many as they swung at his horse. Andrew's horse reared up and fell to the ground sending the knight flying from the saddle. Disoriented, he quickly rose and found his sword as an enemy foot soldier ran toward him with his lance. The two faced each other with their weapons. Andrew struck the legs of the enemy and sent him down. Then he released the anger built up within him and ended the duel once and for all with one swipe of his sword meeting metal to flesh. He stood over his kill only for a moment before he headed onward to yet another foe waiting.

Sir Thomas remained on horseback, slicing his way into the village. His horse leapt over a fence and landed in the burned-out remains of a small house. Thomas drew his sword and thrust it into the back of an enemy foot soldier who was pillaging the house. The soldier screamed in agony as the cold metal entered his body. Sir Thomas withdrew the sword and turned to swipe another of Caragon's soldiers. He and his horse charged from the burned-out house to lead his men further into the battle.

Then came the Zadoks. These large black wolf-like dogs were a creation of Lord Bedlam's evil magic. Their yellow eyes bulged as they showed their wicked teeth. Caragon's men held back the giant beasts on leather leashes as they snarled and begged to be let free. With his arm in the air, Lord Caragon alerted his men to release the Zadoks on his mark. He lowered his arm, the Zadoks ran over the hills without restraint, eager for blood. It was Sir Andrew who spotted the eerie creatures. Raising his lance high into the air, he shouted a warning to the men.

"Dogs!" he screamed. The knights heeded the warning. But for many it was too late. The Zadoks tore into the arms of the men and pulled them down to the ground. These monsters were not dogs, and not wolves. They seemed to be a new breed of animal not seen before. Their teeth easily ripped through armor and mesh as their hot breath met the cold night air. Sir Andrew galloped over to the fight and quickly dismounted his horse. Slicing through the beasts with his sword and lunging at the enemy with his lance, he valiantly defeated many before they killed more of his men.

From the hill, the King watched the heated battle. Through the smoke and fire, he could see to the other side of the village to where Caragon stood, his horse's black mane blowing in the wind and smoke. Both men stared at one another for a moment. Then King Alexander raised his heavy sword high above him and yelled as he reared his horse back in defiance.

All at once, with a swift lunge forward, King Alexander entered into the battle.

§

At the Castle, the garrison of men could hear the trumpet blast from Caragon's army. They could see the fire and smoke rise from the Cardion Valley. They watched as legions of the approaching enemy soldiers hastily made their way on foot to the Blue River, where they set up their positions. The river, the main water source to the Palace and surrounding valleys, flowed west to east outside the castle gate facing the Dragon Forest. The wooden bridge that ran over the river allowed access to the castle's main gate.

Constable Darion knew this bridge needed to be severed. As the tall silhouettes of the catapults rose behind them, Caragon's horsemen gathered nearby, ready to make their run. King Alexander's men knew it would not be long before the enemy made its way to the outer walls of the Castle. The constable stood next to the archers along the curtain wall of the courtyard. He knew the catapults would launch large boulders into the air toward the Castle towers, but whether or not the large towers could withstand the attack he was not sure. Gazing at the bridge over the Blue River, Darion ordered the archers to set it afire in hopes it would give them more time to prepare. Then he made his way down the ladder and off the wall as the bridge burned. The enemy would have to cross the river in order to make their way to the Castle walls.

§

Lady Silith gazed out the window of the steward's tower and saw her village burning in the night. She held a linen handkerchief securely as she watched the men in the courtyard frantically gathering the women and children to send them below the Castle for protection. Her eyes filled with tears. Many of her people were below. She wept for their fate.

Lord Byrén came up behind her and touched her shoulders. Outside the window, the flames from the battle rose into the night sky.

"Do you suppose the King is there, my Lady?" he asked.

"One may only hope," she answered.

The others paced quietly in the large room of the tower patiently waiting for word from below. Just then, Constable Darion burst into the room.

"Quickly!" he shouted. "You must come with me!"

He motioned for them to follow him down the stairs.

"Whatever do you mean?" asked Lady Godden. "What is happening?"

"The enemy is approaching with much haste toward the Blue River," the constable said while he held the large door open.

"The Blue River?" Lady Godden repeated.

"Yes, we haven't much time. I must get you all out of here. You are in grave danger!" he yelled back. "My Lords, my Ladies, please...*hurry!*"

They hastened out of the room and down the spiral staircase where a foot soldier waited with a torch. He led them down the narrow dark staircase toward the dungeon.

"Where are we headed?" asked Lord Byrén.

"To the dungeon," answered Darion.

"The *dungeon*?" Lady Godden asked as she lifted the skirt of her dress so as not to trip in her haste. "Are you sure that is...wise?"

"Yes, my Lady. The King has made the dungeon into a safety room for all the women and children." The constable led them farther and farther down. "He knew this day would come and made arrangements for the gloomy dungeon to be cleaned and prepared to hold as many people as it can for the duration of the siege."

"Wise man, indeed," said Lord Byrén.

They dutifully followed the torch down to their hiding place. They could hear the rumbling of footsteps and voices in front of them. Finally, they spotted others entering into the large room made of brick and stone in the bowels of the Castle lit by many torches and candles. The Ladies entered first, followed by the Lords. As they made their way in, the constable stopped at the doorway and handed the torch to Lord Byrén.

"Stay here. You will be safe. Close the door behind me and no matter what, do not open it. No matter what you hear...*do not open this door*! Understand?" he ordered as his eyes stared sternly at the Lord.

"Yes, of course," Lord Byrén answered. His eyes were serious as if he knew exactly what the constable was saying. If, by chance, the enemy were to enter into the Castle, they would kill everyone in their path.

"Good," the constable said. "Lock it after I close it."

"But what about you?" asked Lady Silith. "Where will you be?"

"I will be with the soldiers." Constable Darion placed his hands on the door to close it. "Just do not open the door. Not even for my voice."

Then he closed the massive door with a resounding thud.

"Oh dear," Lady Silith cried. She buried her face in her hands.

Then she and the others turned to see hundreds of faces watching them. The people of the villages stared at their leaders intently as they wondered what would happen next. Lady Silith regained her composure. She stood tall as she faced her people. A little girl with dark hair approached and gently touched Lady Silith's burgundy velvet gown, gazing at the gold thread. Lady

Silith picked up the little girl into her arms. Then she walked over to the others who were lying down on blankets and huddled together on sacks of grain. She spotted the girl's mother and sat down next to her with the child on her lap.

"We will be safe here." she said, smiling reassuringly, as she sat with the family.

The trumpet blast from Caragon's army could be heard inside the Castle. The people in the dungeon looked up at the ceiling. It trembled slightly from the marching feet on the earth outside, and some dirt made its way down to the ground at Lord Byrén's feet.

"I'm afraid… it has begun," he said.

9 SIR PEREGRINE

Prince Peter sat high on his horse, Titan, watching Sir Peregrine's men make their way through the thick trees of the Dragon Forest. Peter's hands firmly held his new sword and shield as he prepared for whatever lay ahead. He glanced around the forest clearing and noticed that the familiar blue mist was thicker and reached up to Titan's knees. The mist covered the sapphire lake completely. The sight made the forest appear to float high in the clouds. Within the trees, he then saw the yellow eyes of the Dragon waiting patiently to make its move. *What will happen now?* Peter thought as he gripped Titan's mane.

"Hold tight, Peter!" his mother yelled as she led Titan around the corral. The clip clop of the horse's hooves on the dirt made a musical sound as Peter listened to the rhythm. "Try gripping his mane in your hands." Peter obediently grabbed a tuft of mane in his small hands. He was surprised at how thick and rough the hair was in his fingers. He watched his mother walk with the reins in her hands as she led Titan around in circles. "Squeeze tightly around his body with your legs to hold on," she said. "Then you won't fall." She looked back at Peter and smiled as the wind blew her black hair away from her face. "You're wonderful!" she laughed as she watched her son ride his new horse for the first time. The sun was shining brightly on Peter's face as the smell of jasmine filled the air. He could feel the warmth of the sun on his skin.

Titan whinnied and clawed the dirt again with his front hoof, awaking Peter from his memory in time to see Peregrine approach.

Lord Peregrine's voice was faintly heard as he shouted orders to his men. The voice echoed into the night air. Peter couldn't make out what was said because the knight was too far away. But he could see the light from their torches reflect off the trees and their shadows dance along the ground. Peter went over what he would say to the knight when they faced each other. He realized he looked prepared for some sort of confrontation, but he also knew that Peregrine was supposed to be on a rescue mission. Did he truly intend for Peregrine to know that *he knew,* of the plans to capture the Dragon's scales? Peter's mind was spinning as he tried to figure out what to do next. One thing he knew for sure, he would defend the Dragon as his father would were he with them now.

§

Peregrine made his way into the clearing and his eyes met Peter's. He raised his eyebrows as though shocked to see the young boy on his horse with sword and shield in hand. He raised his hand up, signaling to his men to stop where they were. Then he slowly removed his helmet to make sure the young boy in front of him was really Peter.

"Boy, is that you?" he asked.

"Yes." Peter swallowed hard. A large lump had formed in his throat.

Satisfied with recognizing Peter's voice, Peregrine said, "What are you doing out here?"

Peter remained silent.

"I say, what are you doing out here in this forest…alone?" Peregrine asked again while he looked around at the mist covered forest.

"I am—I..." Peter stuttered, searching for an answer. "I am here to..."

"Shouldn't you be on your way back home now?" Peregrine asked. "Your father is very worried. He sent us here to find you." He waited for a response from the Prince. "Do you know what trouble you've caused?" His voice grew louder as his patience drain. Then he saw some strange thing in Peter's hands. He lightly nudged his horse forward to get closer to Peter. Only the sloshing of Peregrine's horse hooves on the damp ground could be heard.

"No, I..." Peter said.

Peregrine was much closer to Peter now. His ruggedly handsome, bearded face, and dark hair were lit only by the torches, but Peter could see his eyes. Peter did not trust Peregrine's eyes.

Peregrine stared at the boy. "What is that you have there, boy?"

Peter looked at the sword and then returned his gaze to the strong knight. "It is my sword," he said.

Then Lord Peregrine's eye switched to the unfamiliar thing in Peter's other hand. He looked closer as the light from the torches was far away. He motioned for one of his men to bring him a torch. The squire galloped over to the knight and quickly handed him his torch. Peregrine took it and raised it up above his head toward Peter. Peter looked down at his shield and grasped it even tighter.

Lord Peregrine's face was now illuminated by the torch. Peter saw the ominous shadows over the knight's deep set eyes and feared him more. Peter had once admired Sir Peregrine as his father's most noble knight. Now he doubted the man's loyalty to his father.

Peregrine squinted in order to see the detail of the shield. Then, realizing exactly what the object was before him, his eyes grew large and his mouth gaped open. He looked amazingly at the boy and then back at the shield. He knew it was a scale...the scale of the Dragon.

"Where did you find that shield?" he demanded of Peter.

"I...did not..." Peter hesitated.

"Answer me! Where did you find that shield?" Peregrine shouted.

"I did not find it," Peter said. "It was given to me."

Peregrine's horse neighed impatiently and tried to turn away. It nervously sensed something unfamiliar in the woods. Peregrine pulled the reins back.

"Given...to you?" Peregrine asked. "By whom? Or what?"

Peter did not answer. This puzzled Peregrine as he knew it had to be a Dragon scale.

"Give it to me." he commanded as he reached out his hand.

Peter motioned Titan to step backward. "No!" Peter yelled. His horse took two steps back, snorted, and shook his mane.

"Give it to me, you silly boy. You don't know what you have there." Peregrine reached out to Peter.

"Yes I do!" shouted Peter. "It's the scale of the Dragon," he said with satisfaction. Peregrine's men gasped and looked at one another. Only then did he realize he should not have made the revelation known.

Peregrine scowled and moved closer to Peter with squinted eyes. He lowered his voice to an intimidating tone. Slowly he said, "Where did you get that scale?"

Peter froze as he watched Peregrine's men inch their way closer to him. Some dismounted their horses and uneasily walked on the blue mist. Titan whinnied and shook his mane as he took a few steps backward. The two stood there as Peter quickly plotted their escape, but nothing came to mind. Peter regretted ever having left the castle.

Lord Peregrine sensed Peter's uneasiness and realized he was approaching this from the wrong direction. He sat straight up in his saddle and seemed more at ease. He released the reins of his horse and handed the torch to the rider next to him. Then he raised his hand toward his men. "Now, now," he said. "We mustn't frighten the boy." He carefully dismounted his horse, and as he turned away from Peter he made eye contact with his men. He whispered to them, "When I give the signal…" And they nodded in agreement.

Slyly, Peregrine ambled over to Peter. He removed his gloves and tried to look pleasant in the darkened forest. He reached for the torch once again and the soldier handed it to him. He gazed at the young Prince's face. He tried in earnest not to look at the beautiful shield made of the Dragon's scale even though it represented all that he had fought for these many months. He kept his eyes on Peter in order to make the boy feel more at ease. But the plan was not working. Peter grew more frightened as Peregrine walked over to him. He slowly grabbed a large chunk of Titan's black mane in his hands.

"Now, my boy…I mean Prince Peter, your Highness." Peregrine bowed his head. "Your father is looking for you. He is very worried about you and gave me, specific orders to bring you home safely." He forced a counterfeit grin.

Peter raised his eyes above Peregrine's head and looked toward the dark trees behind the knights.

"Come now, we do not have much time. There is a battle raging in the Cardion Valley," Peregrine spoke more seriously as he reached out to Peter. "We must get you home so I can help your father."

Peter's eyes were fixated behind the knights as Peregrine spoke. "Help my father?" Peter asked. "My father doesn't trust you."

"Now your Highness," Peregrine said with a sheepish grin and placed his hand over his chest. "Why would he send me out to bring you, his only son, home safely if he did not trust me?"

Peter inspected Peregrine's men. Their armor was darker and heavier than his father's, they did not have the Illiath banner with them. He could barely see their faces in the night. He did not answer Peregrine nor look at him. Instead, he held tightly to the sword as he grabbed the mane with some of his fingers. He knew something was about to happen in those dark trees. He squeezed Titan with his legs, signaling him to be ready.

Peregrine frowned. He was not amused with Peter's silence. Nor did he appreciate the boy's refusal to look at him. "If he trusts me," he said, "so should you."

Realizing he was not getting through to the boy, Peregrine decided to forego the pleasant conversation and get what he wanted after all. Lunging forward in a split second, he yelled to his men, "Now!"

The knights ran toward Peter and Titan as Peregrine tried to snatch the shield from Peter's grasp. But Peter knew what was happening behind them.

The glowing yellow eyes quickly made their way up the trees as the ominous voice came from within the forest walls. "Ride!" was all it said to Peter.

And that is what Peter and Titan did. Peter dug his heels into the sides of Titan, and together they galloped toward the lake. As they made their way, they heard Peregrine yell to his men, "Stop them! Move! Don't let them get away!"

Peter could hear the commotion of the knights as they ran to their horses and began riding toward them. But Peter followed the glowing eyes in the trees. He saw the blue mist rising out of the woods as the great beast began to reveal itself. The blue lake was in front of them and Titan hesitated to enter into the water.

The Dragon yelled, "Do not stop! Ride!" Then blue fire spewed out from its mouth and hissed onto the waters as they approached it.

"What's this?" yelled Peregrine.

The Dragon was sighted at the top of the trees. Some of Peregrine's men sat on their horses staring at the giant spewing the blue fire from its mouth.

Peter kicked Titan even harder as they galloped faster and faster toward the water. Peter closed his eyes as Titan jump up over a log. He fully expected to enter the icy cold waters of the lake when Titan's hooves landed, but they were met with hardened ice instead. Trying not to slip, Titan continued to gallop as fast as he could, leaving Peregrine and his men far behind them. When they made it to the middle of the lake, Peter and Titan stopped and turned to see the knights. Many of them remained in awe at the sight before them. Others were mounted on their horses ready to fight the Dragon. The beast made its way out of the forest deep and revealed itself to the traitorous knights.

Peregrine mounted his horse, pulled his sword from its sheath, and ordered his men to seize the Dragon. His eyes glared at the giant beast, then turned toward Peter who remained in the middle of the icy blue lake. The hatred and anger inside Peregrine built up as he realized he had been tricked.

Many of his knights were mounted and ready to obey their commander's orders. But the Dragon stood ready as well.

Peter asked Titan what they should do. He knew they would be safe on the now hardened lake, but he also wanted to help his new friend.

The Dragon, as if perceiving Peter's concern, turned to him. He spread his massive wings wide open and showed his claws. Then he lifted his head high into the night sky and roared.

Peregrine's men stopped where they stood. They had their weapons in their hands and their shields hiding their bodies, but what match were they for the giant Dragon?

The Dragon made the familiar hissing as it inhaled a large amount of cold night air. The whooshing sound frightened the men's horses, but Titan knew not to be afraid. Deeper and deeper the Dragon inhaled as it reared its head back farther and farther.

"Steady men! Remember your shields!" Peregrine shouted. He reminded them of the magic shields Lord Caragon had provided for them. They were supposed to protect them from the Dragon's breath. He raised his shield up over his head.

But they were no match for the Dragon. A silent pause followed all the hissing and inhaling. Then the Dragon, leaning forward, unleashed all its fury on the knights in one steady stream of glowing yellow fire projecting from its mouth. The unrelenting fire devoured all the men and their horses in one swipe, but the Dragon waved its head from side to side layering the hot fire in row after row. The fire consumed all in its path. It covered the misty ground all the way to Lord Peregrine's armor covered boots. Then it stopped.

Peter had lifted the shield up over his head as a precaution even though he knew the Dragon would not hurt him or Titan. He slowly lowered the sparkling shield to see what had taken place. Fire was burning all over the forest clearing. What was left of Peregrine's men lay smoldering on the ground. Their metal swords and armor smoldered on the hot earth as smoke rose from the burial ground. Peregrine stood breathing heavily, dumbfounded at the sight. Then the Dragon made its way over to the cowering and ignoble Head of the Royal Knights.

Peregrine took a few shaky steps backward as the giant beast stepped toward him. The earth shook with each impact of the huge clawed feet. The snapping of tree trunks was heard throughout the forest. The swishing of its tail fanned the flames that were still burning. Its belly rubbed against the flames, but its scales protected it from harm.

Peter and Titan walked over to the water's edge as the Dragon moved past them. They knew they were safe now.

The hissing sound from the Dragon echoed into the night. No other sound could be heard in the entire forest except the frantic beating of Peregrine's heart. The Dragon lowered its head to the knight. "You dare to approach me?" it hissed.

It continued moving forward as it looked into the eyes of its enemy. Its magnificent scales glistened and reflected the flames around its body. The scales appeared to mesmerize Peregrine. As he fearfully admired the beast's scales, he dropped his pitiful shield to the ground. Still gripping the sword, he knelt before the Dragon's feet. Bowing his head, Peregrine begged for mercy. The Dragon's large mouth was inches away from Peregrine's head. Its hot breath graced the doomed knight's skin and smelled of burning incense.

Peter and Titan stood far away from the spectacle, but they wanted to see what would happen to Sir Peregrine.

Peregrine slowly looked up into the Dragon's eyes. "Please, I beg your forgiveness," he sobbed.

The Dragon answered only with a hiss of his hot breath as he studied the heart of the man before him.

"Mercy," Peregrine said as he remained on bended knee before the Dragon of the Forest. He bowed his head once again to show his respect. "I beg of you."

Peter shook his head. He did not believe Peregrine. He still did not trust him.

The Dragon stayed close to Peregrine for a few moments and then slowly raised its large head. It turned to see Peter and Titan behind its tail. As the Dragon turned toward Peter, Peregrine raised his head to watch the beast's every move. Peregrine's eyes met with the hole in the Dragon's shoulder. He carefully eyed the mysterious gap and realized that a scale was missing. Raising his sword high behind him, Peregrine lunged forward with all his strength. The sword released from his hand and flew into the air, twisting and twirling toward the shoulder of the Dragon.

Lord Peregrine's aim was true. The cold blade entered into the exposed flesh of the Dragon's shoulder and sunk deep into its chest. As the metal met the flesh of the beast, it roared out a painful scream that frightened Peter and Titan. Red blood flowed from the wound. Titan reared up and sent Peter flying to the ground.

Seeing that his aim was indeed accurate, Peregrine grabbed a deserted lance on the ground and hurled it at the wounded beast. The lance pierced the flesh again and sent the Dragon spinning around to face the knight. But Peregrine, in his time of boastful arrogance, forgot his shield on the ground and stood vulnerable to the Dragon's breath. He leapt through the air and rolled on the ground toward his shield. With the celerity, grace, and beauty of a well-trained knight, he quickly grabbed the shield and held it over his body, convinced it would protect him. Spying another sword smoldering on the ground, Peregrine grabbed it and hurled it at the enormous body before him. He ran behind a tree and watched the Dragon as it followed him. Then, Peregrine leapt over to another tree where he hid, hoping the Dragon did not see his maneuver.

But all the armor and promises of greatness and wealth Caragon had sold him and all the training of his youth would betray him that night.

With one exhalation of the Dragon's mighty fire, Peregrine's once proud and strong body was reduced to a simple pile of ashes.

The Dragon, however, was wounded. Peter ran over to see where the beast had been pierced. It lay down on the ground with its head hung low. Peter could hear its heavy breathing. He was afraid.

"We've no time to lose now." The Dragon winced. Peter could see it was in a great deal of pain. "We must go to the battle." Peter lunged forward and quickly removed the lance from the wound. Peregrine's bloody sword had already fallen to the ground. He hoped this would help the Dragon's pain.

The Dragon lowered its head to let Peter climb on top so that they could make their way to the Cardion Valley together. Peter climbed to the back of the massive head and held onto the scales as best he could. The Dragon stood up so quickly that Peter became sick to his stomach from the rapid motion. He regained his strength when the Dragon spread its mighty wings wide open. Peter had not seen the wings spread completely out before and now he realized just how magnificent this Dragon truly was. Peter guessed its wingspan measured almost one hundred feet across with the translucent wings made of thick course leathery skin. .

"Hold on," the Dragon ordered.

Peter obeyed. The giant wings flapped forward and backward in a quick movement. The wind they created blew the trees back and forth as the blue mist rose around them.

Titan reared up and loudly whinnied to Peter as his front legs flared in the air. He looked as if he were trying to say goodbye. "Go back to the castle, boy!" Peter shouted to his horse. Peter smiled as the body of the Dragon rose off the ground. Spotting Titan galloping out of the forest, Peter and the Dragon rose up over the forest and circled above it. Peter looked up and saw the moon. It appeared closer to him than ever before in his young life. He could see mountains and valleys on the moon's surface. He saw the brightness of the stars around them. Then he switched his gaze to the Cardion Valley in the south. He could see the flames of the battle burning brightly and he knew his father needed help.

Together, they flew into battle in order to save his father...in order to save the kingdom.

10 THE BATTLE FOR ILLIATH

The fire lit up the night sky and provided ample competition for the stars in the heavens. King Alexander gazed up to follow the sparks as they floated ever upward into oblivion. The memory of fireflies dancing in the twilight raced across his mind as he drifted back to the many summer nights of his youth. He pictured face of his dear wife appeared among the stars, knowing she would be amused by his nostalgia at such a moment.

The night air was much colder now as dawn approached. His breath could be seen through the visor of his helmet. As he removed it, he noticed just in time the lance of his enemy lunging toward him. King Alexander stared at the bloody spear coming for his life. He grasped his sword with both hands, turned his body slightly to the left. Then, with all his might, he slashed the enemy knight, severing the cursed creature's body almost in two. Alexander stood over the dead creature's broken body. Its hot black blood spewed forth and mixed with the mud on the ground. Realizing the creature was some sort of hybrid between a man and a creation of Caragon's imagination, Alexander knew he and his men were in for long fight.

The King glanced around the smoldering ruins of what was once a lovely village. Yet all that remained in ashes was replaceable. The people of the village had made their way into the Castle walls to safety hours before.

At that moment, Sir Andrew ran, panting, to the King's side.

"Your majesty," he huffed. "You mustn't remain alone like this. You are far too important. No King should fight in battle."

"All is well, Sir Andrew." King Alexander put his gloved hand on the knight's shoulder. "What happened here is not the real battle." He nodded toward the castle as he placed his sword back into its leather sheath. "There is where the battle begins." He looked out over the carnage before them. Many of the enemy lay dead on the muddied earth. Their blood covered the land. The large bodies of the giant Zadoks remained scattered all over the village.

"Strange beasts, indeed," Sir Andrew said. "I've never seen such animals." He tapped one of the dead animals lying nearby with his foot. Its teeth were grotesquely frozen in death snarl.

"Yes," the King answered. "Makes me wonder what Lord Caragon has been up to in those Black Hills." He raised his eyes toward the hills.

"It seems to be some sort of mutation of wolf and dog," Sir Andrew stated.

"There were rumors that Caragon was engaging in experiments of some sort." The King walked over to a dead animal carcass. "I suppose these were part of those experiments."

"Witchcraft?" Sir Andrew asked.

"Perhaps even wizardry," The King answered, shaking his head in disbelief. "I thought I knew Caragon. I was wrong."

The knights sadly walked through the field in the aftermath of battle with their heads hung low and bodies hunched over. Legs and arms were weighted down with muddy armor. Amidst the smoldering ashes, they collected swords, shields, and spears from the dead. The enemy swords were garish twisted pieces of metal that protruded from wooden handles. Their black shields—an inferior grade, almost primitive— were dented and bent from the fight.

Then the survivors, moving as one, gathered their own dead to bring back into the castle when the siege was over. The King watched as his men carefully and respectfully lifted up their dead friends and brothers in order to place them on a carriage. Each man was covered with his cape that bore the insignia of

Alexander: The scarlet and gold coat of arms of a lion rearing up toward the left. Seeing the dead men covered by his family crest made the King pause from a wave of emotion. He found it hard to swallow back his tears. He'd known many of these men since they were young boys.

Obviously, the King's men had won the battle as what was left of Caragon's men retreated into the hills. Lord Caragon himself hastily galloped away toward the Hildron on his black steed. Alexander knew that this small battle, a mere distraction from the main siege at the castle, wouldn't last long. The King wisely left many of his knights as well as a garrison at the castle for protection.

Alexander motioned for his men to gather around him, and, with great respect, they listened intently. "You fought bravely for your King and your people. The battle here is over."

The men seemed relieved, but their relief would only last a moment.

"Yet I am afraid this battle was a distraction meant for us to lose sight of the real war," the King continued. "Right now, as we stand here, Caragon's men are preparing to lay siege to the castle. We must finish here and ride to protect the Kingdom."

As the sound of Caragon's men marching toward the castle could be heard, concern for families and friends washed over each knight's mud-stained face. The once shiny silver armor blotched with blood and dirt looked old and rusted. They reeked of the pungent smell of sweat and sheer exhaustion manifested itself on their faces. King Alexander stared into the intensity of their eyes. Their returned glances seem to go on forever. The hardened and talented fighters knew in their hearts what lay ahead for them. They also knew what would happen if they failed their mission.

Sir Andrew stepped forward and raised his sword high into the air. "Swords high!" he yelled to his fellow knights. "For the King! For the sword of Alexander!"

"For the kingdom of Illiath! For the King!" they all shouted back in unison. Their voices echoed into the cold night air.

King Alexander's heart swelled with pride as he watched his men. But he also feared for his son because he did not know of his whereabouts, and a mighty battle was about to begin. *Could Peter have possibly survived the Dragon Forest?* Alexander did not know the answer to that question, and the incomprehension was almost too much for him to bear.

§

Peter held on securely to its scales as the Dragon made its way higher into the night sky. The night air blew through his brown hair and stung his eyes. The cold rush of wind took Peter's breath away and he found it was hard to breathe let alone speak. He wanted to shout out as they flew together on their new adventure to release his fear and anticipation.

Making their way over the hills of the Cardion Valley, the Dragon and Peter could see the damaged village below. The smoldering ash heaps were all that remained of the little town he had ridden through only hours before. Now it was nearly gone. As he looked over the village, the Dragon landed on top of a hill overlooking the burning ruins.

"This was once a lovely village," Peter exclaimed as he sat upon the Dragon's neck. "I don't know where my father is. But I know that he probably fought here."

"Caragon's men," the Dragon explained. "They began this battle." His claws sunk deep into the cool wet earth with a slushy sound of mud oozing between his toes.

"Yes." Peter viewed the remains of the Zadoks on the ground. "I am glad it is over."

"The real battle is just beginning." The Dragon turned toward the castle. "We must go now to help."

"But when they see you, what will they do?" Peter asked. He knew Caragon's men wanted the Dragon. "Won't they try to destroy you?"

The Dragon struggled to breathe slowly as it spoke. "Don't worry," it said, spreading his wings wide. "They won't see me."

§

The thundering reverberations of the horse hooves meeting with the wet earth shook the castle walls as King Alexander's constable stood atop the outer curtain walls of the mighty fortress. He did not stand alone. Hundreds of the King's finest soldiers stood prepared to meet with the enemy in a battle that would be written about for decades to come. Together they were ready for this moment in time to begin.

"Spy glass," Constable Darion ordered as he reached for the glass instrument used to see hundreds of feet away. The foot soldier handed it to the King's leader, and Darion swallowed hard in anticipation of what would be seen in the darkness. Looking toward the now faint light from the Cardion Valley far into the northeast, he could only see smoke and glimpses of mounted troops approaching. "Ready the catapults!" Darion ordered.

The foot soldiers conveyed the orders below into the courtyard where other soldiers manned the large catapults used for launching large containers of tar. The foot soldiers loaded three catapults with the manmade containers of bark. These containers were to be splattered out onto the earth outside the Blue River surrounding the castle.

"Ready to launch," Constable Darion said. "On my order."

The men eagerly awaited the order to launch their bounty.

"Now!" came the order from above. The catapults were released by cutting the rope holding the arm back. As the rope was cut, the arm swung up and over, launching the tar-filled container high into the sky and over the curtain wall. The constable and the soldiers watched it launch over the Blue River. As it landed on the ground, the bark container split and splattered the black tar all over the soil. With the success of the first launch, several more followed with the same results. Tar now covered many feet across the land to the north of the Blue River.

"Ready the archers!" The constable walked over to the archers. They lit their arrows, and quickly scattered across the curtain wall. "Ready to fire! On my order," he said as they raised their arrows into the night sky.

The fire contrasted brightly against the black night. Behind the small hills of the Cornshire sat the sun waiting to rise. Purple and violet colors weaved across the night. The archers prepared to launch their fire toward the enemy.

"Fire!" Constable Darion called

He watched the hundreds of arrows slice through the blackness and make their way to the ground and the black tar that awaited them. When the arrows met with the tar, fire quickly spread across the tall grasses like a wildfire and lit up the perimeter of the Blue River as if a thousand lanterns had suddenly been lit all at once. It illuminated what the constable had suspected all along. Together he and the King's men saw thousands of Caragon's men making their way toward the River as they prepared to cross its cold waters. Now they were met with a wall of fire which prohibited their journey to the castle. The fire rose nearly thirty feet into the air along with a thick layer of smoke seen from miles away.

Darion could also see giant creatures making their way toward the river's edge. "Ogres," Constable Darion murmured. "Giant beasts loyal to Caragon." This worried him.

He pointed to the giants who were chained like slaves to the massive catapults. Caragon's evil knights whipped the ogres' backs time and again to get them to move faster. With each whipping, the beasts growled in anger.

Constable Darion knew the King's men were no match for these giant monsters. "How did this happen? Caragon must have captured them from the deserts."

The ogres moved each catapult as close as they could to the fires. The fire devoured most of the grasses in its path and would soon lack the fuel it needed to burn. The knights exchanged worried glances.

"Each rock launched at this wall will not penetrate. These walls are far too strong," Constable Darion reassured the men. "We cannot let them into the outer courts!"

The men began to scramble below inside the courtyard to get into position. The soldiers atop the wall prepared to dodge the large boulders that would be tossed by the catapults.

There must be some way to defeat the ogres, Darion thought as he watched the beasts through the spyglass. Each ogre loaded its catapult with large boulders. There were now twelve catapults by the river manned by these obscene monsters. The evil knights rode back and forth on their horses, shouting orders to the foot soldiers.

The constable could see dark shadows behind the soldiers. He wasn't sure what they were, but his body trembled. Suddenly, the soldiers parted and revealed the Zadoks barking ferociously into the night air. The beasts ran to the ogres and barked at their heels. One ogre swung his mighty arm at the wolf-dog and met its head with his large fist. The Zadok flew several feet away but quickly regained its footing. Clearly, the ogres were not too content with being forced to fight in this war. They were being whipped into submission and pestered by these rabid dogs.

"They're slaves," Darion said to the soldiers. "bound to the catapults."

"Yes, and so what?" the captain replied. "What do we care of the plight of the ogres?"

Darion realized the frustration in the soldiers' voices so he quickly made known his plan of attack. "If these ogres are but mere slaves being beaten and ravaged by Caragon's beasts, then perhaps if we free them from their plight they would desire to leave this place and return to their homes. I truly believe that no ogre wants to do battle with the King. They have always lived in peace with us as long as we left them alone in the desert hills of Théadron."

He pointed toward the monsters as they readied their catapults and fought with the grotesque Zadoks. "Perhaps, if we free them, they will return to the Théadron desert. Then our chances for victory increase greatly." Constable Darion considered as he paced back and forth on the wall.

Each captain agreed with the idea of freeing the ogres in hopes that they would run off into the desert toward their homes. "There is no way the Baroks can move those catapults alone," one captain noticed.

"Sir, if we are going to do this, we need to do it now," a soldier said.

Darion agreed. "Tell your soldiers to mount their steeds with swords and shields. I will meet them at the gate to give them their orders."

§

Within the great castle in the musty dungeon, the villagers waited with the Lords and Ladies of the Kingdom. Above them could be heard horses and shouts from the soldiers as they readied for battle. Crusts of dirt fell from the ceiling with each thunderous pound that the approaching army made as it set up its catapults with ogres. Many of the villagers sat and pondered what would happen next. Small children scurried about the dark dungeon, chasing mice into the wall crevices.

Lady Godden paced by a few stacks of hay dampened by the dripping water from above. She tightly gripped her hands one over the other in a nervous way as the others watched. Lord Byrén walked over to her. Her white hair, still pulled back, was glistening in the light of the torch he held as he approached her.

"My lady, please do sit down. There is nothing we can do now, I'm afraid, except wait."

"Yes, I know," she stated as she stopped pacing and looked around at the people. Some were sleeping and others just watching the ceiling for a sign. "I wish I knew what was happening."

"Waiting is the hardest part for those left behind," said Lady Silith as she rose and approached the pair. "Listen...I can hear men's voices." Her eyes darted back and forth along the dirt ceiling.

Above them were the King's soldiers gathering their horses. Shouts from men ordering squires to gather armor could scarcely be heard from beneath the castle grounds. The villagers could hear the approaching enemy. Some women screamed and others clasped their hands over their mouths. Husbands attempted to calmed their wives and children.

"Sounds like men are approaching on foot," Lord Byrén assumed. "Our men are preparing to mount. I can hear the horses' hooves on the dirt. Perhaps the battle will be outside the main walls." He turned his eyes toward the worried Lady Godden. "That's a good thing." He put one hand on her shoulder and her eyes met his. She sighed with relief.

Just then, through the darkness, a loud explosion was heard. The earth shook beneath the people's feet and large clods of dirt fell from the ceiling above them. Children yelled as they ran to find their mothers' arms, and husbands rose as one toward the door that Constable Darion had locked. They banged on the door in a fury of panic.

"Stop that!" Lord Byrén yelled as he ran to the group of men. "They'll hear us! Are you mad? Do you want them to find us down hear? We must remain silent."

The group of men stopped and turned to the Lord. "We can't just stay down here and do nothing!" one man yelled.

"We must," Lord Byrén answered. "That is the only thing we can do."

"But our homes!" another man yelled.

"Gone, I'm afraid." Lord Byrén said bluntly as he shook his head. "Small villages are the first to go in battle. Lord Caragon has destroyed all our homes by now if he is already laying siege upon the castle." He walked back over to the Ladies. "What's done is done."

"That is all too easy for you to say, Lord Byrén," one man said. He jabbed his finger in the air. "Your home isn't the one being destroyed!"

"Calm down!" Lady Godden shouted. "We must remain calm." She put her palms up to gently quiet the crowds.

The men stood in silence as they watched the ceiling for more commotion. But all that could be heard was the deadening thud of horses' hooves meeting the earth in unison.

"Seems they're riding off now," one villager noticed.

"But what was that loud explosion?" another asked.

"Catapults." Lord Byrén stared above. "Probably hit the outer wall of the court then landed inside the court." Sadness lined his face.

"My Lord!" a young woman screamed. "Come quickly!"

The villagers and Lord Byrén all ran toward the young woman. She held in her arms a limp girl no older than three years of age. The child resembled her.

"Oh no!" she cried. "Please help my daughter!"

Apparently, some large rocks from the ceiling had fallen onto the small girl's head. She was unconscious and bleeding. Lady Silith rushed over to her and wrapped the child in her royal robe. Lady Godden ran over to help as well. Together, the three women wept over the small child lying helpless in her mother's arms.

"We have no medicine in here," said another woman from behind. "Only food and water. What shall we do?" She looked at Lord Byrén for help.

"We were told not to leave here. If one of us is seen by the enemy, we all would be discovered. All of us would be slaughtered," he said.

"But the child, my Lord," Lady Godden pleaded.

"Is there anyone here who can help her?" she asked the crowd gathered around her. But no one answered. More explosions could be heard from above, but they were farther away. Everyone looked up at the ceiling and moved back for fear of being struck like the child. Now no one felt safe. Lord Byrén uneasily walked to the door where the men stood. He inspected it as he held the torch in his hand. It was locked from the inside, but he remembered the Constable's orders. He handed the torch over to another man who stared at the Lord in confusion.

Lord Byrén knew what was happening outside the dungeon walls. He also knew there was a physician ready to work on the wounded men in the castle. If they could move the child out of the dungeon without being seen, perhaps they could get her to the physician. But that was too risky. If the enemy were indeed inside the castle court, they could spot them entering into the main castle toward the physician's room, and that would be disastrous for everyone.

"I'm afraid we'll have to wait. It is too risky for us to leave now in the heat of battle," he stated. "We cannot take that chance."

One man spoke up. "But the child is bleeding, my Lord." His voice was met with another loud pounding from above them. Obviously, the catapults were hitting the castle walls repeatedly. Soon the enemy would penetrate the outer walls and enter into the courtyard, where they would be met by waiting soldiers.

All eyes were on Lord Byrén for a decision even though everyone knew what that decision would be.

"No, we cannot risk it. We all must stay here and wait," he finally answered.

The mood of the villagers fell further into despair. Most knew the child would not make it through the night and many battles went on for weeks. People began to move away from the mother and child to give them some air. The mother wept quietly as she held her daughter.

Lady Godden continued to stroke the child's black hair as she held back her tears. It was too much to take in one day. Her village was gone, destroyed by Lord Caragon's men, and now a child may soon also fall victim to his evil wrath. An eerie silence fell over the crowd and engulfed the dark and damp dungeon. It was late now and many people wanted to sleep. The men continued to pace. Then, cutting through the stillness was a voice.

"My Lord," a young man said as he stood from behind a group of villagers. He wasn't yet old enough to be a soldier, but he wasn't a child either. His dark hair and strong handsome facial features were lit by the torch in his hand. He was tall and thin, but muscular in build from working the fields. "I have a plan."

"A what?" a man behind him asked.

"He has a plan!" another young man with curly red hair rose to speak. "We both have been thinking about this since we were locked in here."

"Son!" the young man's father shouted. "Not now. Sit down and be quiet."

"But father," the young man implored. "I know these walls. I know what we can do."

"What is all this?" Lord Byrén asked with a quizzical brow. "Who is this young man?"

"This is my son, Will. He is a bit impetuous at times," his father said. "Please forgive him." The father bowed in respect toward Lord Byrén.

"What plan are you speaking of, boy?" Byron asked.

The young Will stood taller as he spoke to the Lord. His dark brown hair was matted with sweat and dirt. His cotton shirt was worn and so were his brown pants. It was obvious that he was a son of a farmer or a mason. "Sir, I have worked in this dungeon for many months helping the King's men clean it out and prepare it for storage," he explained. "I know these walls as I know my own hand."

"Go on," Lord Byrén said, intrigued.

"My friend Charles and I know there is a secret passage out, up there." He pointed to the back of the dungeon. It was dark so no one could really see where he was pointing. "Back there is a hidden way that leads to the courtyard."

Lord Byrén took the torch from Will's hand and raised it up high into the damp air. The dark walls were illuminated by the torch, but still no passageway could be seen.

"But...we are not supposed to leave here, my boy. We were so ordered," Lord Byrén said.

"Yes, what is it you suppose we do with this passage way?" Will's father asked.

"Charles and I could go into the courtyard and get help," Will said as he made his way to the darkened area. "We can go and find the healer and bring him here to help the girl."

Will's father made his way over to his son. Together they examined the wall. Suddenly, through the firelight of the torch, he exclaimed, "Yes, I see it. Right up there!" He pointed to the passage way high up.

Lord Byrén remained unsure of a plan that had two young men entering into the courtyard unseen by anyone.

"Do you know what is happening out there?" he asked Will. "The enemy is probably already inside the outer walls making their way into the courtyard. There isn't much time until they are already on top of us or mining their way underneath the castle walls. Do you understand?" He stared intently at the Will and Charles.

They looked back at Lord Byrén and then at each other. Without hesitation they answered in unison: "Yes, my Lord."

"No, how could you understand, you both are just boys. What could you possibly know of such things?"

"Please sir, hear us out."

"We were ordered to stay in here for a very good reason, understand?"

"Yes, my Lord."

"Do you know what could happen if one of you were seen? I'd lose my head!" Lord Byrén huffed as he placed his hand over his neck.

Everyone paused for a moment to think about what was happening. Then another explosion occurred just above them, shaking the ground beneath their feet. Children screamed as their mothers held them tightly.

"Alright," Lord Byrén said. "Up and out you go."

Several men rushed haystacks over and rolled barrels toward the two young men as they stacked the materials higher and higher to the passageway. Will and Charles had jokingly entered the secret passage way one afternoon while working in the dungeon. This passage, which was once used by jailers as a quick way to leave the dungeon and enter the courtyard, the boys had laughingly used as a way to scare young maidens out in the courtyard as they milked cows or washed linens. Now they were using it to save a life. There was no joking around this time.

Once all the haystacks and barrels were stacked high enough, Will and Charles began to climb.

"Wait!" Will's father said. He put both hands on his son's lean shoulders and stared into his eyes. "You be careful out there, understand Will? Both of you watch out for the enemy's arrows coming over the walls. Keep a close eye out for the enemy. If just one of those monsters sees you coming out of the dungeon, they'll know."

"They'll know what?" asked Charles.

"They'll know we are all hiding down here and that the secret passage way leads to where we are," Will's father answered. "Now, promise me you'll bring the doctor here and that's all. No heroics, nothing fancy, understand?"

"Yes, father," Will answered. He had never seen his father so serious except for earlier that summer when his wife, Will's mother, had died,

Quickly, both Charles and Will began to climb up toward the passageway. As they climbed, they could hear the soft cries of the little girl's mother as she wept.

"May they be safe," Lord Byrén said as he watched them disappear into the darkness. "May we all be safe," Will's father answered.

11 THE BLACK CROWS

Echoes of the battle could be heard throughout the land surrounding the kingdom as the sun began to rise in the East. Shouts of angry men and horses hooves resounded over the blackened hills of the Cardion Valley and the Cornshire. The colors of the sun light spread across the sky like liquid.

The Dragon Forest was quiet in the stillness of the dawn. The blue mist had left with the Dragon and Peter, and all that remained was a white fog that densely blanketed the lake and trees. Underneath its shelter lay the ashes of Lord Caragon's men. Sir Peregrine's remains were frozen in time as the sun touched the tops of the enormous trees. A black crow cawed and left its perch high atop a pine. The flapping of its wings was all that could be heard in the new morning.

Suddenly, the fog hovering over the damp ground was rudely parted as the black bird made its way to the earth. Its clawed feet touched down as it folded its large wings to its side. The bird's eyes darted back and forth in the early dawn's light. Somehow, the bird seemed to know that all had changed inside the Dragon Forest.

A loud caw reverberated from its open beak, shattering the silence throughout the great forest green. A few sparrows fluttered out of the trees and into the deep violet sky. They circled over the lake and then departed from the forest. The black crow watched them, then slowly turned its head to the pile of ashes next to its claws. Another loud caw broke the silence as the black bird opened its wings once again and prepared to fly into the fog. This time, the "caw" was met with a sudden breeze entering the forest green from the west. The breeze circled over the lake and made its way through the fog, causing it to twist and turn like a small tornado rising over the lake and move toward the damp shore. The twisting and turning moved the fog away from the ashes beneath its white blanket. The black crow perched high above the commotion and patiently watched.

The breeze stirred up the ashes of Caragon's men. Sir Peregrine's remains stirred in the wind and fog and rose higher and higher. As they twisted and turned in the madness of the breeze, they began to take on the shape of a large black bird. The ashes swirled as they formed a body, then wings, followed by a head with open beak. The bird was much larger than the crow that woke the forest with its caw. Its yellow eyes stared firmly and fiercely from within the deep sockets. The leather-like black feathers protruding around its neck stood upright as they made a strange sort of wreath around the face. The breeze continued its mission as it made a path over the other remains of the burned knights. Each pile of grey ashes was swept up into the form of a large black bird with wings spread wide as if ready to take flight in the upsweep of the breeze that gave life to each creature. As the grotesque flock of the undead began to shape, they cawed in unison in the middle of the deep forest green as the moon revealed itself behind a dark cloud. Its stark contrast to the rising sun gave an eerie appearance of glowing light giving off life to the flock of crows below. Each bird noticed the moon's glow and began to ascend into the violet dawn. Their loud caws echoed throughout the Dragon Forest as they rose ever higher above the lake; the wind from their flapping wings moved the fog into the trees. All that remained of the traitorous knights was their swords, shields, and a few scattered pieces of armor stained with soot. There artifacts would remain as a warning to anyone who dared to enter the forest again.

The black birds circled together a few times over the lake and then rose over the trees as one. Caragon's bizarre spell over the remains of his knights was set into motion as they were now large grotesque crows of the night flying toward the castle with sharp beaks and talons of fury. Their black feathers waved in the wind and their yellow eyes searched the night for their master. They flew together in death as they had ridden together in life.

§

Burning arrows continued to make their way over the outer walls of the castle as Constable Darion and the King's men prepared their plan to release the ogres from bondage in an act of desperation and in hopes that the giant beasts, once freed, would abandon the war and return to their lands in the hills.

Soldiers nervously mounted their steeds as the large gate was opened and the bridge lowered. Arrows landed inside the outer courtyard of the castle and found their way into the flesh of several soldiers. Villagers ran screaming for cover. Those who were working in the armory to make more arrows for the King's men helped put out the fires set by the flaming arrows. The wounded were gathered and brought to the physician who had made a makeshift hospital out of the Chapel. He wrapped wounds and helped comfort those who had been penetrated by the the enemy's arrows.

"Where did these men come from?" the physician asked. "Why weren't they inside the dungeon?"

"They stayed outside to help with the wounded, sir," answered the nurse as she helped tend to the men.

"Crazy fools," the physician said under his breath. The air was thick with smoke, making it harder to see and breathe as water was poured onto the small fires all around the courtyard.

The castle walls were hit time and again with large boulders sent into the air by the giant ogres' catapults. The walls held firm for now, but it was only a matter of time before they crumbled. The boulders were larger and larger with each launch. The Black Knights rode back and forth in front of the fire set before them by the King's men. They waited patiently for their orders to ride through the flames and storm the castle walls once an opening was created. Their black steeds reared and screamed with anticipation of the ride.

As the gate opened, Darion met the soldiers as they mounted their horses. "Ride bravely!" he ordered, and they rode into the dawn as a sliver of sun made its way over the horizon. The light made it possible for the knights to see the faces of their wicked enemy. Years of evil service to Lord Caragon had changed the once stern and handsome faces of the men into grotesque visages of pure evil. Their countenances were dark and depraved inside their black armor. The soldiers rode on despite the wickedness that awaited them.

As one, the King's soldiers galloped carefully over the damaged bridge of the Blue River and into the face of battle. Their cries of victory were met with shrills of the enemy. Together they raced toward the catapults, but their horses were attacked by ravenous Zadoks thirsty for blood, biting with their yellow teeth. Each bit deeply into the flesh of the horses and more than one horse fell to the ground, sending its rider tumbling to the earth. Teeth and sharp claws dug into the fallen animals and soldiers. Once other soldiers saw this attack, they changed their direction away from the beasts. They were met by the Baroks on horseback with swords held high above them. The King's men were dealt a heavy blow as the evil Baroks slashed the silver armor of the soldiers. The wicked swords of Lord Caragon's servants were immense pieces of blackened metal that easily sliced through anything in their path. They slashed through the soldiers who were thrown from their horses and swung at the soldiers riding on.

Finally, one of the King's men made his way to an ogre chained to a catapult. As the ogre loaded the catapult with a large boulder, the soldier rode swiftly to the giant with his sword held high. In one swoop, he lowered the sword and cut the chains off the ogre's feet. The monster roared and tried to hit the soldier as he dashed away from his prize. Then, as Darion watched through his looking glass, he saw the ogre run toward the soldier as he galloped away not realizing his chains of bondage had been broken. The ogre stopped and looked down at his feet. Then he shrieked to the other ogres and ran off into the long shadows of the hills toward his home.

Darion smiled. His plan had worked. The ogre cared more about his own freedom than the battle.

This modest victory gave hope and confidence to the other surviving soldiers as, with shouts of victory, they galloped toward the other ogres and freed them in like manner. One by one, the colossal beasts ran away from the battle and toward the hills as the Baroks shot arrows at their fleeing backs.

Lord Caragon watched helplessly as his slaves left his war. He shouted new orders to his men who began riding toward the fleeing giants in an attempt to corral them back into battle, but Caragon could see this was futile. He ordered his knights to lay siege to the castle walls instead. He glanced up and gazed into the deep violet sky. He watched it turn into a blue hue with glimpses of fiery red. Then he shunned his face from the approaching sun. Like a vampire avoiding the strength of the sun's full countenance, he lowered the face mask of his helmet in order to guard his own twisted façade. He squinted his eyes from the pain of the light. Then, with great anticipation and eagerness, he heard something advancing overhead. The sound was like that of mighty winds sweeping over the hills. Beneath his armored helmet, he grinned. Then he ordered his men on toward the castle. What approached in the skies was not the wind, but his returning servant, Sir Peregrine, in the new form of a giant black crow.

§

As the sun slowly made its way over the horizon, King Alexander and his men rode quickly into the hills of the Cardion Valley and the Cornshire toward the battle over his kingdom. Horse hooves beat furiously over the earth dampened while the banner of the King snapped wildly in the wind.

§

Prince Peter, atop the Dragon, gripped the glistening scales of the creature's neck as together they flew high above the farmlands. Peter could see the ocean shore far off to the east with millions of sparkles dancing over the surface as the sun rose above the waters. He could see the black smoke of the battlefield below and wondered where his father was. They were far too high for anyone to see them and recognize the Dragon.

The Dragon circled over the kingdom many times to assess what was happening. Peter's hair flapped in the wind. He turned his small head back toward the Dragon Forest into the wind, but something in the sky caught his attention. The object seemed small, and it was hard for Peter to understand what he was looking at. The black form moved below them as it obviously came from the Dragon Forest. Peter rubbed his sore eyes to try and see what the form was, but the Dragon continued to circle over the kingdom, turning Peter's view away from the approaching form. As the Dragon flew to the north, once again, Peter was able to return his gaze to the black form in the sky below them. As it moved underneath them, Peter was able to realize what the form was: A flock of giant black crows.

"Dragon!" he yelled. "Do you see that?"

"Yes," the Dragon answered. "Hold fast." It flew even higher into the morning sky. The sun had finally eased its way over the horizon and caused the clouds to become red and orange in its glow as night made way for morning.

"Crows! Giant crows!" Peter cried. He gripped the Dragon's neck even tighter as they descended toward the castle. With bodies the size of horses and wingspans to match, the black creatures made their way toward the King's men as they rapidly rode through the farmlands.

"But... how?" Peter asked the Dragon. "Where did they come from?"

"They are Lord Caragon's men. Sir Peregrine is leading them in flight," the Dragon explained.

Peregrine! What sort of wicked magic is this? Peter pondered what he was being told. He had never known such evil as spells cast upon men to turn them into flying creatures after death. The very notion made his skin cold. He watched the black birds fly over his father.

King Alexander led his men over the farmlands when he heard the commotion above him. As his horse galloped, he turned his head back over his shoulder and saw the wicked sight above his men. The large black birds lifted their claws in front of their bodies and lowered themselves over Sir Andrew as his horse galloped. King Alexander watched in horror as one of the crows clasped onto Sir Andrew's body with its sharp talons removing him from his horse and dropping him several feet away.

"No!" the King shouted as he realized what had happened to one of his best knights. Upon hearing the King's shout, the other men turned and saw the crows rapidly descending upon them as well. Talons grasped one knight after the other as the helpless King watched. He pulled on the reins of his horse and stopped it. Then, turning toward the advancing crows, he removed the sword of his fathers and attacked the black birds as they tried to grasp him. He slashed at the talons and drew blood. One crow flew off, but others followed. The other knights stopped to fight as well. Crow after crow swooped down upon the steadfast men as they used their shields and swords to impede the attack. With bleeding talons, the crows did not stop attacking, but their blood was not red. Dark ooze appeared to be coming from the severed arteries of the flying beings. Realizing the creatures had a spell cast over them by Caragon, King Alexander knew they could not be killed by his men. Still, he would not give up.

Peter winced as his father's men being picked up by the giant birds and dropped to their deaths below him. He had hoped the Dragon would interfere and stop the ferocious attack. He covered his eyes when he spotted his father slashing at the crows with his sword. He refused to watch his father die.

King Alexander's arms became weak and heavy as he slashed at the crows repeatedly. Many of his men took out their bows and shot arrows into the creatures as they flew near them. But their efforts were futile. The King rode faster and faster, weaving left and right to avoid the crows above him. Valiant knights, one after one, willingly gave up their lives to ensure their King arrived at the castle safely. They fought off the crows as long as they could.

Peter and the Dragon swerved above through the mist and clouds. The Dragon flew quickly over the castle courtyard and began to descend there.

"What are you doing?" asked Peter.

"Taking you home," answered the giant beast.

§

Will made his way up the shaft and to the small opening in the castle wall. He hesitated to open it, not knowing what was behind the small door. He gazed back at Charles.

"Wait here," he said. "I'll go first."

He pushed open the small wooden hatch and opened it. The glimpse of shadow first appeared and then some movement. Will opened the hatch more; he was near a staircase that led to the courtyard. The stone steps were in the shadow of one of the castle walls. He could feel the cool air from the dawn. He poked his head out slowly and could hear the voices and screams of villagers in the courtyard. He also heard some shouts of commands from the military.

"I am going to find the doctor at the infirmary. Stay here," he whispered to Charles. Charles nodded in agreement.

Hesitating only for a moment, Will stepped out of the secret passage and closed the hatch. He knew his Charles would wait in the dark of the passage way for him. Will stooped down low as he walked up the stone steps. The noises of battle grew louder and louder. A pungent odor hit his nose as a cloud of dark smoke hovered over the ground. As the rays of sun parted the misty clouds, he saw the thick black smoke from the oil fires past the castle walls. Knowing that the battle was raging, Will ran over to the side of the turret and peaked around. Foot soldiers were running while shouting orders. Villagers were screaming. The foot soldiers advanced up the stairs of the outer wall to meet the bowmen on top who were shooting arrows into the sky. Oil, fire, and smoke littered the courtyard as men and women ran for cover from flying fire and arrows. Will saw people hiding under haystacks and wagons. He saw their fear.

In the confusion, he tried to find the infirmary, then remembered it had been set up inside the chapel. His mind raced and his heart beat faster and faster with each scream and shout of the people nearby. He hurried through the smoke filled courtyard with his hand over his mouth for fear of choking. Swiveling his head left and right to see where the wounded were being taken, he finally saw a wounded soldier being carried by two men into a building lit with torches. *That has to be it.* He ran toward the small building. The doorway was open, so he carefully peeked in to make sure it was safe. The surgeon and his nurses ran from one wounded soldier to the next. Many men had arrows poking out from blackened flesh that had been burned by the oil bombs. They screamed in agony. One young soldier held tightly to the arrow in his arm, begging to be sent back out to battle. Will stood there amazed at the bravery.

"Please, my men need me!" the soldier yelled. "I need to get back out there now!" But the surgeon ignored him as he worked on a man bleeding form his chest.

The soldier saw Will in the doorway. Their eyes met. The soldier appeared puzzled, as if he wondered who Will was and why he was there. The fury and desperation in the soldier's eyes frightened Will. He couldn't look away. But the soldier's own plight gave him no chance for pause. He breathed faster and faster and then grabbed the arrow in his upper arm. With one swift yank, the arrow came out of his arm with shredded muscle still on the end of the sharp point. Thick red blood spewed out of the wound. The nurse turned her heard and hastened to wrap the wound with some rags. He got up off his cot and limped over to the doorway. Will's eyes made contact again with the soldier in the doorway. But the soldier looked passed him as if he weren't there and, for an instant, Will thought he saw himself in the young soldier's eyes. Fierce and hardened as they were from the night's battle. Will saw deeply into the gaze of a warrior. He knew he would never be the same.

The young soldier grabbed his belt with his sword and sheath. Then his quiver and arrows, still blackened from the smoke and oil. He ran into the morning mist in the courtyard.

Will watched the warrior disappear amidst all the people running and screaming. He turned back to the nurse and told her of the little girl's wound. She grabbed some rags and some herbs. Then she and Will made their way back to the secret passageway. Will watched behind her to see if anyone had seen them enter the passageway. The lives of many depended on no one seeing where they were hiding.

He opened the hatch for her and saw Charles waiting there. "Take her to the child," he ordered. "I won't be back."

"What?" asked Charles as he led the nurse to the dark passageway. "Where are you going?"

"Into battle," he answered as he looked into the sky.

"But how, Will, you have no sword, no quiver?"

"I know where I can get one," he said. "Stay safe."

Charles watched his friend run up the stone steps then pause. He looked back at Charles.

"Tell my father I will be alright. I need to do this."

Charles nodded and slowly closed the hatch.

Will then ran to the inner ward where the Chapel and the Keep stood. The loud sound of the enemy pounding the outer wall with large stone fireballs made the battle all the more real. Their shouts echoed through the castle grounds. Apparently, they were close. Too close. He knew a battering ram would soon be used to break down the front gate.

Will spotted the blacksmith's hut. He found several large swords, grabbed the largest one, and felt the cold steel and the weight of the sword. Metal helmets lay next to some shields, so he grabbed one of each. He put the helmet on his head but it slid down to his nose. Agitated, he threw it down. He didn't want to be reminded of how young he was. Too much was at stake for self-pity now.

Without a helmet, he ran into the courtyard and stood ready to enter into battle. Just then, he looked up a gust of wind rushed over his face. Clouds of black smoke and mist swirled around in the sky directly above him. The wind rushed faster. Will could not see the cause of the movement. Was it some sort of bird or storm moving above him?

Finally, he heard the flapping of wings, larger than any wings he had seen in his young life, but he still could not see them. Dust, hay, and twigs circled all around him as they danced in the wind. He raised his hand in front of his face as he waited for the wind to stop. All of a sudden, the young Prince appeared out of thin air and dropped to the ground inches before Will. He peered up at the sky, trying to figure out what had happened, but to no avail.

§

Peter stood up and dusted off the dirt from his pants. He looked up at the Dragon who was visible only to him. He feared being left alone in the castle. "What are you going to do?" he asked.

"Fight for your father," the Dragon answered. "Stay here. You will be safe."

Then, with a mighty flap of its giant wings, the Dragon left to enter into the battle for the Kingdom.

Will dropped his sword on the ground next to Peter. Peter stooped down to pick it up. It was far too heavy for him to lift. "Your sword?" he asked Will.

But Will continued to stare at the sky while the wind from the invisible Dragon's wings swished through his hair.

Peter tugged on the young would-be soldier's arm to get his attention. He repeated the question.

"What just happened?" Will asked.

"The Dragon," Peter answered. "It dropped me off here."

"What Dragon?" Will asked.

Peter and Will both stared at the sky as the smoke and clouds swirled in the Dragon's wake. "I suppose it remains unseen by most," Peter said.

"What do you mean?"

"It only reveals itself to those whom it chooses," Peter explained. He looked at Will, expecting to him to fully comprehend the process. But Will just stared with his mouth agape.

"You'd better close your mouth or you'll choke on all this smoke," Peter warned.

"Do you mean to tell me," Will pointed to the sky, "you were dropped here by the Dragon of the Dragon Forest?"

"Precisely," Peter exclaimed rather proudly. "Amazing isn't it?" He folded his arms across his chest and smiled.

"Amazing is hardly the word," Will said. "I thought it was just a legend."

"So did I," Peter said.

§

The invisible Dragon rose higher into the new morning sky and noticed the crows attacking Alexander's Royal Knights. It quickly spotted the King galloping toward the castle over the hills. The time was right for the Dragon to enter into this battle for the kingdom and the forest. Far too much was at stake now.

The Dragon flew quietly over the hills toward the large black crows flying furiously through the sky. As it flew, the change came slowly over its body beginning with the tail. As the change made its way over the back, the scales became soft and long. They fell over the body and covered the entire torso of the giant beast. The leathery wings became covered by the enlarged and softened scales. The rough claws twitched in flight as the sharp talons formed. The Dragon's face jerked with agitation as the softened scales moved over its face. The once prolonged snout shortened drastically as the large eyes became yellow. They began to resemble the eyes of a bird.

The large tongue retracted back into the mouth of the beast as the mouth shortened to form a hardened yellow beak. This beak would know no blue fire or mist.

Softened scales became feathers as the metamorphosis took place. The brown feathered body took on the form of a bird flying through the sky. The Dragon knew it was time for it to be seen. Suddenly, the rush of air under its wings caused him to fly more gracefully and with more speed. On the ground under those giant wings was a darkened shape unfamiliar to its brain. The shape seemed to move over the hills with envied speed as the Dragon flapped its new feathered wings. The shape moved in perfect harmony with the Dragon's transformed body. The Dragon understood the shape to be its own shadow. And that shadow was in the shape of a giant hawk.

§

King Alexander had known fear once or twice in his life, now he knew it more intimately than he cared to know. His men were being slaughtered in the hills, and he knew his men were fighting at the castle. He spurred his horse to move even faster. His sword, high in the air, slashed at any black crow swooping down to attack him. The King's only thought now was on his son. He prayed the boy was safe inside the castle.

A loud screech came from the heavens above them as the knights continued their battle with the giant black crows. One by one, they looked up to find the source of such a loud and grotesque scream. Appearing above them in one large swoop was a giant brown hawk with talons out in front of its wings stretched behind it in an attacking mode.

The men stopped riding long enough to see the giant bird clutch a black crow in its yellow talons. Its beak ripped the flesh buried beneath the black feathers of the crow and ended its life instantly. The giant hawk dropped the dead crow and flew away as the carcass slammed to the earth a few feet away from a knight. The harsh thud startled him. He sat atop his stunned horse and watched the giant hawk continue its way through more and more of the black creatures. As he watched in utter amazement, only one thought went through his mind: The plight of the King.

Avoiding the dead crows falling from the sky, he rode with his sword high in the air and with hope once again flowing through his veins.

§

Will ran with Peter to the castle gate. Peter tried to tell Will all about his adventure with the Dragon, but Will didn't have time to listen. He knew Peter was the Prince and he wanted to make sure he returned to the castle safely.

"You will stay here this time, right?" Will asked. "I have to go and fight now."

"Yes, I will stay here now. Please, try and find my father."

"I will do my best."

Will ran off with his sword and started up one of the ladders that led to the top of the outer wall. Step after step brought him higher and higher into the sky. Finally, he made it to the top and looked over the wall at the scene for the first time. The battle was still raging as Lord Caragon's men fought with the King's men. Hundreds of arrows flew from the top of the castle wall only to be met with more coming from the field below as the bowmen hurriedly fired more arrows into the enemy below. Large wooden ladders were brought to the castle wall by Caragon's men. They desperately tried to raise them up. Will knew that if one of those creatures made their way up the ladder successfully, then all the enemy could make their way into the courtyard and even to the castle. He knew this could not happen. But it was inevitable as the King's men were struggling to maintain a hold in front of the river. The oil fires continued to burn, sending their thick black smoke into the air, but Caragon's men made their way through the river.

Will's blood raced through his body and his heart pounded. He watched the Zadoks fight with the soldiers. He couldn't just watch anymore. He had to do something.

A loud crash come from the turret of the outer wall. Many soldiers shouted for more men to come help them fight near this turret. One of the enemy's ladders had found its way to land against the turret wall. The enemy had finally penetrated the outer wall. He looked down over the wall and saw dozens of the enemy scurrying up the ladder like roaches. Then, he jerked his head toward the courtyard and saw many villagers running for cover. The door of the infirmary was locked up now. With sword drawn, young Will remembered the determined eyes of that warrior he saw in the infirmary.

With all the fierceness his young body could produce, Will shouted, then raised his sword high into the air and ran toward the enemy. Suddenly, he had become the warrior.

The enemy made its way up the wooden ladders. Their blackened faces were twisted and grotesque with bloodied sores covering their skin. The metal shields reflected the fiery arrows from Alexander's men as they flew through the air. Below them, foot soldiers chased the enemy up the ladders swinging their swords at the enemy's feet. The swords sliced the hardened skin and one enemy fighter fell to the ground only to be met by many foot soldiers eager to ensure his swift death. One by one, the foot soldiers fought to keep the enemy from advancing on the castle. To breech the towers would lead to disaster. They had sworn to give their lives to protect the castle.

More foot soldiers left their protective mantlets to climb the ladders. Will noticed one soldier had grabbed a piece of wood and ran to the oil fires still burning the tall grasses. He lit the wood and ran, weaving back and forth to avoid flying arrows from the enemy, but he looked down to find an arrow penetrating the canvas tunic he wore. The stain of red grew bigger and bigger yet he couldn't stop.

"Help me!" he shouted. With his other arm he dropped to the ground near a burning patch of dirt. The stench of oil was powerful as he saw the fire burning the black liquid. He lowered the wooden stick into the fire and quickly ran toward one of the ladders.

Upon seeing the soldier, Will decided to help him. Several enemy fighters ran toward the wounded soldier with swords drawn. The race had begun with each fighter having his own purpose. Turning his head, Will spotted the mutant enemy fighters running after the soldier. The ladder appeared only a few feet away. The pain in his arm caused him to stumble and the enemy fighters gained on him.

"Hurry!" Will shouted to him. He made his way down a ladder and ran to assist.

Running faster amidst the sharpened pain, the soldier began to collapse. Will advanced to the ladder and grabbed the torch in the soldier's hand. He used it to light the ladder and watched as the flame caught instantly and climbed faster and faster up the wood and twine. As the soldier and Will watched the enemy squirm up the ladder trying to escape the flames, they grinned in triumph. Will turned to fight the approaching enemy.

While the fire ate up the wooden ladder, the enemy fighters had no choice but to jump or burn. Those who jumped were met at the bottom by Will, the King's angry foot soldiers, and their swords. Those who remained on the ladder tried to advance to the top and leapt to the castle wall, but the hot steel of the bowmen's arrowheads met their hardened flesh and ended their futile pursuit.

Will climbed back up another ladder to the outer curtain wall. He carried his heavy sword as high above his head as he could with his young arms and brought it down to meet the twisted and grotesque countenance of the enemy. The clanging of steel swords mixed with the agonizing screams of death made Will's skin shiver but he knew he could not give up. Over the castle walls came more and more enemy fighters from below. There seemed to be no end to this supply, yet not one soldier stopped fighting the good fight. Each fought as though they knew what was at stake.

§

King Alexander rode faster toward his castle without stopping to see why the black crows were no longer tormenting him with their sharp claws. He spotted the enemy fighting their way through the oil fires as they ran to the castle walls. The King stopped his horse and shouted to his remaining men. Spotting their leader, the men raised their swords. Seeing him with them gave them renewed strength and hope for victory.

Lord Caragon, mounted on his black horse far off, watched the King arrive to the battle. His wicked plan had worked after all.

King Alexander noticed his dark enemy watching from afar. Realizing now that the plan for this whole battle had nothing to do with obtaining the Dragon scales, his heart became full of hatred for his former friend. There would be no mercy this time for the enemy.

The King's men continued to battle the enemy fighters with all their might. Alexander turned to watch the bowmen's arrows strike down more and more enemy. Just then, a sharp sting entered his side. Below him were three enemy fighters approaching him, swords drawn above them as they ran. The King kicked his horse and ordered it to move. Galloping through the enemy, he sliced through the black flesh of the fighters, severing arms and heads as he made his way to the castle wall. Leaping off his horse, he ran to the main outer gate and helped fight the enemy there. With each thrust of his sword, enemy fighters fell to their deaths.

Will spotted the King from atop the wall and quickly made his way down one of the ladders to meet the King at the gate. Finding the King, Will helped him and the other soldiers keep the enemy from crushing down the gate. Turning and slashing with his heavy sword, Will cut through the enemy like a scythe thrashing through the wheat. He fought near his King, making sure no enemy could touch him. The enemy's black blood marked Will's face with a sting, making it hard to see, but he could not stop now.

Suddenly, the loud screech of a hidden bird alarmed the men in battle as they frantically searched for the source of the noise above them. The giant hawk beat its wings causing dust and smoke to rise up in a funnel cloud. In the giant yellow talons were several enemy fighters screaming from intense pain. Dropping them several hundred feet to their deaths, the giant bird then flew away toward more enemy fighters.

Lord Caragon waved his sword into the air to signal a warning to his men. But it was a futile gesture since his men were being torn apart by the hawk.

King Alexander stared in amazement as the enemy fighters before him ran off to fight the bird at their Lord's command. Their dark and twisted minds seemed to have no will of their own. They were under some sort of spell that only Caragon knew.

Foot soldiers followed the men as their King gave orders to the bowmen to reinforce the castle gate from inside the court.

Will stood near the King as his chest heaved in and out. He bent down to catch his breath when he noticed a dark red stain on the King's side.

"Your majesty!" he shouted. "You are wounded."

Lord Caragon jerked his head around when he heard Will's words. By magic, he could listen to the boy from afar. "I knew I had felt the King's blood spill earlier, but now I know the King is indeed injured," he hissed.

Inside his deadened chest beat the dark and hardened heart of this twisted soul whose only purpose was to see the present and future King dead. Caragon ordered his men to make one final push to the castle gate. With his sword, he waved it over the surviving fighters as they approached him. A mysterious purple mist encircled them. The mist drew higher and higher, taking the forms of the fighters with it into the morning sky. Their bodies grew larger and larger until they were the size of ogres.

King Alexander ignored Will's shouts regarding his injury as he watched Caragon's motions on the hills behind them. The giant hawk circled high above Caragon.

"He cannot see it," the King said.

"What?" asked Will.

"The hawk," the King pointed. "Look!"

Will watched as the giant brown hawk circled above with its huge wings spread out, causing it to glide effortlessly with the wind. Will's eyes gazed downward to the enemy below the hawk. They were covered in the purple mist. Indeed, the King was right. Lord Caragon did not notice the hawk above him. *Perhaps Prince Peter was right*, Will thought, *in that only a chosen few could see the Dragon even when it took the form of a hawk.*

The dark Lord raise his sword high, ordering his new giant fighters toward the castle. The evil fighters turned and began to move.

The ground begin to shake. Staring at the giant fighters moving toward them, Will saw the King order his men to join him in one last surge to defeat the enemy. They raised their arms high and shouted with the King, "To the death!"

Will rushed to the King's side. "No!" he yelled as he grabbed the King's arm. "You are wounded. You cannot do this!" He noticed the red stain on the King's tunic was larger and darker now.

"Join us, young Will. Fight with us, one last time!" the King answered.

"How do you know my name?" Will asked.

The King smiled then was off to the fight. With his royal cloak flying in the wind behind him and with the sword of his fathers glistening in the sun, the King motioned for his men to follow him.

Will stood and watched as his leader made his way through the burning brush and to the Blue River. Death awaited them on the other side. But they had a mighty ally in this fight and the King knew it.

Foot soldiers, shouting and raising swords high in the air, ran past Will to join their King. Will knew it was time to decide what he would do. He could stay behind and climb the ladder to safety on the castle wall, or he could fight alongside his King. He stood for a moment as the soldiers waded across the Blue River into the madness that awaited them. Then, he gripped his sword tightly and ran to meet them on the other side.

§

The hawk gathered more enemy fighters into its fearsome talons, taking them up in one fell swoop. The fighters tried to swing their swords, but it was to no avail. Their foe was mightier than they could handle. Lord Caragon watched as his men were torn to bits before him.

King Alexander moved his men closer to Caragon's men, leading them into the hills and away from the castle. The bowmen's arrows could no longer reach the enemy. The battleground had changed.

The constable atop the castle wall, ordered the bowmen to take up arms and go help the King below. As they hurried down the steps, the blacksmith met them at the bottom, dispersing swords and shields to each man as fast as he could. The main gate opened, and each bowman ran out to meet the King. Shouts of encouragement came from the villagers who remained in the courtyard. They knew that the battle had changed for the better as the enemy ran to the hills. The dark Lord, carrying his banner, had galloped his steed to the hills with his black fighters

King Alexander proceeded ahead of his men to the top of a small hill. Behind him were a hundred or more men ready to end the war with Caragon. Splitting his men up to flank the enemy, the King ordered them to move quickly. One group ran over the hill with swords drawn. The other group waited for the signal to move to the other side.

Will stood ready to run. The blood rushed through his body and his breathing was hard to control. Above them, the hawk circled and waited. One more time it would be needed in the fight.

King Alexander motioned to his men. Will saw the red stain on the King's tunic and knew he was too injured to fight.

The Dragon, still disguised as the giant brown hawk, continued to glide through the morning sky, waiting for the King to order the advance into the hills and into Caragon's men, but the King hesitated. The keen eyes of the hawk spotted the blood stained tunic as the King raised his arms to direct his men. They obeyed the order to flank the enemy and moved into position.

Caragon rode off into the hills to the west, nearing the desert toward the Black Hills. The hawk disrupted its glide and beat its wings as it screeched overhead.

Alexander looked above him at the magnificent sight of this giant creature circling over them as their protector. The tight grip of pain caused him to stumble and lose his breath.

Will grabbed the King's arm. "My Lord, you cannot go on."

"Leave me be. All is well," the King answered as he regained his composure.

"Sire, let us fight this battle for you," Will said. "We need you to remain as King."

But Alexander ignored the plea and watched as his men made their way into position. It was nearly time to give the order to advance. The enemy retreated to the hills.

Alexander smirked. "I suspect Lord Caragon is not finished with this war. His dark role in this battle is larger than I had originally thought." He assumed Caragon had something dark planned over those hills which lay covered in the long shadows caused by the rising sun. Although the King's men were few, they were ready.

Alexander's men ran through the carcasses of the Zadoks and giant black crows. Their bodies lay twisted into grotesque poses with their eyes staring out into oblivion. They spotted dead knights and foot soldiers scattered all over the battlefield. With faces frozen in grimaces of pain, they resembled morbid sculptures.

Some soldiers stopped to put capes over the bodies of the King's soldiers out of respect. But most did not have time to stop. "No time to honor the dead now," one soldier exclaimed. "We'll have time when this war is over."

The blood-stained battlefield would serve as a memorial to the battle. The men knew the importance of this quarrel as, in unison, they marched quick-step to flank the enemy on both sides. The hills were a hard climb for their tired legs, and the distant rumbling of the enemy forces on the other side reverberated through the valley. The sound made them shudder.

As the bowmen from the castle made their way through the bloodied battlefield, their eyes widened from the sight of so many dead. They had not seen the wolf-like creatures and black crows from atop the castle wall due to the thick black smoke covering the Blue River's edge. But now that they were actually there on the field, the sight was more than they could have dreamed. Many of the men were still in their youth and had never entered battle before, but their training had been excellent. They relied on their skills now more than ever as they hastened to meet the rest of the soldiers and surviving knights.

Lord Caragon stopped his horse to turn and see the scene behind him. Before him stood the menacing Black Hills that hid his castle at Hildron. But behind him he could see the King's men trying to set up one last stand. He spotted King Alexander standing atop a small hill as he gave orders. Caragon waited and watched as the men took their places for the advance. His men were low in the desert plains between the lower hills and the Black Hills. They waited with baited breath for their orders to begin the attack. The clanging of their metal weapons created an eerie sort of morbid music that rose over the hills. Their screams and taunts of fury grew louder and louder as they lusted for the blood of their foes. Their tormented wait would soon come to an end.

§

Peter ran as fast as he could to his bedroom window, running past frantic servants rushing to the infirmary to help. He ascended these stairs again, but so much had changed since he last walked these steps only a few hours earlier. He gripped the rail and almost tripped over the steps to get to his window.

Once there, he tore open the wooden shutters that were closed for protection and stood, staring out the open window. Smoke continued to rise over the Blue River valley as the sun made its way higher into the sky. His glance made its way past the Cornshire and over the hills. The small thatched roofs were still smoking from the earlier battle.

But all he wanted to see was the Dragon Forest. Eagerly he searched for it in the distance. So many years he had dreamed of what lay inside the forest green and now he knew. The black smoke blocked his view. He strained his neck to try and see past the smoke. The giant brown hawk cut through the smoke and, as Peter saw its beauty, his heart beat faster. The giant gust of wind coming from its wings blew the smoke away. Peter looked past the commotion, past the battle, smoke, and hills where the Dragon Forest stood guardian over the entire kingdom. Hope remained.

Now to see my father.

12 THE WOUNDED KING

Peter watched out his bedroom window only for a few moments more before he decided what to do. Protecting the Dragon was his mission before, but now he thought about his father. He rushed out of his bedroom, down the tiled floor to the grand entrance hall of the castle, and past the servants hurrying out the main entrance with rags and water buckets to assist at the infirmary.

Then he remembered that Titan had not returned from the Dragon Forest; he had no ride to enter the battle. But Peter could not let that stop him. He understood that Caragon would never let them live in peace. He would have to be stopped. Peter also knew his father, the King, would make sure the end would result in peace.

Peter tore past the main entrance and the infirmary to the outer courtyard. He dashed between servants, wounded soldiers, and panicked villagers. He watched as wounded soldiers were brought down from the castle walls and from the battlefield with bloodied bodies and faces frozen in anguish. For a young boy like Peter, it was almost enough to make him stop and return to the safety of his room. But Peter knew his youthfulness would make no difference to anyone now.

The once black smoke had turned white as the oil fires began to burn out. The sky was now full of darkened clouds. They moved rapidly to the west as the new morning sky was covered. The sun became blocked and no more shadows appeared on the land. A slight breeze filled the air as Peter smelled the coming rain. The slight echo of thunder moved over the shores and to the valleys near the castle. The Cornshire and Cardion valleys smoldered from the early morning fires set by Caragon's men. The little thatched homes were all but skeletal remains of blackened wood and twine. The combined smell of rain, smoke, and oil made the air thick and foggy. The main gate was opened Peter ran through the gate before anyone could stop him.

The smoldering field wreaked of death. The waters were cold as he entered them, but they were not moving swiftly enough to carry him away. Once he made it to the other side, he covered his mouth as the realities of war hit him in the face. Scattered randomly across the once grassy fields were hundreds of torn and battered bodies. He carefully stepped over the dead bodies of his father's brave fighters. Peter had never seen a dead man before. He leaned over the body of a knight as it lay face down. He recognized the coat-of-arms on the cape that was once a cheery red and gold but was now blackened from dirt and oil mixed with blood. Slowly, he turned the heavy body over as far as he could so he might see the face. When he finally saw the death grimace of the dead knight, Peter was stunned with sadness to see it was his father's dear friend Sir George.

A fine knight, Sir George would often tell Peter long stories after supper about faraway lands and ruthless battles with enemies unknown as they sat at the long mahogany table in the dining hall. Peter remembered him as a talented storyteller and knight who served his father well.

But now he lay dead on the battlefield having given all to the cause. Peter lowered Sir George's head back down slowly. The ominous boom of distant thunder made its way over the trees of the Dragon Forest as Peter wiped tears from his eyes.

§

The dark clouds filled the sky with a strange urgency. The shouts of Caragon's men began to rise over the hills. Hearing the clanging of the weapons followed by the threatening shouts of the evil fighters, the King's men took a few steps back. Will stood on the hill by his King as the wind picked up from the east. He watched with confusion as the blue sky became dark as the men prepared for battle. Uneasiness began to take over Will's imagination.

"Steady, men," the King said sensing the uneasiness of the soldiers. "All is well."

He watched his soldiers make their way to the positions he ordered. But the clouds and winds hindered his shouts, causing his men to proceed farther away than he intended. But it was too late now to call them back. He would have to trust their positions.

A slight tingle of moisture touched Will's forearm. Then the scream of the giant hawk gliding above him caused him to look up, and he was met with more rain. *This will make things worse.* But the hawk did not appear to be bothered by the cold rain hitting its wings. Still circling above them, it continued its watch over the men as they prepared.

A slash of light interrupted the preparations as lightning penetrated the dark sky. The lightning was obediently followed by its loud clap of thunder that stirred the horses of the remaining knights. They quickly dismounted and shouted at their horses to head home. The horses ran off toward the castle leaving their masters behind. There would no longer be any need for their horses now; the battle would continue on foot. More lightning bolts followed the first illuminating the obscure skies with flashes of white light.

Peter walked toward the hills in awe of the sight of the lightning show around them. He spotted his father standing on a small hill with Will next to him. Peter knew he could not enter into battle with his father or Will, but he also knew he had to try and help. Peering up into the storm as the rain hit his face, he watched the Dragon continue to glide gracefully as a hawk above them. Peter felt comfort seeing his new friend watching over the King.

The Dragon staggered. It grew tired from flying with its new wings and from the wound in its chest, decided the time was right for the men to begin their advance. The Dragon made its way over to the boy. The screech emanating from its beak startled the King's men, including Peter. He stopped walking when he saw the Dragon approaching him.

With a swoop, the Dragon landed on the ground in front of Peter. The familiar yellow eyes of the giant bird met Peter's eyes as he stood uncertain of what to do in that instant. The bird, eyes blinking, looked to the left and right with its beak apart. Peter knew instinctively what he was supposed to do: climb on the neck of the giant creature, so he obeyed the unspoken order. The bird lowered its neck to allow for Peter to climb and as it felt Peter's small hands grasp the feathers, it began its ascension into the dark and rainy sky.

"What is this?" the King asked as he ran down the hill. But it was too late to interfere. He was forced to watch his son be carried away on the neck of the giant bird.

"No!" he shouted as he waved his arms above his head running toward the bird.

But his gesture was met with a loud screech from the departing hawk as it lifted higher and higher into the rain storm.

Alexander knew there was nothing he could do but trust. This giant beast had helped his men in battle by killing the crows and had also returned his son unscathed to the castle. He knew he would have to trust the giant bird once again. He stopped running and stood still watching his son being taken higher into the sky on the neck of the hawk.

Will saw this sudden movement of the bird as a sign. He knew Peter was too small to be in this battle and perhaps the hawk was removing Peter so they could begin their advance. He went to tell the King his thoughts when, suddenly, Alexander stopped and inspected his men and their positions from the top of the hill.

"It is time," he said. He met Will's confused stare with certainty. "No fear."

Will instantly felt comfort in the King's demeanor. "No fear." He answered back.

Then with a loud shout to his men, King Alexander lifted his sword high into the air. Each squad of soldiers responded to the King's signal with shouts of their own. The banners with Alexander's coat-of-arms printed on them were held high over their heads. They were tattered and torn, but they still remained.

As each squad responded to the other, they began their advance. First, the squads to the west began their march followed by those to the east.

Finally, the King led his men into the valley as the rain pelted their tunics and helmets. The sting of the rain on their faces reminded them that they were still alive. Will followed his King and thoughts of his father and the other villagers still in the castle dungeon ran through his mind. *There is no time for regrets now*, he thought. The battle had begun.

§

The Dragon carried Peter high above the dark rain clouds to speak with him alone. The Dragon left his disguise as the giant hawk as its feathers began to take the shape of the glistening scales so coveted by Sir Peregrine. The once hardened beak transformed back into the long snout of the Dragon as his hissing tongue once again slithered between rows of sharp teeth. But the familiar yellow eyes still gleamed within their sockets. Peter held on tightly to the scales now as he watched the Dragon's body alter itself back to its original state. The hole in its chest also remained and this worried Peter. He knew the Dragon would be needed to help his father win this battle, but how could the beast help when it was wounded?

"Where are we going?" Peter asked as he spotted the Dragon Forest below. "Not back to the forest?"

He was disappointed that the Dragon would place him back in the forest green away from the battlefield, but he also understood why. He wanted the Dragon to destroy the enemy and help his father. He knew that the Dragon was capable of killing all the men, including Caragon with one breath. He had seen the awesome fire firsthand and what it did to Peregrine and his knights. Peter wanted deep in his heart to have the Dragon destroy the enemy of his father. Yet something was causing the Dragon to hesitate there high above the clouds.

Just then they heard the roar of the fighters beneath them. The fighting had started. *Why was the Dragon not watching it?* Peter thought. But he did not want to ask it just yet. He held on even tighter to the scales and waited to see what would happen.

"Peter," it spoke. "The time has come for the battle between what is good and what is evil."

Yes. Peter listened.

"I must wait here before entering in the battle," the Dragon continued.

"But why?" Peter interrupted.

"There will be a signal, I must wait here until the appointed time," it answered.

"But don't you want to even see what is happening?" Peter asked.

"Not yet, Peter. Soon those who fight will see," the Dragon said.

"See what?"

"The Dragon of the Forest," it answered.

§

The rain pelting down on the fighting soldiers made it hard for them to see the approaching enemy, and the dark clouds blocking out the light did not help. But their instinct, training, and skill would serve them well and give them the confidence they needed. So they continued to run toward the sound of the enemy still unseen behind the low hills. As the soldiers and knights made their way up the hills, a bolt of lightning lit up the murky sky. That sudden flash of light revealed the enemy fighters with spears, swords, and axes held high, running at full speed up the other side of the hill. The two forces clashed at the top of the first hill while the wind swept the rain over their faces.

The grotesque clanging of metal with metal mixed with shouts of pain reverberated throughout the valley. Lord Caragon, once again mounted his black steed far away from the battle. His hand gripped his long black spear. The rain blew sideways now, cutting across his helmet and masked face. His red eyes watched his mutant fighters slice away at the King's men. One by one the enemy made headway through the knights and foot soldiers.

King Alexander fought ahead of his men with his sword slashing away. But his wound caused him to stumble. He dropped his sword as his right hand clung to his side. Behind him came a tall brute approaching with a spear held high above its head. This mound of grotesque flesh sighted the unarmed King and knew he this was his chance to kill him. He shifted the spear in his hand for a tighter and he moved closer to the stumbling King. The pain and loss of blood from his wound began to trick the King's mind. He blinked the rain from his eyes and tried to regain his composure by looking around at the fight before him. He spotted his sword lying on the ground and knew he was vulnerable without it. Still crouched over from the sharp pain, the King tried to reach for his sword. Dizziness rushed to his head, making him unable to reach it. He straightened up and took in a deep breath.

The large enemy fighter ran toward the King, his prize kill, and pulled back the spear with each stride. Just then, the King heard the shout of the enemy fighter as he approached. He turned in time to see the giant brute running toward him with spear held high. The King turned back around toward his sword and grasped for it desperately, but fell to the ground as he reached for it. With all of its strength, the enemy fighter lunged forward, releasing the spear into the air. His aim was dead on as the lance soared through the air toward its appointed target.

Will leapt in front of the spear knocking it away with his sword and away from the King. The clang of the two metal weapons hitting each other stirred the King back into action. He stood up in time to find the soft fleshy part of his enemy's torso with his sword. The cold steel blade entered deep into the pit of the fighter's stomach ending its life. Will followed through with his leap forward and almost collided with the fighter as it fell to the earth. The rain poured down on both men as they stood near the dead brute noting its size. With water streaming down their faces, they shared only a few seconds together staring at the thick dark blood oozing from the dead body. Then, without a word, they returned to the battle.

Together, standing back to back, the King and Will slashed at the approaching enemy ducking spears and swords as the battle continued. The rain fell as more soldiers came over the hills to help in the fight. The King's heart swelled with pride. They were making headway against the enemy as they drew the fight farther away from the castle.

§

Will's father paced inside the dungeon, listening to the pounding of boulders against the castle wall. He feared for his son, whose whereabouts he knew nothing of, and yet he felt in his heart Will was still alive.

Charles assisted the nurse administer her herbs to the sick girl. They mixed a potion of dill, mint, hyssop, and fennel together with some water for her to drink. As she drank, her mother and the others noticed how she already showed signs of healing. The little girl opened her eyes to reveal the swelling inside her head was subsiding. Her mother hugged her and wept. Charles felt much better, but the sounds of the fighting outside the dungeon walls made him think of Will.

The little girl silently spoke to her mother through her tired eyes and everyone around her smiled. The dungeon was musty and only lit by the torches on the walls. The villagers were becoming more and more frightened with each passing moment. Charles got up and slowly walked over to Will's father who had stopped pacing.

"I wonder where he is," he asked no one in particular. "I pray he is alright."

"I know Will," Charles responded. "He will return."

Together the two stood looking up at the ceiling as the dust dropped with each pound of the enemy artillery.

§

The rain continued to fall. The ground muddy and slippery, but the soldiers continued to fight into the late afternoon. Minutes seemed like hours as their bodies ached from swinging heavy metal swords and spears. But as they remained, so did the enemy coming over the hills one by one. There seemed to be an endless supply. Where all these mutant creatures were coming from, no one knew. Most of the King's men had seen piles of enemy dead lying on the battlefield near the castle, yet now it seemed as though none had fallen at all.

Will continued his duty to protect the King with each slice of his sword. He lunged forward to insert his steel blade into more and more throats of the enemy as they came for their prize. Their evil faces would twist in pain as their dark blood oozed out onto the earth. The sights and smells made him want to vomit, but he knew one moment of hesitation would be their end. His arms burned from exhaustion, but he knew he could not quit now. Suddenly, he heard his master's voice.

"Will," the King shouted. "This way!" He pointed toward a small hill.

King Alexander wanted to move to better position away from the stench and to help his soldiers.

Together they ran ahead to meet three soldiers who were trapped by several oncoming enemy fighters. Will yelled as loud as he could to frighten the enemy fighters. They turned from slashing at the King's men to meet their fate. With both hands gripping his sword, Will swung it hard left to right severing two heads with one blow. The King stabbed his sword into the back of one fighter as it struggled with a young soldier. The sword went through the enemy and almost stabbed the young soldier whose body was close. But the sword stopped in time to spare the young man's life. The five of them were able to hold off more enemy fighters as they approached. The sight gave hope and encouragement to the other soldiers fighting nearby.

Lord Caragon grimaced. He did not expect the battle to continue this long. He looked around as his men fought, but their deaths sickened him. Some were even retreating from the battle in fear. He roared with anger then lifted his spear high into the air and when it came down, a mysterious green light shot from the top of the lance striking each retreating fighter. Their bodies lurched forward and then fell as dead men onto the earth. As more watched in horror, they stopped their retreat and reluctantly returned to the battle rather than face their evil master's wrath upon them. These evil and twisted creatures had no choice but to fight.

§

Peter sat atop the Dragon's mighty neck as they circled above the battlefield. Peter wondered how long it would be until they could enter into the battle and help his father. But the Dragon still remained far away. Peter knew he would have to trust it once more.

Lightning streaked across the stormy skies, cutting the darkness with its bright light. Thunder claps followed and echo off the hills to the castle where the remaining soldiers stood atop the outer walls. With the darkness upon them, it became harder and harder to see what was occurring. But they knew in their hearts the King would be victorious. No one wanted to think for a moment about the cost of their failure to defeat Caragon. The notion was too painful to bear.

Mud and dirty rain flew off the bodies of each fighter as they twisted and turned with weapons flailing all around them. The enemy approached from the north and the west with their black metal swords glistening in the rain. One squad of the King's soldiers began its advance over the hills to the west. They had defeated the enemy fighters coming from the west, so they decided to follow them. The enemy retreated, only to be met with Lord Caragon's wicked magic. Still they ran deeper into the desert.

The King shouted for his men to stop and not follow them. He knew the closer they got to the Black Hills, the worse it would be for them to ever return. The men heard their master's voice and stopped their advance. They joined their brothers-in-arms near adjoining hills to engage the enemy.

The King grinned. He knew in his heart that they were winning this battle. The hope he had almost lost grew inside him once again. But the pain from his wound quickly brought him back to the reality in front of him as another enemy fighter lunged toward his throat. He raised his sword to block the lance, but the force of the blow caused him to stumble and fall backwards. Yet the sword held back the lance from penetrating his throat, but he knew he could not hold it much longer while on the ground. The weight of the fighter was becoming too much for him as death faced him. His arms quivered as he tried to hold back the fighter who was now on top of him.

The horrid eyes and putrid breath of the creature made his skin crawl from disgust. The rain fell hard on their faces and mixed with their sweat. The salty water ran into the King's eyes, but still he held off the fighter. With one last effort, he pushed with all his strength and lifted the fighter off his chest. The two men rolled downhill together, only to stop at the bottom full of mud. The King leapt to his feet once again, as did his opponent. The fighter growled menacingly as its saliva spewed forth. Its hands tightly grasped its lance as it began to circle the King. With mud soaked armor, King Alexander moved away from his opponent, watching its movements carefully. He grasped his sword firmly as the pain from his side made his vision blurry. He took deeper breaths now to avoid fainting as more blood oozed from the wound. But he remained on his feet.

Waiting for the fighter to make his move, the King continued to move awkwardly. Suddenly, the fighter swung its lance around trying to fell the King, but the King jumped out of the way. The miss caused the fighter to stumble, but he regained his footing in time to meet the King's sword coming down upon him. The clanging of the metal weapons startled Will who fought nearby. He thrust his sword into the enemy fighter near him then, turned to see his King at the bottom of the hill alone. He quickly ran to help...but before he could get there, it was over.

§

"Enough," Lord Caragon snarled. He raised his lance into the dark sky once again. "Lord Bedlam! Now is the time!" he shouted.

He turned his weapon toward the castle and the field nearby. A wicked green light shot across the men as they fought in the rain and mud. The light cut through and hit the battlefield, covering all the dead bodies of the enemy fighters with an eerie green mist. Some of the King's men stopped fighting long enough to see the mysterious light shoot over them, but they continued to fight.

Lord Caragon saw what was happening. He could see his fighters were losing the battle. Once again he would have to intervene to finally destroy Alexander's bloodline. He would have to rid the world of the King and his heir once and for all. This was his mission.

§

The green mist could be seen from atop the outer wall of the castle, where the King's Constable stood wondering what was happening. He ordered for his looking glass once again. As the young foot soldier handed it over to the constable, the green mist began to move around the dead bodies.

Constable Darion peered through the looking glass as the sky grew even darker. The rain pelted down on the lens making it difficult for him to see what was before him, but he strained as hard as he could. He noticed the green mist moving over the dead seemed to have a life of its own. His stomach turned as he watched because he knew something unexplainable was happening and that it had come from Lord Caragon—which is never a good thing.

"Call the surgeon here," he ordered. He knew the King's surgeon and the apothecary were wise and might be able to comprehend what was going on. The constable waited as the young foot soldier ran to the ladder leading down into the castle courtyard. He heard the foot soldier scream for the doctor to be brought up on the outer wall. Then, he waited as the battle continued over the hills.

§

The Dragon circled high above the clouds, where the rain had stopped and the skies were clear all around them. Below them were the dark, mysterious clouds that poured their troubled rain onto the fighting men below. Peter could feel the rhythm of its breathing as the Dragon flapped its leathery wings in the wind.

Peter noticed the rhythm was getting slower and slower as the Dragon circled in the air. He remembered the wound from Peregrine's lance deep in its chest. Peter wondered how much longer the Dragon could remain in the air without rest. He tightened his grip onto the scales.

§

The doctor ran up the ladder to the top of the outer wall. He huffed his way to where Constable Darion stood still peering through the looking glass.

"Yes, my Lord," the doctor huffed.

"Apothecary, look through this glass and tell me what you see," the constable asked as he handed him the brass cylinder.

The doctor looked through the rain and saw the green mist hovering over the battlefield. He strained to understand what he was seeing. "A sort of spell, I'm afraid," he said.

"A spell. That is what I feared."

The two men stood staring at the magic before them.

"Caragon?" the constable asked.

"I believe so," the doctor agreed. "It appears to be focused on the dead mutant fighters, yet avoiding the knights or soldiers, from what I can see."

"Something is about to happen and we haven't much time," Darion said. "We need more men. Call up two more garrisons of soldiers immediately!" he ordered.

The young foot soldier obeyed the order and relayed the message to his sergeant below. But the young soldier knew it would be difficult to find more soldiers now. Some would need to stay behind to guard the castle.

"But the castle, my Lord," the doctor said.

"We'll have to take our chances," Constable Darion answered. He pointed to the green mist ahead of them. "I'm afraid this is most important of all."

The young soldier's request was met with sad news. The sergeant yelled back that there were no men left except the older men and young boys. The foot soldier hesitated to relay the news to the constable, but the sergeant decided to tell him himself. A hardened soldier of many battles, he had little patience left for ineptness. He crept up the ladder and explained his actions to the constable.

Constable Darion met the news from the sergeant with despair. He looked out over the battlefield with the green mist hovering over the dead. They needed a solution—and they needed one now. He turned to the doctor who shook his head because he had nothing to offer. The sergeant and young soldier had blank faces as well. No one knew where they could get more men strong enough to fight and win against the unseen forces of evil about to rise upon them.

"This is an impossible situation." The sergeant rubbed the nape of his neck.

"Nonsense," answered the doctor. "Nothing is impossible.

"Oh really? And what, pray, do you suggest we do?"

"Where there is a will," said the doctor.

"Oh, that's brilliant." The sergeant sighed heavily in disgust and began to pace the castle wall. "Well, whatever we do, we must do it quickly."

"Now that's brilliant," quipped the doctor. He walked over to Darion.

Constable Darion stood by the wall's railing to the courtyard below. He watched as villagers made their way back and forth, trying to put out small oil fires and bring water and supplies to the infirmary. One elderly man was trying hard to lift a large boulder to move it out of the way. As Constable Darion watched the old man struggle to lift the rock, a thought came to mind, and he knew they had to try.

"Ogres," he whispered to himself.

"Ogres?" asked the sergeant.

"Yes!" the constable answered. "They may be our only hope."

"But how?" the young soldier asked.

"Perhaps, by chance, we make them a deal to motivate them to help save the castle."

"But what deal can we make to those beasts?" the sergeant asked.

Constable Darion continued to watch the elderly man move the boulder a few steps. The movement reminded him of the brute strength of the giant ogres.

"If we lose the kingdom to Caragon, he will make slaves of the ogres once again. But if they help us fight and keep the kingdom, they can still live in peace and freedom on their own land," he explained. "Do you see? It is in their best interest to help us."

"But sir," the sergeant interrupted. "How can those beasts possibly understand all this?"

"You underestimate the ogres," the doctor answered as he walked over to the other side of the wall. "They know a good deal when they see one."

"Ha! I've never known an ogre to know much about anything…least of all a war as important as this," said the sergeant.

"Perhaps you are right," Darion said. "I suppose it is too optimistic to depend on such creatures."

"Nonsense!" the doctor said. "I feel it is a great plan and I agree that the ogres will understand the dilemma. Freedom is something all creatures desire."

"How can they possibly understand the plight of the kingdom? All they know is stealing sheep and causing trouble out in the desert plains. Time and again I have been called out there to stop them from setting fires and scaring away game. They're ignorant beasts."

"Perhaps you're the ignorant beast!" yelled the doctor. "All you know is what's in front of you."

"Gentlemen, please," interrupted Darion. "We must remain calm." He understood why the men felt ill at ease. There was little time to prepare, but even less time to quarrel among them. "We've so little time as it is. We mustn't quarrel with each other."

The constable pondered the plan set before them. Could it work? They all seemed to wonder. But the constable was willing to risk it.

"A rider, now!" Constable Darion ordered.

The sergeant found a young man with a horse and swiftly told him the message to take to the ogres. He also found a horse for himself so he could join the boy on the ride. Together they would set out for the desert west of the Black Hills where the ogres made their home. Risky though it was, they knew it might be their last chance.

"You're going along?" asked the doctor.

"Aye, it is the only way to prove you wrong!" the sergeant answered.

"Now, both of you make haste. Do not stop for any reason. If Lord Caragon knows of our plan, he will strike you both down," the Constable said. "Ride now!"

Both the sergeant and the young man mounted their horses at the main gate. As soon as the massive wooden gate was raised and the drawbridge was lowered, they kicked the sides of their horses and galloped quickly away to the west. The green mist circled more rapidly as the men rode past it. The stench of the wet earth and rain, as well as the rotting flesh of the dead, caused them to gasp. But they couldn't stop to mourn or to watch. Over the hills they rode together side by side. The dark clouds continued to hover over the valley as the rain pelted their faces. The battle to the north of them could be heard, but they could not hesitate. Their mission was too important to the kingdom's survival.

13 THE GHOST KNIGHTS

Will spotted his King lying beneath a giant Barok fighter. Both were motionless and seemed to be dead, but Will did not stop moving toward them. When he reached them, he saw the King's chest rise and fall. Will lifted the dead enemy fighter off Alexander only to reveal that the King had thrust his sword into the chest of the creature. Its black blood splattered all over the King's face and tunic.

"My Lord," Will said as he threw the dead fighter off to the side. He watched it roll in the mud as the rain fell. "Are you alright?"

"Yes," the King lied. The loss of blood was great. He knew he should have been dead by now, but a power far greater than his was saving him for something. Would he live to see his son safely home again and the kingdom restored? He did not know the answer.

"Help me get to my feet," he asked.

"Yes Sire," Will answered as he obeyed.

"The battle," the King stuttered. "The men...."

"The battle still rages. The men are making headway, my Lord," Will answered.

The King's men fought hard nearby. But the King knew Caragon would not give in so easily.

"Do you see Lord Caragon?" he asked.

Will strained to see through the pouring rain. "I do not see him, my Lord," he answered.

The King glanced left and right. "He's here," Alexander muttered. "I can feel the icy cold stare of Caragon. I feel his presence." The King turned to Will. "Keep a watchful eye."

Will surveyed the battle and at the men fighting it. Many of them were staring toward the castle with strange looks on their faces, the enemy dead lying near them. He could not tell what they were staring at or why, but he did not want them to lose sight of the battle.

He ran over to a group of soldiers who were standing on a small hill littered with enemy dead. They were pointing toward the castle to the south.

"What is it?" Will asked as he approached them. "What are you looking at?"

The men turned to Will. Their swords dripped with the sticky blood of the enemy.

"Look, over there," Sir Thomas spoke. "Toward the castle, what do you see?"

"Can you see it?" asked another.

Will squinted through the pouring rain. The cloud of mist hovered slightly over the ground. "It moves," he said. "The green mist seems to be moving."

"Yes," Sir Thomas agreed. "Someone needs to inform the King."

Sir Thomas gripped his sword tightly and ran toward the King who was still watching his men from the top of a low hill. Will watched as the knight reached his master and began to point toward the castle. The King stood in the rain listening to his knight explain what he had seen.

Suddenly, a loud horn sounded from the northeast and all the enemy fighters ran toward the sound. They stopped in the middle of their fight and ran off as though they were surrendering. The King's men were so exhausted, they didn't try to follow the fleeing enemy. Some even cheered while they watched the retreat, hoping they had won the final battle.

Alexander watched the enemy fighters run off into the darkness while the horn blast echoed. He made his way down the hill as he tried to figure out what exactly was happening.

Sir Thomas followed him. "Why are they leaving?"

"It is not a retreat," the King answered. "They are being called back. Something is going to happen. Be on the lookout!"

He turned to the hill. He watched his men gather together. Some were celebrating victory, while others were returning to their King for further orders. The King glanced toward the castle and walked toward Will. That's when he spotted what the men were staring at. The green mist had grown larger in dimension and circled faster over the dead. Deep in his heart, the King knew what he was seeing, yet did not know how to describe what he saw. Past experiences had not prepared him for any of this. He knew Lord Caragon was behind the mysterious green mist. Yet no plan for stopping it came to his mind.

§

The two riders heard the horn sound from the north as they rode faster toward the land of the Ogres. Their horses galloped through the rain as it poured. The sting of the rain hitting their faces caused them to close their eyes, but they had to keep going.

"How much farther?" the young rider asked.

"Just keep going!" the sergeant yelled back. The sound of the rain and the horses' hooves in the mud made it hard for the sergeant to hear, but he knew he had to encourage the young man to hold fast.

The Black Hills could be seen in the distance as they rode. The thunderous clamor coming from Hildron grew louder still. The sergeant knew they were close to ogre country. The message he was to take to the ogres was still fervent in his mind, but he remained unconvinced that they would listen to him. His horse galloped as fast as it could as they spotted a few dead trees nearby. The trees thickened into a dead forest like twisted skeletal remains in the lower hills around them. Their horses had trouble running up the muddy hills, but they finally made it to the top. The riders stopped to let their horses rest. The horses panted heavily. Ahead, more dead trees lined the dirt road now thick with mud. To their right they could faintly see the battlefield, which was eerily still.

"Come now, we must continue," the sergeant said. "Be on the lookout for ogres. We are in their country now."

"What do we look for?"

"Well, you won't have to look much. The smell will hit you first!" the sergeant laughed. "By then you will know they are near. They are monstrous beasts with hands that can kill a man, easily."

The young man's eyes grew wide and he nervously rubbed his arms. "I've got goosebumps." His eyes darted left and right. "I've never seen an ogre up close, but I have heard terrible things about their hideous appearance and giant size."

The sergeant chuckled.

"My father spoke of how an ogre could crush the head of a small boy with its hands." The soldier swallowed the large lump in his throat. "Maybe this the idea wasn't so good after all."

As he nudged his horse and the animal began to awkwardly maneuver its way down the muddy hill toward the forest of dead trees. Together the two men rode alongside the muddy path. They rode on into the dark forest.

The sergeant looked over at the young man and noticed the harness on the horse's head was coming off. He tried to tell his companion to stop when suddenly a large tree branch slammed into him and knocked him off his horse.

He hit the ground with such a force that all the air was knocked from his lungs and he could not breath. As he lay there gasping for air, his young companion stopped his horse and dismounted. He ran to his sergeant to see what was wrong. He helped the sergeant sit up and catch his breath, but the sergeant pointed to the space behind the young man. Unable to speak, he just pointed hoping the young man would turn around before it was too late. But he didn't.

Instead, the young man tried to help his friend to his feet but was stopped by the sound of giant footsteps approaching behind him…steps so heavy they slightly shook the earth. The closer the steps got to the two men, the louder they became.

The sergeant's eyes grew bigger and bigger with fear. The young man did not want to turn around but he would eventually have to face the beast behind him. He grasped his sword and pulled it out of its sheath as he stood up and turned to face the source of the giant footsteps.

§

The mysterious green haze began circling faster over the corpses of the mutant fighters, its power growing more and more apparent. It appeared to be stirring something within each dead fighter as well as within the dead crows. The constable continued his watch from atop the castle wall along with the apothecary. Something began to happen on the battlefield.

One of the dead crows started to move and shake. Its body began to twist and turn as it rose slightly above the ground.

"I was afraid of this," said the doctor.

Constable Darion stood still, in fear of the unknown. He narrowed his eyes as if he did not want to consider what he was seeing, but he had no choice.

"We need to prepare the castle," said the doctor.

"For what?" asked the constable.

"For that!" he answered as he pointed toward the green mist working its evil magic on the dead.

Constable Darion turned in time to see a ghostly man rise from the ashes of the dead crow. It appeared to be a knight in an almost transparent form searching for his master. He stood frozen with fright as more and more ghost-like knights rose from where the dead crows had been. Each ghost was gray with a sword and tattered armor clinging to its body. They looked like they had been to the depths of hell and back. One turned toward the castle wall. Constable Darion couldn't help but notice the familiar armor the ghost was wearing. The helmet, tattered tunic, and cape all seemed familiar. But the sword the ghost wielded gave its identity away.

The ghost knight stood on the ground, with sword in hand, while its gray cape lazily flapped in the slight breeze and rain. He seemed to be glowing. More ghost knights took their form on the battlefield.

"No," Constable Darion gasped. "It cannot be."

"Yes," the doctor answered. "I'm afraid it is." He ran to the ladder and shouted to the villagers below to close the gate, reinforce it, and prepare the castle for another siege.

The villagers raced in a panic.

The constable could not stop staring at the ghost knights as they took form from the dead crows. More and more dead fighters arose in ghost form, hovering above ground…glowing with a greenish haze from within.

But it was the lead ghost that caught Darion by surprise. The familiar tunic and cape could only belong to Sir Peregrine. The former head of the King's Royal Knights appeared before them as a ghost knight. "Can this be?" Darion muttered to himself.

"Our only hope is to rely on the ogres now," the doctor mumbled.

§

King Alexander called his men to gather around him immediately. Will shouted the order to the knights on the other hills and they relayed the message to more men. The dark clouds moved swiftly overhead and the wind picked up from the east. The men shivered. A presence in the wind was felt by all as it moved near them like a cold hand touching their wet skin. This sensation caused them to stumble with panic, but the reassuring voice of their King helped calm them.

"Attention!" the King ordered.

The men obeyed and listened to their King but they were interrupted by a noise which came from the green haze still stirring and hovering over the dead. All the men turned to see a ghost-like figure standing over a pile of ashes where a dead crow had been. The ghost-like figure wore a helmet, tunic and cape as it searched for its sword. One by one, these ghost-like knights arose from the dead birds as they were joined by other ghost fighters standing nearby. The green haze began to dissipate into the breeze. It made its way over to the King's men, twisting and turning around them.

The King shook his head. Could it be that all this was caused by an evil spell of Lord Caragon?

"What manner of evil is this?" he asked.

"How could he know this sort of magic?" Will asked.

"Caragon is capable of more evil than we thought," Sir Thomas answered. "We cannot battle the undead!" He hesitated and took a few steps back.

"We cannot stop now," the King said as he touched Sir Thomas' arm. "We must make a stand no matter what."

"But how?" another soldier asked.

"We fight," the King answered gripping the hilt of his sword. "It appears they were brought back from the dead. That means perhaps we can return them to the dead."

The men nodded in response to the light in the King's eyes. Determination appeared on their disheveled faces. His words gave them hope and lit a fire inside them. Their bodies ached from battle and some nursed wounds, but they would once again take up arms to fight an evil they could not explain.

"This evil seeks to take all that we know and love: family, faith, and land," the King said. "They will not negotiate. They will not bargain. This evil cannot be appeased!" He pointed toward the ghost knights as they each rose mysteriously from the ashes.

"If we do not fight now," the King said, "there will be no more tomorrows."

His men lifted up their swords in one accord. "For King and country!" they all shouted in unison.

"For us all," the King said as he watched his brave men gather together around him. His wound began to burn, causing him to stumble. Will caught him and helped him stand straight so that the men could not see the wound. The King was determined to join in the fight.

§

The rain had stopped. The time had come. Suddenly, the Dragon stopped circling and began to fly toward the Dragon Forest. Peter, still gripping to the scales of the Dragon's neck, recognized the direction they were flying. Together they flew below the clouds and entered the realm of the tall trees once again. Peter saw the blue lake in the middle of the forest as the Dragon lowered to meet the ground. He saw his pillow sack still lying on the ground where he had dropped it. Nearby was his sword and shield. As the Dragon's giant claws touched the muddy ground, Peter felt relief that they were safe within the forest once again, but he still needed to know how his father was.

The Dragon lowered its neck to the ground and ordered Peter to dismount. But Peter refused.

"Why? Where are you going?" he asked the Dragon.

"Where I am going you cannot follow," it said as Peter stood on the wet ground before the beast. "There is much I need to do. You must stay here for now."

"But, my father!" Peter shouted as the Dragon turned away from him. "I need to see my father!"

"You will," answered the Dragon as it lifted off the ground for flight. "In time."

The breeze caused by the flapping of its leathery wings hurt Peter's eyes so he raised his hand in front of his face to protect them. Suddenly, the Dragon was high into the sky far above the Dragon Forest. Peter stood and watched his friend fly away. He felt alone and scared. He walked over the glassy blue lake that was calm after the rains. Its mist still hovered over the surface making the forest realm so quiet, so peaceful, it was almost like a temple.

A slight crackling came from behind Peter. The noise caused a few birds to scatter into the air in flight. Peter was startled by their sudden movement, but was quickly reassured when he saw the familiar face of an old friend from within the tall trees.

"Titan!" he shouted as he ran to the horse. "My friend."

He reached out and nuzzled the nose of his faithful horse. Titan whinnied and snorted a hello to his master and the two spent some time silently together.

§

"Do not make any sudden movements," the sergeant advised the young man.

The young rider gripped his sword in his hands as he stood before the giant ogre. The rain had stopped, but the dark sky made it difficult for the rider to see the face of the creature before him. He could hear is breathe, though. The soldier swallowed back his fear.

The ogre roared a mighty roar sending the young rider backwards over the sergeant's legs, throwing his sword far from them. Now they both were on the ground just a few feet away from the giant beast.

"Get up you fool!" the sergeant ordered. "Get up and help me get up."

The two men quickly stood up and faced their new ally. Only, the ogre did not know it was the King's new ally. So, they both began to tell it their message hoping the beast understood what they were saying.

A silent pause came from the ogre when the two men were finished explaining the plight of the kingdom. Then the creature snorted and motioned for them to follow it. Its footsteps were so much bigger than theirs that they had to run to keep up with it. But the ogre led them to the lower hill country where the ogres made their camp.

The smell of fires and the sound of ogres grumbling and snorting could be heard from far away as the two men approached the camp.

As each ogre heard approaching footsteps, it came out of its cave to see what the ruckus was. Sniffing the air, they quickly recognized the human stench, but turned to one another and shrugged. It appeared that they did not understand why their friend was leading two humans into the camp. The ogre shuffled over to two fellow ogres who wore leather vests and had arms full of strange tattoos.

"They must be the leaders of the camp." The sergeant noticed that one had shackles and chains still around its ankles. It listened to the other tell about the two humans and why there were there.

When the two lead ogres raised their arms and let out roars of disapproval, the two men feared for their lives.

"I knew it wouldn't work," the sergeant said, shaking his head. "They don't understand."

"Wait," said the young rider as he noticed the one ogre gesturing and pointing to the Black Hills. "It's telling them of Lord Caragon."

All three ogres turned to look at the Black Hills lying menacingly in the background to the northwest of their camp. The lead ogres seemed to be remembering how they were taken hostage and forced into slavery by Caragon. They slowly turned to look at the two human intruders standing nearby.

The thunderous footsteps of the lead ogre stomping toward them caused the two men to step back a few paces as the giant creature approached. It stood a full four feet above them and had bloodshot eyes. Its grayish green skin was covered in bruises and scars from the many beatings it received from Caragon's men. One eye had been swollen shut and drool leaked from its mouth which could not shut completely from a swollen lip. The two men were suddenly filled with pity for the ogre who had obviously suffered great harm from its evil master.

Ogres were perfect slaves in that they rarely slept and were solid muscle. They ate heartily, but only grew in muscle. They were not very smart compared to humans as far as wisdom and intellect, but they were very good navigators of the lands. They were loyal to each other and would fight to the death for each other. It made great sense for Lord Caragon to take them hostage to be slaves. His evil magic was his tool used to capture them since they were so massive in size compared to Caragon's men.

The ogre's eyes spoke to them. The sergeant realized that the ogre before them wanted to trust them but was hesitating.

"It's having trouble trusting us. Its loss to Lord Caragon must have been great," the sergeant said. So, in a gesture that is universal, the sergeant reached out his arm in a show of faith, friendship, and gratitude for their sacrifice.

The ogre stared at the outstretched human arm before it. Then it carefully studied the sergeant's eyes. Ogres often looked into the eyes of creatures for they were highly capable of sensing danger. Slowly, the giant beast lifted its massive arm and accepted the sergeant's arm in a handshake of trust. The hand grabbed and almost engulfed the sergeant's arm completely, but the gesture was understood by both parties.

One by one, the other ogres left their caves and curiously watched the proceedings. As Grauble, leader of the ogres, grunted and snorted to them, the two men realized Grauble was relaying the plan to its kinsmen. Hope began to fill their hearts once again as they knew the giant beasts were willing to help the kingdom survive.

14 SWORD TO SWORD

Constable Darion waited for word from the sergeant atop the outer wall of the castle. Below him the villagers helped the doctor make rags for wrapping wounds and helped move the recovering soldiers to the dungeon. One by one, each wounded man was led downstairs into the darkened dungeon where hundreds of villagers waited anxiously for a word from outside.

As they pounded on the dungeon door, the village leaders raced over to reinforce the door. They feared the enemy had found them. But the doctor pounded on the door and yelled to them what was happening.

"Do not open it!" ordered Lord Byrén.

"But what if it is the doctor?" one woman asked.

"We cannot take that chance," Lord Byrén said.

The doctor and the others yelled once more that it was not the enemy but the wounded soldiers from above.

Lord Byrén ordered the door to be opened. As the door swung open, the villagers ran to help the doctor and the wounded.

"Is it all over?" Lord Byrén asked the doctor. "Can we come out now?"

"No," the doctor answered as he held the door open. "I am afraid it is not over yet."

Lord Byrén stared at the young wounded soldiers being led into the dungeon for safety. He saw in their faces the determination needed to defeat the enemy. Lord Byrén was shocked at how young the soldiers looked to him, a man over half a century old. Each one could have been his son or perhaps even his grandson.

"What can we do to help?" asked Lady Silith.

"Just give them water when they ask and help them to stay put," said the doctor. "Many of them want to go back and fight with the King. But they cannot."

"Yes, of course. We will help them," said Lord Byrén.

The villagers gathered round the wounded men and helped make beds out of hay for each one, and made things as comfortable as they could.

Lord Byrén anxiously awaited news from the battlefield, especially since the noise had died down. He walked over to the doctor and asked him what was happening above, but the doctor was too focused on getting back outside before the next battle. He did his best to reassure the village leaders that all was well and that the King and his men were fighting valiantly, but the battle was not over.

After ordering the dungeon door locked again for safety purposes, the doctor closed the door. Carrying his torch, he rushed up the long stone hallway. He could not help but worry about the ghost knights outside.

"Could these walls really stop the undead?" he muttered to himself. But no one was able to comprehend the answer. The doctor decided it was not worth his time to think such things. There were already too many things that needed his attention at that moment. He knew more wounded would be coming in once the battle began, and he needed to get his infirmary ready.

§

Charles peeked out from behind a column in the darkened hallway of the dungeon. He waited for the door to close and the doctor to rush out before he began to sneak up the stone steps to the outer courtyard. Having been in the darkened dungeon for so long, his eyes squinted shut when he walked outside. Even though the sky remained darkened from the rain clouds above, his eyes needed time to adjust. Once they adjusted, he watched as the townspeople rushed around, trying to reinforce the main gate. Many ran with buckets of water heading to the infirmary while others helped the blacksmith sharpen more swords and lances. Charles could see the castle was preparing for yet another battle with the enemy.

Entering the blacksmith's quarters, he grabbed a sword, then rushed over to the main gate to help others reinforce it by nailing up planks of wood to the wooden gate to help it hold. Noticing a ladder leading to the top of the gate, he climbed it at once. He ordered some wood be handed to him so he could nail it up high.

After he was finished nailing, two wooden portcullises were lowered in front of the gate. These large wooden structures protected the main gate from enemy buttresses. They resembled cages but were not for trapping anything. The villagers hoped these structures would hold and keep the enemy away.

Charles ran over to the west turret, where a carpenter was hastily hammering and nailing reinforcements to the tower. The wooden hoarding would help protect fighters from the enemy and allow them to drop fire missiles onto the enemy below. Charles ran up the ladder to the top of the tower. Peering over the main outer wall, Charles saw the ghost knights making their way over to the hills, where he could faintly see the King's banner waving in the wind. He watched the clouds move through the sky. It had been awhile since he had seen the sun.

Scanning the tower, he found some rope. Tying the rope to the wooden hoarding, Charles began to repel down the side of the tower without a sound. Slipping and sliding on the way, he finally made it to the bottom. There were cuts and scrapes on his arms and knees, but he did not care. He knew he was where he needed to be.

§

When King Alexander had finished motivating his men to battle, the men began to move into position. They watched as the ghost knights began to gather together to form a line on the battlefield. Some resembled the King's former knights and others were the former Black Knights of Caragon.

"These ghosts were knights, your majesty," Sir Thomas said as he noticed the familiar tunics some of the ghosts were wearing. Even though they were transparent, tattered and torn, he could see the familiar coat-of-arms on the front of the tunics. One particular knight grabbed his attention. He was taller than most and he stood in front of the line with his sword drawn at his side. His face was mostly skeletal, but he could still recognize its features.

"My Lord!" he cried to the King. "Do you see what I see?"

King Alexander turned to his Knight as he pointed to the battlefield and the line of ghost knights forming. The King strained to see what Sir Thomas was shouting about. He scanned the line of ghost knights and enemy fighters and tilted his head. Some did look familiar to him. He focused on their torn tunics and capes stirring in the wind. Then, Alexander's eyes widened. He understood why Sir Thomas was so concerned. He studied the leader of the ghosts who stood out in front of the line in an eerie green mist. The familiar features and stature could not be mistaken. His jaw tightened.

"Sir Peregrine," the King said between his clenched teeth. His suspicions about his former Knight were proven true. Peregrine had been involved with Caragon's evil magic all along.

§

The group of ogres ran together in unison in a single file over the desert hills toward the battlefield. Their long strides made it easy for the sergeant and his young companion to follow along on horseback. Their horses galloped alongside the ogres as they made their way into battle. Each ogre carried a sword and an ax as well as a bow and quiver on its back. They did not know what sort of enemy they would be facing, but they wanted to be prepared.

The loud pounding of their heavy footsteps shook the earth below them as the sound echoed through the valley like thunder. The mud was drying out and turning hard once again but the dark clouds still remained above them. The air was still cool but heavy with moisture. The dense air made it hard to run at full speed, but the ogres knew the importance of the battle. Not only would they be fighting for the kingdom, but for their freedom to live their lives in peace in the desert hills without fear of the evil magic of Lord Caragon.

§

The King called his men to him as they watched the ghost knights begin to form their line. As each one formed, the carcass of the crow disappeared into ashes and was swept away in the wind.

"How can we battle the undead?" Alexander asked Sir Thomas.

The King stood in front of his men as they held their swords out ready to fight. Then, removing his sword from its sheath, their King touched their swords with the sword of his father, Aléon, King of Illiath. The King went down the row of men and blessed their swords one by one.

"This sword of my father's, forged long ago by the Elves of Vulgaard, was part of the Oath made with the Dragon of the Forest. May this sword and the power it holds…the power of honor and truth… now empower your swords to defeat this unnamed evil before you."

Hearing the thunderous footsteps approaching from the desert hills, the men's eyes darted nervously left and right. Was it the sound friend or foe? They did not know, but they did not have time to wait and see. The evil ghost knights roared as one and raised their ghostly swords. They raised their ghostly swords high above their heads. The King and his men prepared themselves for the charge.

"Aim for the head," the King ordered. "And pray that your sword will send them back to where they came from."

He held the sword of Alexander high and pointed it toward his once loyal knight, Sir Peregrine, who stood ready for battle. Peregrine laughed and then stared at the glistening sword in the King's hand. His once handsome and regal face consisted of rotting flesh and bone with glowing eyes within the skull that held the intricate helmet of the King's army. His dead heart no longer pumped life throughout the body. Now only the spell cast by Lord Caragon gave life to the once brave Knight.

It was Caragon who would cause the ghost knights to move like pawns in a game of chess.

Caragon sat mounted on his black horse watching from afar as he ordered his men into position. He, too, could hear the thunderous pounding of the ogres approaching, but he did not care. He only saw his adversary, the King, before him, as he anxiously waited for the battle to begin.

As the King watched his men raise their swords for battle, the sky opened up and a bright ray of light cut through the dark clouds. The intense light of the sun gave hope to the King's men and caused the undead knights to shade their eyes from the light. The King, knowing this was the perfect moment to attack, shouted with all his might for his men to forge ahead into battle with the undead. The horn sounded loudly, and the knights and soldiers made their way down the hills into battle.

§

The ogres could hear the horn as well as the shouts of the King's men as they continued to run through the desert hills. They knew the battle had begun. The drying mud beneath their feet had given way to the grasses that now covered the hills as the ogres made their way out of the desert and into the valleys near the kingdom. They ran onto the top of a steep hill and stopped as the sergeant and his companion reached the top of the hill. Together they stared at the sight before them. The King's men had forged ahead straight on into battle with what appeared to be ghosts.

"What is this?" asked the sergeant as he steadied his horse. He had never seen such a sight.

The ogres just grunted and snorted while looking at the battle before them. They banged together their swords and axes as though eager to fight any enemy of the kingdom. The sun cut through the dark clouds and illuminated the battlefield. Grauble roared fiercely as his fellow ogres raised their weapons up over their heads, hoping to draw attention to themselves. Indeed they did.

Lord Caragon spotted the large gathering of ogres approaching from the west. He did not waste any time. He turned his horse toward the Black Hills. He watched as the ogres spilled over the hills into the battle one after the other. Their massive presence could bring an end to the battle.

The King's men heard the loud grunts and growls of the ogres as they raced toward the ghost knights. They did not have time to wonder if the ogres were there to fight them or not. As each knight approached their ghost counterpart, he prayed that his sword would somehow work on the transparent flesh of the undead.

Sir Thomas led the way toward Sir Peregrine's ghost. He ran with his sword tightly gripped in his hand and, with every footstep, gathered more and more strength. The strength boiling over inside of him seemed to give him courage as he raised his sword high into the air. With baited breath, the other knights watched as Sir Thomas met with his adversary.

The steel sword lifted high into the air and swept back down again toward Sir Peregrine. The ghost knight raised his sword into the air as well and stood ready to meet his enemy's strength. The knights watched as the two swords, one steel and the other spirit, come clashing down onto one another.

A resonating clash sounded from the two blades meeting in the air before them. In that instant, the King's men, the ogres, and the soldiers knew that their swords could stop the ghosts. The King's blessing on the weapons had worked and they could defeat the undead. Peregrine laughed no more.

The loud clash of ghost weapon to steel weapon reverberated, halting Lord Caragon's hasty getaway. He pulled tightly on the reins of his horse and stopped it when heard the familiar sound of metal meeting metal in battle. "No!" he shouted. "This cannot be!" He heeled his horse again and off they rode toward his castle.

§

The constable watched the battle through his eyeglass atop the castle outer wall. He saw the King and his men preparing to enter into the battle with the ghost knights. Then, he heard the roar of the ogres from the west.

"They made it," he said to no one in particular.

The ogres, led by the sergeant and his young companion, with weapons swinging before them like scythes, swept down the grassy hill toward the ghost fighters.

The King's Royal Knights were making headway over the ghosts as their swords cut through the transparent bones and decaying flesh barely attached to the ghosts. But the weapons of the ghosts also ripped through the flesh of the knights and soldiers. Screams of pain and agony could be heard from both sets of fighters, but the King could see victory was near. He ran into the battle, keeping an eye on Peregrine, who was still fighting with Sir Thomas. With each swing of his sword, Sir Thomas met Peregrine's lunge and thrust with cold steel. Their bodies twisted and turned as they tried in vain to outwit each other, but their skills were too similar since they were trained together so long ago.

"You can do better than this, Thomas." Peregrine hissed as he turned to thrust his sword once again.

One mistake would cost one man his life and Sir Thomas did not want it to be his.

"All in time, Peregrine," Thomas answered.

Thrusts overhead were met with sword and lunges toward the heart were stopped by more steel. The battle continued as both man and ghost exhausted all their moves. Sir Thomas grew tired.

Sir Peregrine laughed. "Come now, my old friend!" he shouted. "With grace and balance."

The battle continued.

King Alexander fought two ghost knights at once, even though the pain in his side caused him to stumble from time to time. Suddenly, the roar of the ogres approached from the west. He pierced his enemy with his sword, then watched with caution as the ogres ran with weapons held high above their heads. Their massive bodies pounded the earth as they roared with a vengeance.

They roared with wide grins on their faces. It was as if they knew they would have the chance to defeat Caragon's ghost knights. The ogres had been Caragon's slaves for many years, helping him to build his dark and wicked kingdom in the Black Hills. Now it was time for them to take their vengeance on Caragon.

As the giant beasts slashed their way through the ghost fighters, sending their skeletal remains flying into pieces over the land, the King's knights stood frozen from the awesome sight not knowing what to do. They watched with wide eyes because they had never seen the ogres fight and this time they were certainly glad the ogres fought on the King's side. The scene gave them renewed hope as they continued the assault on the enemy.

One knight picked up a ghost sword, only to discover that once it touched human flesh it returned to its status as a real sword made of steel. Now he had two good swords to use against the enemy. "This magic has limitations after all," the knight said. He thrust it into the chest of one ghost, twisting the cold steel and watching it writhe in agony as it returned to the realm of hell right before his eyes. Then, turning to meet another grotesque mutant fighter running toward him, the knight plunged both swords into its body in a crisscross motion, ripping out the rotting flesh as he pulled the swords out in one swift motion. The deed was over. The dead ghost disappeared from earth into hell.

Will made his way through the assault, slashing and watching the ogres fight. He could not believe he was there fighting with the King on this great day when Lord Caragon would be defeated once and for all time. He thought he heard his name being shouted from within the fight but he was not sure. As he stabbed a ghost fighter in the back, he looked up in time to see his friend Charles running toward him with sword in hand.

"What are you doing here?" he yelled to his friend.

"Will!" Charles ran toward him.

The commotion caused Peregrine to look at the two young friends who were waving to each other across the battlefield. He hovered over the ground, moved toward the two young men, and left Sir Thomas foolishly swinging his sword at empty space.

Will ran toward Charles, shaking his head. "How did you make it out of the dungeon?" Charles got closer and mouthed words to Will, but he could not hear him. "Have you some news of my father?"

Suddenly, a green haze came between the two young friends and, with horror, Will had to watch while the sword of Sir Peregrine was thrust so deep into the chest of Charles that it came out his back. Sir Peregrine kept the sword in Charles, as if waiting for the life of the young man drain from his face.

"No!" Will shouted, but it was too late.

He reached his friend only in time to catch him before he fell to the ground. The ghost of Peregrine departed. Will held his dying friend in his arms as the battle raged around him. He did not have time to look into the face of his friend because another ghost fighter came from behind to slash his back.

In a split second, Will grabbed his sword, as well as Charles', and turned in time to thrust both swords into the chest of the ghost fighter. As he pulled the two swords out of the enemy, his eye caught a glimpse of Sir Peregrine fighting his way back to Sir Thomas, who was protecting the King. Peregrine slashed through soldier after soldier, his glance never left the King. Will knew it was now or never.

15 THE RETURN OF THE OGRES

The Dragon flew over the forest and saw Peter with Titan, his horse. Flapping its giant leathery wings, the Dragon flew over the battlefield in a protective posture. The time was near. Turning its head to the west, the Dragon spotted Caragon riding into the Black Hills toward Hildron, his castle.

Peter could see a glimpse of the sun peeking through the tall trees. His thoughts wandered back to the summers past when he and his parents would ride out to the lakes to picnic in the bright sun. He could see his mother's dark hair in the wind, but it was hard to see her face.

"Hurry, Peter!" She smiled at her find. "Look at the baby squirrels!" She pointed to the ground behind some rocks.

Peter ran over to the shaded area under a tall oak tree overlooking the valley. There where his mother stood, was a small group of tiny baby squirrels.

"They must have fallen out of the tree, don't you think?" she asked.

Peter nodded. Together they placed each little squirrel into the gathered skirt of his mother and placed them near the base of the tree, hoping the momma squirrel would save her young. "I hope she comes soon, before the raccoons or other creatures." She looked up into the tall tree.

Peter stood near her and gazed up at her face. Then he looked down at the small squirrels huddling close together for warmth.

He placed his hand in his mother's hand and held it tightly. He studied their hands intertwined and compared the differences in the flesh. His seven-year-old hand was small within hers. The warmth of her skin and the strength of her grip made him feel safe.

Peter sat on a large cool rock in the shade and remained silent as he cherished the memory of his mother there in the forest. He knew he was safe within the forest, but he wanted to see more. He disobeyed the Dragon and climbed aboard Titan's large back. He squeezed the saddle with his thighs, grabbed a handful of his mane, and motioned Titan to gallop. Titan obeyed, and together they rode out of the green forest once again.

A rush of cold wind followed them like a cape as they rode. Ahead of them was blue sky making the hills brighter than any morning Peter had seen. Together they rode faster and faster toward the battle and toward Peter's father. He could not wait any longer to return home.

§

Like a vulture admiring his prey, Sir Peregrine hovered over the dead bodies of the King's most loyal men before gliding swiftly toward Sir Thomas once again.

An ogre caught a glimpse of the former knight, and swung his fearsome ax. The blade found Peregrine's back just between the shoulder blades. He shrieked from the pain as it entered his dead flesh, yet he continued his pursuit of the King. He reached back and pulled the ax from his skeletal frame. Then, raising it into the air, Peregrine slung it toward the ogre, causing a fatal wound to the beasts head. Now Peregrine could set his sights once again on Sir Thomas.

Will ran quickly behind the evil knight with both swords in his hands and great fury in his heart.

Sir Thomas, still fighting valiantly in front of the King, was unaware of his approaching doom. Greatly fatigued from having to fight hard to protect the King, he knew he could not stop fighting. The ogres were holding off a great many ghost knights, so he paused to ask the King if he was alright. He turned to see that the King was indeed in great pain but still fighting off the enemy.

It was foolish for Sir Thomas to turn his back, if even for a moment for this was all Sir Peregrine needed to down his enemy who was once a friend. He noticed a lance lying next to a dead soldier and grabbed it in his skeletal hand. Then, in his new ghostly appearance, Sir Peregrine swiftly appeared behind Sir Thomas.

The King saw Peregrine's ghost thrust the lance into the back of Thomas, causing Thomas to fall forward as the King caught him. Alexander gazed into the dying face of his loyal and brave knight as he pulled out the lance from Thomas' back. Thomas fell to the ground at the King's feet. Alexander, trying to help him, knelt beside him.

Peregrine watched the scene with anger as he found another lance. Picking it up, he gripped it tightly in his skeletal hand, then he raised it high above his head.

King Alexander, too exhausted to notice his impending death, continued to look down at his friend and loyal Knight. In front of him lay his sword. Alexander slowly moved his hand over the handle and gripped it. He could hear a commotion behind him as he readied himself for one last act before the pain would subdue him.

As Peregrine gripped the lance above his head, he grinned a sickening grin as though thrilled at the thought of finally killing Alexander. He began to lower the lance, but instead of stabbing it into the King's back, his face contorted from the pain of a steel sword entering his own back.

Peregrine turned in time to see Will thrusting the second sword into his ghost chest. Peregrine shouted from the pain. His eyes glared deep into Will's. Then, in agony, Peregrine caught a glimpse of the abyss that awaited him. Its pull was more powerful than the hatred he had in his blackened heart. He reached out for Will in one last chance to hold onto life, but the boy quickly moved away from his grip.

The ghost Knight evaporated before him in a spiral heading downward into hell. For a moment, Will stood there panting, unable to fathom what had just happened.

Alexander, slowly stood up, remembering the Peregrine he had known in his youth. He was filled with sadness that someone so close to him could be so deceived by power, evil, and greed. Succumbing to the pain and exhaustion, the King collapsed from the wound in his side and Will helped him to the ground next to Sir Thomas.

"Thank you, Will," the King said.

"Sire, you will be alright," Will answered as he cupped the King's head in his hand. Gently, he lowered the King's head to the ground.

§

The Dragon kept its eyes on Caragon's castle waiting for what he would try next. Then it turned to see the ogres slashing their way through the ghost knights and fighters far below. It spotted the King lying on the ground near Will, and the Dragon knew the King's time was short.

Peter rode to the top of a hill near the edge of the remains of the once pleasant Cardion Valley. He could see the Dragon gliding over the battle. What he could not see was his father lying on the ground desperately trying to regain his strength to help fight off the undead enemy.

Suddenly, a loud roar rumbled over the hills from the west. In the sky over the looming Black Hills rose a mysterious dark shadow. The shadow moved quickly toward the east, staying low in the sky as it moved, but the cacophony emanating from the shadow made Peter cover his ears and he grabbed his aching stomach. Something evil was approaching.

As the growing shadow loomed in the far off sky, the King heard the strange screeching sound and struggled to his feet. Looking to the west, he noticed the dark clouds were stirring in the clean new sky, but one ominous cloud was moving fast toward the east.

The ogres could see the dark shadow moving quickly toward them. The fury emanating from the darkness caused the ogres to stop fighting and scramble for cover. Many of the King's men lay broken and torn near the dead bodies of their friends and foes. The King noticed the ogres and wanted to assure them that they should remain and fight no matter what the dark mass became. Still holding his wounded side, he made his way to the ogres; they turned to see the King. Grauble, their leader, listened to the King's reasoning as darkness blanketed the hills once again. Grauble's giant body was covered with sweat and dirt from battle as he breathed heavily in and out, but he did honor the King by listening intently to the plan. He knew fighting this unseen enemy would be hard and many ogres would die, but at least they were free now, free to choose whether to stay or leave. The smell of rain and the sounds of distant thunder reclaimed the skies. The ogres decided to stay and fight.

The King ordered all the men to gather before him. Making their way over to the King, the men carefully walked over carcasses and wounded men. The scars on the land were painful reminders of what was done in battle. The ghost knights and Barok fighters had all been defeated in this battle, but they knew another battle was building in the west. They knew this because Lord Caragon was nowhere to be found. The King noticed the weariness in his men's faces along with the dirt and blood caked on their skin. They looked half dead, and yet this was only the beginning.

King Alexander ordered the men to make haste to the castle. The men gathered up their weapons and ran to the castle with the ogres not far behind them. The dark mass still remained over the hills. As it moved, the screaming sound grew louder and louder.

§

The constable watched the King's men run back to the castle along with the ogres. He ordered the main gate to be raised and the bridge to be lowered. Then he ordered the portcullises to be raised in order to allow the men and ogres to enter. Appearing faintly over the horizon, Darion could see the black mass making its way over the hills just behind the men as they ran. The swirling mass circled above the desert hills seeming to be alive as it shifted shape randomly. He did not know what lay ahead for the kingdom, but the sickening feeling inside his body told him that this was Lord Caragon's doing once again.

"What is this evil before us?" he quietly asked.

§

As the main gate lowered a loud rumbling noise echoed throughout the castle courtyard. Many villagers quickly turned to see why the gate they had secured was now being raised. As they ran to see what was happening, many could hear the screams being lifted up by the wind coming from the shadowy mass hovering over the Black Hills.

Before the gate was completely lowered, the villagers spotted the weary and battle worn knights and soldiers approaching with great haste. As they made their way onto the massive wooden bridge, many women met them with water.

The King entered into the courtyard to the relief of his people and his constable. He limped into the courtyard with Will close behind him. The two men reached for a ladle of water and they drank heartily.

"Where is Peter?" the King gasped. "Where is my son?"

"Sire," the constable hesitated. "We have not seen him."

"He is not here?"

"No, sire,"

Will swallowed the water and sighed from the cool taste. Then he said, "My Lord, I have seen the Prince."

The King turned toward him. "Where? When?"

"Before the battle," Will said. "I saw him here, in the courtyard."

"What happened to him?" Constable Darion asked.

"He was brought to the castle," Will explained. "By..."

"By what?" asked the constable.

"Well..." Will hesitated as he remembered the fantastic sight of Peter being plopped down onto the ground by the invisible Dragon of the forest. "By...the," he stuttered.

"By what?" asked the King, frustrated and worried. "Speak clearly." He had his hands on Will's shoulders.

"Tell us," ordered the constable.

"By the Dragon," Will finally answered. "Of the forest."

Upon hearing this, the King sighed in relief.

"By the what?" Constable Darion turned to the King with wide eyes.

"The Dragon of the Dragon Forest," replied Will.

"I see," said Darion incredulously as he watched the King's reaction to the news.

"Where is he now?" asked the King.

"I took him to the castle gate and advised him to remain inside. That was the last that I saw of him."

The King felt at ease as he realized his son must be safe inside the castle walls. He walked over to the courtyard stables and ordered a fresh horse be brought to him. The soldiers all drank and rested, if only briefly.

Will mourned the loss of his friend, Charles, then he inquired as to the condition of the villagers inside the dungeon safe-hold.

"They remain safe," replied Constable Darion.

Will felt his body relax but he knew it would only be for a short while. Meanwhile, the sergeant and the young rider made their way through the gates just as the doctor was heading into the courtyard. As the doctor's eyes met the sergeant's, he grinned with great satisfaction.

The sergeant shook his head. "I'll never hear the end of this."

§

"Take me to the dungeon," ordered the King.

Constable Darion and his party led King Alexander down the musty and dark staircase that led to the former dungeon. As they made their way down the stairs, the King began to limp.

"Your majesty," he said. "You are injured."

"Yes." The King winced. "Slightly."

"The doctor!" yelled Darion. "Call him to the dungeon quickly."

A runner exited the darkened stairway and passed Will, still resting and drinking water nearby. Will saw the runner leave the infirmary with the doctor and decided he would follow them.

The stairway ended with the large door leading to the dungeon that held most of the villagers from the Cornshire and the Cardion Valley.

As the large door was unlocked and pried open, a light from within was seen by the King and his party. They hesitated and then slowly entered. As the King made his presence known, the people gasped when they saw the beleaguered ruler of their land.

Mud and sweat were pasted on his clothing and face, and dark circles appeared under his eyes. The people could see that their King was battle weary. The Sword of his fathers dangled from his belt. The golden handle glistened in the light of the torches.

"Your highness!" someone gasped. The people bowed their heads toward their leader.

Lord Byrén was the first of the rulers to approach.

"King Alexander," he said as he bowed and averted his yes as though trying to hide his shock at the King's condition. "Is the battle over?"

"Is the victory won?" asked Lady Silith who stood nearby. "Tell us, is Lord Caragon defeated?"

All the people began to gather around anxiously anticipating the King's answer. But his concerned expression along with the constable's deflected stare at the floor made them think otherwise.

"No," the King said. "I am afraid the battle has just begun."

"What?' Lord Byrén asked.

The King gazed into the eyes of his many loyal subjects as they stood in the light of the torches. Among the hay stacks and barrels of water and food, the people looked frail and frightened. The King slowly lifted his hands. He imagined how his appearance must be less that reassuring to them. All he could do was look deep into their eyes and remain the leader that he had been all his life.

"All is not lost," he reassured them. "Your brothers, sons, and fathers have fought well."

"But," Lord Byrén said, "it is not over?"

Realizing that trying to hide the urgency of the situation would not work, the King motioned for his constable. Then, he ordered a meeting with the Leaders of the Lands to be held in his chambers immediately.

"Everyone else must remain here," he ordered. "The siege is not over and you are far safer in here than out there."

Families gathered closer together as they watched all the leaders of the kingdom leave with the King. As the door closed behind them, the King could hear the murmurs of the people. "Many of them have never seen their King before," he said to the constable. "I'm certain my appearance was a cause for grave concern."

"They will be alright, Sire," Constable Darion replied. "They are a strong people."

§

The King and his party made their way to the castle entrance. They were met with the King's loyal servants who, just hours earlier, were serving a lavish meal to these very guests and their sovereign. Some servants gasped at the sight of their King limping and bloodied while others averted their eyes. Basins of clean water were hurried into the main chamber as the King eagerly sat down on his large throne. As each loyal Leader sat before him, he began to speak.

"My Lords and Ladies," he said, wiping his face with his hands. "I am afraid the news is far graver than I had anticipated."

His servants began to wash his hands and feet, but the King put an end to it as he stood to reveal the seriousness of the matter. He knew there would be time later for nursing wounds. He waved the servants away.

"What is it, Sire?" Lord Byrén asked.

"Lord Caragon," the King answered. "He has become far more powerful than any of us had imagined."

"What?" asked Lady Silith.

"It is true," the King said. "He has accumulated far greater powers than we thought possible. His time in exile has made way for much evil and darkness there at Hildron castle. It was our mistake to leave him be and now we are paying for that mistake. We are paying with the lives of our sons and brothers." He paced over to the painting of the Dragon Forest. "I do not believe he is working alone. He cannot be. I strongly feel he must have the help of someone far more powerful than he is."

"Helped by whom?" asked Lord Byrén.

The King shook his head. "I am not sure." He stared long and hard at the people before him. "But there is still hope."

The Leaders stood, walked over to the King, and began to discuss the matter. The doctor had made his way over to the castle entrance and was ushered into the main dining chamber toward the King. Constable Darion stopped him and whispered that the meeting was in process and he should wait. Together they stood nearby as the rulers spoke to the King.

"What is the plan, Sire?" Byron asked.

"Yes, what do we do now?" Lady Godden agreed.

The King chose his words carefully. "We must confront this evil. There is no other way."

"My Lord," Lady Godden said. "The time for more bloodshed is over. We have tried your way of fighting and it is not working. We have lost too many lives and there are many frightened people below us who want to return to their homes and rebuild their lives."

The King, with his back toward Lady Godden, listened.

"I say we try and negotiate with Caragon," she continued. "I am sure a delegation of leaders can meet with him at Hildron and discuss his terms."

"What terms?" asked Lord Byrén. "How can you negotiate with that thing?"

"We must try," Lady Godden continued. "For the sake of our people, we must try."

The King turned to interrupt their conversation. "There will be no negotiating."

"But my Lord," Lady Godden interrupted.

"Enough!" shouted the King as he stumbled. He made eye contact with each leader before him. The shock on their faces revealed to him that they were fully aware of his weakened state. "I have seen things you cannot possibly imagine. This man possesses magic the likes of which I have never seen. This magic has taken many lives before me and left me barely able to stand before you now."

"Yes, my Lord, I understand," said Lady Godden.

"No, I am afraid you do not understand," the King interrupted. "Lord Caragon has developed a way to bring the dead back from the realms of hell itself. I have seen it with my own two eyes. I have seen giant black crows sending my men to their deaths before me. And the Zadoks. These wolf-like beasts trampled over my men as if they were nothing. I have seen this wickedness and there is no negotiating with it."

Lady Godden stood frozen in silence as she tried to comprehend what she was hearing. "Zadoks?" She said to the others. "I haven't heard of them for so many years. I thought they were extinct."

"So did I," sighed King Alexander. "But they have been brought back for this battle. And they are fierce."

All the leaders of the lands stared at their King with utter confusion and dismay. Noticing the fear, he decided to reveal to them his plan. "But there is a way out," he said as he sat down on his throne. "We have help."

"What is the plan, my Lord?" asked Lord Byrén.

King Alexander carefully explained his plan to the rulers before him as he motioned for the doctor to enter. Then he dismissed the leaders back to the dungeon room to reassure the villagers that all was well but they needed to remain in hiding. As the rulers left, the doctor removed the ripped tunic from the King's torso and inspected the wound in his side. The deep wound had penetrated through the ribs.

"This should have been a fatal wound, my Lord," the doctor stated.

"Perform your medicine, apothecary, so I can be on my way," the King joked. Knowing that he escaped death on the battlefield, the King mumbled, "My time has not yet come."

The King ordered fresh clothing to be brought to him. He drank a mixture of herbs in a tea made by the doctor. He grimaced from its bitter taste, but he drank it anyway. When he finished dressing, he felt new strength and he knew he could continue.

He ordered a young soldier be brought in for a mission and gave him his orders. "You are to ride out to the Crow Valley to report to the men what has occurred. Do you understand?"

"Yes, sire," the young man bowed before his Lord.

The young rider mounted his fresh horse. He rode through the main gates with haste and, risking his life, he entered into the vastness of the desert plains. At a most rapid pace, they galloped as the clouds darkened the sky like a black sheet being pulled over one's eyes. To the west he could see the glow of fire emanating from the Black Hills and the smoke belching over Hildron castle. To the north he could see the Dragon Forest in its peaceful state. Onward he rode through the barren lands as his horse kicked up clods of dirt into the cool air.

§

King Alexander lifted his tunic and patiently waited as the doctor stitched up his wound. Skilled in healing, the doctor worked swiftly and used anodyne for the pain. With the medicine, the pain was tolerable for the King. But he rubbed his forehead and sighed.

"Do you worry about Peter, Sire?" asked his Constable.

Alexander nodded.

"What will you do know, my Lord?"

"Have we heard from the scouts in the east?" the King asked Darion.

"Yes, my Lord." Darion motioned for the steward to retrieve the scroll they received from the scouts. Darion handed it to the King.

Alexander read the scroll. "From King Mildrir." He managed a smile.

"King Mildrir has responded?" Darion asked.

"Yes. He is on his way," Alexander answered as he rolled up the scroll and handed it to Darion.

King Mildrir, the eldest living ruler, had proved himself a knight in battle and inherited the kingdom at an early age. His villagers built their homes of sparkling white stone on the high ridges along the shore overlooking the ocean. Each residence glistened in the morning sun causing many villagers to name it the Crystal City. King Mildrir insisted on forming a large powerful army after his father's death and so the weapons of Bedlam were highly coveted. But, having learned his lesson from the past, he remained loyal to the Oath.

"What is left of the arsenal?" King Alexander asked.

Constable Darion motioned to have the blacksmith brought into the chamber. "I suppose our resources are quite limited, but I will have the Blacksmith tell us himself," he said. "And Sire, our supply of fighters is depleted, I can assure you of this."

Wincing from the surgery, the King answered, "Yes that is why I asked for the men of the Crow Valley to come help us as well as the men from North shore several days ago."

The doctor finished stitching and began applying an herbal paste to the wound. Then he wrapped it with bandages around his ribs. When the doctor completed his work, the King lowered his tunic and stood. "But only Mildrir from the east has responded so far." He sighed.

"Yes, sire," Darion nodded. The look on the King's face worried him.

"Now, bring me my son," the King ordered.

"The Prince, my Lord?" asked his steward.

"Yes, the Prince," said the King. "My son, bring him to me."

No one said a word.

The blacksmith entered the room and waited to be summoned. The mood of the room was cheerless.

"Your highness, no one has seen Peter since he ran away last night," the steward said.

"What?" the King shouted. "Bring Will to me now!" He stood. "And you have checked his room? The entire castle?"

§

Will sat in the courtyard, deciding whether or not to try and see his father in the dungeon. He knew his father's wrath would be fierce, but he also hoped his father would eventually understand his reasons for fighting. He laid aside the wooden cup of cool water and began walking toward the hidden portal to the secret passageway leading to the dungeon.

A servant to the King approached him. "You there! The King is requesting your presence immediately."

Will followed the servant. Together the two entered into the large foyer of the castle entrance and waited for further orders. Not knowing what he was summoned for, he anxiously waited for news of the King's condition.

Constable Darion walked over to Will and accompanied him to the large dining chamber. There Will saw the King pacing in clean attire looking far better than before. This gave Will great relief.

"Your majesty." He bowed before Alexander.

"Will, come forward and tell my steward where you last saw Peter," he said.

Will turned to the steward and relayed the story he had told the others about how he brought Peter to the castle entrance and departed to the battle. He explained that Peter was in good spirits and understood to remain in the castle for safety.

The servant returned from Peter's sleeping quarters, then returned again to report no one was present in the room.

In absolute despair, the King lowered his head and exhaled loudly. Then he gathered his constable, Will, and the blacksmith together for a conference.

"I must ride to the Dragon Forest." The King motioned for his armor to be brought to him. Several servants entered carrying the clean and polished armor as well as the shield, belt, and sword of the King. As the servants worked, the steward attached the cape bearing the crest of Alexander to his armor.

"But Sire," Constable Darion said, "is that wise?"

"It is the only way," the King said. "I must try and speak with the Dragon. It must know of the urgency." He tightened his belt around his armored waist. "If this kingdom is destroyed, then the forest is destroyed." He looked into the men's eyes. "If the forest is destroyed, all of Théadril is destroyed forever."

The men nodded.

"What is left of the arsenal" the King asked the blacksmith.

"Many swords left, helmets, lances, and axes. Shields I can have ready soon. Bows and arrows are in low supply."

"How much time do you need to arm the men?"

"Not much, my Lord," the blacksmith replied.

"Then get to work," the King replied as he patted the man on the back, dismissing him.

"Will," the King said. "I will need you to stay here and help ready the men. Help reinforce the castle gates and keep watch for the enemy."

Will bowed in compliance to the order then proceeded to head out to the dungeon to see his father.

Darion and the King spoke once more.

"My son is out there," the King said. "I have to trust that he is safe."

"But what if no men from the shores or the Crow Valley come to help us, my Lord? Our supply of men is greatly depleted and the enemy we fight is wicked beyond comprehension."

"What are our choices but to hope in the willingness of our brethren to help us in our hour of need?" the King replied as he walked out of the chamber and into the entrance hall. "Without hope in the brotherhood of man...all else fails."

16 THE DRAGON OF THE FOREST

Hovering above the lands in the ever darkening clouds, the Dragon circled, watching young Prince Peter make his way on horseback toward the Cardion Valley. Not wanting to stop him, it continued to spy from afar.

Peter stopped Titan's stride as they approached the ruins of the once beautiful Cardion hills. The young Prince had never seen the aftermath of battle, but now it stood before him as a hot flame striking at his face. The pain was shocking and intense. He turned his eyes from the horror of the carcasses underfoot. Their grotesquely contorted remains littered the muddied earth. Soot and ash covered the landscape. Blackened wood planks protruding from the ground were all that remained of some houses where children had played and eaten with their families.

As he slowly walked Titan through the carnage, he saw the bodies of the dead Zadoks, some still baring their yellow teeth in a frozen grimace as mud and blackened blood stuck to their thick fur coats. The scene haunted Peter's mind. He turned the other way, only to be met with the remains of his father's loyal knights, their once bright silver armor was now blackened from the rains and mud. He gently booted Titan's sides to move him through the dead bodies. The rage burned inside Peter.

The two made their way out of the Cardion hillside and, as Peter looked up ahead, he noticed something blowing in the wind. He ordered Titan to gallop over to what appeared to be a green cloth. As the cloth whipped and snapped in the wind, Peter dismounted his horse and ran over to what was attached to a stick. He grabbed the muddied cloth between his hands, stared at it, and saw it was printed with a gold lion on the front and gold trim along the sides. Peter realized it was his father's banner. Even though it was covered with soot and ash and mud, the lion on the banner could still be seen. This gave Peter great hope. Yanking the banner off the stick, he gripped it tightly and held it to his chest.

Peter jumped up onto Titan's back and together they headed toward the Cornshire and to the Blue River valley near the castle where still more remnants of the last battle blanketed the ground.

The Dragon spied Prince Peter and Titan galloping toward the Cornshire. Soaring ever higher, the Dragon did not want Peter to see its form in the sky but as it flew the sun parted the clouds again and cast the Dragon's imposing shadow over the earth.

Peter instantly noticed the dark shadow following him as he rode. The shadow was like a comforting spirit bringing guidance and reassurance instead of fear and dread.

§

King Alexander walked into the main courtyard to inspect the arsenal of weapons in the blacksmith's hut. As he inspected their quality, condition, and numbers he felt reassured that his men could still meet the enemy head on in the next and hopefully final battle. He picked up a new sword and held its perfect blade in his hands. The grip felt good in his hand and the weight was exceptionally light and balanced. He twisted the blade around before his eyes and grinned. "I almost envy the soldier who will wield it in battle," he said.

Then King Alexander left the hut and ordered that three fresh horses as well as two riders be brought to him. As he waited, he put on his gloves and helmet over his exhausted face. He could not remember the last time he slept, but he knew there would be time for sleeping only when Caragon was dead.

The King watched the rays of the sun move over the clouds like a herd of white horses flowing over the hills of the Cornshire. Several soldiers and their captains stood nearby the King. As he walked by they stood at attention. Their tunics and armor were stained with blood and wet earth. Their faces were bandaged and still soaked with sweat. Realizing the hellish fight they had just survived, the King stopped to admire his men as more soldiers approached and stood in line awaiting their leader. He tried not to limp as he passed them when he saw that many nursed wounds far worse than his own and yet they were ready to do battle again for their King. Humbled by his men, the King continued his inspection.

Three horses came trotting up to the King alongside the two riders ready for their orders. The King mounted his horse as he looked around the castle courtyard. The villagers were helping the soldiers ready the courtyard for battle once again as many ran to secure the main gate once the King and the riders left.

"Our orders, Sire?" one rider asked.

The King watched as the main gate was raised and the drawbridge was lowered once again. Turning to the young men, he said, "You are to ride out to the Crow Valley, and you ride to the East shore. When you arrive you will tell them we need their men to prepare for battle. Tell them to meet us in the desert hills west of the Cardion Valley. Make certain you tell them of the urgency. Our time for second guessing tactics and plans is over. We must come together as one to defeat Lord Caragon once and for all."

"Yes Sire," the two men answered as they mounted their rides.

"Constable Darion,"

"Your majesty."

"I will send Prince Peter here to the courtyard when I find him. Make sure he is safe during the siege," the King ordered.

Darion accepted the orders and stepped back as the King and the two riders rode to the main gate. As each one rode, they separated in three directions. One rode to the east past the Blue

River. The other rider took the path over the Blue River and galloped into the hills toward the Crow Valley.

But King Alexander heeled his horse and galloped steadily toward the Dragon Forest just opposite the kingdom. There he hoped to meet his fate and secure safety and peace for his people. There he hoped he would find his lost son once and for all.

§

The Dragon spotted the two riders making their way over the Blue River. It also noticed King Alexander riding hard toward the Dragon Forest. As it flew, it closely watched as Peter galloped swiftly over the hills of the Cornshire, not knowing that ahead rode his father coming to find him. As the two rode toward each other, the Dragon hovered, watching the scene. Its shadow, still following near Peter, acted as a phantom guide leading him toward the King.

Alexander spotted the shadow of the giant beast as it moved over the hills and roamed over the burnt remains of the catapults and wooden ladders used by the enemy fighters. Their charcoal remains littered the countryside like a nightmare invading the perfect landscape that was the Cornshire.

He looked up into the sky and for the first time, he watched the Dragon of the Forest fly through the new sky with the sun behind its great wings. Light danced off the jeweled scales sending flashes of light into the King's eyes momentarily blinding him while he rode over hills. Suddenly, he heard something ahead. He glanced down from watching the Dragon fly gracefully above to see what was approaching him in the distance. The familiar gate of the horse and the familiarity of its rider caused the King to pull up on the reins of his horse in order to slow its speed. As he did this, he noticed the rider of the approaching horse slowed down as well. Then he saw who was in front of him. He stopped his horse and rapidly dismounted.

Peter gripped Titan's reins and as the tall horse stopped, Peter dismounted and ran to meet his father. The green banner was still in his hand as the tears welled in his eyes. He ran as fast as he could, but his exhausted body almost could not make the short journey.

King Alexander made the journey for him as he reached out his arms for his son. Grabbing his small body toward his own, the King lifted Peter high into the air and embraced him. Peter's arms wrapped around his neck, tears left the King's eyes and run down his face. He lowered Peter to the ground and removed his helmet to see his son's face better. Kneeling down before his son, the King held Peter's shoulders in his hands and stared at the face of his beloved son.

"Peter!" he said. "Are you alright?"

Peter nodded.

"You look so much like your mother," the King said, smiling through his tears. "I have missed you, son."

"Father," Peter cried. "I am sorry." He said as he wrapped his arms around his father's neck once more. "I am so sorry."

The two held each other there on the hill near the Blue River.

"It is alright, my son," the King cried. "I am just so grateful you are alright." He inspected Peter's face. "You are all that I have left."

Spying the reunion, the Dragon turned in the sky and headed back to its home in the Dragon Forest to once again enter into its realm of solitude. Its shadow glided over the hills of the Cornshire and the Cardion Valley like a deer. Circling the tall trees of the forest, the weary beast lowered itself into the dark coolness of their shadows. A few sparrows quickly dispersed from the treetops, scattering into the sky. The tranquility of the lake welcomed the Dragon as it rested.

King Alexander and Prince Peter stood together looking out over the desert toward the Black Hills where they spotted the dark mass still encircling the Hildron Castle. Father explained to son the coming assault and the hard fighting still to be done before the sun departed the sky. He told of the knights who fought valiantly and of young Will who proved himself a good soldier.

"So, you see, my son," he said. "That is why you must ride back to the castle, find Will, and stay near his side. He will protect you during the siege."

Peter listened.

"No more running away," the King said as he looked at Peter. "Agreed?"

Peter nodded as he held to his father's side. The King spied the green cloth in Peter's hands. "What is this?" he asked.

Peter showed him the torn banner. His father, recognizing the crest of Illiath, smiled.

Alexander walked Peter over to Titan and helped him mount his horse and place his feet into the stirrups. He adjusted them to make sure they fit. Then the King patted Titan on the rear to send them off.

King Alexander watched his son ride off toward the castle in the distance with great relief. The sun was low in the sky now as the clouds moved closer to the Black Hills in the west.

Alexander slowly walked over to his horse and, as he mounted it, he never took his eyes off the Dragon Forest so far to the north. There the forest stood like an emerald in the new sky as the sun began to set on this most unfortunate of days.

§

Peter shouted for Titan to gallop as fast as he could while the sun was still in the sky. He spotted the main gate of the castle with many soldiers atop the long outer wall. Extended hundreds of feet across, the wall housed two towers as well as many holdings for the soldiers to prepare for battle. The castle turrets, made of white limestone, glistened in the sunset. Each tower of the castle, taller than the next, seemed to climb forever into the sky. He could see his room in one of the taller turrets near the western wall overlooking the courtyard. The palace was an impressive sight to the villagers and peasants, but to Peter it was just home.

Peter could see many bowmen lining the walls looking for the best position. He saw them stand ready with their bows in hand and quivers full of sharpened arrows on their backs. As he rode, he tried not to look down at the carcasses being torn and pecked by crows and small birds of prey. Remembering his father's banner, Peter thought he would give it to the constable to raise it up over the outer wall for all to see.

The drawbridge crashed on the ground, sending dust and dirt flying as Titan and Peter galloped onto the bridge and into the courtyard. Peter dismounted and handed Titan's reins to a servant. Shocked at first by the sight of the large ogres helping prepare the castle, Peter then remembered how his father explained their assistance to him in the battle. Removing the tattered banner from his pocket, he handed it to Constable Darion, explaining where he had found it and what to do with it.

Darion smiled at Peter's maturity as he handled the green banner bearing the King's crest in his fingers. Peter asked where Will was as his father had requested. Darion ordered a servant to take Peter to the dungeon to meet with Will.

The constable then climbed to the top of the outer wall where he would oversee the preparations for the siege once again. He watched as the sun set. The day was over, and the night would soon begin bringing with it certain pain and terror before they would see the sun again. He gazed over to the Black Hills toward Hildron Castle, where the looming black mass still circled above the mountains. The dark clouds belched smoke and fire as bursts of lightning shot forth from the enemy stronghold.

"What wickedness has been forged there," Darion asked. "I am afraid no one truly knows."

"How could this have happened?" asked a captain nearby. "Lord Caragon is a mere mortal."

"Yes," Darion answered. "But his powers come from somewhere."

"I will keep a close watch for the King and his signal," said the captain.

"Alert us of any changes," Darion said.

Then he walked the length of the wall and inspected the work of the soldiers and bowmen. There were not more than four hundred men left for this fight and many were wounded and exhausted from the earlier assault. The ogres stood below the wall helping to stack boulders and rocks for the catapults. After receiving food and cool water from the hesitant villagers, the ogres quickly earned their respect. Many ogres rested for the next fight near the main gate as others mended their wounds. Both men and ogres suffered losses at the hands of the wicked enemy fighters. The ghost knights were swift and deadly in their aim, but the ogres' brute strength proved to be most useful to the kingdom. Darion was grateful for their assistance. He knew the siege was not over.

§

Will maneuvered down the darkened steps to where the dungeon entrance stood. The door was open as many villagers raced to the infirmary to bring more wrappings to help mend the wounds of the soldiers. Will slowly entered into the dungeon, bustling with activity. The women were helping the soldiers as the men were nowhere to be found.

"Where are the men?" Will asked.

"Many of them have gone to help prepare the castle courtyard for the siege and others are helping to make more weapons," answered one woman.

Walking around the dungeon, Will searched for his father in earnest. He noticed some smaller children eating and drinking as they watched their mothers talk to the wounded.

"Have you seen my father?" Will asked one of the women.

"Will?" one lady asked. "Is that you?"

He did not realize his appearance had changed since leaving the dungeon to fight. "Yes," he replied. "Where is my father?"

"He went up to help prepare for the next battle," she said. "Are you alright Will? Were you wounded? Your father was so worried about you."

Will lowered his head. "No, I am not wounded."

"Good," she said as she placed her hands on Will's shoulders. "We were all so proud of you."

"The little girl," Will asked. "Is she alright?"

"Yes," answered the lady as she pointed to where the girl was resting with her family. "She is going to be fine."

Will felt relief for a moment, then he remembered Charles and the fact that, only a few short hours ago, they were together in the dungeon. The pain of the memory was too much. He thanked the lady for the good news and ran back upstairs to find his father. The courtyard was busy as well with many men shouting orders and lifting wood up the tower ladders. Others were helping make weapons as well as stacking them. Will watched closely as the villagers worked to help save their kingdom. So much was at stake in this siege. Will became exhausted just pondering what lie ahead. He sat down to rest.

"Will!" He heard his name shouted from across the courtyard. "Will! Is that you?"

"Father!"

The two reunited in the courtyard in the midst of all the chaos. Will explained his actions to his father and told of the assault in the hills by the Blue River valley. He told of the ghost fighters and the Dragon of the Forest returning the Prince to the kingdom. Mostly, he spoke of how he fought alongside their King, Alexander. Then, it was time to speak of Charles and his sacrifice.

The father and son stood talking together for a while as they both realized so much had happened in that short time, and how nothing would ever be the same again.

§

As the trees stood firm forming their ethereal cathedral around the Dragon within, the King slowed his horse by pulling on the reins. Wanting to approach the forest cautiously, he dismounted at the entrance. The pathway leading into the forest was cool in the shadows of the tall trees. The breeze coming from the west was cool as it blew a few dead leaves into the air. His mind raced back to the time of his youth and how he naively entered into the Dragon's lair without hesitation. Alexander stood still for a moment as he strained to hear any sound at all coming from within the trees. His hands gripped the reins of his horse. Since the preceding battles, his senses were on alert for the unknown. His fear and trepidation surprised him, considering all he had seen that day. Perhaps his respect for the Dragon and the oath kept him from rushing in spite of the urgency.

All that could be heard was the wind making its way through the tops of the trees, moving them slightly in a hypnotic swaying motion. The wind carried with it a scent of pine and leaves mixed with the rain that had fallen. The clean scent caused the King to inhale deeply as he walked along the pathway disappearing into the midst of the forest. The stench of death and burnt grasses made any man weary. He grinned as though he welcomed the new scent like a perfume.

Keeping the sword of Alexander in its sheath, he glided his right hand over the grip of the sword, memorizing every detail. Like any good knight, he prepared for any surprise attack. Yet, somehow, he knew he was safe within the trees. He slowly headed down the path into the forest realm. The trees towered over him as though warning him that where he stood was no ordinary place. Golden sunlight cut through their branches illuminating the walls of the trees like stained glass illuminates a holy cathedral. The sight was mesmerizing and frightening at the same time. But he felt he was called to this place for a reason. While walking, all the horror and despair of the day's events seemed far away from this place as the pain dissipated into the crisp evening air. Sparrows sang from high above him as the welcoming breeze blew across his face. He stopped and closed his eyes. He had almost forgotten where he was for a precious few moments as he drank in the tranquility.

The pleasant silence was rudely shattered by the loud caw of a black crow that jarred Alexander from his waking dream as he continued to walk through the sweet smelling forest green. Walking along the winding path toward the center of the forest, there was a sudden heaviness in the air. The change alerted Alexander and he walked more cautiously, remembering where he was. The sun began to make its way lower into the sky sending its golden hues through the trees as their brooding shadows continued to line the pathway. Only the *clip clop* sound of his horse's hooves on the dampened earth could be heard. The King tied his horse's reins onto a nearby tree branch and he headed onward alone. His hand was still gripped the handle of his sword as he stepped into the middle of the forest.

The familiar blue mist still hovered over the lake as a dazzling light from the setting sun glistened on the surface like crystals. Standing still as death, Alexander took in the sight as though it would be his last. He slowly removed his sword from its sheath and held it in front of his face as he took a few steps toward the waters.

Alexander stood fast with his sword ready to slash. The wound in his side began to ache yet again as he stood there. Looking into the sky above the lake, he noticed the light of the westerly sun was dimming quickly.

Then, behind the trees appeared two yellow eyes staring at Alexander from between the darkened branches. The eyes glowed yellow with dark slits running down the center of each eye. Alexander recognized them as the eyes of a dragon. The breath of the Dragon spewed forth from between the trees as Alexander heard the rumpling of leaves and brushes from underneath the belly of the beast. Its huge tail swept from side to side like a serpent easing out of its coil.

Alexander gripped his sword with both hands once again when he realized this was the mighty Dragon of the Forest and then turned the blade down. Kneeling down before the Dragon with the blade of his sword piercing the dampened ground, he lowered his head in humiliation before the giant creature. "I come in peace," he said to the yellow eyes protruding from the trees.

The rising and falling of the beast's belly echoed throughout the forest as no other sound could be heard but its deep breaths. Patiently, the King waited for a response from the Dragon as it was his right. His father before him served as a loyal King to the Dragon Forest and now he was here to do the same. Seeking guidance and counsel from the enigmatic creature before him, Alexander remained there on bended knee.

"What do you seek?" the Dragon quietly asked.

Slowly, Alexander raised his head with intimidation. He sought out the glowing eyes from between the trees once again. "You saved my son and returned him to me. I am eternally grateful for this act of mercy. Now, I seek your counsel," he replied.

The Dragon searched Alexander's heart and found it pure in intent. Gently rising from among the trees, the Dragon's body parted trees and brush sending swallows flying into the air like the down of a thistle. The Dragon moved toward the King with heavy footsteps that sent fear through Alexander's weary body. Each foot hosted sharp black claws still stained with dried blood and plastered with dirt from battle with the giant crows. Each claw dug its way into the damp ground with heaviness. The sheer size of the creature caught the King off guard, but he remained kneeling in humble respect.

Watching in awe as the sinewy muscles twitched beneath the glistening scales, Alexander slowly rose to meet the Dragon he had known since his youth. The long snout stood feet away from the King's head as warm breath eased from the nostrils. The Dragon revealed its numerous teeth as they gave way to a slithering, black spiked tongue moving between them. The creature completed its walk to the Blue Lake in the middle of its fortress amidst the forest green. Its long tail rested gracefully in front of the massive body. Lowering its head to the water's edge, the Dragon lapped up the cool water into its mouth. Then, it paused for a moment and gazed at its surroundings.

Alexander kept a careful eye on the long sharp claws and teeth, knowing his life could end in only a few seconds if the Dragon wished it so. Raising the famous sword before him, he spoke. "Lord Caragon's men are gathering yet again at Hildron castle as we speak. A gathering storm rises over the Black Hills and I do not have enough men to meet the enemy head on in battle. I fear the kingdom will fall. And if the kingdom falls so will the Dragon Forest."

§

Peter watched nearby as Will and his father talked of the battle. Then, Peter was taken over to the men by one of the King's servants.

"Will," the servant interrupted. "His Highness has appointed you to watch over his son, the Prince."

Will accepted the great honor and introduced the Prince to his father. Then the three walked over to the keep to get some food. There they spoke of Lord Caragon and what lay ahead for the King's men.

"Will, I want you to remain in the dungeon with the boy," his father said as he handed Will an apple.

"But father," Will objected.

"Your responsibility is to protect the boy now," his father answered.

Peter just listened. He knew Will wanted to fight again for his King, but he also knew it would be too dangerous.

Will looked down at the ground as the three ate apples from the Keep.

"All is not lost," Will's father said. "Alexander's men will fight to the death to protect the kingdom." He looked at the

Prince. "And then one day it will be yours, Prince Peter." He put his hand on Peter's shoulder. "I pray you will serve the kingdom with honor as your father has."

Peter nodded. He looked at Will, who was still staring at the ground and biting into his apple. The threat of war had made this young man into a warrior who fought with grace and accuracy to protect the King. Peter felt sorry for him, but understood.

§

Constable Darion paced back and forth along the castle wall as the sun began its descent over the Black Hills of the west. The waxing moon began to glow high in the sky above the Cardion Valley as the last golden haze of sunlight cast long shadows over the tormented fields where wheat and hay once thrived. In sorrow, Darion continued to glance toward the Dragon Forest as he awaited word from the King and his riders.

With darkness brooding in the west, Darion noticed light approaching from the desert hills. Tiny points of light flickered from between the clefts in the rocks of the Black Hills.

"Torches!" he screamed. "Torches are coming from the west!"

Bowmen and a garrison of soldiers came running to the wall and up the ladders as they prepared for the attack. The constable showed them the sight as he pointed to the west.

It was true. Tiny flickers of light came from the Black Hills. Above them, the black storm still circled mysteriously.

"Caragon's men are moving," Darion said. "Ready the men and prepare the castle."

"But we have not heard from the King or his riders," one soldier said. "Should we not wait?"

Darion did not know the answer, but he knew it was possible that the King would not return from the Dragon Forest. They would have to fight on without him. Still, he knew they needed assistance since they did not have enough men to take on the enemy as they approached. As the sun sank lower behind the mountains, lightning flashed behind the black clouds heavy with rain. The sight was eerie and foreboding. Darion asked for his looking glass from a soldier. Peering through the lens of the brass looking glass, he searched the horizon for a sign of the two riders making their way back. But he could not see them. Then, he turned his gaze to the Dragon Forest. His eyes saw only small birds rising from the treetops and heading east through the twilight.

"Yes, we will wait," he said. "A few more minutes we will wait for the King. But still we must make sure we are prepared."

17 OF MAPS AND BATTLES

The breathing of the giant beast was labored as it stood before the King. Alexander noticed each breath was causing great strain to the Dragon as it studied its answer to the King's plea.

"We need more help," he said. "What can you give us?'

Realizing how much the Dragon had already done for his men, Alexander felt pangs of guilt in requesting more. But he had no choice now.

The Dragon stared out above the trees as the sun's golden hues turned to violet and then a deep blue as they spoke. The forest grew darker as the mist rose over the lake. The lone black crow still perched on its favorite limb high above the lake. Its black feathers glistened in the moon's glow. Slowly peering from behind the swiftly moving clouds, some stars made their appearance as countless points of flickering lights so far from the earth.

King Alexander noticed the wound in the Dragon's chest. A scale was missing from the wound leaving the creature vulnerable to a sharp weapon.

"Will you help us?" he asked.

"The time for the Dragon has come to an end," the Dragon said.

King Alexander listened.

The Dragon's tail rose and gently fell to the ground darkened now with the long shadows of the trees. The forest grew silent and still. King Alexander looked above for the crow, but it had flown away. The clouds completely covered the stars and swept by the face of the waxing moon.

"Man's time has come," it said with sorrow in its voice.

"One last battle remains," Alexander answered.

Kneeling before the beast once again, the King pleaded for its help. "My son will rule after me. I promise you I will teach him to honor this forest and protect it no matter what comes. I promise you," he urged. He put the sword of Alexander before his face. "I swear on my honor, on the oath of the seven kings, it will be done."

The Dragon turned its countenance toward the King. Staring at the sword of Illiath, he stood up on all four of its giant limbs before the kneeling King. Staring down at the mere mortal in its presence, it studied the subject. He knew the King knew nothing of what he spoke. For Peter to know true honor meant he would have to be tested beyond anything the King could possibly imagine. He would have to face great trials. Yet, the King spoke truth from his heart in all purity.

"This I will do for you King Alexander," the Dragon said with a deep hollow voice. "You have ruled these lands with honor and humility before my eyes. I have watched you for many moons and have been pleased. You have put your very life before sword and lance to protect this forest from evil."

Slowly turning to face the mystical blue waters of the lake, the Dragon motioned for the King to follow it. Carefully, it peered into the still waters as though gazing into a mirror.

Alexander stood and walked over to the waters as he placed his sword into its sheath. There, he hesitated as he watched the Dragon's head hover over the water. Tthe waters began to stir like waves on the sea. The blue mist covering the waters parted to reveal images within the lake.

Alexander took a few steps backward as he saw images appear in the water before him. The reflection of the images bounced off his face as he placed his hand over his eyes. He was frightened.

"Here within these waters lies the truth," the Dragon said. "Here you will see with your own eyes what I have seen. Caragon's army is preparing for battle. Many dark and wicked things have been brought to life within Hildron. Here you will see for yourself."

King Alexander cautiously approached the lake and gazed into the roiling waters at his feet. There, within the water, he saw the images of Caragon's men preparing for battle. Thousands of Barok soldiers lined the hallways of Hildron castle with shields, lances, and swords. Torches, lined up by the thousands, glowed in the darkened hallways as man after man grabbed them one by one to take with them into the night as they began their march toward the Kingdom of Alexander. Fires burned within Hildron's massive courtyard made of black rock from the mountains. The gate to the castle slowly rose as Caragon's twisted Baroks marched through it. Then the images changed to the storm cloud above the castle as it stirred and circled. He saw darkness and winter covering Illiath.

"Caragon has not yet revealed all his weapons for this battle or the source of his power," the Dragon said. "The worst is yet to come."

Alexander's eyes widened. It became apparent that his fears grew as he watched the pictures inside the waters. The images came quickly, one after the other: Peter bound in chains being led away, the ten swords, the leather bound book of Theádril, the castle, dark clouds and rain, a White Forest in the snow, and a glimpse of a white owl flying.

The Dragon explained that behind Hildron Castle is a land so dark and obscure that the mountains surrounding it are blackened from lack of light and water.

"Because the enemy is great with evil," the Dragon continued. "You will need further assistance in this battle if the forest is to remain."

"Then, you will help us?" he asked.

The Dragon gazed into the waters as the images vanished as quickly as they appeared. The waters again returned to their tranquil state. The blue mist once again covered the lake. He stared long and silent into the reflection in the water. Alexander walked up next to the creature. The two stood ever still and quiet.

"My time has come," the Dragon sighed.

Alexander turned to see the face of the Dragon. Its eyes still peered into the water and then up at the moon above them. The rims around its eyes were red and moistened, revealing exhaustion. Alexander studied the scales that lined the face and snout. They were dull and caked with the mud of battle. He looked down at the clawed feet and saw how wrinkled and scarred they were, revealing the Dragon's age.

Suddenly, the King was filled with compassion. *How many years has this creature been faithfully guarding this land? Fighting our enemies time and time again?* Yet now he was asking for its help once again. The sky was dark now and the wind had stopped. The trees stood still around them as they talked.

"What can I do?" Alexander asked. "Can you tell me?"

No answer.

"Will we survive? Will the kingdom go on?" the King asked.

The Dragon turned to face its guest.

"Alexander, King of all the lands from the seas to the Black Hills, I will keep my promise— the Oath I swore to your fathers."

Upon hearing these words, Alexander sighed with relief. He felt youthfulness in his body and lightness in his steps. He ran to his horse. As he mounted the faithful steed, the Dragon turned toward the entrance of the forest.

"As we speak, your rider is returning from the Crow Valley," the Dragon said as it pointed its snout to the west. "Lord Byrén's men are marching forward to meet in battle."

Alexander steadied his horse as he listened with great excitement.

"And to the east, as you ride, you will see the men of the east shore marching toward the Cardion Valley. Do you see, defender of men? You are not alone."

Then the giant beast flapped its massive wings and rose above the ground. The wind from the wings caused the horse to rear up on its hind legs as leaves and twigs danced around them on the ground. Alexander pulled on the reins to steady his horse.

"I will keep my promise," the Dragon said as it rose into the night sky above the King. The deep purple sky surrounded the Dragon as it lifted higher and higher above the King.

King Alexander watched it slowly ascend and as it did, it became smaller and smaller. Its appearance began to change. Once again, the Dragon took on another form: that of a white owl. The owl fluttered its wings while its yellow eyes glowed.

Alexander instinctively held out his right arm for the owl to perch upon. Obediently, the owl landed safely on the arm of the King, gripping him with its sharp claws. The owl slowly folded its wings as its soft downy feathers puffed up when it settled on its new perch. King Alexander kicked his horse and together they galloped from the Dragon Forest toward the Cardion Valley, where his men awaited him.

§

The air was scented with the coming rains as the winds began to stir again from the east. King Alexander rode with great speed over the dark hills toward his castle. As the Dragon had promised, troops marched from the east shore. He could see their torches in the night sky like glittering sparks rising from an open fire. He turned to the right and galloped down a gorge where he had hunted in his youth. Upon exiting the gorge, he rode out on the other side where the hills became rocky. His horse struggled to make it to the top, once they stopped to see the sight.

There, cutting through the darkness of night, he saw thousands of torches lined in rows making their way from the south out of the Crow Valley. Lord Byrén's loyal men had received the call of their King and answered that call to fight with great haste.

King Alexander sat atop his horse with the owl still clinging to his right arm. It flapped its wings in the wind as the King inspected the great and hopeful sign of allegiance. Steering his horse down the hill and through the gorge once again, Alexander rode faster toward his castle with great encouragement. Knowing the impending doom over Hildron was growing fiercer as he rode, he did not desire to gaze upon the darkening force encircling the Black Hills, nor did he see the torches of Caragon's men approaching.

§

Prince Peter walked with Will out of the courtyard and toward the castle entrance as the sky darkened. Looking up, he could see the grey clouds moving fast through the sky as they covered the comforting stars that used to guide him through his night hunts in the summertime with his father. He wondered to himself if life would ever be that simple again.

"Your Highness," Will's father said. "Will and I must take our leave to the dungeon now. The siege will begin soon."

Prince Peter nodded and then turned to enter his father's castle. There he saw the servants waiting in the doorway to finally escort their Prince to the safety of his bedroom. But Peter longed to stay in the courtyard to see the battle between good and evil. He longed to see his father return again, but he remembered his father's orders were for him to return to his room.

"Father," Will interrupted. "May I stay with Peter in the castle?"

"Yes!" Peter said. "That would be excellent!"

"Well," Will's father hesitated. "It is safe inside the dungeon."

"Yes, but I was appointed by the King to look after his son. It is far too dark and damp for the royal Prince stay in the dungeon with the commoners."

Peter stood silent as he waited for Will to continue.

"Please father," Will said. "I want to perform my duty for the King and look after his son."

Will's father smiled with pride in his heart for his son. He hugged his son and patted him on the shoulders in approval. Then he bowed to Peter and went his way to the dungeon.

"Father!" Will yelled as he ran to say goodbye once again. "Thank you. You are... a good father."

Overcome with sorrow and longing for his home, Will embraced his father once again. Not waiting for a response, for he could not stand to look into his father's eyes, he ran back to Peter and together they entered into the massive stone castle that was the kingdom of Alexander.

Will's father stood still for a moment as he watched his only son run off. He hoped his son would somehow find a way to fight in the siege and yet he also knew there was nothing he could do about it now. His son had gone from young boy to warrior in one day's time without his assistance. He frowned with sadness and slowly turned toward the dark hallway that led to the stairs to the dungeon where he would wait for word on the condition of his son. He knew it would be a long night.

§

Inside the castle, Peter noticed Will's temperament had changed. He wondered if Will was thinking the same thing as he was, but did not want to ask until they were alone for fear that the plan would be discovered.

The servants continued to ask Peter if he was hungry or tired or frightened and if he needed anything at all. After Peter answered all the questions negatively, he led Will to his favorite room in the castle. The large dining hall was quiet and cleared of any dishes from the dinner the night before. In Peter's mind, it felt as though years had passed since he played in the room, but he knew it only had a day yet so much had happened.

Will walked into the massive room decorated with tapestries, banners, and paintings. His eyes followed the giant painting of the Dragon Forest. He hypnotically moved toward it, for he had never seen anything of its kind in his sixteen years. Will had never been to the Dragon Forest, but had heard about it since he was a small boy. His father and the townsfolk had spoken of it in hushed tones with warnings and threats of punishment and even certain death to anyone who dared to venture into its realm. Will would often run to the top of the highest hill in the Cardion Valley to gaze upon the tall green woods to the north. There he would dream of someday entering into the mysterious Dragon's fortress as a knight of Alexander's Kingdom to slay the mighty beast for himself. Now, as he stood before the beautiful painting, he had felt the pain of war and smelled the stench of death. He knew from Peter's stories that the Dragon was real and he knew that the King was a mighty warrior who would fight to the death to save his kingdom. Finally, he knew that he had one last battle to engage in before the night was over.

"What are you thinking?" Peter asked his new friend.

"I have never seen anything like this before," Will answered.

The two friends stood before the painting for a moment or two.

"I have never been to the Dragon Forest. Tell me, what was it like?"

"Hard to describe, really." Peter ran his fingers through his matted brown hair as he began to sort his thoughts out one by one. "The trees…are a green I had never seen before. The artist there." He pointed to the large painting. "He has failed to capture it adequately. There were so many black crows hovering above the tree tops." His arms gesticulated above his head as he spoke. "Like guardians to the realm. In the midst of the forest lies a mysterious Blue Lake."

Will could almost see it in his head.

"Magical and mystical waters filled the lake and a mist hovered over it like a blanket. I thought it was the Dragon's breath. The Dragon appeared between the branches of the trees like a prowler waiting to pounce. Its eyes glowed like an owl. Yellow in hue, they followed me wherever I went, yet I felt safe. My horse, Titan, he was frightened, but I wasn't."

"Really?" said Will incredulously.

"It spoke to me," Peter said as he sat down at the enormous dining table where several platters of food awaited him. "Then, with one breath, it turned my wooden sword into a sword made of steel. Its breath was blue fire and cold as ice!" Peter's eyes grew big in their sockets as he spoke.

Will grabbed a chicken leg and ravenously ate the food set out on the table as he listened to Peter's tale. "Tell me more," he said.

"Then, Sir Peregrine came with his men," Peter said and he swallowed some food. "He thought he could fool me, but I knew what he was after."

"What was he after?" Will asked between bites.

"The scales of the Dragon."

"Whatever for?"

"It is said that the scales are more powerful than any weapons forged by man," Peter explained as he ate.

Will listened intently.

"Sir Peregrine came into the forest to slay the Dragon and take the scales."

"And what happened?"

"He failed," Peter smiled. "Miserably."

Will smiled in return.

"He attacked the Dragon, but was met with its powerful hot flaming breath…And he and his men were reduced to ashes in seconds," Peter grinned with satisfaction.

"Amazing." Will eye's grew large at the thought. "I had always heard the legend of the Dragon, but never thought it to be true."

"Oh it is true," Peter said. "And it is real. The Dragon lives. I know, I have seen it."

Together they ate and exchanged stories of the day's events. After they consumed the delicious meal set before them, Peter took Will further into the castle and showed him the table he had hidden under while his father spoke with his knights. Then he showed him all his favorite hiding places.

"This is where I hide when I want to frighten the maid," he said as he opened a closet. "I once put a snake in her mop bucket. I could hear her screaming all the way down the hall."

Peter smiled as he remembered. He told of spiders in pockets and crickets in hairbrushes. They chuckled at the thought. Will found it hard to imagine living in such a large castle. He thought back to the small house he shared with his father and his small room off the kitchen. But here in the palace, with its ornate wood carvings and paneled hallways, he was mesmerized.

As they walked, Peter revealed to Will all the secret passages in the castle halls. In and out of hidden doors they went exploring. "Here!" Peter said as he pointed to a large painting hanging on the paneled wall of the library. "Watch this." He lifted the painting from the wall on one side to reveal a door that led to a secret passage leading to the meeting room of the knights. Peter pressed on the paneled door and it popped opened, revealing a stairway. As they walked down the dark stairway, Peter stopped when he realized they had no torch. They retraced their steps and headed back up and out of the painting doorway.

"What fun it must have been to play here in this castle," Will said as he stared at the high ceilings above them. "So many places to hide." He felt like a small boy again. The images of war left his mind if only for a moment. He felt safe.

"Yes," Peter agreed. They headed out toward the hallway once again.

"I want to show you something," Peter said as he peeked around the corner to see if any of the servants were waiting. When no one was in sight, he motioned Will to follow him down a long darkened hallway. The shiny marble flooring glistened as only a few torches lit their path. Many dusty old tapestries depicting eras long gone hung along the wall. The two young men walked swiftly down the hallway stopping for nothing as they knew their time was limited.

"Where are we going?" Will asked. But Peter remained silent until they stopped before a doorway. Peter reached out, grabbed the brass doorknob, and turned it expecting the door to be unlocked.

"This is my father's private study," Peter said as he opened the door. "He was here a few days ago speaking to his Constable." The two grabbed a torch from the hallway and entered the dark room. Will lit a few candles that were inserted into large brass candlesticks which stood on a wooden table with wide carved legs. As the candles' light grew, more of the room became visible to Will.

On a table were maps and other papers with the King's signet impression set in red wax. Peter opened a large wooden cabinet behind a table, took out a large black leather book that appeared to be too heavy for his ten-year-old arms, and set it down. Will shuffled the maps and papers out of the way. Then he took a lit candlestick and held it closer to the book to read the title.

"Theádril," Will said as he read the book's title. "What is this?"

"This is the book my grandfather wrote," Peter dusted off the leather cover. "It speaks of the legend of Bedlam and the Dragon."

Will nodded. He had heard of the legend and this book as well as the swords of Bedlam, but he understood it to be a myth or tale spoken in hushed tones by the firelight. He never realized it could be true.

"So, this is the book," Will said as he ran his long fingers over the detailed cover. "Open it."

Peter carefully opened the book. The cover stuck to several pages, revealing its age, but Peter turned a few pages to find the part about the Dragon. As he turned pages, Will noticed some illustrations in ink that displayed maps of the ten regions as well as the names of the rulers. He stopped Peter at one page.

"The Swords of Bedlam," he said. The page showed a list of the Kings of Theádril and the swords they received from Lord Bedlam. Each name was listed in the order of the regions. Peter's grandfather was listed second.

"Aléon son of Illiath," Will whispered. "Peter, isn't that is your grandfather?"

Peter nodded. "I had never met him, but had heard about him from his father and mother." Seeing his name listed here made Peter's skin shiver in the darkened room.

"What happened to the swords?" Will asked as they turned the pages of the book.

"Some were lost."

"Lost? How?"

"In battle," Peter answered. "But my father still has his," Peter said. "I will receive it when I become King."

Will knew Peter was the Prince, but he never really understood it until this moment. He became frightened. "Close the book."

Peter did so, then lifted it off the table. As he did, a scrap of paper fell from the pages onto the wooden planked floor. "What is that?" Peter asked.

Will bent down to collect the paper off the floor. When he opened it, he saw that it was not a scrap of paper after all.

"It is a map," he said.

He held the fragile paper in his hands. He could see by candlelight that it was ancient—from generations passed. The paper was brown with age and torn on one side as though it had been ripped in half. It had been carefully folded not to obstruct its contents.

"A map of what?" he asked as he struggled to hold the heavy book.

"A map of a land further west of the Black Hills," Will answered as he studied the paper. "A land of which I have never heard."

Peter put the book down on the floor and stared at the paper in Will's hands. The map showed hills and a compass rose pointing north. Lands were marked in writing unfamiliar to both boys, but they recognized the Black Hills to the west of the kingdom. Will turned the paper around to see if he could read the writing printed at the bottom of the page. But neither could understand the language.

"An ancient language I suppose," Will said.

"What do you think it says?" Peter asked.

Peter stared at the letters that labeled certain areas on the map. Then, suddenly, he realized what the map was. His mouth opened as though he wished to speak but could not.

"What is it?" Will asked.

"I think I know," Peter said as he motioned to the map. Will set it down on the table so Peter could examine it further. The boys carefully studied the map's contents and the writings. At the top of the paper was a symbol that neither boy recognized at first, but as Peter stared at it, he began to remember what it was.

"Well?" Will asked. "What is it?"

"This is a map written in the language of the Dragon." Peter pointed to the map.

"The Dragon?"

"I think so," Peter said. "I remember my father telling me about how the Kings used to live alongside the Dragon in peace long ago until he warned them of an evil presence in the kingdom. I think this is the map that the Dragon gave my grandfather. I think it is a map of where Bedlam ruled. It looks like a map of land near Vulgaard."

"Vulgaard?' Will asked. "I have heard of that land somewhere."

"Your father probably spoke of it at one time or another," Peter said. "Many of the fathers and grandfathers of the kingdom remember, I suppose."

"What is that land?"

"Vulgaard is the land of the Elves, but Lord Bedlam captured the mountains near Vulgaard and has it for himself," Peter said. "Or so I am told."

Will picked up the map and tried again to read its contents.
"I wonder what it says," Will asked. "We had better put it back. I am sure your father will need it one day soon."

He folded the paper and placed it back inside the cover of the book. Afterwards, Peter placed the book back in the cabinet. A loud caw of a crow startled them. Outside the window sat a black crow on the window seal. It flew off.

Will blew out his candle and motioned for Peter to follow him. "We had better go now." Peter blew out his candle and followed his friend.

Together they ran down the hall back to the main entrance foyer of the castle.

18 THE SECRETS OF BEDLAM

Constable Darion scanned the countryside with his looking glass for any sign of the King's approach. Spotting the torches from the east, his heart grew more hopeful.

"More torches," he said. "From the east, I can see them marching. Hundreds upon hundreds of men are marching. This is good."

"Yes," said the captain of the garrison of soldiers who joined the constable on the castle wall. "With the men from the Crow Valley we just might have enough men to do battle. All is not lost," he said as he patted Darion's shoulder.

Then he ordered the bowmen to take positions along the wall with their many arrows and bows at the ready. Buckets of oil were strategically placed near the bowmen by the dutiful foot soldiers for easy access to light their arrow as hundreds of new arrows with sharpened metal heads were allotted to each bowman. Their aim would have to be straight and true from each position in order to stop the enemy they faced.

They scrambled to acquire the best position along the walls. Peering through the crenels of the castle towers and walls, the bowmen were set to fire off their arrows at the enemy through their chosen positions. Foot soldiers ran along the castle wall handing off more arrows and extra bows as well as torches to provide light as they waited.

Darion continued to watch the western sky as the sun made its last appearance of the day over the Black Hills. Fire and lightning still illuminated the darkened skies as the black mass hovered above Hildron castle. Spikes of lightning cut through the clouds sending the piercing clamour of thunder into the air. It's reverberations in the castle courtyard, the sound frightened the many servants still working inside the castle's kitchen and halls. Foot soldiers stood still as they looked into the sky above them. The air was dense. Not wanting them to fear and abandon their preparations, Darion ordered the foot soldiers back to work.

From inside the castle, Peter and Will could hear the thunder claps. Together, they ran to the large picture window that looked over the northern façade of the castle, they could faintly see the trees of the Dragon Forest far off in the distance with what little sunlight they had left.

"I must go now," Will said. "It's time." He sought to find his place either on the castle wall or in the courtyard for the order to fight. "Stay here. You will be safe here inside the castle."

Peter nodded in agreement. He knew this fight was not for him, but he did fear for Will. And he wondered where his father was at this time.

"I mean it," Will said to Peter with sudden authority.

"Are you going to fight now?' he asked Will.

"Yes," Will answered. "Look, I know I told you I would stay here, but…"

"I know," Peter interrupted. "You have to go."

"Don't worry," Will said. "Everything will work out. Your father will defeat the enemy and return."

Peter lowered his head. "I just wish I could go too."

Will smiled. "Haven't you had enough excitement for one day? I mean, riding on a Dragon's back and all?"

Peter laughed.

Will turned and looked for his belt and sword. "I left it in the room!" He raced back down the hallway to the King's study. He returned as quickly as he had left, but with belt in hand. He removed his sword from its sheath and ran to the large doorway.

"I promised your father that I would watch over you," he said to Peter as he turned to leave. "I will be on the castle walls. Please stay here, Peter. Do not make a liar of me."

Peter nodded that he would remain inside.

Then Will ran outside the main castle entrance to the courtyard. Fear and trepidation showed in the people's faces as they quickly carried buckets of water and barrels of food down to the dungeon for storage.

Peter stood at the doorway and watched Will run into the night. He felt as useless as he had a few days ago. Like a child again, he stood there unable to participate in the battle. He turned to walk back into the castle as he had promised and headed up the long stairway leading up to the tower toward his room. His heart was full of sadness once again. He missed his father and wondered where he was. He missed the Dragon and knew it would not live much longer. Peter wondered if he would ever see the Dragon again and tell of his adventures to all the people, but he did know one thing for certain: He would never forget the Dragon of the Forest. This thought brought a smile to his face as he rushed up the stairs to look out the window of the tower.

Then a concern stopped him dead in his tracks. The book. *What was in it?* Now would be the time to take it, hide, and read it until the battle started.

Peter ran toward his father's study when he heard the voices of several people coming down the hall after him. Knowing a secret doorway was behind a statue of his grandfather, Peter dashed across to the marble statue of a man staring down at him from atop a tall pedestal. When no one was in the hallway, he leaned on the statue which opened a doorway in the paneled wall behind him. Peter slipped inside and closed the door. Feeling his way down the dark stairs, Peter found his way to his father's study and pushed on the door into the room with all his strength. The wall opened to reveal his father's table and books.

Peter walked over to the cabinet behind the table and removed the large dusty book with the black leather binding. "Theádril," he said to himself. Then he picked it up and left the room through the doorway once again. The stairway was still darkened but harder to navigate with the large book in his arms. Its heaviness was almost unbearable, so he decided to stop there and begin reading it. But first he knew he needed light. Putting the book down, he raced out through the secret passageway to find a torch in the hallway. But several servants were hurrying down the hallway murmuring to themselves, so a few minutes went by before Peter made his exit. He grabbed a small chair in the hallway, pushed it over to a torch post, climbed on top of it to grab a torch. Then he ran back into the secret passageway.

So, Peter decided to head back to his father's study.

The room was silent as he entered. He lit a few candles with his torch and he scanned the room. All his father's books, leather-bound with gold lettering, faced him from their bookshelves: The history of the kingdom, astronomy, logic, and geography. One day these books would belong to him. But for now, only one book held his interest. With that, Peter found a chair and settled into its soft cushion. Then he peeled open the sticky yellowed pages of the book.

His grandfather's handwriting was hard to decipher at first, so Peter read the maps instead. *The Region of Glaussier* read the first map. Then, it read *Alexander's Region* followed by *Baldrieg Son of Glenthryst's Region.*

"Fascinating," Peter whispered. He had never seen the regions laid out before him in this way before. The lands were great, and he was so small. *Could the world be this big?* He continued to flip through the maps until he reached the section titled, *The Swords of Bedlam.*

"In the beginning, Lord Bedlam's generous gift was graciously received. But in due time the truth behind the gifts was revealed to Aléon son of Illiath," Peter read aloud.

"Ten swords were given to the rulers of the ten regions. These gifts of peace were meant to unite the Kings of Theádril for eternity as a bond of brotherhood from Lord Bedlam," Peter continued reading. He flipped a few more pages until he found illustrations in ink of all the swords. The details of the drawings were impressive. The carvings on each blade were unique to each ruler and the hilts of the swords were made of gold with inlaid ivory. The drawings were labeled according to the ruler of each region. Peter flipped the pages again when suddenly he found the section titled *The Dragon Forest.*

His heart beat faster as he recognized the artist's depiction of the Dragon. Its likeness was exact. Peter recognized the eyes of his friend.

"Until the time of the swords, the skies were clear and the winds were mild. The rains came with such prediction, that the harvests were always plentiful. The moon set the tides and peace ruled the lands. But the times changed. I felt it in the winds. There was no denying this fact: something had changed," Peter read.

"Darkness fell upon the lands as the storms came along with the cold wind. Crops ceased as the earth grew hard from the cold winds. The dark clouds forming over the Black Hills could be seen as far as Niahmir to the sea." The hairs on Peter's neck began to stand up.

"I sought the Dragon of the Forest," Peter read on. He froze. He had forgotten that his grandfather lived in peace with the Dragon. *But I thought no man could enter the forest and live.* Peter thought of the legend. *Perhaps some may enter while others may not.*

"Its wise counsel had helped us before; I believed it could help us again. I wanted to know the truth about the swords of Bedlam."

"'You have been deceived,' the Dragon spoke. 'Bedlam will strike at the opportune moment. You have been warned,' said the beast from the darkness of the forest."

Peter closed the book. *Bedlam,* he thought. He became frightened. He rubbed the leather cover of the large book with his small hand. Peter decided it was time for him to read further about his past. He was older now and he knew he could handle the truth. So, he peered into the ancient book for clues about his father, Bedlam, and the swords.

He opened the cover of the book yet again. He was concerned. The first subject he saw in the book was an overlay of the lands of Theádril. Inside were maps of all ten regions drawn in great detail. "This must have taken them years to complete," Peter whispered. Listed on the maps were the names of each ruler. Peter recognized each name even though he himself never met these men. But he had heard his father speak of them many times. Now they were becoming more real to Peter as he read. His eyes glanced toward Illiath, the land of his father, the land he would someday rule as King. The map showed all the familiar shires and glens Peter had ridden through on Titan, but now these lands were burnt and scarred from battle. *What of this battle?* Peter thought. Lord Caragon came to his mind.

As more pages turned, Peter struggled to read the languages his grandfather had written, but the drawings and delineations of the castles, regions, and dragons were marvelous to see. They stirred his imagination. Suddenly, Peter realized what it was his grandfather and great-grandfather had lived through: the time of the dragons scorching the earth. Images of the battles raced through his mind. The details in the drawings were so precise it was as if the artist had personal knowledge of each sort of dragon. With rows of wickedly sharp teeth and large eyes set deeply in sockets lined with course scales, these beasts looked fierce. Some were small with thin wings while others were larger with longer necks. But the Great Dragon of the Forest was the biggest of them all with a wingspan and body that outmeasured the rest. Peter understood why it was no coincidence that this Dragon ruled over all the land.

More pages revealed more intriguing secrets of the kingdom Peter thought he knew so well. Some pages had notes in a familiar handwriting written in the margins. Peter recognized it as his father's printing. It was scrawled carelessly alongside the writings and drawings. Peter turned the book so he could read what it said. *Near the Cornshire,* the King wrote. Later, down the page, Peter frowned at the name *Peregrine* scribbled in the margin. At the bottom of the page was the word *compass.*

Peter stopped reading. "Compass?" he said. He felt for the compass in his pocket and slowly removed it. Holding it up to the candlelight, he studied it carefully. *Could this be the compass father was writing about?* There was nothing extraordinary about it. It was made of gold with some scroll work along the sides. Peter slowly opened it to reveal its contents. The lid held no writings or scrollwork to be seen and the compass was pointing north as usual. *Guess not*, Peter thought. Then he returned it to his pocket.

He turned a few more pages and noticed drawings of the ogres of the Theádron Desert and a map of the region. He flipped through a few more pages and then, before his eyes, he saw the name of his mother: Laurien. A most beautiful name Peter stopped reading and tried to remember her face. The pages before him told of her marriage to the King, the birth of Peter, her illness, and untimely death in the castle. Peter swallowed hard as he read the words describing his mother and her death. The word *mysterious vial* was scribbled in the margin.

But what disturbed him the most was the name *Peregrine* written in the margin in his father's handwriting. Was his father trying to tell the reader something? Was Peregrine involved somehow in his mother's death? This became too upsetting for Peter as Peregrine's angry face appeared in his mind. Peter slammed the ancient book shut, and dust diffused through the air in that dimly lit room.

He knew there was a reason for the book; it was not just an historical tome written for posterity's sake. It contained secrets meant for certain eyes only, his imagination stirred even more now that he knew. But the maps intrigued him. Drawn so many years before and in such great detail, Peter wanted to study them all the more. *How could someone capture all that detail? It's as if they had hovered above the land and sketched it all. But how?* Peter tried to picture it in his mind.

Then he remembered the map he and Will had found. He opened the book to see the map once again, but he could not find it within the old pages. He turned page after page, but still, no map. He put the book down and looked all around the floor with his candle as his light. He looked on tables, chairs, and in book cases, but still no map. He stood, confused, in the silence of the room. He could faintly hear the sounds of the people in the courtyard preparing for the battle. He wondered about Will and where he was. Then, his eyes widened.

"Will!" He shouted. He remembered that Will had come back to the room for his belt. He searched his father's study—the cabinet, the table, and the papers on the table—but he could not find the map. "He had to have taken it, but why?"

§

Shutters were closed at the Keep and nailed shut. Women who had helped at the infirmary were now being sent down to the dungeon. All those left in the courtyard were some older men who helped the smith get his weapons to the garrisons of soldiers running to take their positions at the east and west gates. The shepherd's gate was being sealed shut as the animals were corralled into their stables. Horses neighed and reared up. Will knew the animals could sense the storm that was coming. He ran over to the captain and asked where he could fight.

"Will!" the captain shouted. "I am glad you are here. Where is the Prince?"

"Safe inside the castle. Where shall I go for the battle?"

"I need you at the east gate. Climb the ladder and wait atop the castle wall. Guard the gate and keep an eye out on anything that tries to topple it. No one enters that gate, understand?" the captain ordered with fierce eyes.

"Yes, sir." Will raced to the east gate with his orders, glad to assist the captain, soldiers, and, ultimately, the King.

Upon reaching the destination, he spotted hundreds of foot soldiers preparing to climb the outer wall over the gate. Many had been wounded in the last fight, but with blood stained bandages over their wounds, they bravely continued to climb the ladders with swords and bows in hand. Their armor, still muddied and dented from battle, made it difficult to climb to the top. Many only wore their breastplates.

At the top of the outer wall, Will stood amazed at the sight of the men preparing for battle. Few had ever seen such a sight. He sighed. "I do believe I will never forget this moment."

The sky was a deep purple. The smell of rain was thick in the air as the wind picked up its strength, sending the clouds racing through the sky at an urgent pace. The clouds swept over the glowing moon, but it remained unveiled. Will grinned at the moon. He knew they would need the illumination of the moon for battle in the dark desert hills.

Below the wall, Will caught sight of the ogres moving many catapult mangonels and mantlets into place near the gate. Their brute strength was greatly appreciated by the captains. They alone could stack several piles of large stones that the soldiers found impossible to move. Each ogre worked hard to help protect the castle wall facing the east. Will surveyed the hills toward Theádron Desert where the ogres made their homes. Darkened from the approaching night, the desert hills lay still and silent. No creature stirred this night. Will shivered and rubbed his arms more from fright than the cold. The terror that awaited the King's men was uncertain and that uncertainty began to paralyze him with fear.

Suddenly, a trumpet blasted, severing the silent stillness of the night. The main drawbridge lowered. Will heard the shouts of the men from the courtyard when a soldier approached from the northern outer wall. Will's courage returned to his body and flowed through his veins.

"The King!" the soldier shouted. "The King has been spotted! He approaches from the north."

Will ran along the stone wall following the young messenger. There, he found Constable Darion ordering the gate to be raised for the King. "Will!" the constable said. "The King rides from the north!" He pointed over the wall and out to the darkened hills. There Will saw the King riding on his tan horse with a white owl perched on his arm. When Will saw the owl, he remembered Peter's description of the Dragon's eyes—"with the eyes of an owl"—and wondered.

Everyone in the kingdom cheered their sovereign as he approached. One soldier ran to tell those in the dungeon that their King had returned. All the fear Will had felt was gone as he watched the King ride swiftly toward the main gate. A soldier grabbed the reins of the King's horse to steady it.

The King did not dismount nor did the white owl leave its perch on his arm. Instead, he spoke with Constable Darion and his captains in the busy courtyard. Will could see the King ordering his men to take their positions. The owl flapped its wings to steady itself as the King spoke.

Then, as swiftly as he entered, the King exited the courtyard. The clopping of the horse's hoofs on the wooden bridge could be heard atop the outer wall. Will and the soldiers watched the King ride toward the desert hills, toward the feint torches of the men from the Crow Valley cutting through the darkness. Farther to the west, the torches of Caragon's men continued to make their way down the rocky Black Hills through the clefts in the stones and gorges of the dark valley.

§

Alexander heeled his horse to gallop faster. Then, lifting his arm high into the air, he gestured for the owl to disembark and fly away into the night. The owl opened its wings and soared high into the air away from the King. Grabbing the reins with both hands, Alexander leaned forward into the horse's stride and disappeared into the desert hills leaving his kingdom behind him.

The fall rains began to fall onto the dry desert land as the soldiers from the east and Crow Valley marched on. The water drops pelted their armor and they leaned into the winds that gathered force as they made their way over the hills. The cold air shocked their exposed skin moistened from sweat, but they kept moving forward, holding their spears and shields. The runner told their captain about the battle in the desert and the castle siege. The people of the Crow Valley had seen the signal fire burning so they waited for word about the siege. They had lived in fear of Caragon's men for many years and they knew the time had come to finally end his reign. The King's messenger explained the plan for attack as the men gathered around him eager for word about the kingdom of Alexander.

He was met with curious faces of men willing to risk all for the sake of the kingdom. The men took up bow and arrows as well as swords and spears as they made their way toward the desert lands. As they marched through all that remained of the Cardion Valley, they were stunned to see the carcasses of the wolf-like creatures and giant crows among the burned homes and stables. The stench of death was thick in the air when the rains came. The winds of autumn blew in from the east, bringing a sting of cold to their faces. Yet they continued their march to the desert hills where they would meet their king. To the north stood the Dragon Forest, silent lo these many years. Not knowing if they would ever hear from the mysterious beast within the walls of the trees, they kept marching. There was too much to lose now to ever turn back.

"Do you think the Dragon will come out and help us?" one man asked.

"Stop talking nonsense," another answered. "There is no Dragon."

The rest kept silent and marched forward to meet their fate. Not one man had ever fought alongside the King. All their fathers and grandfathers had known battle for the land, but while Alexander ruled, they had not known war on these lands. The east shore was their life and livelihood. There was no reason to leave it until now. To the south they saw the castle of Alexander. The younger ones had never seen the fortress, even though their fathers and grandfathers helped build it. Now they would see it rising from the southern hills like the sun at dawn. The skies were dark, but the torches along the outer walls of the castle illuminated it like a beacon.

"Look!" one soldier shouted as he pointed to the south. "The King's castle!"

All the men turned to see the grey stone fortress lined with hundreds of points of light glittering like sunlight on the waters off the eastern shores. The sight brought hope to their hearts as they walked among the ruins of the villages. To know the kingdom had survived the siege was a great comfort to the younger ones. They would soon learn whether or not the King had lived to fight alongside them at all. The march would continue as the waxing moon gave its light through the racing clouds as the storms grew. The rains came down harder now as they went through the gorge. Water began to collect in the deep end of the gorge forming a small running river. Many of the men fell as they waded through the rushing waters, but none were lost that night to the rain. Their fate lay at the hands of Caragon's men who marched down the Black Hills.

Alexander waited at the other end of the gorge. He spotted the men of the east making their way to the other side. Their captain spotted the King and ran to meet him. As the rain pelted his face, he tried to reassure the King that all his men were present and ready to fight. Man after man struggled up the side of the gorge with their weapons and torches held firmly in hand.

The King counted them as each climbed out and stood on the hill beneath him. Then Alexander turned to the west to see the men of the Crow Valley making their way over the hills. Their torches lit up the desert sands and cast their shadows onto the dirt beneath their muddied boots. He counted them as well. The total of men the King counted passed three hundred and fifty from the Crow Valley and nearly four hundred were making their way from the eastern shore, with more coming. Ultimately, they would number in the thousands by nightfall. He knew many men from the east had sailed out to find safer lands that night, but the men who answered his call would suffice. He inspected the men who stood before him with their captains. Their weapons were sturdy and their armor, although wet from the storm, was strong and would hold. But the King knew in his heart that the enemy they all would face was still a mystery. The men did not know of the evil he had seen earlier that day, but they would soon find out what Caragon was devising these many years at Hildron.

King Alexander took the sword of his father out of its sheath. As the light from the torches caught the metal blade, the men saw the mystical sword they had heard about in their youth.

"The sword of Alexander," one young man said in awe.

The men stared at the famous blade given to Aléon of Illiath by Lord Bedlam many moons ago. The gold and ivory handle glistened in the light as Alexander held it up in the air. The sword of Kings, although ancient, still had the carvings on the blade and gave the men hope that they could defeat the evil before them that night. The men around them shivered as their breath rose into the night sky. They lined themselves along the edge of the gorge and awaited word from their captains. Their torches lit up their faces as the King inspected their lines. Their eyes told their tales of eager preparations for this battle. After the inspection, the King ordered his captains to meet with him nearby.

"Alexander, my old friend," shouted a man who came walking from within the ranks.

King Alexander turned to see Aluein, son of Gural, from the Crow Valley, where Glaussier the Brave ruled, walking toward him.

"Aluein," Alexander said as he walked to his old friend with arms extended. "It has been too long." The two men grasped each other hard. "I knew you would answer the call."

"Of course," Aluein said. "When would I pass up a chance to fight? You know me too well."

Aluein of Gural had fought alongside the King when they were but two youths at the Battle of the Cornshire. They, along with Peregrine, had been taught the ways of war with the sword and lance. Shorter and a few years older than Alexander with a full beard of graying brown hair, Aluein was a graceful fighter with the lance and ax, and he was more powerful than any warrior

Alexander had known. Peregrine was more cerebral in his fight, but Aluein had the power, the brute strength. The graying beard was soaked now from the rain. Aluein wore his father's crest on his red tunic and a helmet of a general. He was Alexander's best warrior, now that Peregrine was gone. Alexander was grateful to see his old friend at a time when they needed the best of the lands surrounding the castle.

"We saw the signal coming from the castle. But my father, who received your letter days ago, wanted to wait. Stubborn old fool," Aluein said as he removed his pipe from his belt. Then, he lit the pipe in the cold rain. After a few inhales, the grey silky smoke rose from the pipe into the night air. Alexander noticed two swords and a small ax were attached to Aluein's belt and he remembered these were his friend's weapons of choice.

"I gathered as many of my men as I could," Aluein said. "We hid the women and the children and then left into the dales of the valley yesterday."

Just then, a loud caw of a black crow could be heard above them. All the soldiers looked up to see the bird lift off a branch of a dead tree. As it disappeared into the black sky, its caw echoed throughout the plains.

Aluein's eyes narrowed. "It has followed us since we left our village."

"Caragon," Alexander whispered as he watched the bird fly off.

"What of this mad man?" Aluein asked. "The last time I saw him he was being sent into exile alone and frightened, crying for his mother, if I remember correctly!"

"Frightened, perhaps," Alexander said as he walked back toward the gorge. "But not alone."

As he walked he placed his sword back into its sheath.

"I see you still have your father's sword." Aluein said.

"Aye," Alexander answered. "And yours?"

"Ha!" Aluein grumbled. "Folklore! I stored it away long ago."

"Good," the King said. "The time for the ten swords has not yet come. But it is near."

"As long as you believe," his old friend said. "That's all that matters." He patted his sovereign on the shoulder and puffed his pipe once more. The smoke must not have gone down easily because he gasped and coughed. This made Alexander smile.

"I have to believe, Aluein," Alexander said. "It is all that I have left." Sorrow filled his eyes while he remembered his late wife.

"And the boy?" Aluein asked about Peter.

"He is safe inside the castle," the King answered.

"What of the book?" Aluein asked.

"It is also safe. But I am not certain we will need it. Not yet."

"Good. Peter will make a fine sovereign one day, Alexander," Aluein said.

"Yes, if there is a kingdom left to rule," Alexander said with a sigh.

"Come now, this isn't all that bad, eh?"

Alexander stared deeply into his friend's eyes. "I am afraid it is much worse than we believed."

"Tell me," Aluein insisted.

Alexander went on to explain what they had fought in the Cardion Valley and near the castle. He told of the wild dog-like beasts and the giant crows. Then he explained about the ghost knights and Peregrine rising from the dead before his eyes.

"This is no ordinary magic, Aluein," he said. "This is something I have never seen before: dead men rising and fighting."

"And what of the Dragon?" Aluein said as he puffed his pipe. "Any news of it?"

"Aye," Alexander said as he kicked the ground with his boot. "I have seen it."

"And lived to tell?" Aluein said with a smile.

Alexander grinned back. "It is no folklore, my old friend."

Aleuin motioned for one of his men to come to him where they stood. "I sent many scouts into the Hildron castle," he said. "Nine scouts went in, and only six came back."

The King was enthralled with this news. "And what did they find?"

He was excited to see that Aluein did believe that Caragon was suspiciously planning something in the Black Hills. At times, the King felt he was the only one who sensed it. As Aluein began to tell of what his scouts discovered, one of his men made his way over to the general and the King.

"The scout reported to me of his findings," he said as he patted the young man on the shoulders. "Explain to your King what you found."

The scout bowed before Alexander before beginning his explanation.

"We made our way through the black rock of the hills and into the Hildron kingdom. I was able to climb over the outer wall. The air was thick with smoke and fire. The heat was overwhelming, but I managed to peer over the walls."

"And what did you see?" the King asked.

"Creatures," he said. "Fierce creatures dressed in black armor were marching in rows. They were given swords and lances of a black metal I had never seen before. Their banners were made of black cloth with a crest unfamiliar to me."

Alexander nodded. "Go on," he said.

"The wizard, Caragon, led them toward the gates. They were creatures of every size with twisted faces. They looked like men in former lives, yet they lived."

"Walking dead?" Alexander asked. "I have seen them as well."

"I saw beasts, wolf-like creatures as well as flying creatures," the soldier continued.

"Black crows?" Alexander asked.

"No, my Lord. These creatures were like bats," he explained. "Only larger."

"Flying creatures," Aluein shook his head and murmured as he smoked his pipe. Puffs of smoke rose into the night air as the men talked. "Baroks and Zadoks come back from extinction. Hard to believe."

"And then I made my way down the mountain side before they could see me," the scout finished.

Alexander appreciated the report and told the man so. His eyes stared far off into the distance. Now he knew what they would soon face in battle. Wondering if they were prepared, he walked up and down the ranks inspecting his men. He looked deep into their faces. They were cold. Some had fear in their eyes. Most were ready to begin the surge down the hills.

"So young," he whispered.

"Aye," Aluein said, "But they are ready, my Lord."

Aluein walked over to his sovereign. "I have seen to it that they have been trained for this battle for many moons. I myself have trained them. I can assure you, they are ready for this fight. As for the men of the east that I cannot say."

"We are ready for this fight, my Lord," an experience captain from the east interrupted as he walked over to the King. "I assure you, my men will fight." He glared at Aluein disapprovingly.

"We shall see," Aluein challenged as his teeth held the pipe in his mouth.

The King looked at the men before him with gratitude. He knew not all would return home. He also knew they understood the cost of this battle. "You are free men now," he said pointing to the west. "Caragon breeds slaves on his mountain. These creatures have no souls, but you do. You know what you left behind and what awaits you should you fail."

The men raised their swords and shouted in one accord. This pleased the King.

"Caragon has nothing to lose in this battle," he continued. "He is a mindless slave of another. But you, you know what you have to lose." He paced back and forth in front of the ranks. "Think back to your homes, your families. Think long and hard on the life you had before you marched here. I have seen the enemy we face. They are wicked and dark. There is no life in their eyes...only death. I have fought against the dead. They fight with swords and spears as you do, but yet they are dead."

The men eyed each other in the cold night air.

"Caragon uses his twisted magic to forge weapons. But they are primitive. I have seen them. They are no match for our swords or our spears...and our hearts. His fighters are not the warriors I see before me now," Alexander shouted.

The men raised their swords once again and whooped loudly.

"You are the warriors here. You have trained to fight this day to preserve all that you have waiting for you at home. I know you will fight for your King, for your lands, and for your honor. Because I know, that *you* know what will happen if you do not fight and answer this call!"

With that he raised his sword, the sword of his father, high into the air to rally his men. Their eyes caught the shining blade as it lifted into the black sky lit only by the faint light of the torches. Many of them had heard of the Swords of Bedlam, but they had never seen one. The skin on their necks shivered in the cold air and from the excitement. They answered with a rallying call that could be heard at the castle.

The King and Aluein strode past the soldiers and up a small hill, from which they could see the plains and the torches of the approaching enemy through the light rain. "I cannot count how many there are," Alexander said. "But I do know we did not kill all the men in the last battle. Many fled back into the desert plains toward Hildron."

As they watched, the lights of the torches lined up straight in rows.

"Battle positions," Aluein said. "They are preparing to advance. We should extinguish our torches. No need giving them our numbers now."

He ordered the captains to extinguish all the torches of his men. Unfortunately, this would remove any warmth the men derived from them. They obeyed and shivered in the night air.

"The cold and rain will hinder us," Alexander said. "We must line the men up now before they become too cold."

"What of the castle?" Aluein asked.

"My constable is preparing for the siege."

"And Lord Byrén and the others?"

"They are hidden in the dungeon," the King answered. "All preparations have been made."

"Good," Aluein said. "Then let us get this bloody thing over with." He extinguished his pipe and tufted it back into his belt.

And with that he shouted orders to his men to form lines. The men ran into place with their swords ready. The sloshing of boots in the mud echoed in the night. The bowmen ran up ahead and knelt down in front of the line. The foot soldiers were next in line with their lances and shields ready. The sound of hundreds of men running into place in squads echoed through the plains as the shouts of their captains could be heard in the distance. Their footsteps were lit only by the faint moonlight above them.

A loud screech came from the darkness. The men looked up to see a white owl piercing through the dark like the full moon. Its eyes glowed in the darkness as it watched them. The sight was familiar to many of the men and gave them hope.

"The owl of winter," Aluein said as he pointed to the bird circling above them. "A good omen!"

The men shouted with approval and raised their swords into the air. King Alexander watched the owl fly in circles over the men, but he knew it was not the omen of the coming of winter. He knew it was a sign of something else. Deep in his heart, he knew the Dragon would be with them this night.

19 THE MARCH TO WAR

Will watched eagerly as his King rode off toward the desert plains. As he stood on the castle wall, he knew he was ready to face the beast: the enemy of Caragon's making. He gripped his sword as the rain pelted his face with its sting and cold. He took only a moment to turn toward the castle and gaze into the windows, looking for Peter inside. But as he inspected each window facing the outer wall, he did not see the ten-year-old boy pressed against the glass as he suspected he might. Instead, he saw Peter running out the main castle entrance into the courtyard with his arm raised above his head as he shouted something. *Oh no,* Will thought. *I told him to stay put!*

Will put his sword into its sheath and headed toward the ladders, but his captain stopped him.

"Will, where are you going? The battle is about to begin!" The captain shouted as he pointed toward the darkened desert.

The torches of the approaching enemy had begun to line up into battle positions and the King's men could be seen extinguishing their torches. Will knew this was the sign that the siege was starting, but he also knew he had to stop Peter and get him back inside the castle to safety. He had promised the King he would protect Peter.

Suddenly, as Will was about to explain his position on the ladder to his captain, both men stopped in their tracks as they listened to a most frightening noise from far above the castle courtyard. It seemed to come from the darkness and through the rain. The high pitched squealing sound was unlike any animal they had heard, but it was not of a dragon either.

"What in heaven's name was that?" The captain asked as he searched the black skies above him. Eerily, the rains stopped and the air was still. The screech sounded again but this time it seemed closer.

Will froze as he, too, searched through the blackness for the source of the wicked sound. "It sounds like a dying animal of some sort," he said.

The others agreed as they searched the darkness as well.

Then Will scanned the hills and saw the enemy moving. "Look!" He shouted as he pointed out toward the torches as they moved. Some soldiers ran to the edge of the wall and stared at the sight of all the torches in the distance. Not one of them imagined so many enemy troops advancing at once, especially after so many had been killed in the last battle.

In that instance, the high pitched squeal pierced the silence yet again, causing the men to cover their ears from the pain.

"Where is the creature?" some of the men asked. "Put it out of its misery!"

Silence followed. The men waited. The next squeal sounded closer. So close, in fact, that some of the men began to recognize what it was.

"Gizor," said the captain as he slowly backed away from the edge of the wall. His eyes never left the darkness as he searched for the mysterious creatures.

"What?" asked Will. "What is Gizor?"

"That!" the captain said as he pointed to the flying creature hovering before them. "Lord Bedlam's creation," the captain explained as he stared into the glowing eyes of the creature. He began to shout orders to his men to ready themselves. "I have seen these before," he shouted to the men. "Ready your bows and arrows!"

Will forgot Peter and everything else when he saw the flock of Gizor hovering above him. The creature, unlike anything he had ever seen, floated in midair. The sound of wings flapping and the smell of rotting flesh made Will shiver. He could not believe what he was seeing, but then he remembered the enemy they were fighting. The creature above him circled like a bat, but its wingspan was larger and its body was almost like that of a small man. The screech came again from the open mouth filled with rows of tiny sharpened teeth; it sent some men scrambling from fear.

The thunderous marching of the enemy came up over the hills. The creature glided through the air, keeping its yellow eyes on Will. A slight grin stretched over its grotesquely gaunt face as it flapped its leathery wings and curled its clawed feet. Then, as quickly as it appeared, it was gone. Will frantically looked back and forth trying to spot the creature, but he lost it in the darkness. Then suddenly there appeared before the castle walls several dozen of the flying Gizor making their high pitched squeal as though they were laughing at the sight of the King's men scrambling for cover.

The Gizor seemed to be waiting for orders to attack. Will tried to steady the men in response, but it was no use. They were too frightened by what they saw. The creatures continued to hover and wait with great patience.

Finally, they dove in like birds of prey with no mercy. Their clawed feet grabbed and scraped at the men as they ran and the creatures quickly grabbed swords and arrows from the frightened soldiers, dropping them to the ground outside the castle walls. Panic spread across the walls as men covered their ears in pain from the loud screeches. Will and the captain yelled to the men not to leave their posts, but to stand and fight. The captain ordered the bowmen to begin firing their arrows into the air to try and hit the creatures.

But it was no use. The Gizor numbered into the hundreds and flew far too fast, like bats. They dipped and fell through the air, then rose again on the wind beneath their leathery wings. Clumsy as they were, they were fast, too fast for the arrows. So the captain had to think of another way to stop the flying pests. Will waved his arms above his head to scare off the creatures as they swooped and screeched toward him. He gripped his sword and sliced through the air as one Gizor dove to him with its teeth gleaming in the night. Its yellow eyes with black pupils stared at Will almost daring him to strike its body.

Will met the challenge and lowered his sword through the air in one swift motion. The screech he heard wasn't like the ones before. It was a scream of pain. Will turned his head as hot black blood spattered his face and a leathery wing fell with a thump at his feet. The Gizor wing twitched before him without its owner.

Will ran to the wall and peered down over it to see the creature with one wing meet the ground with a sickening thud. But there was no time to celebrate as more of the mutant creatures swooped down and tore men's flesh with their claws and teeth. The soldiers swiped at the night with their swords, but the Gizor were too quick.

Will ran along the wall and grabbed a lit torch. He swiped at the creatures with the fire and with his sword as he ran. He ordered the men to stand still and let the creatures come to them. But the men mostly ran for their lives from the sight of the evil monsters coming at them. They were young and had never seen an enemy like this before.

Will decided to show them how to fight the flying monsters, so he stood firm with his sword and spotted a creature as it dipped toward him. He felt the cold air on his sweaty arms and in his lungs. His heart pounded so fast he thought it would surely burst from his chest, but he continued to stand firm as he waited.

"Come on!" He shouted. "Come and get me!" He stared into the eyes of the beast when it spotted him. It growled with claws opened and teeth glaring. Will waited for it to fly closer and it did. Then, with both hands tight around the grip of his sword, he swiped at the monster as it dove in for the kill. Once again, the hot blood of the Gizor splattered his skin. He opened his eyes in time to see the creature's body cut in half as it fell from the sky.

"That, my friends," Will huffed, "is how you kill a Gizor!"

The men around him shouted in unison, and then stood still there on the wall, waiting for the creatures to try and strike them. One by one the creatures did the only thing they knew how; they dove in to try and kill the soldiers. But their attempts failed one by one. The soldiers swiped with swords and torches and cut the Gizor down. Will grinned at the sight.

It was then he remembered Peter.

§

As the soldiers marched in darkness through the hills to meet the enemy, the rain stopped pelting their skin. But the cold air continued to weigh heavy in their lungs as their boots treaded through thick mud and slush. King Alexander led his men on horseback with his friend Aluein by his side. The breath of the horses appeared in the darkness, reminding the men of the cold. Yet they continued to march and settle into battle positions. Torches extinguished, men at the ready, and King Alexander with sword drawn, the battle was about to begin when the white owl screeched above the men, awakening the fear and trepidation within their souls. This was their time.

Ahead of them, the torches of the enemy stopped marching and formed battle positions. They were many in number. The King scanned the area. He sensed there would be more wickedness coming. The white owl continued to circle above them, and with a final screech, flew away toward the castle, signaling to the King to start the battle for Theádril now or forever lose what was rightfully his.

He watched the owl fly away toward the lights of the torches along the castle walls, hoping that it would keep his son safe. His thoughts flashed to the blue lake deep within the Dragon Forest and the images the Dragon had shown him. The face of his late wife came to the front of his mind. He could see her mouth moving as though trying to speak, but he could not hear her voice. His chest tightened as he remembered her untimely death on that sad night when he held her tightly until she breathed her last...

Alexander shook his head. He could not let himself think of such things at this time. Turning toward the enemy, and with a loud yell from the depths of his soul, he raised the sword of his father high above his head. His men answered the call with shouts in unison. But the enemy also met their calls with shouts of their own.

Suddenly, a loud, sickening screeching came from above them in the dark sky. The men searched the skies for the source of the screams, but couldn't see anything. The King was afraid the screams would distract his men from the fight. "Look lively, men!" he shouted to them.

Their gazes returned to their King mounted on his nervous horse. It whinnied and neighed its disapproval.

"Now, men! Move!" he ordered as he lowered his sword. The men dutifully began their march down the hills as they watched the enemy fighters begin their march.

"Move!" Aluein yelled to his men as he kicked his horse's ribs. The beast hesitantly moved forward as more screams echoed above in the night sky. Aluein had to hold tightly to the reins to keep control of his mount. He knew it was spooked by something unseen, but he also that knew the unseen had to be ignored. Caragon's desire was for the men to be afraid as they came over the hills, and Aluein knew this. "Keep marching, men!" he yelled.

The cadence of several thousand men marching in unison could be heard from the castle walls. Will watched as the King's men moved ahead into battle. "For King Alexander!" he yelled.

The soldiers along the wall shouted back in unison for their King.

§

Alexander, hearing the yelps coming from the castle, knew his men were fighting already. He could not see what it was they were fighting, but he knew he could not and would not let them down. He watched his men cautiously make their way down the muddy hills and into the desert valleys before the Black Hills.

Hildron Castle remained surrounded by glowing red fire and billows of smoke rising within its walls. He could faintly see some sort of activity rising from the castle, but he could not allow his focus to be on Hildron when he knew he had to maintain focus on the grotesque enemy put before him and his men. The soldiers were in place. Their positions were good.

Alexander prodded his horse, and it ran down the hill near the soldiers. They shouted as they watched their King gallop ahead of them to the front lines. He stopped his horse and turned it toward his men. He could not believe the sight before his eyes: thousands of men stood ready with swords and shields in hands stretching wide in the desert valley. Some had spears and others had bows and arrows ready to launch. Alexander ordered the arrows to be released into the night air. Then he and his men stood silent as the bowmen knelt and loaded their bows. Together they raised their bows and, on command, released the arrows toward the marching enemy.

Alexander turned to see the result of the arrows filtering down out of the sky. Some enemy fighters gripped the arrows as they penetrated their rotting flesh and fell to the ground twisting in agony. Others were able to dodge the falling arrows and continue marching.

"Steady, men," Alexander said. "Release the next round of arrows!"

More arrows shot through the sky as they watched more enemy fighters fall to the wet earth. But the King watched the surviving enemy fighters continue their march.

"Ready to fight?" he shouted.

All the men shouted back in return as they raised their swords high into the air. The sight gave Alexander great hope. He was young again in his heart. He was a lion ready to kill for the first time. His mind raced to Knight Training when he stood ready for his first joust.

Nudging his horse forward, he raised his sword and gave the order for them to move forward. Man after man ran with shouts of glory and swords glistening in the fire glow from the enemy torches. But it was Alexander who led them on his horse. It galloped fast through the mud and the King leaned forward to help it gain speed. He gripped his sword tighter as not to lose it in the fight. He knew he would need the sword of his father's when this was all over. He knew his son would wield it to keep the Theádril from falling.

§

Constable Darion grabbed his sword and swiped at the flying monsters diving at the men atop the castle walls. He sliced off a few wings and watched the wounded creatures fall to the ground. Their blood splattered the castle walls. The Gizor became macabre confetti littering the ground.

Darion then ran down to the ladder leading into the castle courtyard. As he grabbed it, his eyes caught a glimpse of Peter running into the courtyard. "Prince Peter!" He shouted hoping to get the young boy's attention.

Will heard the shout and searched the courtyard for Peter. He saw Darion quickly climbing down the ladder. Will decided to meet Darion at the ladder, but as he began to move, he felt a sharp pain in his shoulder. The pain was met with a tugging sensation when his tunic was pulled from behind. A creature had him by its claws. He could feel the black claws digging deep within his flesh and it burned. He screamed and tried to swipe his sword behind him, but the creature began to flap its wings. His feet leave the castle wall.

"No!" he shouted.

He knew that if the creature took him off the wall, he would be dropped to his death. Will grabbed at anything that he could find on the wall, but nothing was secured. Still the creature stubbornly flapped its wings and Will could feel the breeze lifting him. He decided to see if he could slip out of his tunic. He lifted up his arms and began to ease out of the fabric. He could feel his body moving downward, but the claws were still in his shoulder. He wriggled his body and used his arms to punch the legs of the creature all the while shifting out of his tunic. The creature screamed as its legs were being punched and pulled. Will finally used his sword to swipe at the Gizor's legs and it worked. He could smell the familiar pungent stench of the black blood as it spattered. He felt the claw open and release his shoulder. He fell to the ground and watched the wounded monster fly off with his tunic still in its claws, but it was bleeding and falling to the ground. Will sat on the castle wall heaving and clenching his shoulder. He knew he was bleeding, but he still had to reach Peter. He stood up and felt a rush of dizziness come over him. He fell to the right, but grabbed the wall to steady himself.

Darion made his way down the ladder clumsily, grasping his sword in his right hand. But he lost its grip and it fell to the ground. Just then, he could hear the screech of a creature above him. Gripping the ladder, Darion looked up toward the top rung only to find a Gizor wickedly grinning back at him while it held the ladder within its grasp. For a moment, the two stared at each other knowing what was about to happen.

Will regained his composure in time to see the creature grab hold of the ladder. Will looked over the wall to see Constable Darion still on the ladder several feet above the ground. He knew what the creature was going to do.

"No!" he shouted as he ran to stop the creature from releasing the ladder. It turned when it heard Will shout, but Will stumbled from the pain in his shoulder.

Darion, still twenty feet from the ground, began to quickly climb down, but it was too late. He felt the ladder pull away from the castle wall as he turned to see the courtyard. He decided to jump and improve his chances of landing safely on the ground. But when he hit the dirt, he could feel his bones break and his legs go numb.

Will helplessly watched Darion fall to the ground as the creature flew down to meet the wounded constable. It tore at his flesh with its claws and teeth. Darion screamed. Will looked for another ladder but could not find one. All he could do was watch the King's faithful servant be attacked by the evil creature. Darion kicked and jabbed at the creature until his strength left his body and he could fight no more. The Gizor dove in for the last time to end the fight, but something stopped it midflight. It hovered over Darion's still and wounded body, but its eyes had caught a glimpse of something else.

At that instant, Will turned and saw a young boy running in the courtyard. He knew that if *he* saw Peter, the creature also saw Peter.

§

Peter made his way through the courtyard, all the while hearing the screeching from the creatures as they flew. He knew he had made a mistake. He had promised Will he would stay inside the castle, yet here he was once again in harm's way. Stopping to find a hiding place, Peter heard his name being shouted above all the noise. He looked up at the castle wall in time to see Constable Darion climbing down the ladder.

Peter did not know what to do. *Should I stay and hide or run to meet the constable?* That's when the creature had grabbed the ladder and hurled it to the ground with the constable still on it. Peter had watched as Darion hit the ground with a loud thud, then searched frantically for a place to hide from the creature. Only buckets and barrels could be found. He turned to see the blacksmith's hut and decided whether to hide inside. He could hear Darion's groans of pain.

Peter took off and ran toward the blacksmith's hut, but he tripped over a small bucket filled with water. Picking himself up off the ground, he felt something staring at him. He looked to his left and then to his right, but did not see anyone. He glanced down at his knee and watched a trickle of blood drop from a small scrape. Then the feeling of someone or something watching him grew stronger. He slowly raised his head. There, hovering above the courtyard, was a hideous flying creature with wings flapping and sinewy legs dangling from its body. It had the body of a small human but with the skin and head like that of a bat. Its glowing yellow eyes were fixed on Peter's every movement. As their eyes met, the Gizor's skin stretched over its bony face, forming a menacing grin revealing sharp teeth still stained with the constable's blood. Peter's entire body shook at the sight. There was nowhere to hide from this thing, but he also knew he had to try.

Still in a staring contest with the creature, Peter's mind raced. Perhaps he could make it to the blacksmith's hut and find a weapon. He knew he had to try. He counted in his head. *One, two, three...*

§

With Gizor screeches still permeating the cold night sky, King Alexander rode on swiping through the air with his sword. He could hear his men behind him running toward the enemy fighters who were now running to meet them. As his heart pounded and his horse galloped, Peter's face came to Alexander's mind. He could see his son and he remembered why he was fighting. With a lunge forward, the King lowered his sword and met the flesh of an enemy fighter. Its arm flew off at the shoulder sending its spear into the sky. Leaning to the left, Alexander repeated the swipe and sent another limb flying. He yelled loudly as more fighters ran to him, only to be cut underfoot by his horse's hooves. He could hear Aluein's steed gaining on him from behind as well as the yells from his men as their metal weapons clashed with the enemy.

"For Theádril!" yelled Aluein as he sliced through the enemy with his ax, sending dead fighters flying left and right. He felt a sharp pain in his arm as he raised his ax. He winced as an arrow had met his flesh, but he could not let it stop him. He yanked the reins to turn his horse, but he felt dizzy and lost his balance. Off his horse he flew.

Alexander pivoted in time to see his friend in peril. "No!" the King screamed.

He yanked the reins and turned his horse around. The beast panted from exhaustion, but it galloped to where Aluein lay. Alexander dismounted and ran to his friend's aid. Aluein slowly rose to his feet in time to meet an enemy fighter as he lunged toward him with a sharp lance. The blade just missed his jaw as Aluein moved to the right. Then he lowered his ax with all the strength he had left and found its resting place in the sinewy shoulder of the enemy. He watched it land on the wet ground with a splash. But another of Caragon's Barok fighters was behind it with a sharp spear.

Alexander arrived in time to meet the enemy's spear as it was thrown toward Aluein. The King swiped the spear with his sword and sent it flying away from his friend.

But Aluein fell to the ground in pain from the arrow. "The enemy's a good shot, I'm afraid."

"My friend," Alexander cried. He held Aluein in his arms. Several soldiers came to his aid and protected him from the approaching enemy. He had to leave his friend and fight the good fight for the kingdom.

Aluein stumbled to his feet again and grabbed his ax out of the dead creature just in time to meet an approaching mutant fighter. He flung the ax, and it met the enemy's chest dead on, sinking deeply into bone and muscle and splattering thick blood all over the ground. The dead Barok fell back, clutching his chest in one last act of futility.

"You see, I am a good shot too," Aluein joked to the soldiers as he gathered his strength. The arrow in his arm ached, but he could not let that stop his fight. He grabbed the wood sticking out of his arm and broke it off with a loud yelp. Then, he removed his knife from his belt, and, sighting Alexander ahead, ran into the enemy. He lifted his head and ordered his men to fight with him. As he ran by the dead Barok, he pulled his small ax out of its chest with a sickening sound and sprinted toward the King.

Together Aluein and his men ran into the approaching enemy head on with swords raised. The enemy fought with fierce yet controlled anger. Their eyes were glowing red. They appeared to be men and yet they did not look like any men Aluein had ever seen. They seemed neither alive nor dead, but they fought as though under a spell. Something more powerful than Caragon was behind their existence.

Aluein ran with the ax in one hand and knife in the other, slashing his way through the Baroks coming toward him. He lowered his knife and cut through the wooden handle of a spear, then swung his ax into the soft underbelly of the creature as he tried to run. When he retrieved the blade, more dark blood gushed out as the creature fell dead in the mud.

"Hideous beasts!" Aluein picked up his ax. He turned to see Alexander fighting off several enemy fighters, so he ran to help.

Still slicing through the air at anything that moved toward them, Alexander and his men fought off the enemy fighters as they pushed them back toward Hildron. Lances flew through the air and swords clashed together sending men to the ground dead. Alexander turned to the left to thwart off an attack. He pushed the fighter off his body with his legs and thrust his sword into its chest. He retracted the blade from the beast and immediately turned to the right and pushed it into another fighter as it lowered its sword. Alexander's blade met the creature's neck, sending it to the ground. He stared into the Barok's glowing eyes as they suddenly went dark.

Breathing heavily, Alexander could see they were advancing even closer to Hildron. He could feel the heat from the fire within the castle walls. He turned to see his men fighting behind him. They cut through the enemy with ease. Yet, deep inside, he knew this was only the beginning. Caragon was drawing them in closer, but why? The King had yet to figure out Caragon's plan. He felt a twinge of pain coming from his battle wound and it made him wince. But he knew he had to continue.

"We shouldn't be so close to the castle!" the King shouted.

"Why not?" Aluein asked.

"I do not trust Caragon. Who knows what evil he will unleash next? We should pull the men back," said the King. He did not want to order a retreat, but he shouted to his men, "Pull back!"

They turned to see their King looking at the castle walls. The men were shocked at how close they were to Hildron and the Black Hills already. The orange glow from the inferno that was the castle lit up the area around them and cast long shadows over the hills. The whole desert valley seemed aglow with fire. The men felt uneasy about their position.

Immediately, they obeyed their King's orders. The enemy, exhausted from the fight, pulled back as well. There were no shouts of victory or glory. Both sides were too tired to shout.

Aluein looked for his horse, but could not spot it in the battle. Alexander called for his and the animal came running toward him. He quickly mounted the horse and galloped off to direct his men back into the hills.

Aluein ran as fast as he could while shouting orders to his men to pull back. Suddenly, he spotted his horse lying dead in the mud. Several arrows had pierced its large grey body. His shoulders sank at the sight, but he shook his grief off, knowing there was no time to grieve. The battle waged on.

§

Peter leapt with all his might toward the small hut as the Gizor screeched and dove toward him, teeth glaring and its claws ready to grab Peter's flesh. But Peter made it inside the hut in time. The creature to swooped away from the blacksmith's hut. Peter frantically searched inside for a weapon of some sort. He finally found a dagger lying on the ground. As he reached for it, the creature swept down and grabbed Peter's foot with its sharp claws. Peter screamed at the pain. With wings flapping, it pulled Peter out of the hut and into the courtyard, but Peter turned on his back and swiped its foot with the sharp blade. The cut made the Gizor screech loudly.

Will watched from atop the castle wall. He turned to his right to find a ladder, but he could not see one. He saw Peter still fighting off the strange creature. Its wings flapped as it pulled harder and harder, but Peter still slashed with his knife. Will couldn't wait any longer. He grabbed a thick rope lying on the wall and wrapped it around his waist. Then he called to a soldier to hold it securely as he climbed down the wall. The soldier gripped the rope and helped Will rappel down the castle wall. Slipping and scraping his knees several times in his haste to save Peter, Will made it to the ground in one piece.

Untying the rope from his waist, Will ran to Peter's aid. His bare shoulder was still bleeding from his own encounter with a Gizor, but he knew he couldn't stop for pain. He had forgotten his sword on the wall, so when he made it to the creature, he grabbed one of its legs and yanked as hard as he could. The creature had small hands at the ends of the wings and these small hands had very small but very sharp claws. Out of fear for its life, it scraped Will across his face with a swipe of the small hand. Will let go of the leg and grabbed his cheek. He could feel his blood seep out of the cut, but he continued to fight. Peter continued slicing at the leg of the creature with his small knife and the Gizor's screams could be heard from the top of the wall.

A bowman turned to see the fight between Will, Peter, and the flying monster. He also spotted several more of the Gizor flying over the courtyard; they seemed ready to dive in on the action below. So, the bowman grabbed an arrow from his quiver and loaded his bow. He aimed at the beast with Peter in its grasp, but it was moving too frantically. He didn't want to hit Peter or Will, but he also knew he had to try and stop the fight before the Prince was hurt or killed. Taking a deep breath and holding it in, he carefully took aim. Then, slowly pulling the arrow back, exhaled, and released it. It soared through the air toward its mark.

The arrow hit the creature square in the middle of its back. It screeched a high-pitched scream and tried to grab the arrow from between its shoulders, but it could not reach it. Letting go of Peter's foot, the creature tried to fly away, but Will grabbed Peter's knife and ended the incessant screaming once and for all. He dug the knife deep within the body of the flying monster and its wings stopped sputtering instantly.

Will then grabbed Peter up into his arms and ran toward the stairway leading to the dungeon. He knew there were more creatures waiting to dive in for the kill and there was no time to waste. Peter held tightly to Will's neck as they headed to the darkened stairway. He spotted the blood pouring out of Will's cheek. Suddenly, there were more screams. The screams were louder and fiercer. Will stopped and slowly turned with Peter still in his arms. He raised his eyes and saw before him the most frightening sight.

Hovering above the courtyard, like ghouls from a nightmare, were hundreds more of the wicked Gizor ready to attack what were left of the soldiers and bowmen.

A shiver went up Will's spine from fear and the cold night air on his bare back. He knew he had to get Peter to safety. He spotted the staircase and ran down the stone steps groping for the door. Upon finding the door in the darkened hallway, he put Peter down and together they pounded on the door and begged for it to be opened.

The commotion out in the courtyard—the screeches of the creatures and the flapping of their wings in the night air—was too hard for the curious villagers to ignore. When they opened the door and raised their torches to see who was knocking, they saw the Prince and Will and quickly helped them inside. But before they closed the wooden door, they heard a different sound coming from the courtyard. It didn't sound like the screams of the Gizor from before. The screeching came from each corner of the castle, as though it were moving through the sky.

Will ran back up the darkened stone steps and halted the top of the stairway, his mouth agape. Flying over the courtyard were hundreds of falcons with talons glaring, led by the whitest owl he had ever seen. Will walked farther out into the castle courtyard and watched as the falcons fiercely attacked the flying Gizor one by one. Each creature would twist and turn in midair as several falcons tore at the leathery flesh with their sharp talons and beaks. The birds gripped the creatures and pulled them down to the ground then peck at them furiously. The falcons seemed possessed by some spell that Will didn't understand. He wondered where they came from. Dead Gizor bodies littered the ground as the falcons followed through and made sure each one was finished off for good.

"What is it?" Peter asked from the bottom of the steps.

"I don't know," Will hesitated. "Something is happening." He spied the white bird again—the white owl.

"Peter!" Will yelled. "Come see this!"

Peter ran up the stone steps to Will's side and eagerly looked where Will was pointing.

There, perched on a wooden crate amidst all the fighting between the falcons and the creature, sat a beautiful owl with glowing yellow eyes. As Peter stared into its eyes, he could feel a familiar sensation.

"It's him," he whispered.

"I saw that owl once before," Will said. "I saw it with the King."

"It's the Dragon!" Peter shouted.

Creatures in death poses littered the ground. Others still writhed in their last moments. Peter ran to the owl. Standing before it, he held out his arm. The bird turned its head and flapped its wings. Flying to Peter's arm, it perched carefully as not to tear his skin with its sharp talons. Using its wings to settle into the perch, the white owl turned its head and scanned the courtyard at the successful raid of its brother falcons. Soldiers were shooting arrows into the hideous Gizor as they fought off the falcons attacking them.

Soon, this phase of the siege was over. Many soldiers turned to each other and embraced with relief. Dead Gizor and wounded falcons littered the courtyard inside and outside the castle walls.

"Will!" Peter cried. "It's safe now."

Will ran out to meet Peter, searching the skies above. He glimpsed more falcons scattering Gizor away. Whoops of victory could be heard from the castle wall as the soldiers celebrated.

But Will knew victory was not yet in their grasp. He could hear the ogres on the outside of the walls growling and grumbling. He knew they could see the battle in the hills as well as the fire from Hildron. No, Will knew the battle was just beginning and Caragon would try another siege on the castle soon enough. But what form of sinister magic would he use this time?

The large white owl perched on his arm was heavy, but he was so joyful to see the Dragon—to help save the castle once again—that he didn't mind. "I didn't think I'd see you again," he mumbled.

"Peter, we have to get you safe inside the dungeon," Will said as he motioned for them to move. "It isn't safe out here yet."

"But the attack is over."

"Caragon isn't finished yet," Will explained. "The King's men are fighting now in the hills outside of Hildron. I have to join them. Caragon will try and attack the castle again. Come now, we have to get you inside."

"The castle" Peter pointed to his room in the tower of the castle. He knew he wanted to wait there for his father's return.

Will and Peter once again ran to the castle. As they entered the large doorway, a loyal servant stood waiting. "Master Peter," he said with an exhausted look.

"Don't worry," Will said. "He isn't going anywhere this time."

§

Inside the dungeon, the doctor quickly made his way to the wounded soldiers coming in from the battle. Many suffered from deep scratches and flesh wounds that were treated with herbs, then wrapped in bandages. Constable Darion moaned from the pain of his deep cuts and scratches.

"What happened young man?" the doctor asked Darion. "Whatever was it that attacked outside?"

"Yes, we could hear the horrid screeches," said Lady Godden.

"Gizor," Darion uttered as the doctor removes what shreds of clothing were left on the constable. "Hideous flying creatures sent by Caragon."

The women gasped as they listened. "But how did it end, my friend?" Lady Godden asked as she held Darion's hand.

"All is well," he whispered as he closed his eyes.

"He needs rest," the doctor said as he began to clean the wounds. He shuttered when he saw teeth marks and large deep scratches on Darion's back.

§

Along the eastern wall of the castle stood many of the ogres ready to fight. As they hastily moved into battle positions to face the enemy, they could easily spot the battle in the distance near Hildron castle. Now that the castle was secure for a moment, they concentrated their efforts on the approaching enemy fighters.

The surviving soldiers realigned themselves along the castle walls and prepared for another siege. Their bodies ached from the day's battles, but they knew they had to continue. In the distance, they could see and hear the battle being waged in the desert hills of Theádron.

Inside the castle, the servant cleaned the wound on Will's face and applied some bandages around his shoulder. Then he fit Will with a clean tunic. As Will bid farewell to Peter, he ran out into the night to return to his position along the castle wall. He ran around the grotesque creatures as they lay stiff and dead. Several of the local men had come out of the dungeon to carry survivors to the doctor. Some of the villagers were taking Constable Darion to the infirmary. As Will passed by, he reached out and grabbed Darion's hand and squeezed it slightly to let his friend know he was there for him. Darion gently squeezed back. Will wanted to stay with the constable, but his King needed him now more than ever.

"Will!"

He turned to see his father running toward him. "Father!"

Will answered ran to meet him. Together they embraced.

"I never thought I'd see you again, my son," his father cried.

They gazed at one another for only a moment before Will explained that he must return to his position on the wall.

On the outer wall, Will tried to find his captain. Many of the soldiers, wounded as they were, still maintained their positions. Fatigued and weary, they stood and watched the battle off in the distant hills knowing that soon the enemy would try and take the castle again. Will walked by the bowmen who were gathering up as many arrows as they could find. With so many arrows spent in battle, supplies were few. So the blacksmith returned to his hut to try and make more. He ordered what he had to be sent up by rope. The bowmen passed around the supply, hoping it would be enough, but they shook their heads as though they knew they would need more.

Will stood along the wall and felt the cold stone on his hands. The breeze chilled him, but the new clean and dry tunic brought some warmth. His hands were cut and bruised from the battle and his shoulder ached. He kept his eyes on the hills, waiting for the King's return. If he spotted the King, then he knew all would be well. If another was leading the men home, then he would know the battle was lost. All that he could do was wait and see.

20 SECRET CHAMBERS

"Fall back, men!" the captains shouted to their soldiers as they made their way back toward Theádron's desert hills. The desert floor remained damp from the night's rain, but the mud began to dry in the cold wind. This made the marching easier. The men were confused as to why they were retreating when they were successfully pushing the enemy back toward Hildron castle. Their blistered feet ached in their wet boots. Still, they marched on.

"The captain doesn't want us too close to the castle," one soldier explained as the others grumbled their displeasure. "There's something happening inside that dark place and he wants us far away from it."

"Aye, bring the enemy to where we want them and not the other way around," answered another man.

The soldiers agreed as they marched back and helped the wounded make their way to the ranks. Sweat dripped from their foreheads even as their breath could be seen in the cold night air. Fire belched out of Hildron as the sky around it reddened.

King Alexander remained nearby on his horse, ready to lead his men back into the desert hills toward his castle. He knew the last battle had to be fought there and not here near the dreaded domain of Caragon. Behind him, the men continued their march, carrying wounded with them. Alexander yanked the reins and galloped his horse out in front of the men. He found a soldier to sound the trumpet to the castle.

The young man removed his horn from his bag around his shoulder and put it to his lips. With a gasp of air, he sent the alarm into the night sky with one breath. The trumpet was carried off toward the castle and all who waited within its walls.

§

Will heard the blast along with the others soldiers and bowmen standing on the curtain wall of the castle. The captain understood what it meant.

"The King," he said. "The King has ordered the trumpet sound!"

This was good news to the men. Now they knew their sovereign was alive and bringing the men to the castle. But then a second blast came. This one was longer followed by two shorter tones.

"He is requesting help," the captain said.

"Requesting us to go to him?" Will asked.

"No, he is asking for some to help them return," the captain hurried to the west gate. "Ogres!" he yelled. "March to the hills of Theádron. Your King commands you!"

With that order, Grauble, the commander of the great giant ogres, nodded in agreement. He led the way as dozens of his kind followed. Together they headed through the raised gates and over the drawbridge wearing their leather armor with bucklers, swords, and axes. Easily crossing the Blue River, they made their way into the low lying hills toward Hildron and the King's men.

"Why send them?" Will asked.

"The King can use their brute strength for whatever it is he needs," the captain answered. "For now, we are safe here as we wait." Then the captain ordered his trumpeter to send a blast back into the night sky to answer the King.

As the trumpet blast echoed through the sky, King Alexander heard it. He knew that his captain was sending assistance to the battle.

§

Aluein huffed his way through the mud and muck to meet with Alexander. Out of shape and out of breath, he stood by his sovereign as they watched their men march back to the hill country of Theádron.

"Call for assistance, eh?" he asked the King.

"Yes," Alexander said. "How is your wound?"

"Fine," Aluein answered. "And yours?"

Alexander realized his friend must have seen him wince with pain from the wound in his side. "It is an old wound…nothing to worry about."

"What assistance can the captain send? Not many men left at the castle,"

"No," the King answered. "I have not asked for men."

"Well, what are they going to send us then? Women?" Aluein laughed.

"No, my old friend," Alexander chuckled. "Ogres."

"Ogres?" Aluein asked incredulously. "What ogres would serve the likes of men?"

"Grauble," Alexander answered. "He has been set free from Caragon and will help us. He knows it is the only way to free the land from its terrible curse."

"You are giving them far too much credit," Aluein said as he took out his pipe from his belt and lit it. "Never knew ogres to help out man before…not even Grauble."

Puffs of smoke rose into the night sky as the two friends enjoyed a respite from the battle. "But, I trust you, my friend," he said as he puffed on his pipe. "And if the ogres are what you have requested, then we will fight alongside the ogres here tonight."

Alexander dismounted his horse. He walked to the edge of the hill and inspected his men marching back into lines. Ahead of them was Hildron, still belching out fire into the sky. He knew the fight was only beginning. Above the men, a high-pitched screech pierced the night. They gazed up as they made their way into line.

Faintly seen through the darkness was a falcon circling above them. Another joined it, and together they flew to a tree without leaves. In that instant, the moon appeared again from behind the clouds and lit the entire field before them. The soldiers could see more falcons circling above as they made their way through the face of the waxing moon.

The King watched the sight of the smaller birds of prey hovering above them. Each bird made its way over to a tree branch and waited as though some orders were coming to move them to action. "What do you make of this?" he asked his friend as he walked back to the top of the hill. He pointed to the tree behind them with its long bare branches twitching in the slight breeze. The air was crisp and chilled.

"Another good omen," sighed Aluein. "Winter is coming."

"No," King Alexander said. "Something else is coming."

§

Inside the castle, Peter carried the owl on his arm into the large hallway near the dining room. The servants scurried around him, bringing water and bandages made from torn sheets to the infirmary in the dungeon.

"Stay here, your highness. I will be back soon," said the butler. He then ran out into the courtyard surrounding the main entrance to help carry wounded below.

Peter's body ached from the fight with the creature and from the day's adventures. He hadn't slept in a while, but he was too excited to stop and rest now. He found a large wooden chair and placed the owl on the back of the chair. The large white bird hopped onto its new perch and sat patiently.

Peter studied the bird for a few moments. "Are you going to stay with me now? I wish you could speak now."

The owl fluttered its wings and looked around the hall.

"I know you cannot stay, but I want to...thank you for all you have done," Peter said. "The falcons coming and attacking...brilliant!" he smiled. "Friends of yours?"

He found another chair in the large open hall. Above the chair which held the owl hung the portrait of Peter's mother in a large gilt frame. Lit only by a lone torch in the hall, the haunting image moved Peter. "Quite a room isn't it?" he asked his silent friend. "I feel as though I am new to this place after all that has happened recently." He yawned from exhaustion. His sleepy eyes met the owl's bright and glowing yellow eyes as it inspected the surrounding area. "I've never been up this late before." He smiled as his eyelids grew heavier.

"I know you must return to my father's side to protect him. I appreciate that." Peter stared down at the shiny marble flooring. "I also know you are hurt and tired. But my father needs you. We need you...I need you," he stuttered.

But the bird remained silent. Peter leaned one arm on a small table next to his chair and rested a bit. The owl remained still.

"Just awhile longer..." Peter slowly dozed off to sleep.

The owl, still perched on the chair back, watched as Peter's eyes twitched in their sockets as he dreamed. Images of the Dragon Forest raced through his mind. He saw the ruggedly handsome face of Peregrine before him, and his body jerked at the sight.

The owl watched.

Then, the mystical blue lake appeared in front of Peter as the mist rose all around him. The dining hall disappeared. Peter stood up, out of the chair, and walked toward the lake. As he approached the shore, he heard a faint voice whisper his name. The voice was that of a woman. There, in the lake's surface, appeared several images as clear as life. Peter froze as he studied each image.

He saw a field of lavender blowing in the wind. A person, a woman, stood far off in the distance surrounded by lavender. Next, an image of the horse his mother rode, Sweyn, a white stallion given to her by the King. It was running. Suddenly, the image of his mother appeared in the glassy lake causing Peter's body to shake from the shock of seeing her face again. She spoke to him, but he could not hear what she was saying. He saw his own arm reach out to touch the water. His mother reached out her arm and stopped him from touching the water. Behind her appeared a sword hovering in the air over the surface of the lake. Peter tried desperately to walk toward her, but her image was gone before he could reach her.

"Remember the compass," the voice whispered. With that, the owl flapped its wings vigorously, startling Peter awake. He looked up, surprised that he had fallen asleep, and rubbed his eyes. He swiveled to look at the white owl by the Queen's portrait, but it was gone.

§

The falcons flew above the soldiers as they stood in straight lines awaiting their orders to attack. The sporadic screeches of the small birds cut through the silence from time to time, causing each man's eyes to follow the sound. A thunderous noise was heard off in the distance, coming from the castle. Several captains located torches and lit them to see what was coming. There, along the gorge near the men, came several giant ogres running to meet their King in battle. Some of the men staggered backwards when they saw the giant man-like beasts coming toward them, but they held the line when they saw their King galloping to greet the ogres.

"Grauble," Alexander said. He rode over to the ogres. "I thank you for responding."

The leader of the ogres grumbled and groaned in his own language. An interpreter for the King approached to speak for the ogres. "They say they are ready to fight, my Lord," he interpreted. Each ogre wore a leather breastplate over a linen tunic to help stop arrows from piercing their tough flesh as well as leather helmets of their own design.

Alexander was impressed with their armor. "I am encouraged by this sight," he said. "It gives me great joy to see how seriously your ogres are taking this war with Caragon."

Grauble growled in approval.

Alexander turned to the interpreter. "Explain to them the strategy. Then tell them we need them to stay in the back until I give the order to advance," the King instructed.

"Yes, Sire." Then the interpreter went on to explain the battle, what had occurred and what they were waiting for. Grauble nodded his comprehension of the orders. But then he went on to testify as to what happened at the castle.

"My Lord," the interpreter said. "Grauble has informed me of the battle at the castle walls. It appears several hundred flying Gizor, mutant creatures from Hildron, attacked and greatly wounded many men. But hundreds of falcons, brothers of the white owl, came and fought off the flying monsters to great victory."

"Good grief!" Aluein shook his head upon hearing the news. He puffed on his pipe as he walked toward the Ogre commander. "What sorcery is this?" he asked as he exhaled smoke into the air.

Grauble smelled the sweet tobacco and motioned for a puff of the pipe. "Don't have a pipe on you, eh?" Aluein asked. Grauble shook his head. "Well, alright then."

Aluein handed the pipe to the giant ogre. It disappeared in his large hands, but he was able to puff a few bits of the sweet tobacco into his mouth. Grinning, he handed the pipe back to his friend. "It has been a long time, my old friend," said Aluein.

He chuckled, and then walked back to Alexander who was studying the falcons still perched on the branches of the tree near them. "Flying creatures? Man-like fighters with foul black blood? What is this, Aluein?" asked the King.

"I do believe we have walked into something that we may not be able to walk out of..." Aluein hesitated. "I have not heard of such wickedness since before the Dark Times.

"I have the sword of my father, my son is safe, and the Dragon is with us." Alexander removed his sword from its sheath. "We can still win this fight. Caragon is strong, but he has shown us his weaknesses."

"Yes, but what of Bedlam?" Aluein asked. "If he is behind all this as we suspect, what shall we do when he decides to appear and end all this once and for all?"

"He cannot do anything to Theádril as long as the seven swords remain," King Alexander answered.

"But do they all remain?" Aluein answered.

§

Half awake, Peter leapt out of the chair and ran to the entrance of the castle. He arrived in time to catch a glimpse of the white owl flying above the courtyard and into the night sky. With that, Peter ran to the stairs and headed up to his bedroom. He slammed the door open and ran to his window. Unhinging the center window, he pushed it open and leaned out. Peter could see the white owl reaching higher and higher into the sky. He knew it was flying out to the desert hills of Theádron to meet his father in the battle. Peter watched the Dragon fly off in the form of the special nocturnal bird, then turned toward the east to see shades of violet permeate the sky appear low near the hills at first. He knew it would be daytime soon, but he wondered what the day would hold for Will, his father, the soldiers, and the Dragon.

Not satisfied with the view from his bedroom, Peter shot out of his room with such speed that all his toys flew off the feathered bed where he had left them. The toys no longer held his interest, not after all that he had recently encountered. He knew there was a righteous battle about to begin and he needed to witness it. Peter knew one day he would be needed to write down all that was happening in this time and place as King of Illiath.

In the hallway lit by only one torch, Peter made his way to the set of stairs leading up to one of the towers of the castle. He quickly climbed up the stone steps leading to the small turret where scouts and lookouts perched. He was tired from running up the steps, so he leaned against the wall and rested. The door to the turret was narrow and wooden. He grabbed the brass knob, hoping it was unlocked. With a twist of the knob, the small door opened revealing the room with one window overlooking the entire kingdom. He ran to the window and pushed it open. As the sun began to rise in the east, Peter could see all the torches aligned in the desert valley and the fire still atop Hildron carved out of the Black Hills. The storm clouds still hovered over the castle and Peter knew his father was there among the torches.

The white owl was nowhere to be seen and this saddened Peter, but he remembered the compass in his pocket and the voice he had heard in his dream. Reaching in his pocket, Peter grabbed the compass and held it up near the window. The arrow bounced a bit and then pointed north. He closed it. Deciding to head back to the great hall, he hurried down the stone steps and groped for the heavy door. As he opened it, several scullery maids with white sheets in their arms hastened by him, mumbling about the infirmary and the wounded soldiers. They quickly passed out of sight.

Peter closed the door and walked down the hallway, peering over the balcony to make sure no one was around. He headed down the grand staircase that led to the great hall. No one was near, so Peter carefully approached the portrait of his mother. He stood before the elegant painting in the gilt frame lit only by a torch. He removed the compass from his pocket once again and held it in his palm. Nothing happened. So he decided to open it. The lid opened, the small arrow bounced around yet again, then settled on north as usual.

But this time, Peter heard a creaking sound coming from the paneled wall behind the portrait. The creaking grew louder as the painting move toward Peter. It seemed to be on hinges like a door.

It opened slowly. Peter peered behind the painting and saw a darkened hallway. He cautiously scanned the large open room for a candle, but the only light he found was the torch on the wall. on a chair and grabbed the torch, then poked it inside the dark hallway behind the painting.

"Hello?" Peter whispered.

No answer came from behind the portrait. The way was dark and it sounded hollow with stone walls and floors. Peter placed his right hand gently on the gilt frame and opened the passageway enough so he could walk into it. Placing the compass in his pocket, he entered the passageway. Thick damp air enveloped him. He hesitated to close the "door" behind him for fear that it would never open again, but he took the chance. The torch amply lit the passage as Peter used his hands to guide himself along. The stone wall was cold and damp and the passageway was long and winding. He could not see what lay ahead, but he kept walking.

He passed several closed wooden doors in the stone walls. He did not try to open them. He just kept walking. The only sound he heard was a slow drip of water and the whistle of the wind coming through the cracks in the stone walls where the mortar was missing.

"Hello?" Peter said to no one.

His voice echoed several times, revealing how long the passageway was. He began to think he had made a mistake entering into the unknown until finally he spotted a light ahead. The warm glow welcomed Peter, but he was curious as to its source. So, he continued toward it with his torch held high. The sound of something hitting the stone floor startled Peter and he stopped. The noise resembled a book landing on the floor with a loud thud. Then, he heard someone mumbling to himself.

"Hello? Is anyone there?" he asked. He found it hard to swallow as his body shook.

"Yes," someone answered. "Master Peter. Is that you?' It was the voice of a man.

Peter stood there, confused. He did not know whether to answer or not, so he didn't.

"Hello?" the gruff voice asked. "Master Peter? Are you there?"

Peter decided to answer since the voice seemed friendly. "Yes," he said, nervously.

"Oh good, bring me your torch. I can use the extra light in here," the man said. Peter carefully walked toward the light until he saw the source of the voice. It was a tall, thin older man with a short white beard and white hair underneath a pointed nightcap. The man wore a thick dark robe and underneath the robe he was dressed in nightclothes as though he were ready for bed. He peered at Peter through his wire-rimmed spectacles and grinned.

"Good," he said as he bent over to pick up a book off the floor. "I am glad you made it."

Peter did not know what to say to the stranger who seemed to know him, so he stood cautiously still near the door. The room where the man stood contained a large wooden table with carved legs. Around the table were bookcases filled with numerous volumes of leather-bound books and stacks of papers rolled into scrolls. Atop the table was a candle in its wooden holder as well as more books stacked on top of one another in several clumsy piles. Papers and scrolls were strewn on the table without care. Peter carefully studied the contents of the room, wondering what it was and why it was hidden. Several unlit torches hung along the wall in their brass holders ready to receive fire.

"Who are you?" Peter asked the tall thin man standing before him. "And what is this place?"

"I am Sir Theodore Sirus III at your service," the man answered and politely bowed. "But you may call me Theo. And this place...well, it is a special place, Peter."

He climbed up a small stepping ladder and pulled down one of the tomes on the bookshelf. He blew the dust off the book and handed it to Peter. "Your Highnes."

Peter studied the man's face in the firelight of the torch then examined the book in his hands. Bound in black leather, the title on the book said simply, *Prince Peter* in gold letters embossed into the leather. Peter raised a quizzical eyebrow and took the book into his hands.

"These books, Peter," the man said as he spread his arms wide, "are all yours. Well, one day they will be all yours." He winked. "But for now, they are here, safe from the siege until then."

Peter, still cautious and confused, moved into the room then placed the book on the table. He used the torch to read the titles of the books on the shelves. History, geography, maps, astronomy, and logic were all written in gold on the books. Then he read the names of the ten rulers of the regions including his great grandfather and grandfather.

Theo stood by and watched Prince Peter read through the titles. "This room, Peter, holds the archives of the kingdom. I have sworn to protect them here in this hidden passage so that they may serve you as they have served your father."

Peter, feeling more comfortable, decided to ask some questions. "Who are you, again?" he asked.

"I am a tutor of sorts. I taught your father and his father before him. And soon I will teach you," he said as he slowly stroked his beard. "The time has come for you to learn all about your part in history."

"My part?" Peter asked. "I assumed I would be king one day…and that was it. Is there more?"

"Well, being king is one thing, Peter," Theo said as he pulled out a chair. "But, yes, there is more to it than just ruling."

Peter's arm ached from holding the torch. He walked over and placed it into a wall mount. But Theo took it and lit two more torches giving the room a brighter appeal. Afterwards, Peter walked over to inspect the books that would one day belong to him. He pulled out a scroll that lay on a shelf near him. As he unrolled it, dust diffused all around him.

"Careful," Theo said. "These scrolls are ancient and fragile."

Peter nodded. He read the writings on the scrolls. This particular one was about the dragons of all kinds. He glanced it over, shrugged, and then rolled it up and placed it back on the shelf.

"Don't like dragons?" Theo asked.

"No, I do," Peter replied. "I already know all there is to know about dragons. That's all."

Theo grinned a slight grin.

Peter only had one question for Sir Theodore this night, so he bravely decided to ask it.

"Did you know my mother?" he asked.

Theo's eyes widened as though surprised by the question. "Why yes. Queen Laurien," he answered. "I did."

"How?"

"She was...well, I suppose, in a way, she was family," Theo said. "I was there when she met your father. I tutored them both when they were no older than you are now." He smiled at the memory. "They sat right there," he pointed, "at this table. They sat in these chairs." He rose and pulled up another wooden chair for Peter, who dutifully sat down, enthralled to hear more. "They studied many of these books."

Peter removed the compass from his pocket and placed it on the table. "Did you know about this?"

Theo chuckled. "Why yes," he said. "Yes I do." He picked up the gold trinket and gazed at it over his rimmed glasses. "It belonged to your mother...she made it for you. She bade me to give it to you."

Peter sat back in the chair, at ease knowing that there was a purpose behind all this. "Why?" he asked.

"So one day you would find this place and come here," Theo said. "And meet me."

"So you will tutor me then?" Peter asked.

"Yes," Theo answered. "But tonight I am here to answer your questions."

"Are there more hidden passages in this castle?"

"Yes, many."

"Why did my father make hidden passages?"

"For protection during wars like this one." Theo adjusted his glasses.

"Do you know about the Dragon?"

Theo smiled widely. "Oh, yes," he said.

"Do you know about the swords?"

"Of course," he answered. He folded his long thin arms across his chest and waited for the next question.

"I have seen the Dragon," Peter said proudly.

"Yes, I know," Theo said. "And you rode on its back, didn't you?"

Peter nodded enthusiastically. "How did you know?"

Theo smiled as he removed a pipe from his robe pocket. He found a match, inspected it, and used the candle to light it. Then he inhaled and puffed as he lit the pipe. The smoke rose around him like a wreath.

"I watched you from the window," he said. "In fact, you've had quite an adventure with the Dragon these last few days, haven't you?"

Theo rose from the chair and walked over to the shelves. He pulled one scroll from the shelf and placed it on the table. He carefully unrolled it and placed the candle on top of the antiquated paper to hold it. Written on the scroll was the tale of the Dragon Forest. Theo held his pipe between his teeth. "What do you think?" he asked.

"I was glad to enter into the forest," Peter answered. "I wish everyone would."

"Ah, but not everyone can, Peter," Theo said. A serious look came across his face.

"What do you mean?" Peter asked.

"You see, only those chosen may enter into its realm and live," he answered. "And you, Peter, have been chosen. You are heir to the throne of Illiath in the land of Théadril. Your line — and only your line—can enter into the Dragon Forest." Theo said as he reached over and pulled out a book. He placed it on the table and thumbed through it as though searching for a certain passage to read. "Yours is a great purpose, Peter," he said, "and the Dragon knows this. Now, it is time you knew it as well."

§

Lord Byrén paced back and forth inside the dungeon that soon resembled a hospital as maids and villagers tended to the wounded. Soldier after soldier was bandaged but each one rose up to return to the castle wall.

"Sit down!" yelled one nurse maid as she grabbed a foot soldier's arm. "You are too hurt to return to your post."

"Nonsense," the man moaned as he secured his belt around his waist. "I must return to my post." His arm was bandaged tightly as was his thigh, but he still walked out of the dungeon to take his place among his friends. Others followed suit even though their bandaged bodies ached.

"All of you sit down and rest!" ordered the doctor, but each man returned his command with a stern and determined look that silenced him instantly.

"Doctor," said the nurse. "You cannot possibly let them go like this!"

But the doctor saw that they were determined to return to their posts and engage in the battle no matter what he said or did. And this fact left him utterly speechless.

Lord Byrén worried for his son, Sir Lucas, a brave Knight of the Crow regiment. He continued to pace. "Rest, my friend," said Lady Godden.

"Rest?" Lord Byrén asked. "How can I when my son…*our* sons…are in battle with that wicked enemy."

"Yes, I know," she said as she gently touched his hand. "But that is where they long to be. My son has been training for knighthood since he was thirteen years of age. Now he is twenty-one. He is by his King's side, serving his country in honor."

"And if he dies?"

"Then he dies doing what he was destined to do," she answered.

Lord Byrén looked into her blue eyes in her gentle face surrounded by white hair. "You are a brave woman. I know you have lost two sons already from battle long ago." Not wanting to insult her or hurt her any further by causing her to remember the loss, he nodded and touched her hand as gently as she had touched his. As she walked away, his thoughts continued to race and unsettle him.

"Don't fret, my old friend," whispered Darion who lay nearby. "Your son has trained with the best knights of the kingdom. They will all be victorious in battle."

Lord Byrén walked over to his friend the constable and looked deep into his tired eyes. "Are we doing the right thing?" he asked. "Should we have tried aggressive diplomacy instead?"

"You know as well as I do what Caragon was doing to the land," Darion answered.

"Yes, but all this bloodshed, and for what? The forest? The Dragon no one has ever seen? Look around you, constable. These people have suffered. I cannot help but think we have made a grave error in not trying to find a compromise somewhere somehow. Some sort of negotiation or treaty."

Constable Darion tried to sit up. With a stern expression on his face, he said, "As the King said so elegantly before, there is no appeasing evil. There is no compromise. There is no negotiating with a man who creates such creatures as those Gizor that attacked us today. No amount of appeasement will ever halt Caragon's lust for power. He does not seek peace. He does not wish to share the Dragon Forest or Théadril. He wants to destroy it.... completely."

Lord Byrén nodded as he listened. He wrung his hands over and over again in a nervous twitch.

"And he will not stop until he sees the end of Alexander's line," Darion said.

Silently, Lord Byrén turned away and walked off into the darkest part of the dungeon Keep. He knew his friend was right, but he couldn't bring himself to say it knowing that only hours earlier he was saying it himself in the castle. But now his son was facing this horrible enemy. Now he would face the realities of war itself. And he was not sure he could.

"You know what he has done to the Crow Valley," Darion said as Lord Byrén walk away. "You have seen your own people suffer, Byron, at the hands of Caragon!"

But it was no use. Byron remained aloof and grief stricken.

§

"But why? Why does Caragon wish to destroy the Dragon Forest?" Peter asked.

"Caragon knows the secrets of the forest," Theo answered. "Do you?"

Peter shook his head.

"You see, long ago, before you were born, before your father was born, man lived in peace with the Dragon of the Forest. Man swore to protect it because he knew the secrets and man knew the Dragon fought to protect the lands," he said as he chewed on the tip of his pipe. "But vanity, lust for power, greed, and the idleness that comes with prosperity allowed the oath to be long forgotten, I'm afraid."

"And now, as a result, Peter, your generation is completely ignorant of the Oath and the Dragon. The people fear the Dragon or they want to kill it for its scales. Others think it a myth or legend of folklore." Theo shook his head. "And the swords? Most people believe they are lost or hidden away somewhere. King Aléon was the only king who instructed his heir on the ways of the Dragon. Your father, Peter, desires for you to know and carry on the Oath sworn by your fathers before you."

Peter listened intently.

"Caragon knows this and has created a plan to keep your father from instructing you: through the constant threat of war. By keeping you and your father separated, how can he instruct you, Peter? He longs to kill your father and then kill you. That is why I am here. I am a servant to the King, to the Oath." He winked.

Peter was saddened and somewhat afraid to know Caragon was planning against him. "But, will he kill my father?" Peter asked.

"Do not be afraid, Peter," Theo said. "Your destiny is great and no mere man can stop it. By teaching you the history of Théadril, about the Oath of your fathers, and all that the Dragon has done for this land, we will be securing the line of Alexander forever. You will teach it to your heirs." Theo smiled. "But you still have a long and arduous journey before you, Peter."

Peter's eyelids grew heavier and heavier. He sighed a deep sigh and sunk lower into the chair.

"When was the last time you slept?" Theo asked.

"Two days ago, I think," he answered.

"Well, we had better get you upstairs to bed."

"No!" Peter shouted. His voice echoed through the long dark hallway. "I cannot rest until my father comes home. I must see him. There is something important I have to tell him."

Theo placed his long thin arm on Peter's shoulder. "He knows, Peter," he said.

"None of this is your fault. Lord Caragon has been planning this raid for many months and it would have happened even if you hadn't run away."

Peter looked down at his feet in shame.

"Don't worry yourself, my young boy," Theo said reassuringly.

Peter's head swam with dragons and swords and flying creatures until he could no longer hold his head up. He rested it on the table top and quickly fell asleep.

Theodore walked over to a large wooden chest hidden in a corner of the room. Opening it, he removed a woolen blanket. Placing it around Peter's shoulders, the old man sat down with a groan and played with a quill on the table. He winced once in a while because his tall bony frame was sore from all the stacking of books and scrolls. Satisfied with his work, he continued to puff on his pipe a few more times until a wisp of smoke rose up to the ceiling.

Then, Theodore Sirus III, the great Chronicler of the King, found a book, opened it, and began to read as he kept a careful eye over his most important pupil.

§

King Alexander watched the luminous white owl fly away into the violet sky as the moon faded and the sun began to rise in the east. He sighed heavily as he realized the next battle was about to begin. His body was tired as well as his spirit, but he, like his men, had to endure this. The ogres, mighty in appearance and in strength, had taken their positions and each one carried a large hammer-like weapon in their hands. They were anxious to start and so were the soldiers. They longed to return to their homes and resume their lives after this fight, but deep inside their hearts they knew Illiath, and perhaps all of Théadril, would be forever altered.

Aluein stood nearby thumping his pipe into the palm of his hand to shake lose the used tobacco. As the tobacco clump finally fell to the ground, he placed it into the small pouch on his belt and readied his ax. Without his grey horse, he felt odd, but he was glad to be among the men, ready to fight. He was reminded of his time spent in the regiment as a young man long ago. Aluein smiled at the memory. Ahead of him, he spotted his eldest son, Sir Roen, a fine Knight, inspecting the ranks. Sir Roen wanted to make sure the men were ready. They were tired, but they were ready.

Alexander mounted his horse once again as he felt the twinge of pain from the wound in his side. But he paid no heed to the pain. He pulled on his horse's reins nudging it down the hill through the lines of men until he was in front. Alexander turned to view his men's faces in the early morning light. Behind him, thousands of enemy fighters from Hildron were making their way to the base of the hill with the castle behind them. They roared as they lifted up their weapons in defiance and rage.

But this did not alarm Alexander. "Steady men," he ordered. Then he removed the sword of Alexander from its sheath and held it high. His men cheered and roared their approval. Wanting to move forward, his horse whinnied at the commotion. Alexander had to steady him.

The storm clouds lingered above the castle of Hildron and the mutant enemy fighters still shouted and challenged the King's men to advance, but Alexander ordered them to remain still. He wanted to bring the enemy to his position this time.

Moving from within the ranks of the enemy, a mounted figurehead moved forward parting the wicked fighters as it went. Alexander tried to make out the figure, but he couldn't. The figure was silhouetted against the red fire glow from Hildron.

As the mounted rider came closer, Alexander could see he was clothed in black and his horse was as black as night as well. The man wore a metal helmet that hid his face. He sat tall on a horse draped in a black cloth with a crest embroidered on the side. As he came even closer, finally Alexander could read the crest and decipher who the rider was.

The man they had been battling these many hours now sat before Alexander at the bottom of the hill surrounded by his evil fighters. Lord Caragon stared at the King's men as though they were a prize he had already won.

But the King did not move from his place as his enemy sat before him in clear defiance of the rules of law. In bold confidence, King Alexander motioned his horse forward to face Caragon. Alexander thought that perhaps the two could settle this matter in one fight, sparing his men the battle, but he knew it was not to happen. As he approached, he could see the eyes of the former servant to Illiath. It was clear to Alexander that this man was possessed or under a spell of some sort. Yet Alexander was not afraid. Instead, he patiently waited to hear what this man had to say.

"This resistance is futile," Lord Caragon said quietly. "A waste of good men."

"The end of your reign of terror and injustice is over, Caragon," Alexander replied.

"What you have witnessed so far is only a small portion of my power, son of Aléon," he answered.

Alexander winced at the obvious refusal of Caragon to address him as his King. "Your magic has failed you. I have seen enough of it tonight. Time and time again you have used your powers to attack my men, my castle, and time and time again my men have come through victorious." He smirked. "Your plan has failed, Lord Caragon."

The horses neighed nervously.

"The Dragon and the Forest remain," the King said.

Lord Caragon listened as the King finished his statement. Then he hissed. "Prepare yourselves. This is far from over. Your time as ruler of Illiath is over, son of Aléon. But I am merciful. Lay down your weapons, give me the sword of Alexander, and I will spare your men. Bow down to me and join with us and you will live. If you obey me as the other rulers have done, there will be peace in all of Théadril. They were wise. They have surrendered to me and spared their people pain and suffering unlike you. You have caused great misery for your people and the land. You have put your vanity, your ideals, and your precious throne ahead of your people. Your impetuous actions have cost your kingdom dearly."

Alexander's horse jerked its head up and down.

"They will see me as merciful and you as careless, proud, and arrogant," Caragon said. His men roared in approval clanging their metal weapons together creating an eerie cacophony. "They will forget all that you have done for them and turn against you. The other rulers have placed their people ahead of themselves. They have joined with us because they understand what will happen to the land if they resist…unlike you, son of Aléon."

King Alexander could feel the weight of his men's eyes on him. They waited for his reply.

With the sword still in his right hand, Alexander stared at the fine piece of artistry. It had been forged by a sorcerer's magic, redeemed by victory in battle, and was now a clue to the source of peace in the land. Alexander knew he could not let the sword of his fathers be destroyed. He tightened his grip around the handle of the sword.

Steadying his horse, Alexander pointed his sword defiantly at the dark Lord. "I have but one reply to you, Lord Caragon…ride!" Alexander shouted to his men with all his heart and soul. The lion was back. The men, ready to fight now more than ever, picked up their weapons and ran toward the enemy.

Caragon, shouting in his anger and fury, raised his arms above his head to signal his men to attack. Then, in a black cloud of smoke his body rose up into the air growing larger and larger. His form began to change right before the King's eyes. The once human body turned in the air and became another being altogether. Black mist rose higher into the sky before all the men gathered there that dawn.

Lord Caragon was now took the form of a black dragon spreading its leathery wings wide. Its mouth opened to reveal a red spiked tongue shooting out between rows of sharpened teeth as long as swords. Its long tail whipped around, scraped the earth, and send rocks and pebbles flying like shrapnel. The beast rose higher into the night as it roared its fury and sent it echoing into the darkness.

§

A tremendous roar made its way to the castle as the men on the curtain wall witnessed the phenomenon in the western hills. They could see the fire and smoke in the light of Hildron as well as the giant black dragon rising into the sky.

"What's this?" said the captain on the castle wall when he saw the dragon flying into the air. He knew it would make its way to the castle.

Alexander's heart sank as he realized there was no time to respond to the magic of Caragon. He knew they had to advance now or it would be too late. His men followed him as he rode into the enemy.

Suddenly, the Baroks, running toward Alexander and his men with their teeth clenching, slowed as a commotion could be heard behind them. Between their ranks came the giant wolf-like beasts: the Zadoks. These all too-familiar monsters ran at full speed toward Alexander, snarling for fresh meat. They leapt at the King's horse, but the King slashed a Zadok in half with his sword. One slice forward killed one beast and one slice backward killed another. And yet the Zadoks still came from behind the enemy. The ogres hammered away at them sending them, whimpering to their deaths one by one. Grauble shouted orders to his fellow ogres telling them to keep moving forward until the King ordered otherwise. His ogres fought bravely as arrows and lances raced passed them. Caragon's Baroks were fierce fighters in hand to hand combat, but they were cursed with bad aim.

Aluein and his men stayed put on the hill and forced the Baroks to meet them where they were. His plan was to make sure they maintained their distance from Hildron and the black dragon circling above. He and his men did not have to wait long, the Baroks ran to meet them on the small hill with their weapons drawn. But Aluein and Sir Roen sliced their way through the enemy with ease.

One fighter made his way toward Roen with his sword of black metal drawn. Roen waited patiently in a wide stance as his enemy came closer. He raised his sword high above his head as the drooling creature approached. Part man and part beast, the Barok ran up to Roen and tried to shove his sword into his chest. Roen lowered his sword down on the creature's skull, killing it instantly.

Then he turned and shoved his sword into the chest of another creature approaching from behind. As the beast fell, Roen turned to the right in time to place his sword into the body of a Zadok leaping toward him. The wolf-beast fell to the ground taking Roen with it. In its final struggle, it clawed and gnashed at him with its teeth and feet. His blood sprayed into the air, so he twisted his sword in deeper and felt the metal blade sever the heart of the wolf-beast.

Rising to his feet, Sir Roen pulled the sword out of the beast, and turned to rammed it into the chest of another approaching Barok. The creature leapt into the air and fell right onto the blade.

Aluein watched his son kill several enemy fighters. Then, a fighter screamed as he lunged for Aluein, but his small ax blade flew through the air ending the feeble attempt of the Barok. Aluein ran and retrieved his ax quickly.

"Not much time for resting now, eh?" he shouted at Roen.

"Too busy now to talk, father," he smiled. Then he turned in time to sever the arm of another approaching fighter. "They seem to come from all sides!" he laughed. Together, the men made quite a pair of warriors.

Alexander stopped his horse and leapt off in time to slice through the matted black fur of a Zadok tearing at a soldier. The beast cried out in pain then perished. He helped the young man to his feet. He had deep cuts and lacerations, but he continued to fight. Together, he and the King used their swords to fight through many more enemy as the black dragon still hovered above them. They could feel the wind from its wings, but the King did not pay any heed to its course.

But when the black dragon roared from the skies and the men stopped out of fear. "Do not stop, men!" Alexander shouted, but their attention was focused on the ranks of enemy fighters. They could hear and feel a rumbling of the earth beneath their feet. The Baroks parted their lines to reveal something coming from behind them. Something no one had expected.

21 THE BLACK DRAGON

Atop the curtain wall of the castle, the wind died down as the sun slowly and peacefully made its way over the horizon—a stark contrast to the carnage of battle on the earth below. Will watched the commotion in the desert hills. He could view the firestorm above Hildron and he could scarcely see the torches of the Baroks as they advanced. There was unsettledness in the air as the men waited on the castle wall for their orders. Many still nursed wounds from the last attack, but they stayed true to the King. Will carefully searched their faces. Many were older than he, but he felt safe among them. They were now forever brothers, bonded by their battlefield experiences there along the castle wall.

Below, the villagers and servants were helping to move more wounded into the dungeon as bandaged soldiers came out to take their places in the fight. As the last wounded man was taken inside, Will heard the order to seal the dungeon door. As it grew eerily quiet in the courtyard, the chaos of moments ago was scarcely remembered by Will as he turned to face the hill valley outside of the castle. The fields nearby were still scattered with the carcasses of the wicked Gizor fighters rotting in the night. He could still spot some fires burning the tall grasses near the Blue River where he had fought off ghost fighters with the King. To Will, it seemed a lifetime ago. He knew he was ready to face whatever came from those black mountains in the west.

"Steady men!" he yelled.

They all took their positions with wounds bound and weapons drawn, ready to fight. Their eyes were bloodshot from exhaustion and their muscles ached throughout. But they still held their positions. Ahead, they could see and smell the putrid fire from Hildron as it moved through the air. They also could faintly hear the cries of the men fighting the Baroks.

"Whatever happens," he said. "We fight as one!"

The men shouted together a battle cry.

Suddenly, in the sky above the battle, a wave of blackness rose high and hover above the mountains. When lightning struck behind it, the blackness was silhouetted to reveal its true form: a black dragon.

When the men on the castle wall saw the form far off in the distant sky, panic filled their hearts, for many of them had never before seen a dragon. It had been many decades since the horrid beasts attacked Théadril. They were only myths to the villagers, but the elders remembered the dragons of their youth. They remembered the attacks and the destruction.

"A dragon!" One man as he pointed to the western horizon.

When some of the others heard the warning, they immediately dropped their weapons and ran to the ladders. They pushed and shoved so hard to climb down that some of them fell over the wall to their deaths. As they hastily made their way down the ladder and into the courtyard, their captain shouted orders for them to return to their posts or face death by hanging. Some stopped and hesitantly made their way back up the ladder, but others still ran to the dungeon, only to be met by a locked door. In their fear, they hid trembling in the darkened stairway.

"Cowards," their captain said and turned to sternly watch the other men return to their posts.

They reluctantly picked up their weapons and stood with the others who had not wavered. Among them, stood Will.

"Steady, men," the captain said. The black dragon hover over the battle. Its size was immense with a wide wingspan of several feet. The front legs were attached to the wings to provide a more streamline approach to flight. It dove faster and swooped up over the courtyard so fast that many did not even see it pass by. Its tail whipped from side to side as it flew.

"It's going to come here and attack," Will said.

"Most certainly," the captain said as he walked by.

He inspected all the men along the wall to ensure they were ready.

"Load your bows!" he shouted to the bowmen.

They obeyed with trembling hands as they aimed the arrows high into the sky.

All they could do was wait.

§

The Baroks, still roaring and banging their weapons, parted their ranks to allow the trolls through. These giant beasts with their humped backs and grotesquely long arms, held axes in their hands as they stomped through the lines. Grauble saw the enemy and growled an order to his fellow ogres to advance and meet the trolls to fight. The King's men ran back to let the ogres through the lines. Some were thrown aside by the thunderous race between the two giant peoples. Trolls, with their long beards, large noses, and long arms, were more brutal in battle. Ogres, with their stout muscular bodies and giant arms and hands, fought more wisely. Still, the men had to stop and watch the commotion of the two peoples meeting in the battle.

The awesome sound of axes meeting with hammers echoed throughout the hills as Grauble wrestled with Thorg, the leader of the trolls. Dropping their weapons on the ground, their arms intertwined as one tried to throw the other down. Each growled and bit at the other's arms and neck as they fought. Alexander watched from afar as Grauble fought. For a moment, he wasn't sure what to do, but an attacking Zadok quickly reminded him of his purpose. He drew his sword and sliced off the creature's head as it lunged at him. Its hot blood splattered on his face and stung his eyes. When his men saw this attack, they immediately entered back into the fight, paying no heed to the black dragon above them.

Grauble moved quickly to grab Thorg's head in his arm. He began choking the troll leader as it struggled to break free. Another troll, defending its leader, came up behind Grauble with its ax held high. Grauble still twisted Thorg's head tighter, feeling its life leaving its body, but he did not see the enemy behind him.

King Alexander did see the troll behind Grauble, so he grabbed a spear from the ground and threw it at the troll in time to stop it from lowering the ax into Grauble's back. The creature fell to the ground as the spear entered its thick barreled chest sending its ax flying behind it. Grauble finished his work on Thorg and threw its body to the ground in defiance. Then, he continued to fight the next troll advancing toward him.

The black dragon roared again from the air as he saw the ogres killing the trolls. With a loud roar, the beast ordered the Zadoks to attack and follow him to the castle. The wolf-like beasts ran through the King's men, throwing some down and tearing at their flesh. Then, as commanded, they continued running past the line of men to the desert hills and toward the castle. Alexander followed them with his eyes. He could see the black dragon flying off toward his castle as the sun appeared over the eastern horizon. He knew what was going to happen. Then, without warning, the dragon opened its mouth and spewed out its fire lighting up the desert and setting it afire. It then turned to the left and spewed out more fire sending a stream down to the ground. The fires illuminated the way for the Zadoks as they ran with their Master.

"To the castle!" Aluein ordered.

Alexander nodded in agreement. He knew the men and ogres were making progress against the Baroks in the hills. He motioned for his knights to head up a garrison of soldiers and move to the castle. The black dragon circled high into the new skylight as the rising sun glistened off its scales. Alexander felt sure that the beast would spew its fire on the castle. He thought of Peter.

Running over the smoldering hills with his men, Aluein and his son, Sir Roen, led the way as their men followed. Swords held high and shouts of glory sent chills through their King's body as he knew these men would die for him and their lands. Behind him stood hundreds of soldiers ready to advance toward the castle. The fire in their eyes matched the fire in the desert hills ahead of them. Bloodied and torn from battle, they were indefatigable in their quest to rid their beloved land of the wicked Lord Caragon.

From among their ranks stepped a knight loyal to the King. His armor was stained with blood and dried mud and his hands revealed torn flesh. In one of those hands, firmly gripped, was the sword of a warrior. King Alexander watched as the young knight approached him.

"My Lord," he spoke. Then he kneeled before his King. "All of us are ready to follow you into battle."

Alexander beamed with gratitude as he searched the faces of those surrounding the Knight. "Rise, Sir Leonius," he said. Recognizing the young man from Aluein's ranks in the Crow Valley, Alexander placed his hand on the shoulder of the brave knight and again ordered him to rise. Then, nodding to the men, King Alexander raised the sword of Illiath, the sword of his father and grandfather, high into the morning sky and together they ran into the desert hills to protect the castle.

§

Soft stirring echoes of the chaos outside in the courtyard came miraculously through the thick stone walls of the hidden room where Peter slept and where Theodore kept watch. Only, the old man wasn't watching his liege, but instead he too slept slouched back in the ornate wooden chair as the candle slowly burned out.

Peter heard what he thought to be a thump of something impacting the wall of the castle. Opening his eyes slowly, he suddenly remembered where he was. He looked over to where

Theo sat sleeping in the chair. Then, he slowly allowed his eyes to roam over the scores of books stacked neatly on shelves before him. As the candle glistened in the darkness, spreading its light over the books and scrolls on the table, Peter decided to take advantage of this time alone and do some research of his own.

Grabbing the candle, he walked over to the shelves and tried to read each title when he was interrupted by another thump that seemed to be coming from the outer walls of the castle. But Peter kept reading. He glanced over the leather bound books with gilt lettering, one by one, simply amazed at how many books there were in this small hidden room. Suddenly, one particular title stood out from among the many. Peter saw that it was out of his reach, so he grabbed the ladder that Theo had used to reach the higher shelves and rolled it toward the book on the shelf. The ladder, on a set of wheels so it was easy to navigate, was sturdy as Peter climbed near the top wrung. Holding the candlelight higher, Peter inspected the tome closely. "The Dragon," he mumbled quietly to himself. He pulled out the large book and realized he could not carry it while carrying the candle, so he placed the candle down on one shelf and carried the book down the ladder carefully so not to wake Theo.

With the book on the table, Peter retrieved the candle so he could read the printing inside the book. Then, he quietly began to flip the ancient pages one by one. It had been written by Theo, but he seemed to be dictating the words of someone else, the words of some sort of chronicle about a pact or covenant between a people.

Maps and course delineations lined the margins. One in particular caught the eye of Peter: that of his father's sword. The drawing had great detail.

Suddenly, another thump made Peter jump and Theo squirm a little in his chair. Peter sat very still hoping that his new tutor wouldn't wake to find him thumbing through something secret. But the noise coming from outside began to worry Peter. He could slightly make out sounds that resembled people screaming and running. Deep in his heart, he knew that another battle was being waged outside and he worried for his friend, Will. And he knew that his father was out there somewhere. Feeling helpless, Peter hoped that the Dragon would return and help in this battle.

His eyes returned to the pages before him and he read through the writings carefully. One by one, they listed parts of a pact or promise between men and Dragon. Each man, supposedly, promised not to harm the Dragon nor enter into the forest green. The Dragon, in return, promised to protect the people and all the kingdoms. Then, the rulers of the regions brought their swords together and sealed the promise. Yet, Peter had remembered how his father had told him that only some of the kings kept the promise. Some had decided not to protect the Dragon and others coveted its scales for themselves. He remembered the meeting with the knights in which they argued for entering into the forest to retrieve the scales. *What happened to the covenant?* Peter thought.

But it was the next few paragraphs he read that made it all come together for him at this time in the history of the kingdom of Alexander. As he continued, the sound that reverberated through the walls was not a scream nor a thump, but a roar that sounded threatening. The sound started low and deep and Peter knew instantly what it was: a dragon. He knew it was not *his* Dragon, the one he flew with and the one mentioned in this book. Peter knew the dragon roar he heard coming from the courtyard was the dragon his father was battling and now the people were battling outside the stone walls surrounding the secret hidden room of books.

Worried, Peter quickly read and what he read brought the day's and night's events to a sudden and alarming halt:

"What the rulers of men did not understand on that day, nor could they truly comprehend it, for their minds were feeble and full of avarice, was that the course of action taken by the Great Dragon was more drastic and dramatic than the mere acts of men. The Dragon had committed itself by a pact between itself and man, to laying down its life in order to save the line of Alexander, Illiath, and all of Théadril from any force set on destroying or severing that lineage so pure and true.

"By its virtue alone, the Great Dragon, entering into this pure covenant with impure man, would keep this promise and that by making this promise would do this one particular thing...no matter what occurred."

When Peter read these words, something inside him changed. The passage continued:

"The gratuitous and astounding part of this covenant with man, in this Chronicler's opinion, was that the great sacrifice of the Dragon was not necessary for the Dragon itself. For it had proven time and time again that it had no need for man. It alone had defeated all the enemies that had arisen to strike down Illiath and all of Théadril with its power. Yet, on that fateful day near the forest green in the region of Baldrieg, son of Glenthryst, the Dragon swore the Oath to protect this lineage of Alexander with its life."

With its life.

Peter read the words over and over as the sounds from outside the courtyard became louder still. So loud, that Theodore awoke. As he took his spectacles off his forehead and placed them over his tired eyes, he focused them on Peter whose face was pale and whose mouth was agape in sudden awareness. Then, glancing at the open book before Peter, Theo began to understand why.

Peter's eyes met with Theodore's and the two sat eerily still, considering the chaos outside.

"Why?" Peter asked as tears began to fill his eyes. He swallowed hard to stop the emotions he refused to show.

But Theodore knew the answer to that question had to come from the Dragon itself. So he shook his head as though he did not know the answer.

Peter raced out of the room and up the darkened stairs toward the painting of his mother. The makeshift door remained open releasing light into the darkened passageway. Peter raced through the doorway and up the familiar stairs leading to his bed chamber with thoughts, frightening thoughts racing through his mind. But, as he entered his bed chamber, there was only one thing he sought at this moment. Only one thing he realized he needed: the scale shield that the Dragon had given him.

Peter now understood why it was given to him. He now understood why all the events had been set in motion. And now was the time to act, for the roars of the black dragon were louder than ever before. And Peter knew that he, alone, must save the Dragon of the Forest.

§

Out in the courtyard mayhem ensued. The black dragon had made its way toward the castle and began its siege on all therein. The soldiers released their arrows into the sky in vain as the beast swiftly escaped each one in flight. The early morning light illuminated the fields below as the dragon breathed its fire and set ablaze all the wet grasses sending smoke into the air like giant clouds rising from the earth. This caused great confusion for the men trying to make their way back to the castle. Their metal shields, as strong as they were, would not be able to stop the dragon's fire for long. They knew they would be most vulnerable, but they also knew they must not give up. The screams of the women trying to find cover could be heard from the fields where Aluein and his men finally climbed out of the gorge. The smoke hit them hard in their exhausted state, but they kept moving. They could hear the ominous growl of the dragon above them and the menacing presence of the Zadoks near them. It was too much to take for some of the men, but Sir Roen kept them steady.

"Come here and strike *us* you absurd beast!" Aluein shouted. "We're the warriors, not the villagers!"

King Alexander came running with his men not too far behind.

The captains near the castle walls ordered the remaining ogres to load catapults with large stones soaked in oil. They lit the stones with the torches and released them into the twilight sky, but the dragon easily swerved to miss each fiery stone. As the stones landed, they spread more fire into the wet grassy fields.

"This is useless," Aluein said as he inspected the sight.

§

Peter made his way into the scramble of the courtyard in time to see the hideous black beast fly over the walls and hover above. He stepped back into the castle entrance so the dragon could not see him with the shield. He knew Caragon would know that the shield was a scale from the Dragon of the forest. Peter waited for the dragon to fly away and when it did, he ran out to find Will. But the panicked people made it difficult for Peter to make it through the yard. Women and men ran to the dungeon as soldiers leapt from their posts to escape the fire from the dragon.

"Will!" Peter screamed, but Will would not be able to hear him.

As the villagers made their way back into the dungeon, Peter again waited for another chance to climb to the wall and watch for the Dragon, the knights, and his father.

Behind them, the approaching Baroks could be heard, but King Alexander gave no order to advance toward the castle while the black dragon circled above them. He knew they would have to take their chances where they stood amidst the smoke and fire. He turned to see the frightened faces of his men. They knew they were surrounded by Zadoks and Baroks.

Suddenly, out of the smoky clouds around them, a Zadok leapt toward the King with its teeth bared and its wild eyes gleaming. Its black fur was soaked with sweat and mud. A hideous sight it was, but the King was ready as he held the sword of his fathers out in time to slice the throat of the wolf-like beast, sending its black blood splattering into the new day's light. As the dead beast fell to the ground motionless, the men cheered and headed into the smoke to fight more of the beasts. Not wanting to wait for the attack, the men chose to meet the enemy where they were, no matter what happened. They knew in their hearts the end of the battle was near.

§

Peter ran through the yard as fast as he could before the black dragon made another pass. He suspected the beast was searching for something and deep down, he knew it might be searching for him. Peter hid by a ladder and searched the skies for the dragon. Not finding it anywhere, he began to climb up the wooden ladder. Carrying his shield and sword, climbing was harder than he thought, but he made it to the top, where he found many soldiers had remained at their posts. Many continued to shoot arrows at the black beast, but others were staring down over the outer walls into the fields below. Peter crept over to the wall's edge and hesitated. He had never been on the walls of his father's castle before; only now did he realize how towering they were. Looking down. He could see the fields were ablaze and the smoke was thick from the wet grasses. The fighting of the knights and Caragon's Baroks could be heard in the morning air. Peter tried to catch a glimpse of his father's men in the distance, but the smoke was too thick. Instead, he turned his gaze toward the Dragon Forest. So peaceful, it stood in the distance with the rising sun spreading its warm hues across the tall trees like an artist's brush across a canvas. The forest would assuage his fears instead of produce them. A few sparrows took flight high above the trees as if startled by something. Peter hoped it was the movements of the Dragon of the Forest.

§

Will ran along the outer wall shouting orders at the men to remain still and wait for their orders to descend and fight in the fields. The captains were preparing the men to leave the wall and fight alongside the King below, but they waited until the black dragon had made its way back to the desert plains. As the beast turned midair toward the battle, the soldiers quickly shuffled down the ladders and into the courtyard near the closed gates. Running with his sword, Will stopped when he spotted Peter.

"No!" he shouted. "Not again!" He ran to Peter and grabbed his shoulder.

"Will, please!" Peter shouted. "I have to help the Dragon."

"What are you talking about?" Will asked as he pushed Peter toward the ladder. "I've got to get you out of here."

"No," Peter said. "I have to get down there and help the Dragon."

Then Will saw it. He spotted the scale on Peter's arm. As the sunlight glistened off the surface of the iridescent scale, its reflection hurt Will's eyes and he squinted to get a closer look.

"What is that?" He gently ran his fingers over the glassy surface. "Is it glass?"

"No," Peter answered. "It is a shield. It is a scale from the Dragon." He turned it so Will could see that it was once attached to the Dragon. "It gave this scale to me to use. I have to protect my father. I have to help the Dragon."

Will stared almost hypnotized by the luminous shield as it changed colors in the sunlight. Peter wrestled free from Will's grip and headed down the ladder. Will followed thinking that he could get Peter into the dungeon once and for all. But Peter ran toward the gates before Will's feet hit the ground. As the gates opened, Peter scurried through them.

"No!" Will yelled. "Peter, stop!" Will ran toward the open gates. "That's the King's son, stop him!"

But it was no use. The soldiers marched out and Peter ran between them unnoticed. All eyes were on the skies watching for the black dragon to appear at any moment.

§

"We will not last in this smoke for long," shouted Aluein to the King. He could feel the smoke clog his throat and he knew the men would soon suffocate if they did not leave the area. "We must move."

"No, we have to wait," Alexander answered. He was convinced the Dragon would remain faithful to the oath. "Remain still."

Some men ran into the smoke still fighting the unseen enemy. Others stood by their King not wanting him to fall in battle. True knights, they were willing to risk their lives to ensure the line of Alexander continued.

But Alexander knew the black dragon was using his smoke and fire to trap his men. He could see the flames covering the fields around the castle as the smoke thickened. He knew they had minutes only before the dragon decided to incinerate them once and for all.

Aluein shook his head as he watched his stubborn sovereign hold fast in his position.

"Hold fast, men!" he shouted to the soldiers and knights around him. Then, in front of them came a dreaded sound of the approaching black dragon. The breeze from its wings caused the smoke to circle around them and rise only to reveal its deep black presence in the new sky. Aluein knew they were vulnerable.

He ran over to Alexander. "We've nothing to buffet its fire," he shouted. "Our shields will not stop the flames."

Alexander nodded in agreement. His men had few shields and only helmets and breastplates to protect from man-made weaponry. But this enemy was not man. It was a supernatural being with powers unlike any Alexander had seen before. Only supernatural means could stop this fiend. But he still remained in his position as the black beast made eye contact with the King. Alexander did not flinch. He did not breathe. He gripped the sword of his father in his hands.

"Your majesty," Aluein said. "What do you want us to do?"

"Hold fast, my old friend," he answered. "Hold fast."

Aluein sighed. "I suspect we shall die this day." He turned to Alexander. "Perhaps that is the only proper death for two men of war."

So, he turned to face the flying beast above them as it hovered and flapped its mighty wings fanning the flames around creating a sort of halo of fire. Behind them he could hear the fight between the approaching Baroks and his men. The sound of swords clinging together blended with the shouts of his men far off in the distance to create the all too familiar cacophony. Aléon removed his ax and sword in his hands and signaled to his men to stand firm on this small hill that would forever remain as the place where their brave and honorable King was slain while trying to protect the kingdom from absolute evil.

§

Peter, sword and shield in hand, kept running between the marching soldiers as he spotted the black dragon hovering in the distance. The sun was higher in the sky now and the fires in the fields around the castle spewed their thick smoke into the air and blotted out the new sun. He gripped his sword and his shield in his hands as he ran. He could hear Will shouting his name behind him, yet he could not stop. He had to meet his father and help the Dragon of the Forest.

The captains shouted orders for the men to stop and take positions. There weren't many men left, but they obeyed their commanders and took battle positions. The archers raised their arrows into the sky and released them. As the arrows pierced its leathery skin, the dragon released into the air a scream of pain and anger. King Alexander watched the beast flinch from the arrows in its back. The presence of hope in his soul once again as he knew his men were still in the fight.

But the black dragon turned to see the soldiers approaching from the castle. In its anger, it inhaled deeply, producing a horrible a hissing sound. As it released its breath, fire spewed forth onto the men. The men hid behind their tenuous shields, but they could not hold back the intense heat. The flames consumed them.

§

Peter took his shield and held it high over his body as he knelt on the ground, trying to remain as small as he could behind the scale. He could feel the pressure from the flames hit the shield but to no avail. The scale held fast and protected him from the deathly fires.

Unfortunately, all around him the men were burned one by one. The dragon inhaled again. Peter ran closer to the beast before it could spit its fire. Behind him, the captains gave orders to the men along the walls to load their arrows again.

The dragon spotted Peter kneeling before him. He exhaled his fire hitting Peter's shield directly. The scale held fast once again sending the flames to the left and right of Peter's body. He could feel the immense pressure, but not the heat. He patiently waited for the dragon to finish and inhale again. As it gave in to its need for air, Peter ran closer to the beast. He could hear and feel the wings flapping above him as the breeze sent twigs and leaves flying through the air like shrapnel. Peter kept the shield near his face lowering it only once to see his position near the dragon. He was much closer now. So close, that he could see his father's men through the smoke and hear them fighting. He also could spot the underbelly of the black dragon as it flew near. Peter gripped his sword tightly.

The dragon inhaled yet again and released its fire on Peter's shield. Perplexed that this tactic was not working on this shield, the beast flew higher and circled around Peter. Peter turned his shield and followed the monster's path. The dragon tried to attack from behind, but it was no use. Its fire could not penetrate the shield. It roared its frustration and the sound hurt Peter's ears. He squinted from the pain in his head, but he still did not let go of the shield. He lowered it slightly to see where the monster had gone, but it was no longer in the air. He turned all around, searching for the dragon, but he could not see it. Peter decided to try and run through the smoke to find his father.

"Father!" he shouted. But there was no answer from the smoke.

"Father! Are you there?" Peter shouted.

"Peter!" the King answered from inside the ring of smoke.

"Yes, father," Peter said as he searched the smoke for a sign of his father. "It is me!" Then, he saw a glimmer of gold from inside the smoke directly in front of him. He knew it was his father's sword, so he quickly ran toward it.

But at that moment, the giant black dragon landed right in front of Peter, blocking his path. The ominous beast stood twenty feet into the sky as its chest heaved in and out sending its hot breath near Peter's face. Its black scales glistened as the fire reflected off its giant body. Its wings were still spread out as though trying to trap the boy. Caragon's dragon knew its prize was the Prince of Illiath.

Without hesitation, Peter raised his shield yet again and prepared for the flames to hit, but instead the beast took its long tail and swiped Peter with it, sending him flying into the air. The young boy landed hard on the ground and lost his bearings for a second or two. When he awoke, he realized his shield was nowhere near him. In a panic, he groped for it through the smoke. But he knew he still had his sword because he felt the cold blade with his hand.

Glimpsing the grotesque black dragon still in front of him, he stood up and raised his sword. The smoke from the fire began to sting his eyes, but he knew he had to stay still. The dragon lowered its head and opened its jaws. It roared and began to inhale with the same hissing sound. In the distance, Peter could still hear his father's voice shouting his name. Peter was ready to die protecting his father. He was finally a dragon slayer.

The dragon's gaze, fierce and evil, caught Peter's eyes. Both of his hands gripped the sword even tighter now as he waited for the dragon's move. The eyes were hollow and soulless. The head, large and grotesque with jagged scales covering the snout, tilted back as it took in more air. As it leaned forward to spew its fire forth, it suddenly stopped and let out a piercing scream sending the fire into the sky instead of onto Peter.

Realizing that his father's men had attacked the dragon from behind, Peter used the opportunity to find his scale. He spotted the shield lying near him so he ran to pick it up in time to meet the dragon's fire yet again. As the beast began to fly up into the air, it continued to spit its lethal venom in a steady stream onto Peter's shield, but it was still unable to penetrate it. It flew off into the sky leaving Peter alone for a moment.

"Peter!" Alexander shouted. "Son, are you alright?"

"Father!" Peter shouted as he ran toward the King. It seemed a lifetime since he had seen him. Together they held each other in the midst of the fire and smoke there on the hill.

"Are you alright? Were you burned at all?" the King asked.

"No father," Peter answered. "The scale, it acted as a shield. It saved me." He held the shield up and showed it to his father.

King Alexander stood amazed that his son was safe after facing the dragon. "You are brave." he said. "You saved us, Peter. You saved all of us from the dragon." He smiled at his small son and then searched the skies for Caragon's beast.

"Now, come with me," he said as they ran into the smoke for cover.

"Father," Peter said. "We're not safe out here. It will be back."

"We wounded it," Alexander answered. "We can kill it."

"No father," Peter interrupted. "Not without shields. We need these shields for the men."

"But where do we find them?" asked Aluein as he inspected Peter's scale. "I've never seen anything quite like this before."

Behind them they could still hear the shouts and screams of the men fighting the Baroks. "We've not much time," Alexander said. "The enemy will be here soon."

"What do we do?" Peter asked. He could feel the trepidation rising inside yet again.

"Wait," the King answered. "We'll wait for the Dragon of the Forest."

22 THE SAVIOR OF THÉADRIL

Will stopped at the open gates as soon as he felt the extreme heat from the black dragon's fire. Then, hesitantly, he stood and watched as many of the King's men ran for their lives. He wanted to come to their aid, but he heard the dragon's hissing as it inhaled more air to spew out its fiery venom. But it was no use.

Will ran back inside the courtyard as more people scurried, tripped, and fell over each other as they tried to get inside the dungeon. The courtyard was filled with small burning fires leftover from the dragon's breath. Will ran to the blacksmith's hut and frantically searched for a shield, but to no avail. There were none. He would have to face the dragon without a shield.

Peter was out there now along with the King. Will knew he had to do something. He had promised the King he would watch over the Prince and keep him safe. He grabbed two swords and ran out of the hut toward the open gates. The surviving soldiers were scampering to close the giant wooden door, so Will ran through the gate and over the bridge as fast as he could. Once outside the mighty walls of the castle, all were vulnerable to the dragon. He knew Peter would head there. Will sloshed through the Blue River with its cold waters stinging his skin under his leather boots. The waters reached up to his knees, but it was easy to cross. His eyes continued to search the sky for the dragon. As the flames from the beast's breath caused small fires to burn near the Blue River and the castle walls, Will used them as a cover to make his way near the hills where he knew the King was fighting

Through the smoke, Will spotted the large black dragon as it searched for Peter. Time and again it spit out its fire at Peter, but the shield saved him from the intense heat. Will crouched low near the ground and waited to see if Peter was alright. He watched as the dragon roared in pain and flew up into the air. Peter ran from underneath the beast and into the billows of smoke. The dragon hovered in the air and then flew away. Will could see that it had been wounded. He knew the King's men were near and had fired upon the dragon.

Will continued to stay low to the ground as he moved from fire to fire trying to spot Peter. Suddenly, he heard voices in the distance. He recognized the King's voice as he heard shouts and screams from fighting nearby. Will knew he had entered the battle scene.

Making his way into the smoke clouds that surrounded the King, Will entered enthusiastically knowing that soon he would be reunited with his sovereign and with Peter.

Peter stood near his father. He gazed up into the sky hoping the dragon would not return and watched for the Dragon of the Forest to come as it had promised. Then he heard a thrashing sound come from the smoky clouds nearby. He became frightened when he realized a Zadok could be approaching.

"Father," he whispered. "What is it?"

The King grabbed Peter's shoulder with one hand and gripped his sword with the other. Aluein turned with his ax held in front of his chest, ready to throw it at any approaching creature.

"Stand still," Alexander ordered, holding his breath.

A shadow formed within the smoke clouds. It was that of a man and not a beast. Still, the King raised his sword to attack whatever came through the smoke. But just as they prepared for the worst, they spotted Will coming through the smoke clouds with his swords drawn.

Peter smiled when he saw his friend. "Will!" he shouted. "You made it."

The two friends ran toward each other. Will put his hand on Peter's shoulder as a sign of their friendship. "I am glad you are safe," he said as he spotted the King. "My Lord." He said as he began to kneel.

"Hush!" the King said as he pushed Will and Peter behind him. Just then, a Zadok leapt into the air and through the smoke clouds with its teeth and yellow eyes glaring. As Peter and Will were shoved back, Aluein threw his ax forward where it met with the head of the black wolf-like dog, sending it to its death.

"We cannot stay here much longer," Aluein said as he retrieved his ax from the Zadok's skull. He wiped the black blood onto the soil and replaced his ax back onto his belt. "The enemy will find us and the dragon will be back."

"We mustn't move," King Alexander warned. "We need to wait. The Dragon will show as it promised. I know it will. I feel it in my heart." He winced from pain and the rims around his eyes were red from exhaustion.

"Aye," answered Aluein in obvious disapproval. But he was a servant of the King. So, he stood nearby with his son, Sir Roen, and a few dozen knights along with mercenaries who were anxious to fight again. All this waiting was not good for a warrior used to attacking at random until the battle ended. But if they were ordered to wait, then they would wait.

Together they waited as the battle raged around them with the impending return of the black dragon looming over them. Their fear intensified.

Will stood next to Peter wishing he were back in the dungeon. He had seen enough battle and death to last a lifetime and he was all of sixteen years old. Peter gripped his shield and sword tightly as they stared into the distance where the castle walls rose out of the horizon.

As the fires died down and the smoke clouds began to lift, King Alexander turned toward Hildron where he spotted his men successfully fighting off the Barok troops and trolls. The fire over

Hildron could still be seen as the sun made its way higher into the new morning sky.

The black dragon had returned. The men came together in a tight formation, knowing that without shields they were too vulnerable to do any good. Still, the soldiers and knights came together for a last fight. They were good soldiers.

"Hold steady, men," the King ordered.

Alexander's eyes searched the sky for any sign of the beast. He pushed Peter behind him in an attempt to protect his son, but Peter wouldn't have it. He stepped forward trying in earnest to see the Dragon of the Forest return. Only Peter knew the screech was the white owl. The screech echoed once again from above and this time it was louder. Peter smiled as he watched the skies. A breeze came from the east and spread the smoke all around the men in wisps. The men covered their eyes as twigs and grass spun around them in whirlwinds. They all became afraid except Peter. His eyes never left the sky. He knew the Dragon was near.

And then the Dragon of the Forest appeared—hovering above the men with its wings spread out flapping gently. It began to lower itself to the ground rather hastily and as it did, Peter ran towards it.

"I knew it!" Peter yelled. "I knew you would come."

King Alexander felt his body and countenance relax at the sight of the Dragon. He knew it would remember its Oath to his father and Théadril. And it finally appeared to honor that ancient Oath sworn so long ago. The King exhaled.

The knights and the men raised their weapons as they saw Peter run to the Dragon, but Aluein raised his hand and ordered them to stand down. Even he could not believe the sight before his tired eyes. The Dragon of the Forest did exist just as his sovereign had told him.

"Peter," Alexander yelled. "Wait!" But it was no use. The boy made his way over to the Dragon's face and looked deeply into its eyes.

"We've not much time," it whispered to Peter. He could see the Dragon was not well. The wound in its chest remained.

"I knew you would come back," Peter smiled as he touched the Dragon's snout. It felt cool as the scales glistened in the morning sun rising in the east.

Alexander walked over to the Dragon and touched his son's shoulder. "What do you want us to do?" he asked it.

"Take these scales and use them as shields," it answered as many of its scales fell from its back and shoulders. As they plunked to the ground, King Alexander motioned for his men to grab them and they obeyed. Hesitantly and gingerly, they approached the Dragon never taking their eyes off the giant beast. All their lives they were told of the Dragon in the Forest, but now they were seeing the myth come to life right before their eyes. The sinewy muscles twitched underneath the leathery skin as the men bent to grab the scales. They gathered them up and quickly began to disperse them out to one another inspecting the glistening armor in their hands.

"I've never seen such a thing as this," one soldier exclaimed as he gazed at his reflection in the scale. The shield was not cumbrous or awkward at all. It was no heavier than his sword, but yet it was made of a strong substance. One by one the scales were distributed among the men. Each young man stared in amazement at their new armor. On the inside of each scale was a grip made from a tendon of the Dragon's flesh. The men could place their forearms inside the grips and maneuver the shields to protect their vital areas.

"Amazing," the men exclaimed as they raised their new shields. Peter noticed the Dragon's vulnerability as the scales fell from its body.

"But you will not have the protection," Peter said.

"It is too late for me," the Dragon answered. "These scales will be of better use here protecting these men." Its large glowing eyes met with the King's eyes and together they understood what must happen next. The Dragon could see the great fatigue in the

King's face. There was no time to lose. "Use these shields against the fire of the black dragon."

Alexander nodded as one scale was handed to him by Aluein. His friend stood near and carefully watched the Dragon. Alexander grabbed the shield and held it firmly in his grasp. The iridescent surface of the scale was remarkable. It sent sparkling reflections onto Alexander's face. Then, he turned to his son. "We must go now, Peter."

But Peter stood near the Dragon and never stopped staring at its face.

"No," Peter said. "Not now."

His father sighed and tried to pull his son away from the Dragon. "We do not have much time. The black dragon is returning. We must go now, son," he said.

But Peter did not move.

The Dragon shifted its tail along the ground which startled the men and made them stumble back into rows. Then it slowly lifted its giant head up to examine its surroundings. The castle had been hit hard by the fires and no men stood along the walls any longer. Hildron was still belching its black smoke and red fire. The Baroks were still fighting off the King's men in the hills of Théadron. As it lowered its head to look at Peter, it opened its mouth to speak yet again.

"One last ride to safety," it whispered to Peter.

He smiled and climbed onto the neck of the Dragon. As the beast lifted him up high into the air, it glanced at Alexander who stood nearby. "To the castle," it said to the relieved King.

Alexander had wanted his son out of the battlefield and now his son would be safe from Caragon's last stand. As he watched the Dragon lift off the ground, the King felt a surge of strength flow through his body. He no longer felt weak, but strong. As the wind from the Dragon's wings blew around him, he could almost feel his body rising off the ground with it as though he were an eagle taking flight. He would not be weary any longer. He would not feel the pain from his battle wound again. With this renewed strength, he, the King, was new again.

Peter gripped the scales as the leathery wings flapped one more time and lifted the two high into the air. Peter watched his father and all the men including Will grow smaller and smaller underneath its feet. He was able to obtain an overview of the whole battlefront. All the shields held by the men sparkled as the sunlight hit them, creating an incredible sight that Peter had never seen before. The wind blew through his hair as they flew toward the castle and into the courtyard where the people ran and screamed when they spotted the Dragon. Many villagers took up rocks and large stones to hurl at the Dragon. Some soldiers raised their arrows to shoot it until they spotted Peter. He waved his arms to stop them and they obeyed.

The Dragon lowered Peter to the ground gently in a cloud of dust and hay. As all the dust settled, Peter hopped off and ran to meet the beast's eyes. Deep inside he knew it would be their last meeting, but he didn't want to say it. He simply stood near its moistened eyes and remained silent. With labored breath, the Dragon returned Peter's gaze. A bit of smoke snorted out of its nostrils making some women scream and run, but Peter knew all was safe.

"I will miss you…my friend," he said.

The Dragon raised its leathery wings. "I kept my Oath, Prince of men," it answered. Peter nodded. "Now, you must keep yours."

"I will," Peter answered. "The forest will remain."

"Remember, it is now the time of man," the Dragon said.

And with that, it stood up on all four of its limbs folding its wings back and creating a menacing sight for the villagers. More scales fell off its body onto the ground nearby leaving more of its skin exposed. As the scales fell, Peter instantly knew what the Dragon was doing.

When it was finished, the elongated wings unfolded and began to flap as the giant torso rose off the ground sending more villagers running for cover.

Peter watched his friend fly over the castle walls.

"A dragon!" someone shouted.

"Stone it!" yelled one man as he threw a rock. "Kill it!"

More men grabbed rocks to throw at the Dragon as it flew. Peter covered his face as more dirt and twigs scattered in the wind around him. He watched as the villagers came closer with rocks to hurl.

"Stand down!" Peter ordered. He ran over to the men and raised his arms. "Stand down!"

The men froze in place at the voice of their young sovereign. They stared at him and then watched the Dragon fly off. Each man dropped the stones. Soldiers ran over to Peter to protect him from the angry villagers. But Peter held his own ground as he glared at the men who dared to harm the Dragon of the Forest.

"It is not going to harm you," he said. "It is going to save us all."

The men remained silent as they stood incredulously nearby.

Peter's time had come. "Now, do as I say," he ordered. "Each man, pick up one scale and use it as a shield. Hurry!"

The soldiers quickly obeyed, but the men of the village hesitated.

Lord Byrén, great leader of the Crow Valley, climbed up the steps leading away from the dungeon in time to see the Dragon fly high into the air and Peter order the men to gather the scales. He could not believe his eyes. Stepping toward the scales on the ground and stooped over to pick one up. The surface of the scale was smooth in his hands as he inspected it. Then, he turned toward the men and began to pass the scales to them one at a time just as Peter had ordered. The men of the village followed suit and took the shields.

"The black dragon is coming back soon," Peter explained. "We've no time to lose." As he finished speaking, the roar of the black dragon echoed once again through the new morning sky sending the men running to retrieve scales. "Only these shields can protect you from the flames."

"To your posts!" Peter ordered the soldiers.

Climbing the ladders to the outer walls of the castle once more, each man took his place ready to fight. The bowmen found their quivers and arrows. As they prepared to load them, one man shouted, "Look!" He pointed out over the walls and into the air where they all spotted the Dragon of the forest circling high and near the enormous beast flew the black dragon following closely behind.

§

The King's men aligned into battle formations quickly with their new shields in front. King Alexander and Aluein inspected the formations. They only minutes to spare, but all was ready. Alexander stood out in front to lead his men. The Dragon circled above them. Then the black dragon approached.

Behind them, they could hear the marching of the Baroks in the hills nearby. Before them, the fires in the grasses had burned out in the morning sun. The smoke had dissipated and the castle could be clearly seen as could the dead of previous battles. The remains stood as a memorial to all that had happened up to this one defining moment.

"Alexander," Aluein said as he stood next to his King. "Your name means 'defender of men.'" He placed his arm on Alexander's shoulder. "You have lived up to your name, my friend."

The King smiled and drew his sword, the sword of his father, out of its sheath one more time. Then, he turned to his men to steady them. "At my signal!"

All the men drew their swords in unison, waiting behind their shields for the start of the battle. Aluein took his place with the men, lifting his shield near his neck. It fascinated him how the shields protected all the men from neck to thigh as though they were designed that way from the beginning.

"Steady men!" shouted the King.

The men raised their shields higher as they prepared for the intense heat of the fire.

The black dragon circled, but it spotted the men below in their formations. It dove lower and swiftly passed by the men sending some flying through the air from the wind of his wings.

"Hold fast!" Aluein shouted as he struggled to stay afoot himself. The men quickly regained their footing and grasped their shields tightly as their hearts beat faster. But the black beast passed again this time even lower to the earth.

King Alexander raised his sword above his head with the intent to strike at the dragon as it flew by. He timed his swipe carefully. As the beast came near, the King took his sword and threw it handle first at the dragon. The blade soared through the air and found its place in the belly of Caragon's black dragon. Grabbing the sword with its talons, the black dragon twisted in the air from the pain and removed the blade from its belly. This time it reached greater heights as it flapped its wings faster and faster. Suddenly, the black dragon flew away toward Hildron behind them. But the King ordered them not to move. The men grew nervous with the black dragon out of sight, but they obeyed their King.

As quickly as the dragon was gone, it reappeared behind them to burn the men with its fiery breath. King Alexander sensed its approach and so ordered his men to raise shields and turn in unison. As they heard the order and obeyed, they all turned in time to meet the fire spewing forth toward them. The shields all blocked the fire as the dragon passed overhead. With shields raised high above their heads, they all were able to follow its fiery path until they were once again facing the castle. Amazed at how the shields protected them, Aluein smiled and cheered the Dragon of the Forest. The men followed with shouts of exuberance as they realized they survived. All celebrated, except King Alexander, whose eyes never left the black dragon's flight.

He knew the black dragon now had the sword of his father.

Having failed to successfully stop the men, Caragon now focused on the castle. The King could see the fire spewing down into the courtyard and he shuttered for fear of his people's safety.

Then he thought of Peter.

His eyes lifted up to the sky and spotted the loyal Dragon still there, circling above them. The men stood silently as they watched the black dragon hover above the castle still spewing forth its demon breath.

§

Peter knelt behind his shield as he watched the others do the same as the black dragon continued to spew out his fire onto all in its path. *Surely it must need a breath by now*. He glanced over to see Lord Byrén holding his shield in front of his body to ward off the flames. Lord Byrén spotted Peter and grinned approvingly at him. When the fire stopped and the hissing sound of the dragon was heard, the men scurried to load their arrows and fire them at the dragon's belly as it hovered over them, but they were too late. Lord Caragon flew away and then repositioned himself over the west wall of the castle to burn more of the walls.

As King Alexander watched his castle burn, he grew angrier and angrier. "No other kingdoms have come to our aide," he said. Aluein heard him. "Not one region has come to help us." Alexander turned to his friend. "Do you think it is true, what Caragon said? That all the other kings have joined him"

"Cannot possibly be true," Aluein answered. "Besides, we do not need them."

He turned his eyes upward toward the Great Dragon of the Forest. It flew lower now, as though to taunt Caragon back away from the castle. Alexander exhaled with relief.

Will stood steady with his shield in his hand as he watched the castle burn. He hoped all the villagers and Peter were inside the dungeon. But when the dragon stopped his fiery attack yet again, a shout of victory was heard emanating from the castle walls.

"Listen!" he yelled to the men. "Do you hear that?"

"Yes!" Sir Roen answered. "The men are shouting! I can hear them!"

He smiled as he realized they were still there. They were still fighting.

King Alexander and Aluein stared intently at the castle as the black dragon flew away once more. The shouts of the men were victorious indeed. He looked at the Dragon once more and noticed more of its scales were gone from its body. "They must have its scales," he said. "They must have shields!" He pointed to the Dragon.

"Aye," said Aluein with a smile. "It appears to be that way. We are protected. We should march toward the castle. What have we to lose?"

"Yes," Alexander agreed.

He ordered the men to slowly approach the castle in unison with shields high. As they moved, Caragon's dragon spotted them marching. It turned its wicked fire on them in order to stop them, but as they marched with their shields, they could not be stopped. Each time the black dragon stopped to inhale, the men made more progress toward the castle. And as the dragon turned away from the castle, the men on the walls shot their arrows hitting the beast's back sending it reeling with pain. Catching itself before hitting the hard ground below, the dragon swooped up and used its wings to try and stop the King. The wind from its wings caused dust and dirt to rise up from the ground and swirl over the men, pelting their bodies with pebbles. But the men held fast and marched forward as the intense wind and fire gushed at them time and time again until, finally, they stood outside the castle walls before the Blue River. Crossing it would be a challenge for the men who still held their swords high to protect their bodies.

Alexander strained to see if the black beast still had his sword, but he could not see it in its belly.

The Dragon, patiently hovering over the desert hills of Théadron, waited as the black dragon landed between the men and the Blue River. Caragon roared his displeasure at the men's progress and signaled his Baroks to attack without mercy. They had followed closely behind the King's men. Coming from the hills, the grotesque creatures ran with swords drawn.

Alexander knew that it would be impossible for them to fight and protect themselves from Caragon at the same time. He could hear the black dragon's hiss as it inhaled for yet another slow burn.

"Focus all your arrows on the Baroks!" he ordered the bowmen on the walls of the castle. As the Baroks approached, the arrows flew toward them sending many to the ground, but many more followed behind. This worried Alexander.

He ordered half his knights and men to turn and fight and the other half to use their shields to protect them from the fiery breath.

As they turned to meet the Baroks in battle, Will ran up ahead and threw his sword deep into the chest of one of Caragon's beast-like fighters only to find the monster had been stricken with several arrows. As Will stood over the black fighter, he wondered how it was pierced with so many arrows at once. Looking up, and toward the east, he spotted a sight he could not believe. Coming from the Cornshire hills, he saw hundreds of men on horseback riding with loaded crossbows firing at the Baroks and hitting dozens of them. Will turned to see that the King and knights had spotted the approaching men as well. More exuberant shouts of victory came from the castle walls as the Baroks were being stopped.

Standing with his shield, Alexander gazed upon the sight of King Mildrir the Warrior leading his men into the Barok formations. Colliding near the Blue River, the clash of beast and man happened yet again. Alexander's eyes welled at the sight and he knew that they were not alone after all. But there was no time for celebrating with the black dragon still standing between him and his castle. As Mildrir and his men fought valiantly near the Blue River, King Alexander ordered his men to turn and face the black dragon. As they did so, the beast spread its wings and inhaled again deeply with a loud hiss. The men raised their shields high and prepared for the fire. As that fire met their shields yet again, they could feel the pressure on their shields as it hit them with a fierce intensity. Alexander felt Caragon's desperation.

The black dragon flapped its wings and spit its fire onto the men. It rose off the ground and flew toward King Mildrir's men knowing they had no shields to protect themselves. All Alexander could do was watch Mildrir and his men burn to death as they fought for his kingdom.

The King had never felt so helpless.

§

Climbing the ladder to the outer wall, Peter frantically made his way to the top and ran to see what was happening to his father. Still carrying his shield, he spotted his father below near the river. He could see King Mildrir's men battling the Baroks in the field near the castle. A feeling of relief ran through his body as he sensed his father's safety. But he arrived on the wall in time to see the black dragon lift into the air and fly to the battle. The beast still had arrows in its back and Peter spotted blood spewing from its belly yet it flew away. All the soldiers on the wall stood in silence as they knew the dragon was going to end the battle with its fire. There was nothing they could do as their arrows could not fly that far into the air. Peter stared down at his father and the knights below.

At that moment, as Caragon flew to the battle, Peter spotted something coming from above them all. With one rapid swoop, the Dragon of the Forest spit out its blue fire, sending Caragon spiraling out of control. Then, with its talons, the Dragon grabbed the neck of the ferocious beast and sent it soaring to the ground with a loud thud. Dirt and dust flew when the beast landed and quickly regained its footing. With its long neck twisting like a goose, Caragon's dragon awkwardly returned to the skies. It attacked the Dragon with rapid fire, causing it to roar from the pain of the heat meeting its exposed flesh. But it did not stop fighting. The Dragon inhaled and spewed forth its blue fire once again hitting the evil dragon in the face.

Peter watched in horror as the two dragons fought in midair before him. He knew the Dragon was too vulnerable to withstand Caragon's fire, yet there was nothing he could do but watch.

King Alexander ordered the gates to be opened and the bridge lowered. When the order was obeyed, he led his men through the cold rushing water of the river to the drawbridge. Soon they were safely inside the castle grounds. Climbing the ladder to the top of the wall, the King stood watching the fight of the dragons in the sky with his son, Peter.

Will wasn't too far behind, and when he reached the wall, he stood nearby the King and Peter.

Mildrir's men were finishing off the Baroks when the black dragon spit fire onto the knights sending many to their deaths. King Mildrir knew the Dragon could only protect his men from Caragon's black dragon for only a few moments more. He ordered his surviving men to ride to the castle for safety. As they sliced through the Baroks, the men quickly found their way to the river. Crossing it quickly, Mildrir's men finally escaped inside castle gates and entered into the courtyard.

Meanwhile, the battle in the skies continued. Caragon's fire found the Dragon's exposed skin time and again sending it reeling through the air. The Dragon tried to inhale again to send its blue fire out, but it could not find the strength. Finally, it landed onto the ground barely able to move. Its breath was heavy and greatly labored now, and its leathery skin was burnt and bleeding. Its wings were damaged from the fire.

Caragon landed in front of the Dragon and hissed once again. As he inhaled, the Dragon lurched forward and ripped Caragon's skin with its talons. Using its tail, it hit Caragon across the face sending him flying backwards. But when he regained his footing, he turned and spewed out more fire burning the Dragon's face and exposed neck.

"No!" Peter shouted as he tried to climb down the wall. Restrained by his father, Peter struggled to break free. He did not want to watch the Dragon die.

"Peter," Alexander said. "There is nothing we can do now!"

Lord Caragon's black dragon continued to spit his fire at the Dragon as the men on the castle wall watched helplessy. The few surviving Baroks stood by cheering as their leader burned the Dragon of the Forest. With roars from the pain of the fire and now unable to fly, the Dragon tried to attack Caragon, but when it stopped to inhale yet again, the Dragon could barely see its foe in as the blinding smoke. Caragon's dragon roared and flapped its wings, sensing the battle was almost over. He hissed again sending more air into his dragon lungs.

The Dragon of the Forest, hunched down and barely able to look up into the bright sunlight, slowly glanced over to the castle wall where its eyes, now dimmed, searched for Peter. The new morning sun was higher in the sky at that time of day.

Peter, still restrained by his father, saw the Dragon searching for him. "It's looking for me!" he shouted. "Let me go!" With that, the King released Peter and watched his son run to the wall's edge. Peter waved his arms as the Dragon spotted him. Their eyes met once more. Peter saw that the familiar yellow glow of its eyes was fading.

King Alexander stood nearby and watched the painful sight.

With only a few breaths left, the Dragon spread its damaged wings wide and flapped them as it looked deep into Peter's eyes. As it returned its gaze to the enemy before it, the Dragon lifted its torn and burnt body off the ground, and with one last bit of strength it lunged at Caragon's black dragon before he could spew his fire. The Dragon of the Forest wrapped its sharp talons tightly around the neck of the black beast sending it backwards and onto the desert floor. With its body weight far greater than Caragon's lithe black beast, the Dragon had the advantage. It gripped the neck with all its strength as the dragon tried to breathe in. The pulse in the neck was strong and the Dragon could feel it in its grasp, but with each passing moment, the pulse grew weaker and weaker as Caragon could no longer breathe in air. The Dragon gripped as Caragon swiped with his claws and talons to try and break free. The claws ripped open the Dragon's flesh yet it still would not release the neck until finally, finally, Caragon's wicked black dragon of his own creation kicked no more, the pulse in the neck was gone.

Lord Caragon was dead.

The fires that belched over Hildron castle finally ceased. As the Dragon let loose the neck of Caragon's dragon, the beast began to disintegrate, to turn to ashes, to dissipate into the morning breeze. And then it was gone.

§

The Great Dragon of the Forest stood bleeding and wounded. Its massive sides heaved in and out. Peter headed for the ladder and slipped by his shocked father, the King. He slid down the familiar ladder, ran over the lowered bridge, and through the open gates toward his dying friend. He crossed the Blue River with its ice cold waters reaching his waist but did not stop. His eyes remained focused on the Dragon.

The roar of the Baroks making their way toward the feeble Dragon stopped Peter. He quickly hid behind a bush so they would not find him. He could hear his father's footsteps coming from behind, but he did not want to move or leave that place.

"Peter," the King whispered. "Do not move."

He knelt with his son and placed his hand on his shoulder. He knew his son had to be near the Dragon in its final moments, but he also knew the Baroks wanted blood for the death of their leader. Together, King and Prince knelt nearby as the Baroks ran up to the Dragon with their weapons drawn.

As the Baroks reached the Great Dragon, they climbed on its back and thrust their spears and swords deep into its back causing it to roar from the pain. It twitched as it tried to inhale and spew forth its blue fire, but there was no strength left in its broken body. One after the other, the Baroks sliced at the Dragon. Its blood soaked red into the ground. The leader, a black armor-wearing Barok, ran to where Caragon's dead dragon once lay and picked up the Sword of Alexander from the desert ground. Running back toward its fellow Baroks, it held in its hand the Sword of Alexander. The Baroks roared with pleasure at the sight of the famous enemy sword. Their leader climbed up the dying Dragon's body and stood on its burnt back. Then, as the King and Prince watched nearby, it turned the blade downward and thrust it deep into the Dragon's back.

"No!" Peter shouted. His father covered his mouth before the Baroks could hear him. Tears streamed down Peter's face as he watched his friend being killed before him. His father turned him away from the sight and held him close as he tried to break free from his father's hold.

§

From the castle wall, Will and the soldiers tacitly watched the sight of the great Dragon of the Forest, willingly give up its life to save the kingdom. Aluein joined Will and the soldiers along the outer wall of the palace and caught the sight of the Baroks claiming victory over the Dragon of the Forest.

"Let us show those monsters a thing or two about victory," he said as he ordered the men back out to the battlefield.

King Mildrir also ordered his men to battle and together the two kingdoms rode as one and made their way across the Blue River to the valley where they would finally finish off the Baroks once and for all.

The final battle was swift and easy as the King's men caught the Baroks off guard. As the creatures were slaughtered, their leader escaped on horseback into the hills, arrogantly carrying the King's sword, the great Sword of Alexander. Sir Roen loaded his bow with an arrow and aimed it at the fleeing beast as it ran to the hills. But he noticed a crow flying above the Barok leader. As Roen quickly released his arrow into the air, the Barok flung the sword into the air where the crow caught it in its talons and flew away toward the Black Hills. Sir Roen's aim was true. The arrow pierced the last Barok between the shoulders, sending it to its death there in the desert hills of Théadron.

But the sword of Illiath was gone.

Among the dead and dying Baroks there in the low desert hills outside the castle, all the knights and soldiers stood silently near the Dragon. But they feared they were too late. It lay still on the ground surrounded by its blood and the bodies of dead Baroks. King Mildrir, sword drawn and breathing heavily, dismounted and made his way to the still beast and, as he approached, he noticed it was not yet dead as he had thought. Indeed it was barely breathing. He motioned to King Alexander. He cautiously made his way over while still holding a weary Peter in his arms. As they approached the Dragon, Alexander set Peter down and allowed him to walk over to his dying friend.

Its red-rimmed eyes slowly opened as it greatly labored to breathe, but it mustered enough strength to turn its massive head to meet Peter's eyes as he approached. Puffs of smoke left its nostrils. Its leathery skin shivered from the cold air and intense pain. Its mouth slowly opened to speak. Its lips were painfully dry with thirst, but the Dragon strained to speak.

"You are my friend, Peter," it whispered. "You and I are brothers."

Peter nodded through his tears.

"Man and dragon once lived as brothers long ago. It is time for that peace again. As I have sworn…a son of Alexander…will sit on the throne of Illiath forever," the Dragon declared. "Your father, King Alexander…was called to be the protector of that covenant Oath. He has fulfilled his duty with honor. And now," it hesitated. "You are the heir of that promise."

"But, why me?" Peter asked as he looked into the Dragon's weary eyes.

"This... is your purpose, Peter. This... is your burden."

Peter nodded.

The Dragon turned its head toward Hildron. "Do not seek glory for yourself, Peter. That... is what Peregrine did. And that is what Caragon did."

The Dragon turned its gaze toward the castle. More smoke lifted from its nostrils. "The palace...it faces the Dragon Forest," it whispered. "All others built their castles away from it. They cannot see it, Peter. Always remember... to keep the Dragon Forest in your sight."

"Why?" Peter asked.

"That is where your purpose dwells," the Dragon said. "That is where you will get your strength."

Peter nodded once again as the tears welled up in his eyes. He quickly wiped them. Then, walking up to the Dragon, he gently laid his hand upon its rough snout. No more glistening scales lined the face of the beast. They were dull and muddied. And no more words came from its mouth. It remained closed. Peter gazed into its eyes. They stared at one another for a moment longer.

Peter tried to remember the first time he entered into the Dragon Forest that cold night. It seemed so long ago. He remembered the first time he saw the glowing yellow eyes appear from between the trees that were so black and eerie. Now, those eyes were dimming forever. Peter gently stroked the snout as the Dragon closed its eyes from exhaustion. It seemed to like the gentle touch.

"I will never forget you," Peter faintly whispered. Then, realizing there was no longer a reason to whisper or feel ashamed anymore, he stated firmly and plainly for all to hear. "*I will never forget you.*"

And with that, as Peter slowly lifted his hand away from the snout, the Great Dragon of the Forest, the savior of Théadril, the covenant maker, breathed its last breath and died there on the desert hills near the Blue River in the kingdom of Illiath.

23 A NEW DAY

All was silent in the new morning. All was still.

The shocked men along the outer palace walls stood staring at the sight. The villagers in the courtyard waited for a word from them, but their stares were met with quiet stillness. They gazed up into the morning sky for a sign. The soldiers along the wall gave them no signal. Yet many more ran to the dungeon to guide more people out into the morning sun. They covered their eyes as they left the shadows of the stairway and felt the sun's warmth on their faces. One by one, the villagers entered the courtyard and for the first time saw the results of the battle.

In the desert hills, the stunned men of both kingdoms stood staring at the Dragon, their King, and young Peter. No one dared to move. Suddenly, a soldier took his sword and turned it upside down. He thrust it into the ground where it settled to stillness and he knelt behind it out of respect. Other soldiers and knights spied the man and they took their swords and knelt with heads bowed. For most, this was the first and last time they ever saw the Dragon of the Forest. It had existed only in tales, myths, and stories told to them by their families. But now they were witnessing for themselves the truth: The Dragon did exist and it gave up its life that they might live.

King Alexander hesitated. For the first time he was unsure of what to do next. Taking in a deep breath, he walked up to his tired son and picked him up.

With his tired limp body in his father's arms, Peter cried. He only allowed himself to weep for only a few moments and then he lifted his head up and motioned for his father to release him. King Alexander lowered his son to the ground. As Peter stood before the men he would one day lead, he straightened up his shoulders and tried to stand as tall as he could. He was a Prince, after all, the future King of Illiath, heir to the throne. He would not be carried away from this site as a child, he decided he would walk away as the sovereign that he was.

Leading his father and with chest out, Peter boldly made his way between the men as they knelt silently. The knights and soldiers watched as both royals passed by them. The soldiers along the palace wall followed both Peter and the King with their eyes as they slowly came to the river's edge. Together they crossed the waters and stood in front of the castle.

Will stepped toward the ladder and quickly climbed down as Peter and his father entered through the castle gates. The villagers watched as their brave King entered into the courtyard with his bold son leading the way. As they approached, men and women along with their children bowed their heads as their sovereign leaders walked by. Only the cool wind softly blowing through the trees could be heard on this new day.

But above them, as the sun made its way higher into the sky, a little girl standing with her mother spotted something more beautiful than anything she had ever seen before. "Look!" she called, pointing to the sky. Her mother turned her gaze to the sky in time to spot a multi-colored prism stretched out across the firmament making its way from the south to the north.

"It's a rainbow," the mother said to her daughter as she smiled.

"A rainbow," the little girl repeated. Then, she grasped her mother's hand in hers as a few sparrows fluttered across the sky toward the Dragon Forest.

§

As the dust from battle settled over the land, a peace befell the kingdom as the villagers began to return to their homes. Family after family made the sorrowful journey home to their villages. Some returned to burnt houses and found farms in disarray, and others returned to discover their homes were damaged, yet still standing. The area looked as though some wicked storm of nature had befallen them instead of war. The farmers of the villages would have to work to rebuild their lands and return to the life they knew before the siege.

One night soon after, the King gathered a few of his men to follow him out to the desert. Together they stood near the Dragon's body which still lay in the desert hills west of the castle. Logs of wood were brought and stacked alongside the massive body of the Dragon. When enough wood was stacked, it was lit with a torch held by the knights. The fire quickly spread, its intense heat giving warmth as the night air turned bitter cold. Lastly, King Alexander, holding his lit torch, walked up to the fire and, with Peter by his side, threw his torch into the blaze.

There, they all stood and watched as the Great Dragon's body burned down to ashes. The legend of the Dragon would live on forever.

And the night slowly turned to morning.

§

Finally, the time had come for the many funerals honoring the fallen who had given their lives to defend the kingdom of Théadril. The somber villagers from the Cornshire held their funerals and memorials in the rolling green hills outside the castle walls. The regal Lady Godden walked slowly behind the wooden coffins carried in horse drawn carriages through the small towns toward the cemetery high overlooking the valley.

At the Cardion Valley, Lady Silith participated in the memorials held for the Royal knights who died protecting the Cardion Valley from the evils of Lord Caragon. Her townspeople suffered the most from this most grievous war. As she walked alongside family members of the fallen, she clasped their hands tightly as though they were her own family. She sought to unite herself with their pain and anguish. All the people of Cardion suffered heartfelt loss. Most lost their homes, all had lost their livelihoods when their fields were burned by Caragon's tumultuous creatures, the Baroks.

But Lady Silith understood the resolve of her people. She knew they would rise again from the ashes and rebuild their small town. Yet on this day of mourning, it was hard to imagine a time when all would be normal.

§

General Aluein led the somber procession in the Crow Valley alongside Lord Byrén as the many soldiers and knights marched in unison to memorialize the fallen from their small community. This proud community, known for its training of knights and mercenaries for the King's service, stood along the road with banners held high flapping in the breeze as their brave men strolled together marking this day in history. The Crow Valley had been enslaved by Lord Caragon's fallacious madness for many moons as he overtaxed the people, mislead them, and withheld commodities in order to starve them into submission.

Now, with silent Hildron in the distance, the people vowed never to forget and never to allow such oppression to happen again. The fires over Hildron were snuffed, but the dark storm clouds still hovered over the mysterious castle carved out of the Black Hills. Once built and possessed by Hildron the Mighty, the castle was used to house Caragon in his exile. But somehow he claimed it as his own and now it served as a constant reminder to all people of what injustice and cupidity can do.

§

Back at the palace of Alexander in Illiath, the many memorials had come to an end. The courtyard was rebuilt and the dungeon became a storage facility yet again. The merchants began to return to their commerce and trade as the people of the nearby towns felt safe again. Exhausted, King Alexander took refuge inside his castle for many weeks as he recovered from the wounds he suffered in battle. But finally, he felt the time had come for his kingdom to move forward with some good and fruitful celebrations. He had decided to Knight some of the brave soldiers who had so gallantly fought to protect the lands and the King in a grand ceremony to be held in the throne room of the palace for all the villagers in the nearby lands. It was to be a grand celebration of bravery indeed. Alexander felt deep in his heart that his people needed a time of commemoration.

As the invitations were delivered throughout Théadril, the festivities were planned and prepared by a recovering Constable Darion. Upon retaking his post as head over all the cares and concerns of the castle again, Darion's pride in his King and country swelled inside his heart. His King was safe, the castle remained, and the lands were healing.

The Kings from the outer regions came to witness the event. Eulrik, son of Glausser the Brave, came from the southern region as did Thorgaerd, son of Théadron. Alexander had not seen these men in many years.

King Mildrir the Warrior, the eldest living King, attended to honor his men. He rode in from the East Shore port where his mighty castle stood on Mount Thorgest. Mildrir's ancestors founded the land by the sea and defended it with a mighty navy created by Mildrir's father, Melkorn. The name, Thorgest, derived its meaning from the word "warrior" and so Mildrir was aptly named after the land of his father.

Thorgest boasted some four thousand residents of both farmers and mariners. Its history is undistinguished and ordinary. The land was settled at the time of Théadril as each leader rose to power. Melkorn was a reclusive man of the sea. He wanted his kingdom to remain set apart from the others as he vowed to protect the eastern shore. Now, as the only living King of the original Leaders of the Oath on this momentous occasion, he had come to honor the son of Illiath at his time of commemoration for he had kept the Oath and assisted him in time of battle. Alexander would come to remember this allegiant act in the future.

King Mildrir recalled how his men alerted him to the signal fire atop Illiath's castle. As he approached Alexander, he could see the relief in his eyes.

"My old friend," Alexander said as he extended his arm. "It is so good to see you once again." The men grasped forearms in a gesture of friendship.

"A time of peace," Mildrir said. "It is good to be here."

"Tell me of the sword of your father," he continued. "Any signs of it yet?"

"No," Alexander sighed. "I am afraid it is still lost."

Mildrir walked with Alexander and placed his arm around the King's shoulder.

"Any plans to go after it?" he asked.

"In the making," Alexander said. "I am organizing a meeting of the rulers soon to discuss the next steps to retrieving all the lost swords once and for all."

"Good. We cannot waste any more time," Mildrir answered as he retrieved his pipe from his belt. "This meeting will be most beneficial for all the kingdoms."

Alexander smiled. "I hope so, my Lord." He felt safe in the presence of his father's oldest friend. Mildrir often reminded him of his father with the same brow and white hair. Not as broad as Aléon, but Mildrir's personality was larger than life.

"I have ordered a conscription sent out to all the leaders for this quest. Surely many men will step forward to be part of something so historic," said Alexander.

"One can only hope," replied Mildrir.

Isleif, son of King Bœrn, arrived on a white horse given to him by King Aléon, Alexander's father. He had come from the serene north shore valley to partake of this celebration. It was his people who provided the sturdy limestone blocks that built the palace of Illiath. As he walked toward the mighty structure, he carefully examined the craftsmanship of the builders remembering the toil and cost of constructing such a fortress. But it stood out as one of the finest in all the land. He grinned.

Having been an old friend of Aléon, he now wanted to give his blessing to Alexander and Peter. "I always enjoy coming to the palace of Illiath," he smiled as he greeted the King. "Though it has been too long, my friend." The two grasped forearms.

Finally, King Beátann the Wise, the elder and still great leader from the southeast region, rode in on his prize black stallion, Audun. Missing were the fallen Kings, Hildron the Mighty, Niahm, son of Egan, and Naá,l son of Leámahn. But their sons and daughters came to represent each kingdom and to pay their respect to Alexander.

Lady Aemilia, the youngest and fairest daughter of Naál, came to Alexander with a gift of gold. She had flowing blonde hair like that of the sunlight and was dressed in the finest blue silk from across the sea. He smiled as he remembered her from his childhood. Alexander found himself staring at her rare beauty before him.

They embraced. Her lithe body felt soft in his arms and her scent lingered in the air near him. Such a pleasant contrast to harsh battle.

She placed a small chest of carved mahogany into his hands. Inside the chest was the gift of gold from her lands. When their eyes met, Alexander felt something inside his heart he had not felt since Laurien had passed. He gladly retrieved the gift from Aemilia's soft hands and thanked her. She bowed her head in respect, and as her face slowly lifted, she smiled at Alexander silently. He raised his arm and she reached for it. With her hand resting on his forearm, the two walked into the throne room together. The leaders, representatives, and townspeople watched and soon followed.

The celebrations began in the great hall of the castle as all the Kings stood together for the first time in many years. The sight was grand indeed. Each leader represented hope that their lands would be rebuilt and life would return to normal. All the leaders raised their swords high into the air. All the swords except for those lost, including the sword of Illiath which was taken in what would forever be known as the Battle of Caragon. As Alexander gazed down at his empty hand, he felt strange not to have his father's sword. His became shiny with tears as he became stricken with the sudden sense of loss and failure. But he was grateful to still have his son, the heir to the throne, before him. Peter, dressed in his finest royal robe with his brown hair combed and a crown of gold resting on his brow, stood proudly beside his father during the procession of all the Kings and leaders of the nearby lands.

Lady Godden and Lord Byrén approached the King first bowing in respect as they made their way across the glistening marble floor. Lady Silith with her regal velvet gown of burgundy bowed her head before her sovereign. Behind her were all the villagers representing each land.

The sight was most impressive to Peter, one he knew he would never forget as long as he lived. He had seen battle and entered the Dragon Forest. He had ridden on the Great Dragon's back and watched it give up its life that others might live. Now he was seeing the results of their struggle to rid the land of evil. It was a great time of prosperity for all.

As the Kings, leaders, and townspeople stood along the walls of the grand hall in the palace of Illiath, several young men approached King Alexander as he stood in the middle of the great room. His royal robe and train of scarlet-dyed fox fur were removed by Constable Darion revealing his embroidered canvas tunic and pants. He slowly removed his sword-less belt from his hip and handed it to Darion as a symbol of the lost sword of his father. Several of the King's servants approached with his battle armor. One by one they helped attach the armor to the King as the people watched.

When they finished, the King stood regally dressed in his silver battle armor, polished to that of a mirror reflecting the torches and candles aligning all the walls. Darion returned with the King's scarlet robe and train almost ten feet in length and placed it on the shoulders of his sovereign. Following close by Darion was a young peasant boy holding a long wooden box of cherry wood intricately carved by a craftsman with the King's crest. Finished with the task of attaching the royal robe, Darion turned to the boy and opened the box to reveal a dazzling gift of steel and gold. The crowd gasped at the sight of the sword's ivory inlaid handle. Darion lifted the new sword of Alexander, still in its leather sheath, from its holding and stood at the ready next to the King.

With the gold crown of his grandfather, Illiath, resting on his brow, King Alexander was the epitome of regal splendor and youth in the midst of his grandfather's castle. He was the lion once again.

Standing before his throne of red velvet and carved wood, the King motioned for the men to be brought forward. Each young man, dressed in cadet armor, stood before the throne underneath the chandelier filled with dozens of burning torches. Each man knelt before his sovereign Lord as the King turned to Darion and took the sword from his grasp. Then, King Alexander slowly removed from its sheath the new sword bestowed upon him by Aluein, his most trusted General and friend.

The glistening steel blade, filigreed with a unique pattern chosen by Aluein himself, sparkled in the light as the King raised it high only to lower it onto the shoulder of Will kneeling before him. When the blade touched the armored shoulder of the young man, his father smiled with pride as he watched in the grand hall. Alexander pronounced him a Knight of the Royal Order of Illiath. Will was ordered to stand before his sovereign Lord, and as he did he gazed into the eyes of Alexander.

"You have proven yourself in battle alongside the knights of this palace," Alexander said, "and alongside your King."

Will lowered his eyes.

"I thank you, Sir William," the King said. "For protecting my son, for protecting this castle, and…"

Will looked up once again.

"For saving my life," the King finished.

Will grinned and felt the sting of tears forming in his eyes, but he refrained from shedding them in the midst of so many people. Yet he knew he loved his King as a father.

Peter beamed with excitement at the sight of his friend being knighted that special evening. Will stood before his King dressed in his new silver cadet armor, constructed especially for him by the silversmith, to be used for Knight Training.

Bowing his head once more as a sign of respect, Will then turned to see Peter grinning proudly for him. Will smiled too as he tried to believe that this was not a dream but that this evening was truly happening to him. Only a few weeks earlier that he was a peasant farmer helping his father harvest the corn. Now he would be leaving the valley to attend Knight Training in the Crow Valley with the finest knights in all the lands.

One by one, King Alexander knighted each young man there in the great hall. Afterwards, food was served and wine was poured as great stories of battle were exchanged that night.

Peter finally had his audience and his long awaited chance to tell his own tale of how he was a dragon-slayer if only for a moment in time. As each leader listened intently to Peter tell of the Dragon Forest and his adventures, they couldn't help but smile at how much this young boy had changed.

§

"As we gather here today to set forth a plan to retain the missing swords, may we never forget those who gave their lives for our lands," King Alexander said as he ushered in the leaders from the ten regions to the dining hall of the palace. "This historic meeting will be recorded by the Secretary of Archives for posterity sake."

With that announcement, the rulers of the ten regions sat down along the large mahogany table adorned with the red banner of Alexander. Servants brought in bowls of fruit and pitchers of wine as the leaders mingled and ate. Alexander sat next to King Mildrir as he began to discuss the agenda of the meeting.

"First, we must decide who shall undertake this quest to retrieve the swords," Mildrir said as he drank his wine from a golden goblet.

"Yes, your highness," Alexander answered. "I have my ideas."

"Before we begin," King Beátann rose to speak. "I have something to say."

All the leaders sat silently as they watched King Beátann lean on the large table. He motioned for his squire to come toward him. The leaders noticed the young man was carrying a wooden case covered in the banner of the late Naál, son of King Leámahn. All hushed at the sight of the approaching squire. He stood next to the King who quickly took the long rectangular box from the squire and pushed him aside. Resting the box on the table, King Beátann continued.

"I come to present to you, King Alexander and all the other rulers and their representatives," he said as he removed the black banner from the box only to reveal the polished cherry wood case closed by a golden clasp. He carefully lifted the clasp and raised the lid. As he put his hand inside the box, all eyes strained to see what was inside.

Then, it was revealed. He gently lifted the prize out of the cherry wood box: The sword of the late King Naál. As he held the sword by its ivory handle, his intrigued audience gasped.

"The sword of Naál," King Beátann said. "Found at last."

King Alexander rose to his feet as his eyes never left the steel blade glistening in the light of the torches. The golden details decorating the ivory handle were polished to newness. The sword looked as though it had never been used. Everyone in the meeting stood to inspect it. All the rulers quickly gathered round King Beátann as he cradled the sword.

"Are you sure this is the sword?" Thorgaerd, son of Théadron, asked. "How can we be sure?"

"Yes," asked Eulrik, son of Glaussier. "How can we be sure this is the missing sword?"

Alexander walked over to see for himself if the magnificent blade was indeed the true sword of King Naál. "There is only one way to know for sure."

"Aye," said King Beátann. He said as he twisted it in the light. He smiled and handed the sword to King Alexander.

He took the sword into his right hand and gripped the handle. It was warm in his fingers and the grip felt good in his hand as it was similar to his own. The weight of the sword was perfectly balanced. "She knew how to make a sword that is for certain." Alexander smiled.

"Excuse me?" Eulrik asked.

Alexander didn't answer. Instead, he held the sword high into the air and then read the inscription on the blade. Each sword was inscribed with a secret message. Bedlam was unaware of the inscriptions added by the Elves of Vulgaard. Partakers of the Oath for their protection and that of their heirs, the Elves assisted in making the swords.

"The inscription is on the blade," Alexander said

"What does it say?" asked Thorgaerd.

"It is in the elfin language from the lands of Vulgaard. Their craftsmen were hired to inscribe all the swords with a secret code," Alexander explained as he handed the sword back to Beátann.

"The secret code?" Eulrik asked.

Alexander nodded. "For a secret purpose."

"But these were gifts bestowed upon the rulers by Lord Bedlam," Thorgaerd replied.

"Exactly." Alexander glanced at the blade. "I am afraid I cannot tell you what it says."

Thorgaerd frowned.

All the Kings present felt great relief that one of the missing swords was found at last. This was indeed the lost sword of King Naál lying in the carved box. The members of the audience applauded the great find.

"Wherever did you find it?" Alexander asked as he sat down.

"It is a long story, but I shall try to explain it," King Beátann said. "One of my scouts was sent to the Black Hills to spy on Hildron. He spent many a cold night trapped in the mountains waiting for a chance to return to our castle. Finally, a break came when he spotted the gates of Hildron opening to release the black knights of Caragon. As they rode off into the deserts of Théadron, my scout made his way out of the mountains and followed them. When the dark creatures stopped to rest, my scout spotted a sword being carried by one of the leaders of the tribe. He recognized the blade and handle as that of the sword of Naál."

"But how could he know the sword?" Thorgaerd asked with incredulous skepticism. "Had he ever seen it before?"

"Yes," Beátann explained. "Before I sent out my scouts, I showed them the etchings made of the each lost sword. Their mission was to find those swords or never return."

Thorgaerd embarrassingly returned his gaze to the plate of food placed before him.

"He charged Caragon's Baroks, killed them all, and returned with the mysterious sword," King Beátann said has he sat down. "Upon my inspection of the blade, he was overjoyed to know of his miraculous find."

"Still, Beátann, why was Caragon in possession of the sword? How could he be so foolish as to allow one of his men to use it and take it out of the kingdom risking its loss?" asked Mildrir.

"Well, I suspect he did not know it was being taken and used by one of his men," Beátann said as he placed the priceless sword back into its case. "As foolish and surreptitious as Caragon was, I cannot imagine he would have allowed it."

But Alexander was not comforted by this tale. Deep inside he felt there was more to the story. *How did Caragon come into possession of the sword in the first place?* He thought, not wanting to ask Beátann at this time. He knew it was a story for another time.

The dinner continued until it was time to begin discussion about the quest for the missing swords. Alexander put forth his ideas as did the others present. One by one, the ideas were exchanged but no agreement was reached.

"My biggest fear," King Mildrir said. "Is that Lord Bedlam continues to hide in the mountains past Vulgaard. I know from elfin scouts that they believe Bedlam abducts elves from time to time and holds them as slaves in his mountain prison. But to prove it and hold him in a court of law, that I cannot do. He is too illusive as he still has many leaders under his spell. They hide him and his works"

"My father assured us before his death that Bedlam was long gone," Thorgaerd said. "And that he would no longer be of any threat to Théadril. Why then do we still bring this wretched creature's name up at this meeting? Why do we not seek the swords in the other regions beyond Vulgaard?"

"Why search for the swords then if Bedlam is no longer a threat?" Alexander asked. "I tell you this here and now, while those swords exist, Bedlam's spell is still cast."

The men nodded in agreement, but Thorgaerd was still not convinced.

"The magic, the wickedness I witnessed on the battlefield could not have come from one man, Lord Caragon." Alexander said. "The madness in the eyes of the Baroks was not of human origin but of the supernatural. The ability to raise fallen knights from the dead and cause them to fight again did not come from Caragon's will."

"Aye," Aluein grunted through his pipe as its scented smoke rose up to the beamed ceiling. His eyes had a faraway look as though the memories of the battle raced through his mind.

"I concur," King Mildrir stated. "If there is no threat from Bedlam, then this meeting is futile. I say Bedlam lives and only because the swords remain. He must have the missing swords and desires the others to complete his reign. The Dragon of the Forest is gone now and with it the scales. He has nothing to lose now except those swords."

"Yes," Isleif rose to speak. "All this talk is nonsense. Let us put forth an assembly of men and send them on this quest for the good of all of Théadril. I, for one, will go."

The group of men erupted in a loud squabble as most disagreed with Isleif's pledge. "A regional leader must not participate on this quest!" one man shouted.

"I have volunteered," Isleif argued. "It is of my own volition!"

"If he wants to go, he must go," Aluein said as he puffed on his pipe.

"Yes, but a regional leader?" Mildrir asked. "Is it wise to send leaders when the knights will gladly go?"

"What say you, my Lord?" Isleif asked Alexander.

King Alexander stood silent for a moment pondering the impulsive act of Isleif. Prince Isleif was still a young man not yet crowned king. He inherited the kingdom at his father's passing and Alexander knew that King Byron would not have wanted his only son sent on such a dangerous mission. Isleif had not yet married and produced an heir to the throne of Gundrehd. If he fell in battle, Gundrehd would be in disarray.

Alexander slowly walked over to his friend and placed his hand on his shoulder. "Isleif, my friend," he said. "Your courage is admirable and will not be forgotten. But I am afraid Gundrehd could not bear to lose you at this time when there is no heir to the throne." "Aye, marry, produce a son, and then you may go to battle," Aluein said as the others laughed. "After a few months of marriage…you will prefer to go to battle!"

More laughter erupted. Isleif frowned at the laughter because he despised his youth and ignorance at this time in history, yet he sat down knowing what Alexander spoke was truth. His time had not yet come.

"There will always be wars to fight, my friend," King Alexander said as he walked around the table. "Now then, whom shall we send?"

24 THE DRAGON FOREST

"But why are there ten rulers from the ten regions?' Peter asked Theodore as he poured another cup of hot tea and placed it on the large wooden table before Peter. They had a lot of reading and studying to do before Peter would be ready to head off to train as a knight just as his father and grandfather had done before him. "Why was I given the realm of the forest?" he asked as he sipped his tea.

"Each region has a purpose," Theo said as he poured cream into his tea. "Unfortunately, not all the regions fulfilled their purpose. Many turned against the Dragon and Illiath when it was discovered Bedlam wasn't pure in his intentions." Theo skimmed through a large book searching for a paragraph for Peter to read.

"Bedlam's magic is wicked, isn't it?" Peter asked.

"Well, all magic is wicked, but his is the most wicked magic of all," Theo responded. "Of all the magic I have seen, that is. In fact, I believe what makes him the most evil is that he once was a friend of King Illiath and all of Théadril."

"Even to my father?"

"Your father wasn't born yet, but your grandfather witnessed the friendship between Bedlam and King Illiath. They were trusted friends."

"What changed everything?"

"Well, what changes most men?" Theo said as he placed a book before his student. "Avarice, lust, and desire for power; all these blended together make for the most dangerous of ideas."

"When did King Illiath realize who Bedlam truly was?"

"Around the time of the swords, King Illiath realized how easy it was to manipulate men just by bestowing elaborate gifts and promises upon them, along with promises of greatness. The swords were magnificent indeed, but not worthy of abandoning all reason, integrity, and logic."

"You saw the swords? You were there?"

"Aye," Theo said. "I happened to be there at the time of the swords. I saw them, studied them. They were resplendent each to its own, but together…they glistened like rare jewels."

Peter tried to imagine all the swords together. "But what about the Dragon scales?"

"The swords were neither as beautiful as the scales nor as powerful. I must admit, those scales are far and above anything I had ever seen in my lifetime. No other surface shines as they do."

Peter nodded. "But what about Bedlam wanting the scales for his own purposes?"

"Incidental to his cause, I am afraid," Theo lit his pipe and puffed it a few times sending sweet smelling smoke into the air. "Now we know his true intentions were not *only* the scales, but to destroy all of Théadril once and for all."

"Including my father?"

"Including you as well Peter,"

Peter's eyes glazed over at the thought of Bedlam setting out to destroy him and, one day, his heir.

"That is why you are here, my Lord," Theo smiled with his pipe between his teeth. "The more you know, the more prepared you will be to do battle."

"Battle with my mind?"

"Yes, before the battle on the field,"

"Let's begin then," Peter said as he flipped through the book before him.

Peter had many more years to spend with his new tutor as his father had before him. The fire in the fireplace created a most comfortable warmth in the cold, dark, secret room where Theodore tutored Peter.

"Yes, well, before we begin," Theo said as he rose from his large wooden chair. "I have a surprise for you…"

Theo walked over to the bookcase facing Peter and gently pushed it back. The bookcase slid open revealing a passageway that led to a larger, grander library. Theo's private quarters were next to this room. The wood paneled library resembled other rooms in the palace—a humble room lined with still more books, tapestries, tables, and chairs. It was lit with a few torches and ancient rugs befell the wooden floors. As Peter studied the room, he heard voices coming from the hallway that led to yet another room. The voices were younger, not adult at all. Peter was intrigued.

Theo disappeared into the mysterious quarters and quickly reappeared with three young students: a girl and two boys.

"Peter," he said as he motioned for the three youngsters to follow him. "These are your fellow classmates."

They were introduced as Annika, Simon, and Crispin, none of whom Peter recognized as relatives or children of the palace staff. Standing nearby, Peter looked confused.

"Yes, well, you see Peter, I have asked that these young people be tutored alongside you because they too will someday lead one of the ten regions of Théadril. Annika is the only heir to Baldrieg of Glenthryst, Simon is heir in line to the throne of Glaussier the Brave, and Crispin is grandson to King Béatann, the Wise.

Interesting, Peter thought. "Where did they come from?"

"I hid them in the library behind these bookcases until the time was right to introduce them today."

"So, if you will all take your seats, we will begin," Theo directed.

Each student walked over to the large table and found enough chairs to seat themselves around it. Peter, still standing, watched them carefully. Being an only child, he was not accustomed to sharing anything with anyone near his own age and these three strangers were all sharing the books, the room, and his tutor. Suddenly, Peter did not know what to feel about what was happening. So he stood aloof.

"Peter," Theo said, startling the boy, "won't you join us?"

He pulled out an empty seat for Peter to employ. Peter hesitantly sat in the chair next to Annika, a girl of ten years with long blonde hair and the bluest eyes he had ever seen. Her hair was tangled and stuffed into a ribbon behind her head.

"I went riding this morning," Annika said as she sensed Peter staring at her. "So my hair is a mess this morning." She tried to straighten her hair, but it was of no use.

"You look fine, my dear," Theo said. "Peter, say hello to your new classmates."

"Hello."

"Hello, my Lord," Crispin spoke up as he reached across the table to shake Peter's hand. "Hello to you all." He said as he made eye contact with each one. Peter shook the extended hand weakly as he was still unsure of the whole arrangement.

"My, Lord," Simon said as he stood and bowed to Peter and then, subsequently, to each student.

"Hello," Peter said again.

Theo watched Peter's awkward reaction. "Let's get started," he interrupted. "We've a lot of work to do."

§

"This is my favorite book." Peter held a large leather bound tome in his fingers. "*The Dragon Forest.*" He read the title on the

336

spine of the book and fingered the golden letters on the front cover with great care as though they responded to his touch.

"Yes, I know." Theo smiled as he drank his tea. "Now, let's delve deeper into its pages today, shall we?"

"Is it true, then?" Crispin asked. "That you actually entered into the forest and saw the Dragon?"

Peter nodded.

"And is it true that you rode on the Dragon's back?" Annika asked.

Again, Peter nodded.

"Amazing," said Simon. "I thought the Dragon was myth."

"Oh no," Theo said. "It is no myth."

"I was told of the legend, but I did not believe it." Crispin thumbed through another book he found near his hands. "I still find it hard to believe it at times, but my father said he rode right by the dying Dragon and saw it with his own eyes."

"Yes, and the knights all stood along the wall watching as well," Annika said. "How can anyone dispute that it actually happened?"

"Well, I am told some still question that Dragon's existence to this day." Theo puffed on his pipe.

"He said we were brothers," Peter whispered as he slowly opened the book.

The others watched.

Theo sat silently as he listened.

The eyes of the Dragon appeared in Peter's mind.

"He said he was my friend."

"He spoke to you?" Simon whispered as he thumbed through the book. His eyes widened. "Fantastic."

Peter stared into the pages of the book saying nothing for a few moments.

"Hmmm. A noble act." Theo said, referring to the Dragon's sacrifice.

"But why?" Peter asked as he gazed up at Theo.

"You know the answer, Peter," Theo said. "More than I do."

Peter nodded.

"Now, let's read again about the forest," Theo said.

They turned the pages together studying the illustrations on the pages. "These drawings do not do it justice," Peter said. "The forest is more beautiful than anything I have ever seen. Here it looks so plain and ordinary."

"It is not the outward beauty that matters, Peter," Theo said, "but the inward beauty. The deeper one goes into the forest, the more beautiful it becomes."

"Yes," Peter answered. "And not everyone may enter."

"Only those chosen." Theo adjusted his spectacles.

Peter nodded as a grin crept over his face for he knew he was one of the few who were chosen to enter.

"Here we read about why King Illiath ordered the castle to face the Dragon Forest," Theo said. "Here we see the plans that were drawn by the royal architects."

The students looked at the illustrations on the pages, but Peter's mind was elsewhere. He was off...

...traveling to faraway places on the back of the Dragon while the wind swept over his face and his hands grasped the scales on the Dragon's neck. Over the valleys and through the clouds together again they soared on some adventure to rid the land of pure evil.

Peter closed his eyes. He could hear the birds singing and the wind through the trees. He could smell the crisp scent of fall in the air. And barely, ever so slightly, could he see the glowing yellow eyes peering from between the trees like beacons leading a ship to shore and to safety. Yes, he could see those eyes leading him home again.

He knew he would study with these students for a time, but they could never understand what he had been through. They could never know what it meant to be inside the Dragon Forest. That secret was his to keep forever.

§

As Peter sat on his feather bed reading a book, he spied his sword leaning on the wardrobe near the entrance to his room. A few cobwebs had formed on the blade for many months had passed since the death of the Dragon and the end of Caragon. Peter remembered the night they burned the Dragon's body in the field where it died.

He watched the garrison of Royal Knights lead by his father, the King, walk toward the Dragon with their torches lit. One by one the knights leaned down and lit the fire. Finally, King Alexander reached forward and placed his torch into the fire. Peter noticed his father hesitated before throwing his torch in with the others. The reality of the moment hit Peter hard as he knew it was the end of the Dragon forever. Then all the villagers and knights stood silently as they watched the fire reach high into the night sky. The sparks circled high like stars.

He remembered his mother's funeral procession. She had died when he was almost six years old.

As he walked with his father behind her casket, pulled by her lovely black horse, he glimpsed the sad faces of the villagers lined the streets. They threw flowers onto her casket and onto the road as they walked to the highest hill south of the palace. The images still haunted his mind.

Suddenly, Peter felt older and wiser. No more toys lined the shelves of his room, only books and etchings of the forest he had made. His brass telescope stood near the window which overlooked the forest green off in the distance. He thumbed through his book pleasantly realizing how much he liked studying with the others students.

Annika, who was annoying at times with her talk of wanting to be the "first female knight to serve the King," was the best horsewoman he had ever seen. Peter knew he could learn a lot from her about riding. Her riding skills had at once forced him to become a better rider and as a result a better Knight candidate. He was grateful.

Crispin will be a challenge academically, he thought, *but a little competition is good.* Crispin, a thin boy with thick reddish brown hair and an immense knowledge in history and physics, was good at debating, and Peter knew he could learn a lot about reasoning and debating from him. Crispin had eleven brothers and sisters, yet he welcomed Peter as though they alone were brothers.

Simon, smaller than the others, with light brown hair that hid his blue eyes, was brilliant in astronomy and had the best and most powerful telescope Peter had ever seen.

Peter felt he outdid them all in war strategy since he alone had experience with battle. *Yes, studying with these three will be fun and rewarding.* Peter smiled at the thought.

A knock on his door interrupted his reading.

"Yes," Peter said as the door opened. "Father!" He leapt up from his bed and ran to greet the King.

"You've grown a lot this spring," Alexander said as he hugged Peter. He studied his son's new height. Peter's body was changing from a young boy to a young man. His baby face was gone only to reveal stronger facial muscles and chiseled good looks. His longer arms and legs caused him to be much taller than his peers, which gave him the confidence he had always lacked. His brown hair was longer, and Alexander noticed it resembled Will's carefree hairstyle. He smiled.

Together they sat on the bed near the window. "A good book?" he asked.

Peter nodded.

"And how do you like your studies with Theodore and the other students?"

"Fantastic," Peter answered as he closed the book. "It will be a challenge, but fun too. I am looking forward to it."

"Good," said the King. "Summer is coming. Will you fish and hunt this year as you did last year?"

"No," Peter said. "I have much studying to do before heading off to train."

The King smiled. "Ah, well, yes, studying is important," he said as he thumbed through Peter's book. "But you mustn't forget that you are still a boy." He said as he rubbed his son's hair, sending it falling over his eyes. "There will always be time for studying, but not enough time to fish and hunt. The summers come and go so quickly. Enjoy them while you can."

"Will you come along with me?" Peter dared to ask fearing the answer would be disappointing. He looked down at the wooden floor and noticed a small spider crawling near his foot.

"Of course I will," The King answered. "There is a new watering hole we'll try this year." He smiled at his son.

"Oh really?" Peter asked as he watched the spider. "Where is this one?"

The King walked to the window and peeked through the telescope eyepiece to discover it was pointed at the Dragon Forest instead of the night sky. "Near the North Shore on the other side of the Dragon Forest there is a large pond that's good for fishing."

Peter nodded. The spider made its way under his bed.

King Alexander continued to peer through the telescope. "Anything new out there?" he asked.

"No," Peter sighed. "Nothing yet." He walked over to his father near the window.

Together they stood as the sun began to set over the hills near Hildron castle. "Although..." Peter hesitated.

"What?" asked his father as he continued to peer into the telescope.

"I thought I saw..." Peter stopped himself.

King Alexander turned to look at his son. "What?"

"I thought I saw a blue light coming from within the forest one night not too long ago," Peter said as he pointed to the forest off in the distance.

Alexander turned to look at the forest as well. He watched the wind blow through the green grasses on the hills outside the castle walls. "Interesting. A *blue* light you say?"

Peter nodded.

They stood in silence for a moment as the forest stood silently still in the distance. Alexander noticed something shiny peeking out from under Peter's pillow. "What's this?" he asked as he pulled the object out.

"My compass," Peter answered.

"Ah, the one your mother gave you."

"Yes."

"Good, I am glad you have it," Alexander said as he studied the gold compass in his hands. He opened the lid slowly to reveal the intricate design of the compass inside. The arrow at once pointed north. "It still works!" He smiled and handed the compass to Peter. "You know, your mother made this for you, don't you?"

"Really?" Peter said as he held the compass with greater interest.

"Yes," the King smiled. "She was very technical, very creative...more so than most of us knew. She was a brilliant woman who loved making things like this. And she made this one especially for you."

"I remember when she gave it to me. It led me to Theodore and the secret room."

His father chuckled. "Yes, I know, and as long as you have it with you, you will never be lost. You will always know where you are supposed to go and how to find your way home."

"I miss her," Peter sighed.

"We all do," said Alexander.

Suddenly, below them and near the western castle wall, they heard someone calling out Peter's name. The sound seemed to be coming from the castle wall outside Peter's window.

"Who is that shouting for you?" the King asked. Together they walked over to the window and spotted Will on the outer wall.

"Look, father," he said pointing out. "It's Will saying goodbye."

Peter quickly opened the window to shout back at Will. He stood waving at them.

"Ah yes, there he is," Alexander spotted the young man and waved in return. "He is heading out to the Crow Valley to begin his training."

"Peter! I am leaving now to go train!" Will shouted. Then he spotted the King. "My Lord," he said as he bowed.

"Goodbye, Will!" Peter shouted. "Good luck!" He waved his hand as Will waved back in return.

"I'll see you soon!" Will shouted back.

"Goodbye, Will," the King said as he waved.

Then Will ran over to a waiting ladder and slid down it with great speed. When he reached the courtyard, he met his horse and squire. He quickly mounted his horse with ease and kicked its ribs. Together they made their way through the gates and over the drawn bridge. As Will rode off into the hills followed by his squire, King Alexander and Peter watched them disappear over the dale and fade into the sunset.

"He has a lot of training still ahead of him," the King said.

"I envy him," Peter sighed. He imagined what Knight Training was like with the jousting and swordplay.

"It's not an easy life," Alexander said. "But it will serve him well. Serving a King is a great honor."

Peter leaned over to close the window. "Father?" Peter asked. "Tell me, about your training as a knight."

Alexander walked over to sit on the soft feather bed. He winced as he sat down on the bed as his torso bent where his wound was still. "Oh Peter, that was many years ago."

"Come now, you remember," Peter pressed.

"Well, let's see if I can remember. It was *so* long ago." He chuckled as he felt every bit his age. Rubbing his bearded chin, the King grinned when he remembered meeting Aluein for the first time. "Training was hard, but fun too. It's always fun to brawl and joust with your friends…"

Peter gently closed the window as his father began to speak. Off in the distance he could still see Will riding into the hills toward his destiny. *Will I ever see him again?* He wasn't sure of the answer. He stared for a moment, still gripping the window latch in his fingers.

Then, just before he closed the window, Peter gazed one more time over at the Dragon Forest. There it stood, regal as ever, with the sunset highlighting the treetops. At the exact moment his eyes found it, a burst of white doves quickly dispersed over the tops of the trees creating a cloudlike form rising high above and out of the forest. Peter smiled at the sight. Such peace, such solitude. The Forest continued to assuage all his fears and give him tranquility. As he slowly turned away, he caught a glimpse of what appeared to be a flash of blue light emanating from within the dark trees. Peter studied the sight. *Is it real or imagined?* But nothing else happened.

Perplexed, he secured the window. He realized it must have been the glare of the setting sun on the window panes, so he turned to listen to his father's tales.

But when Peter closed the window and the latch caught, a white owl flew onto the turret of the outer wall near Peter's window. It sat there for a moment on its stone perch gazing out toward the sunset. With intense eyes glowing yellow, its white feathers blew in the breeze.

As quickly as it landed, it suddenly took off in flight, the wind catching its wings and causing it to gently glide its way over the grassy hills. The sturdy wings navigated the white bird over the flowing Blue River then over the Cornshire and Cardion Valley with the little thatched-roof houses and farmlands settling in for the night. The owl flapped its wings with more effort in order to ensure it reached a final destination of security, rest, and solitude unlike any other place in the land.

And as it approached its destination with the swift ease of familiarity and placidity, the white owl circled the treetops once around as if to inspect them as a general inspects his troops, looking for any sign of weakness or vulnerability. Then, only then, when completely satisfied, did the owl finally and gracefully enter into its realm...the realm of the Dragon Forest.

THE END

ABOUT THE AUTHOR

Award-winning author, R. A. Douthitt has also written *The Dragon Forest* trilogy and *The Children* series, winner of the Bronze medal Moonbeam Children's Book Award, Best Book Series. All artwork was created by the author.

When she isn't drawing or dreaming of dragons, R. A. Douthitt lives in Phoenix with her husband Scott, who still inspires her to keep on writing no matter what. For more information on R. A. Douthitt and her books, visit: www.thedragonforest.com

Made in the USA
Las Vegas, NV
17 September 2024